A century before the term "crossover" became a buzzword in popular culture, Edgar Rice Burroughs created the first expansive, fully cohesive literary universe. Coexisting in this vast cosmos was a pantheon of immortal heroes and heroines—Tarzan of the Apes®, Jane Porter®, John Carter®, Dejah Thoris®, Carson Napier™, and David Innes™ being only the best known among them. In Burroughs' 80-plus novels, their epic adventures transported them to the strange and exotic worlds of Barsoom®, Amtor™, Pellucidar®, Caspak™, and Va-nah™, as well as the lost civilizations of Earth and even realms Beyond the Farthest Star™. Now the Edgar Rice Burroughs Universe expands in an all-new series of canonical novels written by today's talented authors, plus new editions of the Master of Adventure's classic works!

RETURN OF THE MONSTER MEN™

EDGAR RICE BURROUGHS UNIVERSE™

The Edgar Rice Burroughs Universe is the interconnected and cohesive literary cosmos created by the Master of Adventure and continued in new canonical works authorized by Edgar Rice Burroughs, Inc., the corporation based in Tarzana, California, that was founded by Burroughs in 1923. Unravel the mysteries and explore the wonders of the Edgar Rice Burroughs Universe alongside the pantheon of heroes and heroines that inhabit it in both classic tales of adventure penned by Burroughs and brand-new epics from today's talented authors.

TARZAN® SERIES

Tarzan of the Apes
The Return of Tarzan
The Beasts of Tarzan
The Son of Tarzan
Tarzan and the Jewels of Opar
Jungle Tales of Tarzan
Tarzan the Untamed
Tarzan the Terrible
Tarzan and the Golden Lion
Tarzan and the Ant Men
Tarzan, Lord of the Jungle
Tarzan and the Lost Empire
Tarzan at the Earth's Core
Tarzan the Invincible
Tarzan Triumphant
Tarzan and the City of Gold
Tarzan and the Lion Man
Tarzan and the Leopard Men
Tarzan's Quest
Tarzan and the Forbidden City
Tarzan the Magnificent
Tarzan and "The Foreign Legion"
Tarzan and the Madman
Tarzan and the Castaways
Tarzan and the Tarzan Twins
Tarzan: The Lost Adventure (with Joe R. Lansdale)

BARSOOM® SERIES

A Princess of Mars
The Gods of Mars
The Warlord of Mars
Thuvia, Maid of Mars
The Chessmen of Mars
The Master Mind of Mars
A Fighting Man of Mars
Swords of Mars
Synthetic Men of Mars
Llana of Gathol
John Carter of Mars

PELLUCIDAR® SERIES

At the Earth's Core
Pellucidar
Tanar of Pellucidar
Tarzan at the Earth's Core
Back to the Stone Age
Land of Terror
Savage Pellucidar

AMTOR™ SERIES

Pirates of Venus
Lost on Venus
Carson of Venus
Escape on Venus
The Wizard of Venus

ERB UNIVERSE™

SWORDS OF ETERNITY SUPER-ARC

Carson of Venus:
The Edge of All Worlds
by Matt Betts

Tarzan: Battle for Pellucidar
by Win Scott Eckert

John Carter of Mars:
Gods of the Forgotten
by Geary Gravel

Victory Harben: Fires of Halos
by Christopher Paul Carey

Victory Harben: Tales from the Void
Edited by Christopher Paul Carey

DEAD MOON SUPER-ARC
by Win Scott Eckert

Korak at the Earth's Core

Pellucidar: Land of Awful Shadow

Tarzan Unleashed

OTHER ERB UNIVERSE BOOKS

Victory Harben and
the Reaver of Worlds
by Christopher Paul Carey

Beyond Thirty: A World Reborn
by Jeffrey J. Mariotte

The Land That Time Forgot:
Fortress Primeval
by Mike Wolfer

A Princess of Mars:
Shadow of the Assassins
by Ann Tonsor Zeddies

Mahars of Pellucidar
by John Eric Holmes

Red Axe of Pellucidar
by John Eric Holmes

Tarzan and the Forest of Stone
by Jeffrey J. Mariotte

Tarzan and the Dark Heart of Time
by Philip José Farmer

Tarzan and the Valley of Gold
by Fritz Leiber

ERB UNIVERSE ILLUSTRATED EPICS

Comic Books

Jane Porter: The Primordial Peril

Graphic Novels

Jane Porter: City of Fire

The Moon Maid: The Three Keys

Victory Harben: Warriors of Zandar

Victory Harben: Ghosts of Omos

EDGARRICEBURROUGHS.COM

EDGAR RICE BURROUGHS UNIVERSE™
RETURN OF THE MONSTER MEN™

JOSH REYNOLDS

Includes the bonus novelette

WEIRD WORLDS™
DEAD ON VENUS
BY
MIKE WOLFER

EDGAR RICE BURROUGHS, INC.
Publishers
TARZANA   CALIFORNIA

RETURN OF THE MONSTER MEN

© 2025 Edgar Rice Burroughs, Inc.

WEIRD WORLDS: DEAD ON VENUS

© 2025 Edgar Rice Burroughs, Inc.

Cover art by Brian LeBlanc © 2025 Edgar Rice Burroughs, Inc.

Map of The Island by Mike Wolfer © 2025 Edgar Rice Burroughs, Inc.

The Favonia and The Favonia Cargo Crawler illustrations by Mike Wolfer
© 2025 Edgar Rice Burroughs, Inc.

Return of the Monster Men is based on the Monster Men comic books
written by Mike Wolfer and © Edgar Rice Burroughs, Inc.

ERB Universe Creative Director: Christopher Paul Carey

Special thanks to Kathleen Bonnaud, Llana Jane Burroughs, Brian LeBlanc,
Janet Mann, Ryan Okabayashi, Josh Reynolds, James Sullos, Jess Terrell,
Cathy Wilbanks, Charlotte Wilbanks, Mike Wolfer, and Bill Wormstedt
for their valuable assistance in producing this book.

First standard paperback edition

Published by Edgar Rice Burroughs, Inc.
Tarzana, California
EdgarRiceBurroughs.com

ISBN-13: 978-1-945462-91-7

- 9 8 7 6 5 4 3 2 1 -

CONTENTS

THE ISLAND

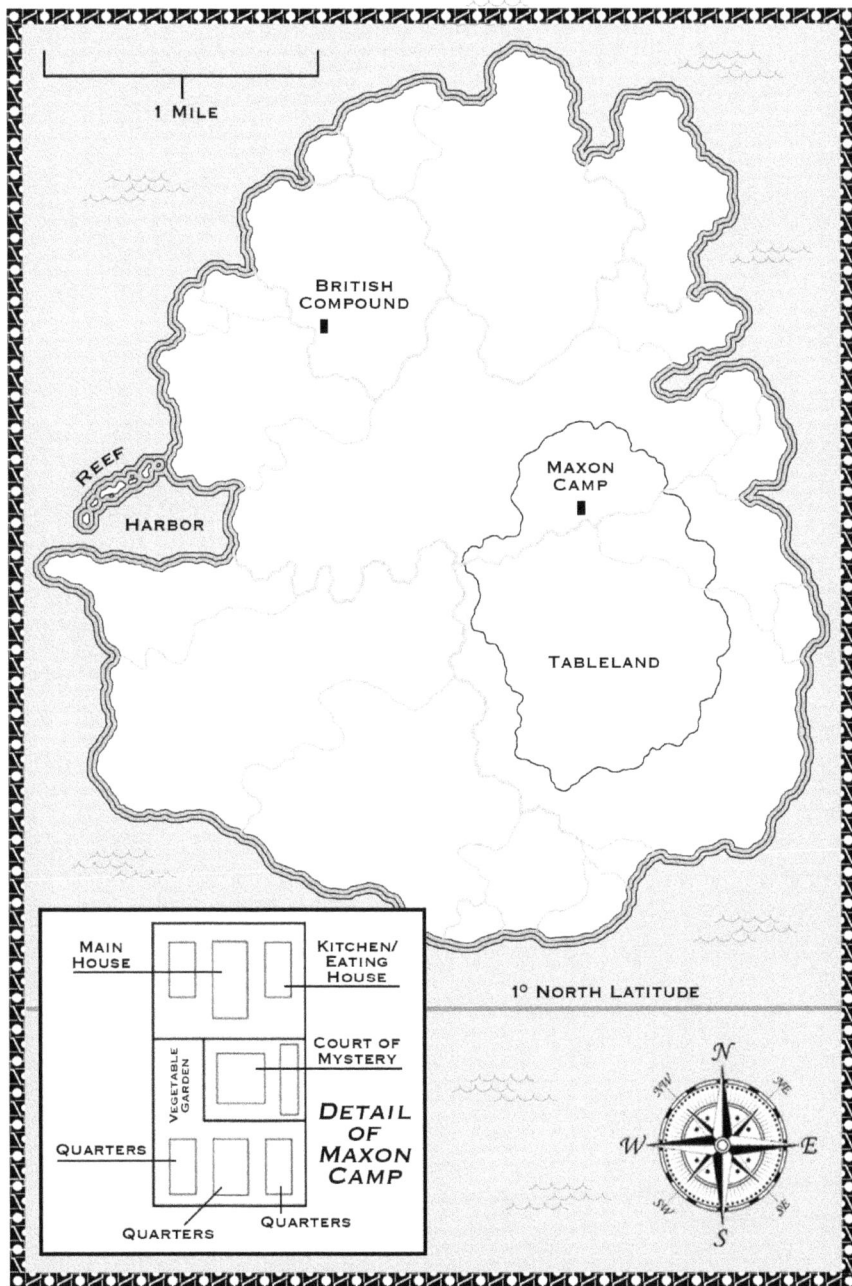

1 MILE

BRITISH
COMPOUND

MAXON
CAMP

REEF

HARBOR

TABLELAND

1° NORTH LATITUDE

MAIN
HOUSE

KITCHEN/
EATING
HOUSE

VEGETABLE GARDEN

COURT OF
MYSTERY

QUARTERS

DETAIL
OF
MAXON
CAMP

QUARTERS

QUARTERS

N
NW   NE
W   E
SW   SE
S

MAP BY MIKE WOLFER BASED ON AN ORIGINAL
DRAWING BY EDGAR RICE BURROUGHS.

RETURN OF THE MONSTER MEN ™

Prologue
Forest of the Night

THE RAINFOREST FELL SILENT.

Tijilik paused, alert to the sudden change. The Dayak turned slowly, surveying the twisting trail behind him. The trees crowded close, like the walls of some great green longhouse, and fleshy orchids dripped softly, overfull with captured water. The night air was damp and still, heavy with the memory of one storm and the promise of another. At any other time it would have been teeming with life. But now, nothing moved; no animals called out. The forest was as still as death.

Tijilik's hand instinctively fell to the deer horn hilt of his niabor, where it hung against his hip. The curved sword had belonged to his father, and his father's father. In its time, it had taken the heads of rival tribesmen, Dutchmen, and Portuguese sailors. He resisted the urge to draw the weapon, however. Better to wait and see.

Something—someone—was following him, he was certain of it. He felt no fear, for as far as he was concerned, he was the fiercest thing in the forest. Still, it puzzled him. His unseen pursuer wasn't one of the British, he thought. The foreigners had no sense of how to move in the forest, and could not help but trumpet their location for miles, without even realizing it. Their clumsiness made them easy to avoid—and even easier to kill.

Not that he'd had the opportunity of late, more was the pity. He was not here to collect heads, but information.

Muda Saffir had commanded that no blood was to be shed; not until he deemed the time right. And so Tijilik's niabor remained sheathed, and no heads decorated his belt. Instead, he had spent lonely, uncomfortable days prowling the forest and keeping a close watch on the British compound and its inhabitants. Soldiers, mostly. Why they were all the way out here, Tijilik could not fathom. Then, the ways of the foreigners were a mystery to him.

In any event, he was bored now and eager to return to the others to deliver his report. Muda Saffir would be angry, but so what? If there was no plunder to be had, they ought to leave. And if there was plunder, as their captain swore there was, why had they not yet taken it? A question to ask the man himself, perhaps. Tijilik grinned slightly at the thought.

Of late, Muda Saffir had made himself increasingly un-popular with his crew. Wild tales of monsters and treasure were all well and good when told in the comfort of the longhouse, but they lost some of their luster when proof was so lacking. The time was coming when Saffir's captaincy would come to an ignominious end. Tijilik wondered if it might fall to himself to strike the final blow. The thought was a pleasant one.

Out in the dark, a branch snapped.

All thought of taking Muda Saffir's head vanished, and Tijilik froze, senses straining against the now-oppressive silence. His eyes darted from tree to tree, searching for the telltale gleam of a weapon or the shining eye of a beast. But nothing revealed itself to his alert gaze. He felt his skin prickle with alarm.

Uneasy, he stepped off the trail and into the shadow of a towering Benuang tree. Best to see who it was before he acted. Only a fool did otherwise. Perhaps Muda Saffir had sent someone to find him. Perhaps they were going to attack tonight. The thought quickened his blood, and he almost called out to his mysterious pursuer. But at the last moment, common sense asserted itself.

Another crack of wood—closer. Too close. He risked a quick glance around the side of the tree, but saw nothing. His fingers tightened about the hilt of his blade. He felt eyes on him, studying him. Calculating. He swallowed down a sudden rush of fear as he heard the hiss of movement behind him.

Tijilik was not a coward. Yet when he saw what awaited him, he turned and ran. The thing crashed in immediate pursuit of him, tearing through the undergrowth with a speed and fury that turned his blood to water. It made no sound, unless one counted the harsh rasp of its rancid breath, but that only made it worse.

It was not a man, and did not run as a man. Rather it moved something like one of the great orangs of the forest, with a rolling gallop first on two legs, then four or sometimes three. At times, it sprang into the trees and moved from branch to branch above him, until it grew weary of this route and dropped back down. Nor did it seem to tire; his breath burned in his lungs and his legs felt like grass, but he forced himself on when he realized that it hadn't slowed. He cursed it and prayed in the same breath, but it responded to neither.

As he burst through the heavy undergrowth, Muda Saffir's stories came back to him—not the tales of treasure and mysterious lockboxes, but those of the monsters. The things that had supposedly torn apart Saffir's old crew, save a few survivors who refused to sail with him again and who were equally reticent to speak of the creatures they had faced . . . beings that resembled men, but were all twisted up out of their proper shape in ways that could not be described. Awful things, out of a child's nightmares.

Was the thing behind him one of these, then? It seemed impossible, yet the stink of it was all too real—a pungent-yet-sweet odor, as of sour blood and rotten meat. A predator-reek, like that of one of the great tigers that haunted the islands near Borneo. But this was no tiger.

Tijilik stumbled—turned—snatched his niabor from its sheath, knowing as he did so that the thing would be in midleap even as he cleared the scabbard. His blade whistled out in a silvery arc . . . but sliced only the humid air.

His pursuer had vanished.

Tijilik stared into the darkness, his pulse pounding in his ears. Behind him, something gave a wet chuckle. "Ich bin jetzt hungrig," it growled, softly. He did not understand the words, but the intent was clear. Tijilik spun, niabor slashing. An iron grip snapped shut on his wrist. Bone snapped and Tijilik's blade tumbled from nerveless fingers as pain from his broken wrist flooded through him.

In the gloom of night, he saw two rows of shark's teeth rising from within a tangle of greasy hair. Something that might have been an eye flashed, reflecting the faint light of the moon. Unable to look away from that hideous countenance, Tijilik blindly groped for his knife. He didn't reach it in time. Instead, a malformed hand fastened itself about his throat. Tightened. The shark's teeth drew close.

"Otto! Nein!"

The teeth paused. Past the grotesque form of his opponent, he saw a curious figure striding down the trail. A little man, a white man, dressed for the city. He had flyaway white hair and a beard, and a pair of spectacles hid his eyes. He did not seem shocked by the sight before him, or frightened. Rather he seemed . . . disappointed.

"Let him go, boy. Please." Tijilik knew some English. That was why he had been given the onerous task of watching the British. The old man spoke English now, but with a heavy accent that reminded Tijilik of the few Dutchmen he'd spoken to.

The monster glanced down at Tijilik and then at the old man. "Dayak," it growled.

The old man shook his head slowly. "Ja, ja, ja. And so? That means he is to be eaten? No. For shame. Let him go now."

Incredibly, impossibly, the monster did as he bade and Tijilik fell back onto the ground. He jarred his injured arm in the process and bit back a groan. The monster shot him a look and Tijilik shuddered. The creature clearly still hoped to devour him. Only the old man stepped between them.

"You must not, Otto. It is not good to—to give in to such desires."

"Hungrig," the monster rumbled. Then, in guttural English, "Hungry, Doctor."

"Yes, yes. Find a pig, Otto. A deer. A civilized repast, as befitting a gentleman." The old man glanced at Tijilik. "You are one of Muda Saffir's headhunters, ja? Is he still around then, the thieving fool?"

Tijilik tried to rise, but paused as the monster tensed, as if preparing to spring. The old man adjusted his spectacles and gave the briefest of smiles. "I will take your silence as assent. My friend here wishes to—to devour you, do you understand?" he asked, expectantly.

"Yes," Tijilik said, hesitantly.

The old man nodded, pleased. "Good, good. I will convince him otherwise, but in return you must take a message to our friend Muda Saffir for me, yes?"

Tijilik stared at the old man in bewilderment. So too, he thought, did the monster, if such a thing were possible. The old man ignored the creature and picked up Tijilik's niabor. He gave it a few experimental swings, showing a startling degree of skill in the process. Then he extended the bone hilt to Tijilik. The Dayak hesitated, but only for a moment. He took the sword and used it as a crutch to lever himself to his feet. Cradling his injured hand to his chest, he said, "What is the message that you wish Muda Saffir to hear?"

The old man's smile widened. "Tell him that he was right. That his treasure does indeed exist, that it is here—and that I can show it to him. Tell him that. I expect he will be most pleased. He might even reward you." He gestured. "Now go. Quickly."

Tijilik did so. He glanced back only once, to see man and monster standing together in the moonlight. But then, as he turned a bend in the trail, the forest swallowed them up and it was as if they had never been there at all.

1

The Island

TOWNSEND HARPER, JR., the man sometimes known as Bulan, stood on the deck of the schooner, and breathed in the salty tang of evening as he tried to steady his nerves. There was a taste of rain on the air; a storm had lashed the schooner the night before and dark clouds pressed close overhead, all but blotting out the sunset, promising more to come.

He wasn't afraid, for fear had largely been burned out of him by the various travails of the last year. He had lived among monsters—as a monster—and had killed, and been nearly killed in turn, more times than he felt comfortable attempting to count.

Not fear, then, but a sort of atavistic tingle—the inherent wariness of a wild animal, sensing danger. A part of him was convinced that he was sailing into a trap . . . though what kind, exactly, he could not say with any certainty. Yet the feeling remained and grew stronger the closer the schooner drew to the island.

He studied the slowly swelling black blotch of the island on the horizon. He thought they'd seen the last of it a year ago. Had hoped, in fact. But it seemed this part of their story was not yet concluded. "Thirteen," he murmured. He tensed instinctively as he felt someone approach him from behind.

"What are you mumbling about?"

Bulan—for that was how he thought of himself—turned. Virginia Maxon stood behind him, as lovely as the day he'd

1

first set eyes on her. He forced a smile. "It's been thirteen months since we were last here. Doesn't bode well, does it?"

Virginia laughed softly. "Numerology doesn't suit you, darling." She ran her hands through her short-cropped blonde curls, shaking them out. A casual gesture that nonetheless never failed to set his heart racing.

He chuckled. "I suppose not. Then, numbers and I don't exactly get along—save for the ones on the scoreboard. Those I can make go up without much trouble, unlike the grades on my architecture exams, sadly." His expression turned rueful. Harper men had been attending Cornell since its investiture, as his father often liked to remind him. He smiled at his fiancée. "Those sad, lonely little grades."

Virginia smiled up at him and stroked his square jaw. He'd once thought himself quite handsome, but his time on the island had taught him that there was more to someone than looks. Even the ugliest frame might hold a soul, and the prettiest face could hide a lifetime of sins. The woman before him was the exception—Virginia was beautiful inside and out, and a better woman than he deserved. "No one could expect you to bounce back immediately; not after what you experienced."

Bulan looked away, out over the water. "My father did." Townsend Harper had expected a lot of things of his son. Not just that he would graduate, but that he would follow in the footsteps of his father and grandfather, maintaining and expanding the family fortune.

"Your father was—is—worried. Just as mine is." She leaned against his chest, turning slightly in his arms so that she could see the island. He felt her shiver. He wasn't the only one with bad memories of this place. "They think we're a pair of fools."

"They could be right," Bulan said, softly. His father had argued against the expedition, as had Virginia's father. The former, perhaps, more strenuously than the latter, but both had their reasons. His father wanted him to just—forget everything. To pretend that the whole horrific episode was nothing more than some fever dream, now finished and done. Only, that wasn't how the world worked.

Some things couldn't be forgotten. No matter how hard one tried.

Virginia snorted. "Sometimes a bit of foolishness is the only way to get things done." She turned and pulled his face to hers. Her eyes flashed with steely resolve, and he was reminded again of that spark that had first drawn him to her. Virginia had never met a problem she couldn't solve, through sheer determination if nothing else. "And when this is done, we'll return to New York, you'll get your degree, we'll be married and live happily ever after. How does that sound?"

"Like paradise, Virginia," Bulan said. They kissed, slowly, deeply.

The moment ended all too quickly. A polite cough caused them to separate, if only reluctantly. They turned to see the small, thin form of Sing Lee, standing at the schooner's rail. The old Singaporean was dressed as ever in his traditional linen coat, with a frayed homburg perched on his head, and his long queue trailing down his back. He had a Lee-Enfield bolt-action rifle nestled casually in the crook of one arm, and with the other, he indicated something in the shallows ahead.

"Excuse the interruption, Miss Ginny," he said, glancing back at them. Sing spoke with the precision of someone who'd learned English late in life, and but for a faint accent might have passed for an overly educated academic. "I thought you might wish to see this."

Bulan and Virginia joined Sing at the rail. Out ahead of them lay the island. The shoreline was as oppressive and overgrown as Bulan remembered, with trees hanging low over the water in places, creating shadowed inlets. Elsewhere, escarpments of greenery-shrouded rock rose high above the forest canopy, to loom like great headstones over the island and all those who dared dwell upon it.

"Not a friendly place, eh Bulan?" Sing murmured, at his elbow.

Bulan glanced at the smaller man. "No, not in the least," he replied. When they'd first met, Sing had been a cook employed by Virginia's father, Professor Arthur Maxon, and Bulan—well. He'd been an amnesiac, convinced of his own monstrousness by an odd arrangement of circumstances, some of which could be laid at Sing's feet. Since then, the old man had become more than just a faithful retainer; rather, he was a friend and trusted confidant, as well as a fellow survivor of the horrors they'd experienced on the island.

He looked at Virginia. "Last chance, my love. We can leave now, and put it all behind us—for good."

She smiled sadly. "We can't, and you know it. Not until we find him." Her gaze strayed back to the island, and the softness was replaced by resolve. "Not until we know whether Number Thirteen is dead . . . or alive."

Bulan could not say which of those options he preferred. From the look on Sing's face, however, he favored the former. "If it—he—is alive, Miss Ginny, he may not be pleased to see us, eh? Especially if he knows who we are."

Virginia nodded. "I know. But it is my responsibility. My father created those wretched creatures, and I cannot—I will not—abandon one, if I can help it." She looked at them. "My father left many debts unpaid on this island. It's up to me to rectify that."

"Us," Bulan corrected, gently. He pulled her close. "It's up to us."

It had all begun with Professor Arthur Maxon's theories: specifically, the artificial creation of life. Two years earlier, he'd sailed the *Ithaca* from Singapore to the Pamarung Islands, hoping to achieve his goals far from the prying eyes of the greater scientific community. He'd eventually succeeded, despite the madness that gripped him—that still gripped him, to this day.

Thirteen times Maxon had created life, drawing it from his vats like a modern-day alchemist. But not life as most knew it. Instead of men, Maxon had created horrors . . . twisted mockeries of the human form, driven by bestial impulses and possessing a ferocity that outstripped even the most savage of animals.

For a time, Bulan had lived among them. Had thought himself one of them; had known himself only as Number Thirteen. It had been an accident of fate; a coincidence that he still found hard to believe, despite the physical evidence. He glanced down at his forearms, where white trails of scar tissue stood out against the tanned skin. More scars decorated his chest and shoulders; mementos of his time as self-appointed leader of Maxon's monster men. Virginia followed his gaze, and idly traced one of the scars.

"Which one gave you that?" she asked.

Bulan looked away. "Number Twelve, I think." He felt a flicker of old guilt as he recalled how he'd led the pack of brutes into battle against the Dayak pirates who'd attempted to spirit Virginia away. They'd died on his behalf; not out of love, but fear of the whip he'd carried. The whip he'd used to brutalize them, as mercilessly as a slave driver. He could still sometimes hear its vicious snap in his dreams.

He feared he would carry that stain on his soul forever and a day. That was part of the reason why he'd agreed to Virginia's plan to find the real Number Thirteen, whom she believed to have been left on the island, alone and forgotten. Sing had sworn the creature was dead—born dead. But Virginia believed otherwise, and Bulan feared she was correct.

Maxon was mad, but he was a genius even so. The creatures he'd created were nothing if not hardy. And Maxon had sworn that Number Thirteen would have been the greatest of them—a man, among monsters. A Caesar of the inhuman. After all, nothing less would have made for a suitable husband for Virginia. Or so Maxon had intended.

Bulan shied from the thought, not wishing to consider the awful possibilities it brought with it. Maxon had dragged himself back from the periphery at the last moment, and upon their return to New York, had voluntarily committed himself to a sanitarium.

But even so, the question of Thirteen's fate remained. And Virginia was determined to answer it—one way or another.

They dropped anchor a safe distance from the island. The crew of the schooner consisted of seven Lascar sailors, hired in Singapore. An older man named Kazin was their leader, and he and Sing seemed to have some history. The old man claimed to have worked with him before; doing what, Bulan hadn't asked, and Sing had not volunteered. The Lascars had experience plying the pirate-infested waters, and moreover could be trusted to follow orders—or so Kazin, and Sing, insisted.

Kazin eyed the island warily. "It is almost dark," he said, to Sing. Kazin rarely spoke, save to the other man, or to bark orders to his crew. Sing nodded and looked at Virginia.

"He is right. Would you not rather do this in the morning?"

Bulan spoke up. "There are headhunters and pirates in these waters. It's best if we go in, see if we can find what we're looking for and get back to the schooner as quickly as possible. We have the cover of darkness, but the longer the schooner sits anchored out here, the more likely we'll be spotted by someone with bad intentions."

Virginia nodded. "I'd rather not wind up a guest of someone like Muda Saffir again, if it can be avoided." She gave a quick grin. "I didn't much enjoy his idea of hospitality."

Kazin grunted. "Muda Saffir is a very bad man," he said, with almost comedic seriousness. Then, he shrugged. "Perhaps it is not so dark as all that."

It was decided that three of the Lascars would stay with the schooner to keep watch on it. The others, led by Kazin, would accompany Bulan, Virginia, and Sing onto the island. Bulan felt some of his uneasiness abate as they lowered the lifeboat into the water. The Lascars were all armed, and knew their business. They were perfectly safe.

But even so, as he considered the island he could not help but wonder what horrors might be lying in wait for them beneath the dark palms.

2

THE COMPOUND

NIGHT HAD FALLEN FULL AND HEAVY by the time they found the compound. Virginia studied the palisades, somehow still intact if now covered in places by opportunistic greenery, and felt a chill run through her. Something that had once been as familiar to her as her own hands now seemed incomprehensibly alien in the light of the electric torches the Lascars held.

The last redoubt, her father had called it. His citadel of reason, against the enemies of progress, but by the end it had been nothing more than a chamber of horrors. She closed her eyes, recalling for a moment the last time they'd spoken, just before they'd left for Singapore. Arthur Maxon had never been a robust man, and his time in the sanitarium had only made him dwindle further into himself.

They had met in a white room, a table between them. Clad in his dressing gown, his palsied hands scratching notes onto a pad as he spoke, he had resembled a wizened child. "Leave it, Ginny," he had said, not meeting her gaze. "Leave it be. If he lives, he is a monster—like the rest of them. Reflections of my—my insanity." He spat the words like bullets. Lucidity had brought self-recrimination with it.

"And what if he isn't?" she'd asked. "What if . . . ?"

He'd looked at her then, for the first time in what felt like months. "Then he is something worse. A devil. A soulless thing. Leave him to his green hell." He'd called for the nurse, then, and that was that. Only it wasn't, and she wouldn't.

Virginia had been horrified when she learned the truth of her father's work, she didn't deny it. She felt a spiritual revulsion at the thought of the monstrous engines of flesh he'd brewed in his vats, but she also felt shame for her disgust, and pity for those wretched beings that had not asked to be made. She had not been able to help the others. But if Thirteen still lived, however unlikely that seemed, she was determined to do the right thing by him—whatever the cost. It was the only way she could think of to balance the scales.

But first, she had to muster the courage to step through the open gate and into the place where she'd spent the worst two years of her life. It was harder than she'd expected. The compound, so still and silent amid the tumult of forest at night, reminded her of some great predator, crouched and waiting. Thankfully, she wasn't the only one who was intimidated by the mere sight of the place.

She glanced at the others. Sing was as unreadable as ever. Kazin and his Lascars, on the other hand, looked distinctly unsettled. And Bulan . . . Bulan might as well have been a statue. His face was stiff and waxy, but his eyes spoke volumes. Her heart went out to him. They had both endured so much here. So much awfulness—so much fear.

Virginia touched her fiancé's arm, startling him. "What do you think?" she asked.

"Bigger than I remember," Bulan murmured, half in jest. He looked at her. "We could turn around and go back to the schooner. No one would blame us."

Out in the dark, something crashed through the undergrowth, heading away from the group. Everyone tensed, and one of the Lascars cursed softly. Virginia took a deep breath. "No. We're here. We might as well see what there is to see."

Kazin and one of his men led the way, advancing slowly through the wide-open gates into the compound, rifles at the ready. Virginia and the others followed, moving with paranoid caution. Virginia left her hand on the Colt M1900 she'd acquired before they'd left New York. Bulan carried one as well, and they'd both trained with the weapon—as well as rifles—before undertaking their expedition.

She was reasonably comfortable with the notion of shooting another living thing, even a man come to that. The pirate, Muda Saffir, for instance. Or the late, unlamented Von Horn, who'd caused them all so much trouble.

Sometimes she worried whether this willingness was a sign that the tribulations they'd endured had hardened her in ways she couldn't fathom. Other times, she thought it was no bad thing to be ready for violence. Especially in places like this, where danger was around every corner.

"It is quiet," Sing said, in a low voice. He sounded almost worried, or as close to it as Sing got. Though he'd been hired as a cook, she'd always had the feeling that there was more to Sing than recipes.

"Better than the alternative," Virginia replied. The old man snorted. She reflected, and not for the first time, that they knew little about his life prior to his signing on with her father and Von Horn in Singapore. He shared even less. Sometimes, she found herself wondering what circumstances had brought so capable a man into their lives.

"And to think, for a time I believed that I was created here," Bulan said. There was something almost wistful in his tone. He glanced at Sing. "Thanks for that, by the way."

Sing sniffed. "It turned out all right in the end, eh?"

It had been Sing who'd substituted the unconscious form of her fiancé for that of the being known as Number Thirteen, dragging the latter from its vat of chemical fluids and leaving it outside the palisade, in the forest. Sing had gone back to bury the piteous thing, only to find the body missing— dragged off by animals, or so he'd assumed at the time. But Virginia knew better. So too did Bulan, though he didn't like to admit it.

As the men dawdled behind, Virginia strode ahead. Each of the buildings was perched atop a series of posts, save the smaller outbuildings. The compound was split by an internal palisade, separating the gardens and general quarters from the so-called "court of mystery," as her father had called it, which consisted of the main building, where they'd resided, her father's laboratory, and the oversized outbuilding used to house the creatures.

A wave of remorse and melancholy filled her as she considered the latter. Her father had created his monsters without any thought as to their futures. To him, they had simply been stops on the road of progress. The poor brutes had desired nothing more than to walk free under the sun. Instead, all of them had died in the steaming jungles of Borneo.

All but one.

Virginia turned her attention to the peaked roof of her father's old lab. For a moment, she thought she glimpsed something there, against the faint gleam of the moon. But as clouds obscured the night sky, the moment passed, and she decided it had simply been a trick of the light. Even so, she knew that if there were answers to be had, that was where they'd find them. But she couldn't face it; not yet.

She turned back to the others. "Let's check the main building first," she said, indicating the central structure of the compound.

Bulan and Sing shared a look, and Sing turned to Kazin. "Two men on the gate," he said, to the Lascar. "Two with us."

Kazin grunted. "Esmail and I will stay here." He gestured to the other two Lascars. "Hamad, Comjee. You see pirates, you shoot," he said, and, with a glance at Sing, added, "You see anything else—you call for help."

One of the men frowned. "Like what?"

"Monsters," said Sing, flatly.

The Lascars chuckled, but fell silent at a sharp gesture from Kazin. Sing gave them a hard stare. "Laugh all you like, but if you want Mister Harper's money, you do what you are told." He paused. "You have not seen what I have seen. Be thankful."

Virginia left them to it. The main building was differentiated from the others by the narrow veranda that encircled it.

A set of plank steps led up to the veranda and the main entrance, a pair of heavy doors on the front face of the building. She remembered Von Horn opining once that the doors were heavy enough to resist anything short of a cannon. The compound had been built to resist attack from pirates and headhunters, neither of which were known for their artillery.

She started up the steps. "Wait, Ginny," Sing barked. "Not without us." She paused and gave the old man a smile as he and Bulan hurried to join her.

"No need to mother hen me, Sing. I'm quite capable of looking after myself." She patted the Colt on her hip as she spoke. Sing didn't look convinced. The old man was a traditionalist in some ways. Bulan, thankfully, was more open-minded.

He looked at her. "Are you sure about this, my love?"

"It's as I told you on the deck of the Navy ship that took us home last year: we were made for one another, and no power on Earth can keep us apart." She pulled him close, and kissed his cheek. He smiled.

"Glad to hear it, though you didn't exactly answer my question." He stepped back. "Just to be on the safe side, I'll go in first."

Virginia laughed. "If you insist."

The doors hung open, their hinges rusted through and swollen stiff. The wood was scored by thin marks—fingers? Or claws? It was hard to say. Virginia saw nothing but darkness within. She tensed as Bulan stepped past her. "We need some light," she said. Sing obliged, extending his electric torch toward the entrance.

"Do you see anything?" Bulan asked, warily. He had his hand on his pistol, ready to snatch it from its holster at a moment's notice.

Sing frowned, peering into the darkened interior. His light did precious little to dispel the shadows. "No." He swung the light around as Bulan stepped inside.

Virginia heard the creak of weathered boards an instant

before the stultifying air was split by a querulous, simian grunt. "Down!" Bulan roared and dropped to the floor.

Sing dropped his light and pushed her aside as something massive and rust-hued launched itself toward the interlopers. The heavy shape leaped easily over Bulan's prone form and out onto the veranda, separating Virginia and Sing. Virginia had her sidearm half drawn when the creature jumped from the veranda to the ground below. She snatched up Sing's fallen light and caught the beast full in its beam.

The orangutan shielded its eyes with one wide hand and gave a low, throaty rumble of discontent. Then, it knuckled swiftly toward the main gate. "Don't shoot," Virginia called out to Kazin and the other Lascar at the bottom of the steps. "Let him go!"

"Those things move far too swiftly when they're of a mind," Bulan said, leaning over the rail to watch the animal vanish into the jungle. They turned to the open door, where Sing was dusting off his homburg with a look of annoyance. "They must have moved in when we left. I'm surprised we haven't run across more of them."

"One is more than enough," Sing said. He pinched his nose and indicated the main room behind him. "It does not smell pleasant in there."

Virginia rubbed her arms. She felt a sudden chill, as if they were being watched. Maybe there were more of the apes lurking about. "The orangutans are welcome to the place, after we've gone," she said, loudly. "They'll put it to better use than we ever did."

Sing moved aside and she stepped inside. The main room was overgrown like everything else in the compound. The detritus of its former inhabitants littered the floor. She saw bits and pieces that she recognized. Here, a chair, there a table . . . a bookshelf, its contents warped and moldering in the tropical climate. The feeling of being watched grew stronger and she found herself peering into the shadowed corners, half expecting to find something or someone looking back at her.

"If Number Thirteen is alive, I can't imagine him choosing to live here. Maxon's creations didn't get along well with the wildlife, as I recall."

"Unnatural," Sing muttered. Virginia glanced at him, but said nothing. Sing's opinion of her father's work was well known to her at this point. The old man had done his level best to protect her both from the dangers of Borneo as well as her father's madness. As he was determined to protect her here. Something crunched beneath her feet and she looked down. It was a tarnished picture frame, bits of mold-spotted glass still clinging to it.

"Look at this," she said, to the others, as she stooped to retrieve it. "My photograph was in this frame." She looked at Bulan. "I wonder where . . . or who . . ."

He frowned. "Let's look in the lab."

3

PIRATE OR MONSTER?

HE ORANGUTAN BURST THROUGH the open gates, moving with determined swiftness. Comjee was knocked sprawling by the beast's sudden rush, and Hamad yelped, startled. The latter swung his rifle after the departing beast, but refrained from firing. Instead, he began to laugh. "What do you think, eh?" he hooted, as Comjee clambered gracelessly to his feet. "Was that a pirate . . . or a monster?"

Comjee glared at him. "I once saw an orangutan rip a man's arm off in Borneo," he said, retrieving his watch cap from where it had fallen. He slapped it against his thigh to dislodge the dirt. "I'd say that's a monster, wouldn't you?"

Hamad grinned at the other man. Comjee was infamously pessimistic. Superstitious as well. He saw death portents in every cup of tea, and jinn in every twist of smoke. "In my experience, if you leave them alone, they'll leave you alone."

"You do not fill me with confidence," Comjee said, dubiously. He was staring at the trees where the animal had vanished. "What if it comes back?"

Hamad rolled his eyes. "It won't. Come—have a smoke with me."

Comjee was still watching the forest. "Kazin wouldn't like it."

"Kazin isn't out here. He's in there, with young Esmail. If he was concerned, we'd know it." Hamad found his cigarettes and extracted one with his lips. The Turkish brand was acrid, but affordable on a sailor's wages. Kazin wasn't as much a cheapskate as some, but neither was he particularly generous.

Not like their current employer, the young Mister Harper and his bride-to-be. Hamad didn't know what to make of the Americans. Harper seemed a decent enough sort, and Americans weren't as bad as Englishmen, when it came to formality. The young woman, Harper's fiancée, was pretty enough but—well. There was iron in that one; even a fool could see that. Then there was the Singaporean. That little man was dangerous. Hamad had faced his share of pirates across bloody decks, and knew a killer when he saw one.

Yes, it was an interesting crew, all things considered. He was almost sorry to turn the lot of them over to Muda Saffir. He comforted himself with the thought of the money he was being paid to feed his charges to the pirate rajah and his pet Dayaks.

It wasn't the first time Hamad had led lambs to the slaughter, but he hoped it might be the last. He wasn't Saffir's only spy in Singapore by a long shot; every pirate worth the name had a handful of men they could trust to warn them of likely targets. But he felt with some confidence that he was the luckiest.

Saffir wasn't just after plunder these days. No, he was obsessed with these islands, or so Hamad had heard. Perhaps obsession enough to pay double, for the successful acquisition of these mysterious Americans who seemed to know so much about this unpleasant place. He'd sent the pirate a message in the usual fashion the day they'd left Singapore. No doubt Saffir was already prowling somewhere close by, waiting to strike when Hamad sent the signal—two rifle shots, in close succession.

The only question was, when to do it. Too early, and he risked exposure. Too late, and Saffir might miss his opportunity. He would not be pleased if that were to happen. He might even decide to take it out on Hamad. Having seen what a man like Saffir did to those who displeased him, Hamad had no intention of suffering such a fate.

Even so, he couldn't help but wonder why Saffir was so interested in this place. There were rumors about what had taken place here a year ago, of course. There were always rumors. Monsters and buried treasure. Children's stories. Everyone knew you didn't bury treasure—you spent it. Quickly and irresponsibly, if possible.

Still, Americans were odd. Who knew what they'd gotten up to, the last time they were here. Maybe that was why they'd come back—to retrieve something valuable that they'd had to leave behind. Perhaps there was indeed a treasure. Maybe he wouldn't send the signal until he was certain. There might be more than enough to go around. Why turn it all over to Saffir, after all?

Hamad smiled thinly, thinking of how he'd spend such impossible wealth. He had debts, but those could wait until last. No, there were more pleasant activities a man of means could indulge in, in Singapore.

He was still entertaining himself with such thoughts when he realized that Comjee had vanished. "Comjee?" he called. Where had the overeager fool gotten to? He took a last pull on the cigarette and pinched it out, sliding what was left behind his ear for later. "Comjee, answer me. If this is a joke, it is not an amusing one."

Hamad hesitated. Only an idiot wandered off into the forest at night. Comjee had never struck him as that sort of fool. Too scared of night-devils, for one thing. He cursed under his breath, hefted his rifle, and hurried to where he'd last seen the other man.

It wasn't that he was concerned on Comjee's behalf, particularly. He and Kazin and even Esmail would likely be killed when Muda Saffir came for the Americans. He felt a small prickle of guilt as he considered his fellow Lascars.

Comjee and those they'd left behind to guard the schooner were no loss, and Kazin was too stubborn to turn his charges over to Saffir when the time came. But Esmail was young, and Hamad had served with both his brother and father. It seemed a shame that the boy had to die, but—well. Sometimes sacrifices were necessary.

"Comjee," he called again. Perhaps the idiot had chased after the orangutan. "I said not to worry about the ape. Where are you?" A wall of trees now separated him from the compound. Only a few steps, really, but it seemed an impossible distance somehow. As if he'd stepped from one world into another. Hamad was a man of the city and the docks. He didn't care for the forest, and didn't see why anyone with any sense would bother coming this far inland. It was noisier than any city street, in its own savage way.

As if to prove him right, a sound—the muffled snap of a branch—caught his ear. He froze. Someone was out there. Not Comjee. No, whoever it was, was trying not to be heard. Maybe they had good reason to be quiet. He hesitated, and then called out, "If you are here on the orders of Muda Saffir, then we have much to discuss."

A risk, but better a risk than a Dayak blade in the guts.

No answer came. Hamad swallowed a sudden rush of panic. Saffir might well have decided he no longer required Hamad's services. That would be unfortunate. He tightened his grip on his rifle. "Who is out there? Answer me, or I will shoot."

Branches rustled and cracked above him, and he leaped back, only just avoiding something that came crashing down. It slammed hard into the forest floor, and he heard the telltale snap of bones. Hamad stared at the body, pulse thundering with such rapidity that he could barely think. It was Comjee—what was left of Comjee.

His fellow Lascar was very dead; but not because of the fall. Numbly, Hamad noted that Comjee's throat had been laid open to the bone, and with such force that his head was only barely attached to the rest of him. Hamad stepped back. This was not the doing of any Dayak. The orangutan . . . ?

Something heavy flashed through the canopy above him, moving so fast that he barely glimpsed it. But he saw enough to know it wasn't any orangutan. He turned, trying to follow the shape, but it vanished as quickly as it had appeared. He felt a coldness in his chest and raised his rifle. Monsters—that was what Sing had said. And the stories he'd heard in Singapore. Maybe there was something to those tales after all.

Hamad brushed the thought away. It didn't matter. All that mattered now was getting back to the compound and the others in one piece. Hang Saffir. Hang the treasure, if it even existed. Money did a dead man no good. Despite his rising terror, he didn't run. It was too quick, whatever it was. No, he needed to stay calm.

Calm—

A low growl sounded to his left. He spun, his finger on the rifle's trigger. But it was too fast. Too strong. The weapon was snatched from his grip, breaking his finger in the process. He stumbled, biting back a wail.

Hamad stared up at the thing, as it examined his rifle with what he could only assume was curiosity. In the darkness, it could have passed for a man, albeit a large one. But here, up close, it reminded him of nothing so much as a fiend out of one of Comjee's tales.

Its skin had the pallor of a water-bloated corpse, and its bloody hands had too many fingers, and all in the wrong positions. The malformed digits flicked up and down the surface of the rifle like the questing legs of a spider. Its face was partially obscured by a curtain of matted, greasy hair, save for a shark's grin of yellowing fangs. There was red on its chin—Comjee's blood, he knew.

"Wer bist du?" it gurgled, in a voice like dirt falling into an open grave. Then, a moment later, in English, "Who are you?" It raised its head, and the curtain of hair parted briefly to reveal a yellow eye—like that of some great cat.

Hamad took an awkward step back, cradling his injured hand. The thing followed. "Who are you?" it growled, teeth snapping off the end of each word. "Why are you here?"

Hamad found himself unable to reply. The words dried in his throat as he stared in incomprehension at the grotesque being before him. He wanted to beg, to plead, to say something, anything to buy himself a moment more. But instead, instinct took over. Driven by fear, he went for his knife.

The monster gave a grunt of annoyance and shoved Hamad's rifle forward like a spear. The barrel punched through his chest and out between his shoulder blades. Hamad felt no pain—only shock. He fell to his knees, trying to breathe through lungs rapidly filling with blood. His dreams of treasure fled, along with his strength. The knife slipped from his fingers, and the world went black and red at the edges.

The monster crouched before him, watching him gasp out his life. "I . . . am sorry," it rumbled softly, looking down at its hands, as if in puzzlement. Hamad toppled over, the monster's next words following him into the dark.

"I meant no harm."

4
Laboratory

BULAN STOOD IN THE ENTRANCE to Maxon's lab, overcome by a surge of—what? Not fear, not exactly. Sadness,
maybe. Or perhaps despair. As their lights played across
the interior, memories of the last time he'd been here came
back in a rush, washing over him like a black cloud. He remembered Maxon and Von Horn, the touch of the bull whip
and the pathetic snarls of his fellow monsters—the creatures
he'd believed were his fellow monsters.

They'd been like children, in a way. Abused and neglected
by their creator who saw them as failures or worse, they had
made their own society and welcomed him into it, if grudgingly and, at times, violently. And in return, he had led them
straight to their deaths. He closed his eyes, fighting back the
regret that suddenly threatened to overwhelm him.

The laboratory was much as he recalled, save for its general
state of degradation. Like the other buildings, it had suffered
from neglect. The windows were open to the muggy air, albeit
covered by tattered curtains, and green shoots nestled in the
floorboards and the walls. Sagging workbenches lined the
walls beneath tall cabinets. The floor was covered in debris—
broken cabinet facings, shattered bottles and flasks, books
that had been left to rot.

And at the far end, shrouded in shadow—the birthing vats.

He felt Virginia take his hand. He released a shuddery
breath and looked at her. He thought of the first time he'd
seen her, at the train station in Ithaca. She and her father had

been about to depart for the first leg of their journey to the Pamarung Islands. He had fallen instantly and madly in love, and made immediate preparations to follow—despite the strongly worded protestations of friends and family.

"It's okay," Virginia murmured, leaning against him. He kissed the top of her head.

"It's not, but thank you." Sometimes, he wondered what would have happened had he listened to his family. He'd have graduated, gone into the family business . . . possibly even have married. He certainly wouldn't have pursued Virginia and her father across the Pacific, only to be waylaid by pirates and left senseless and adrift in a lifeboat.

His gaze found Sing. The old man had found him unconscious—amnesiac—and rescued him. Sing had nursed him back to health in secret, all in the hope of somehow thwarting Maxon in his lunatic design to wed his own daughter to his newest creation. Sing had substituted Bulan for the insensate occupant of Number Thirteen's birthing vat, and neither Maxon nor Von Horn had suspected anything was amiss.

Sing met his gaze and a slight smile creased the old man's features. "I should have burned this place to the ground," he said.

"There was hardly the time," Virginia said, stepping away from Bulan to examine one of the collapsed shelves that lined the walls. "Besides, my father would never have allowed it. He always assumed we would bring him back to—to . . . I don't know. Collect his notes, I suppose. For posterity."

"We should burn them too," Sing said, examining one of the work benches. "All of it. Anything relating to your father's experiments."

Virginia and Bulan looked at him. "Burn them . . . ?" Bulan began, though he found that he agreed with the old man. "We can't simply—"

"He's right," Virginia said, as she looked through a shattered cabinet. She turned to face them. "I love my father, but his notes might as well be a grimoire of black magic. Von Horn lost his life trying to possess them, and he wasn't the only one who thought they might be valuable . . ."

Bulan frowned. According to Virginia, her father had maintained a staggering web of correspondence before his mental state had degraded into blind paranoia. He'd shared his theories with anyone who'd listen—anyone he thought might be able to help.

Once Maxon had returned to Ithaca and committed himself, it wasn't long before men claiming to be from the government had paid him a visit. Some had been accompanied by Maxon's former colleagues at Cornell, others alone. There'd even been a foreign visitors from parts unknown. All of them had come looking to pick Maxon's brain; all of them had gone away unhappy.

Bulan couldn't say whether Maxon himself held out any hope of ever successfully completing his experiments. Maybe some part of him did. Maybe that was why he'd warned Virginia against coming back to the island.

"Perhaps you're both right. Maybe we ought to burn the whole wretched place, after we're done. Leave nothing to chance."

"It may be too late for that," Sing said. "There is something missing."

"Several somethings," Virginia said. "There were six incubation vats originally. Now there's only one. And the shelves . . ."

Bulan followed her gaze and saw telltale gaps in the books that remained. Places where something had been moved, possibly. "Have you found your father's notes, Virginia?" he asked, as a suspicion began to bloom in his mind. Perhaps the damage to the buildings wasn't simply due to opportunistic orangutans.

"No. And they should be in here—some of them, at least." She looked at him. "Do you think . . . ?"

"Someone has been here," Sing said, kneeling beside the remaining incubation vat. "Look here—there are tool marks on the pipework. Someone tried to dismantle it, as they no doubt dismantled the others."

"Dismantled . . ." Bulan murmured. "You mean someone ransacked this place and removed the vats. But why? Without the notes . . ." He paused and looked at Virginia. "Unless they found the notes as well. Our old friend Muda Saffir, perhaps? There's no telling what Von Horn told him, before he was killed."

"Saffir was—is—a pirate," Virginia said. "Why would a pirate steal lab equipment?"

"To sell, perhaps?" Bulan looked around, trying to spot something—anything—that might give them a clue as to what had happened. As he did so, he heard a soft thump somewhere above them, as of a loose branch striking the roof. He glanced at Sing, and the old man narrowed his eyes and nodded, indicating that he'd heard it as well.

But as Sing played his torch across the roof beams, it flickered and died, casting them all into an oppressive gloom. Virginia headed for the closest window. "We need some light. The moon should be up. I'll pull down some of these curtains."

Bulan spun, as his instincts screamed a warning. "Virginia— wait . . . !"

Too late. Virginia tore the curtain aside—and stumbled back, eyes wide with shock. Something large crouched in the window. At first, he thought it was a man, but what man had such a corpse-like pallor, or teeth like serrated razors?

The thing stared down at Virginia, as if equally shocked by the suddenness of its exposure. It tilted its shaggy head, studying her with an intensity that sent a chill through Bulan, and he reached for his sidearm. "Virginia, get back," he called out. "Sing . . . is that . . . ?"

"Yes, yes," Sing barked. "Number Thirteen!"

At the sound of the old man's voice, the creature's head whipped around and its yellow gaze narrowed with menace. Sing lifted his rifle as it sprang toward him with a guttural growl, arms spread wide. He was forced to leap aside as the creature crashed down where he'd been standing. It whirled and faced the old man.

Virginia took a step toward the creature, as if to interpose herself. "We were right, Bulan," she called out. "He is alive!"

The monster turned, as if startled, and Bulan wondered if it had recognized his name. It glanced at him, and he saw a flicker of something—regret, or perhaps fear—in its flat, yellow gaze as it studied him. Its malformed hands twitched and clenched. Then, with a grunt, it leaped toward the remaining incubation vat and, in a display of inhuman strength, it tore the tank from its housings and hefted it over its head.

With a roar, Number Thirteen hurled the vat toward Bulan. He threw himself flat, narrowly avoiding the flying piece of machinery. He heard Sing cry out, and spied Number Thirteen bounding toward Virginia. Before she could go for her own weapon, the monster had scooped her up in its long arms and escaped out the open window.

Bulan cursed and gave chase. As he reached the window, he saw Number Thirteen lope across the compound courtyard, Virginia cradled to its—his—chest. He also saw Kazin and the other Lascar raise their rifles and take aim at the creature charging toward them. Panic seized him. "Don't shoot," he roared. As before, he was a half second too late, and Kazin fired as Number Thirteen swatted the younger Lascar aside.

Thankfully, the shot went wide and Number Thirteen was already racing for the palisade, Virginia still clutched tightly in his grip. But Kazin began to line up another shot—one he wouldn't miss.

Bulan had little time to act. He dropped out of the window and sprang toward Kazin, tackling the Lascar to the ground even as the rifle barked. Instead of hitting Number Thirteen, the shot punched into the palisade. Kazin cursed and flailed as Bulan released him and rose to his feet. Sing was a half step behind him. "We will get him, Mister Harper," the old man shouted. "He will not get far!"

"No, I'll go after him alone," Bulan said, already moving

in pursuit. "You get to the ship and get the other Lascars. I'll fire a shot or two so you can find me. Hurry, Sing!" He didn't slow to wait for an answer. He holstered his pistol and chased after Number Thirteen, pelting into the darkness of the jungle. As he left the gate behind, he barely paused to wonder where the other two Lascars had gotten to.

He heard the harsh rasp of the monster's breathing, not like a man's at all—more like the panting of a tiger—and Virginia's voice, muffled, pleading. A red haze descended and he ducked his head, picking up speed. If the creature had hurt her . . .

Bulan burst through a curtain of vegetation and saw his quarry just ahead. Virginia was free and on her feet, the monster circling her. She was trying to talk to it, but it wasn't listening. It began to turn as Bulan burst onto the scene, and knowing he had only one chance, he flung himself at the creature with a bellow worthy of a bull elephant.

They collided with a bone-rattling thump, and went down in a frenzied tangle. Bulan rained blow after blow down on the hideous countenance, and Number Thirteen responded in kind. The creature was strong—stronger than any of the others Bulan had grappled with, even Number Twelve—and it had soon tossed him aside as if he were a sack of potatoes. He hit the ground hard, but immediately rolled to his feet, his pulse singing in his ears. "I don't want to hurt you," he said, as they began to circle one another. "We're friends."

Number Thirteen snarled, showing what it thought of that. It pounced and bore him backward, its clawed fingers digging into his scalp like iron nails. It was so strong—so impossibly strong—he felt the bones of his skull beginning to part beneath that awful pressure and gagged on the rancid stink of the creature's breath, as he clutched vainly at its thick wrists. If he could break its hold, maybe—

The cold click of a pistol being readied made both combatants pause in their struggle. Both man and monster turned to see Virginia staring at them over the barrel of her pistol.

"Let him go," she said, with an icy calm. "And don't give me that mute shtick. You understand me well enough. I saw it in your eyes earlier."

Number Thirteen released Bulan and stepped back, hands raised. "Bitte . . . nicht . . ." he gurgled, taking another step back. Virginia froze, startled.

"He can speak," she began, her tone one of wonder. Her pistol dipped, forgotten. Bulan clambered to his feet as Number Thirteen whirled and pelted into the jungle. He took a step after the creature, but stopped and turned to Virginia. "Are you . . . ?"

"I'm—I'm fine." She looked at him, confusion on her face.

"He said 'no, please' . . . in German."

5
RAJAH

REASURE," MUDA SAFFIR SAID, rolling the word around in his mouth. He liked the taste of it. "You are certain the old man said this?" he asked, looking down at the injured Dayak. Tijilik had come creeping back into camp a few hours ago, looking as if the ghosts of the forest were close at his heels.

Tijilik nodded and winced. "Yes, Rajah." The young warrior had his injured arm bound in a sling against his chest. Ordinarily, a one-handed man would be of little use to Saffir, but Tijilik was the cousin of an important chieftain. To dispose of him would be to draw the ire of said chieftain, something Saffir could not risk.

His position was a tenuous one at the moment. His influence among the local chieftains was not what it once had been, and many among his own crew questioned his fitness to command. Once, he might have settled such matters with the sharp edge of a blade. But he was older now, and wiser.

Saffir had first made his name in the Strait of Malacca, plundering Dutch traders. But in the years since the end of the Infidel War, he had done his best to stay out of the eyes of the Dutch and the British. He had contented himself with small raids against easy targets—at least until last year, when he had stumbled across Maxon, and his fabled treasure.

The American was still regarded as something of a legend among the tribes inhabiting the Pamarung Islands. They thought him a sorcerer, a conjurer of jinn and other devils.

28

As such, few doubted that he had also possessed a great treasure, which was still hidden on the island.

Acquiring the latter, if it truly existed, would do much to restore his reputation among his peers. The name of Muda Saffir would once more be feared in these waters. If the treasure was real. If he wasn't deluding himself, as some claimed.

He sat back on his stool, pondering the news Tijilik had brought him. Around him, the war camp hummed with life. He'd claimed an isolated cove on the island as his headquarters. Far enough from the British compound to avoid the notice of their intermittent patrols, but close enough to be within striking range of the next supply ship.

That ship would no doubt be carrying much of value, especially ammunition, which his crew was in sore need of. He'd intended to find a new cove to shelter in once they'd ransacked the ship; the British would no doubt come hunting for them at that point, and he had no intention of being here when they did. But now, if what Tijilik was saying was true, it might be wiser to stay.

He had feared that he'd missed his chance when the British had arrived, and had kept close watch on them for that very reason. A few tentative sorties had shown him that their strength was not negligible, and it was best to leave them be for the time being. He would need more men, or better weapons, if he wanted to take their compound for his own. But unless it brought him closer to his goal there was no point in expending the resources he possessed in such a brash endeavor. A successful pirate was one who did not strike save when victory was certain, and the reward was great.

Rewards like Maxon's treasure. It seemed that it was real after all, even as the renegade, Von Horn, had assured him during their all-too-brief alliance a year ago. Von Horn was dead now, his head decorating some longhouse on the coast. Saffir did not mourn him. The American had been clever and ruthless, qualities that he valued in an ally, but absolutely untrustworthy otherwise. No, better he was dead and Saffir free to search without any further complications.

"Tell me again about the monster," Saffir said, leaning toward Tijilik. Once again, Tijilik described the thing—its strength and swiftness, its raw ferocity. A man-eater. But a domesticated one. Much like the fiends Maxon had created—or so Von Horn had insisted. Guardians for Maxon's treasure, summoned like jinn from great vats.

Saffir had given much thought to the monsters since his first encounter with them. That Maxon had some dark wisdom was obvious. With a crew of such beasts as the mad American had created at his beck and call, a man might become a power to rival even the greatest of chieftains. To become a rajah in truth, rather than merely playing the part. Moreover, what might the British or the Dutch or even the Germans pay for such knowledge?

The latter held more appeal. Saffir had survived in these contentious waters for as long as he had because he knew his limits. A man could only carry what he could hold.

Saffir rose abruptly to his feet and flexed his big hands. He felt a pulse of eagerness, as at the end of a successful raid. It was as if all the fortunes of the world were aligning just for him. Truly was there a more blessed man in all of existence than Muda Saffir? He laughed and thumped his chest with his fists before dismissing Tijilik. "Get some rest, boy. There will be killing to do soon enough, and I need your sword ready."

As Tijilik slunk away, Saffir turned to his second-in-command, Riwut. The big Dayak was an exile from one of the sea-tribes, and had taken to the life of a pirate with aplomb. It was Riwut who had brokered many of Saffir's alliances with the local tribes. In return for a share of the spoils, the chieftains would send him their best warriors. They made for formidable crewmen, and the terror of their reputation was often enough to see a ship's crew surrender without a shot fired.

"Have we heard from that dog of a Lascar yet?" Saffir asked. The Lascar, Hamad, had alerted Saffir's people in Singapore to an American yacht heading for the island. It had seemed too much of a coincidence to Saffir, especially given Hamad's description of the young woman. He had half feared they would make for the British compound, but it did not seem so. A kernel of suspicion began to grow in his mind.

Riwut shook his head.

"No, though we did hear gunshots."

Saffir turned. "But not the signal?" If the woman was the same one he was thinking of, he knew exactly where she was going. He suddenly recalled the glint in her eyes, the gold of her hair, and felt a familiar flutter in his chest. She had been a vision—and fierce! A tigress, in the very flesh. Of course she had returned, for was the treasure not hers? Yes, it was all beginning to make sense now.

"No."

Saffir paused. "Are you certain?"

Riwut hesitated. Saffir sighed and clapped the Dayak on the shoulder. He tightened his grip after a moment, causing Riwut to wince. Saffir was older, but still a strong man, honed to lethality by a dangerous life. "Riwut, I ask again—are you certain that you did not hear the signal?"

Riwut grimaced. "It is possible."

Saffir gave him a more gentle squeeze and released him. "As I thought. Hamad is a fool. He probably gave himself away, and is even now fleeing into the jungle." More likely, someone had been startled by an orangutan or another animal. But he needed to give Riwut a good reason for mustering the men, if only to avoid protest.

"That does us little good," Riwut said, surreptitiously rubbing his shoulder. "We do not even know where they are."

"I know exactly where they are," Saffir said, giving his beard a thoughtful tug. He smiled at the look on Riwut's face. "The compound I told you about? The one the British were so interested in?"

Riwut grunted. "There is nothing there but orangutans."

Saffir laughed. "And have you looked? No."

"The British beat us to it," Riwut protested. Saffir nodded.

"Yes—exactly! And who is to say they did not find something?"

"Then why do the Americans matter at all?"

Saffir sighed. "Because the British may not have found what is hidden there." It would not do to reveal his true interest in the Americans, and the woman in particular. "The man who built that compound was mad, but clever in the way of some madmen."

"He is the one who tricked you," Riwut said, with a slight smile. Saffir frowned. He did not care to be reminded of the great sea chest that he had risked so much for, only to find it full of worthless paper, and not even the kind that could be spent.

"Yes," he said, grudgingly. He choked down his anger and added, "Perhaps he tricked the British as well." He decided to change the subject. "If the Americans are at the compound, that means their vessel is likely anchored in the cove closest to it—you know the one I mean?"

Riwut sucked on his teeth. "It is not far from here."

"Not far at all." Saffir rubbed his chin. "How many Lascars are with them?"

"That old reprobate, Kazin . . . a handful of others." Riwut frowned. "Not more than six, I think. Five, if we do not count Hamad."

"And why would we?" Saffir murmured, tugging on his beard. Hamad was useful, but often had an overinflated idea of his importance in Saffir's plans. The Lascar had too many debts for Saffir's taste. Perhaps it was time to dispense with his services once and for all.

"And what of the old man that Tijilik met?" Riwut asked. "What of his claims?"

Saffir paused. The old man—a German, at that—was a mystery, and he did not care for mysteries. It was clear that he had come with the British, but who was he? And what did he know of the treasure? The questions nagged at him. "I do not know," he said, finally. "He claims that he wants to talk. Perhaps he is tired of British hospitality. Or perhaps he knows something the others do not."

"Do we meet him?"

Saffir raised an eyebrow. "We?"

Riwut grunted. "I assumed you would not wish to go alone. It might be a trap."

Saffir dismissed this with a wave of his hand. "No, I do not think so."

"It would not be wise to attract the notice of the British," Riwut continued. "Not after last time." Saffir nodded reluctantly. The attacks against the British compound had been necessary, if only to gauge the threat the invaders posed, but they'd lost a good many men and left the remainder of the Dayaks grumbling and unhappy.

"The Americans, then," Saffir said, rubbing his hands together. He looked out over the camp, and its assemblage of tents and lean-tos. He had a single prahu under his command currently, and just enough crew to man it, if not well. Not an army, by any means. Less than sixty men, and a third of them wounded. But it was more than enough to handle six or seven Lascars and a pair of Americans. Even the woman, however fierce she was.

"When?" Riwut asked.

"Tonight," Saffir said, decisively. "We will take their vessel first, and then capture them when they return." He grinned at his subordinate. "We will let them come to us, yes? And then we will see what they know about this treasure."

6

SOULLESS

BULAN STARED INTO THE DARKNESS beyond the palisades and imagined what might be looking back. He rubbed the marks left on his throat by Number Thirteen's impossibly strong fingers. Everything hurt after his brief encounter. The creature had been stronger than his predecessors, and faster as well.

Smarter.

"Well, we have our answer," he said, in a rough voice.

Virginia nodded, her attention torn between him and the forest. "We do. I can't say it's the one I hoped for." She touched his bruised neck, brushing gently at the red marks as if hoping to wipe them away. "I don't know what I was thinking."

Bulan took her in his arms, and crushed her to him. "You wanted to help him. As you helped me. We both wanted to help him, but . . ." He fell silent. What was there to say? Neither of them had been prepared for what awaited them. He had imagined some cowering brute, a child in mind if not body. A pathetic grotesque, in need of pity and kindness.

Instead, Number Thirteen was a monster. A true monster; strong and fast and as silent as death. Hostile, of base and brutal disposition. Or so it had seemed to him as the creature's grip had tightened about his throat, and he had stared up into those hungry eyes. Those awful, hungry eyes. The worst of it was, Number Thirteen was no feral animal.

34

There was intelligence in that horrid skull; an intelligence apparently unleavened by the milk of human kindness. It had been like looking into the eyes of Lucifer himself.

He shuddered and Virginia looked at him in concern. "Are you all right?"

"Honestly? No." He sighed and turned away. "In the weeks it took us to get here, I had a lot of time to think. Too much, even."

Down below, Sing was overseeing the burial of the dead Lascar. One of them was still missing, but none of them held out much hope of Hamad's survival. All they'd found of him was his rifle—covered in blood.

Bulan took a deep breath. "In my heart, I knew we would find him. But I hoped we would find him dead." He looked at her. "What I endured when I thought I was Number Thirteen was horrendous. Torturous. Agony, in body and mind."

"Oh Bulan." She tightened her grip on him. For a moment, he wanted nothing more than to take her and flee. To go back to the schooner, back to New York. To pretend none of this had ever happened. That it was all just a terrible dream. Instead, he went on.

"I've imagined him, hiding in the forest like a frightened animal. A child, confused and alone. Abandoned. I pitied him." He paused. "I still do. For a time, I lived as one of your father's creations . . . but I was not one of them. Despite any tutoring or nurturing they could have received had they been treated more humanely, Number Twelve and the others could never be men. I know that, in my heart. And that knowledge haunts me. That but for a soul, they could have been men."

He closed his eyes, seeing again that shark's grin—those eyes—and knew that the next time they met, one or the other might have to die. "I hoped we would find him dead," he repeated. "I hoped that when we found his body, my conscience would be at peace. But now, having seen him, I feel a hundred times worse. I should never have left the island without proof of his life or death. I should not have abandoned him. What might he have become, if I hadn't? What has he become, because I did?"

Virginia was silent for long moments. Then, "If you abandoned him, then so did I. And as to the rest—well." She laughed softly, bitterly. "What is a soul?" she asked, tilting his face so that he looked at her. "You, my father, even Sing, say that they didn't have souls, but what does that mean, really? Tell me, Bulan. What is a soul—and how do you know that they didn't have it? Or that Number Thirteen doesn't?" Her gaze was as hard and sharp as diamond. "Does my father have a soul? Did Von Horn? Or Muda Saffir? They were as much monsters as those poor creatures, but somehow they are different?"

Bulan looked away, unable to meet her gaze. She continued, remorseless. Unrelenting. "Who are we to say a man is soulless?" She shook her head and looked away. "I don't know about you, but I'm not comfortable bearing that responsibility."

Unsettled by the turn the conversation had taken, Bulan decided to change the subject. "Why do you think he took you?" he asked. "What was the point of it?"

"Instinct, perhaps," Virginia said, pushing away from him. She rubbed her arms and walked a little ways away, her expression one of cool calculation. It was not the first time he had seen that look on her face, though it never failed to disconcert him. At such times, Virginia reminded him very much of her father. The same determination, the same will that had enabled Maxon to create his abominations was present in Virginia. Once she had chosen a course, very little could alter it. "It is a good question, though. We'll add it to the pile."

Bulan nodded. It was obvious what she was referring to. "The missing vats, you mean." Another worry, though not quite as pressing as the monster stalking them.

"Among other things. Time and neglect account for much

of this place's condition, but—look there." She pointed to the ground near the main gates. "Those rutted tracks there. Something heavy was pulled through the courtyard, and recently."

Bulan followed her gesture and saw the furrowed ground. They hadn't noticed it before because of the overgrowth, but from atop the palisade it was clearly visible. A trail of deep ruts, carved into the soft earth, leading from the gates to the main buildings. "I don't recall any wagons or carts from before," he said, thoughtfully.

Virginia shook her head. "No, we broke down the ones we used to bring in father's equipment, and used them as building materials." She smiled sadly. "He didn't intend to leave, you see, so no need for a way to transport anything anywhere."

Bulan sank to his haunches and scanned the compound. "I noticed weak spots in the palisade during our initial exploration. I chalked it up to neglect or foraging animals, but—were the gates closed when we left?"

"Yes," Virginia said, in a quiet voice. "I didn't think of it earlier, but—yes."

Bulan glanced at her. "You were right, someone was here. Someone took the vats."

"A German," she said. "Number Thirteen spoke to us in German. I can't imagine where he might have picked it up, unless . . ." She trailed off, frowning. Before she could continue, they were interrupted by Sing and Kazin, who joined them on the palisade.

"I tell you, I hear thunder," Kazin was saying, to Sing. He looked to Bulan, as if seeking support. "If there is a storm, sailing into it will be a very bad idea. Tell him, Mr. Harper. Tell him it is foolish."

Sing grunted dubiously and looked at Bulan and Virginia. "If we wish to leave, now is the time. If we start now, we can reach the schooner before the storm hits."

"Who says we're leaving?" Bulan asked.

Sing's expression was mulish. "I understand why you

came here, sir. You wanted to know if Number Thirteen
was alive. We know now. He is alive and he does not want
us here. We should leave before he decides to take offense
to our presence."

"If Kazin is right, trying to leave tonight would be foolhardy," Virginia said.

Sing shot her a look of betrayal. "Oh no, not you too," he
began, clearly exasperated by her hesitation. "Miss Ginny,
please . . ."

Virginia overrode him. "We'll be safe in the compound
tonight, won't we? The Lascars can—" She hesitated, and
looked to Kazin. "I'm sorry. There's still no sign of Hamad,
is there? And how is Esmail?" The younger seaman's wits had
been thoroughly rattled by Number Thirteen's blow, though
he was otherwise uninjured.

"He will recover," Kazin said. "Sing brought Habiboola
and Ameer. They left Jabal to watch the schooner. He is a
good man." He hesitated. "We can protect this place. The
gates can be barred, the brush cleared away. But . . . that
thing was so quick, so strong. I do not know that gates will
be enough. I do not know that we will be enough."

Sing spoke up. "Which is why we should go. Number
Thirteen may well return to try his luck again." He looked
at Virginia as he spoke.

"And I will be safer here, surrounded by armed men, than
running around out in the forest, in the dark." She turned.
"Kazin, we will stay in the main building. I'll show you where
we kept the tools when we lived here. If they're not completely
rusted, they might be of some use in helping us get this place
shipshape." She descended from the palisade, Kazin at her heels.

Bulan turned back to the forest. "Shipshape," he murmured.

Sing chuckled grimly. "We will be secure enough. The walls
are still solid. We will cut back any overhanging branches, to
prevent Number Thirteen from getting in that way."

"I wouldn't be so sure," Bulan said. "If he wants to get in,
I'm sure he'll find a way."

"Then we will be waiting for him. This time, he will not catch us unawares." Sing frowned, then added, "I am sorry, Mr. Harper. I should have made sure he was dead, when I pulled him from the vat. I should have slit his throat then and there."

Bulan blinked, startled by this sudden display of vehemence. "You couldn't have known, Sing. None of us could have known."

"I should have. I saw the professor make the others; I should have known Number Thirteen was made of sterner stuff than that." Sing's frown deepened. "It was evil, that business. To make such things, to let them loose on the world—it was a foul act."

"Maxon was—is—a troubled man," Bulan said.

"Troubled men make trouble," Sing said, sharply. He rested his rifle in the crook of his arm. "And now that trouble is ours. He has killed two of our people; there is no telling how many others have suffered a similar fate. I do not wish for us to join them."

Bulan looked at the older man. "I know you're worried, Sing. I am as well." He hesitated. "You didn't have to come, but I'm glad you're here."

Sing was silent for a moment. Then, "I came because I wanted to, Mr. Harper. I owe you that much. You arranged for me to enter the United States, though we Chinese are no longer welcome. You treat me like a man, rather than a railroad worker. For that, I will go anywhere with you."

Bulan hesitated, surprised again by Sing's uncharacteristic openness. The Singaporean was a mystery to him, in many ways. Sing rarely spoke of his life prior to his signing on with Maxon. Had he always been a cook, or was there more to him?

That Sing knew his way around a rifle was self-evident. And Kazin, old salt that he was, seemed to have great respect for him. From little he'd gleaned from their conversations, Bulan suspected they'd served together in battle, though when and where that might have been, he couldn't say. He didn't even know whether the other man had any family at all.

Sing checked his rifle and said, "You go rest, Mr. Harper. You and Miss Ginny both. I will keep watch tonight." As he spoke, thunder rumbled and the first pattering of rain descended.

Bulan paused, and then stretched out his hand. Sing looked at it for a moment, and then took it. "I will, Sing," Bulan said. "But I can't guarantee that we'll sleep." He looked out at the dark forest, and wondered again if Number Thirteen was out there somewhere, looking back at them. Planning his next move. Bulan turned away.

"Not until we've settled this, one way or another."

7
JU–LONG

JU-LONG! DO YOU SEE ANYTHING?"

Ju-Long turned from the forest to look down into the courtyard of the compound. Lieutenant Arkwright stood below, sheltered from the rain by an umbrella. The Englishman was narrow; a needle in uniform. Ju-Long had grown up on the docks of Singapore, around hard men and rough ones, around Lascars and Malays.

Arkwright was harder than any of them. It was why Ju-Long respected him, though he did not particularly like the man. "Nothing, Lieutenant," he replied, stepping back from the Maxim gun he'd been manning. He patted the weapon fondly. It was a favorite of his, and he was the only man in Arkwright's command capable of firing it without difficulty—a point of pride, though he was careful not to show it around the enlisted men.

"Perhaps it was just thunder," Arkwright said, looking up at him.

Ju-Long shook his head, rainwater sliding from the brim of his straw hat. "I am certain I heard a gunshot." He paused, as a thought occurred to him. "Maybe Muda Saffir and his pirates were fool enough not to heed our warnings." The wily Malay and his Dayaks had been a thorn in their side since they'd come to the island. After the first few probing attacks they'd contented themselves with harassing the occasional patrols Arkwright dispatched. "If they have returned . . ."

"Then they will pay the price," Arkwright said. He turned

away. "Notify me if you see anything. I will be in the laboratory with Professor Vogel."

"Sir," Ju-Long called. Arkwright paused. "I think a patrol should be sent to the Maxon compound. The Dayaks might have decided to loot it, finally. It would be best if we discourage them."

Arkwright peered up at him, his expression unreadable. Then he nodded. "Pragmatic as ever, Ju-Long. I will let you see to it."

Ju-Long hesitated. "Perhaps it would be better if you gave the order, sir."

Arkwright chuckled. "Still giving you lip, are they? They'll never respect you, if you don't show them your teeth every so often. No—I trust you to give the order, and ensure it is obeyed. Carry on, there's a good fellow." With that, he departed.

Ju-Long sighed and turned back to the forest, one big hand resting on the Maxim gun. Some days he regretted ever introducing Vogel to Arkwright. He'd hoped to make his fortune—the fortune Von Horn had promised him, and then reneged on.

His hands clenched abruptly as he thought of the American. Von Horn was dead, but he still owed many debts. But one could not collect from a ghost. He had thought that Arkwright might make good on what Von Horn owed, but instead he had insisted that Ju-Long accompany his expedition. Whether he feared trickery, or simply desired another hand, Ju-Long could not say.

Arkwright was smart; cunning, even. He was not simply a soldier. He might well go far in the world, and if Ju-Long was wise—if he too was cunning—he might be carried along in the other man's wake.

The ladder of the watch post creaked. Ju-Long turned to see one of the soldiers, a sergeant named Higgs, climbing up toward him. "What are you doing here?" he asked, warily. Ju-Long and the enlisted men kept a careful distance from each other. For all intents and purposes, he was outside the chain of command, answerable only to Arkwright. Higgs and the others didn't like that, but feared Arkwright too much to do anything about it.

Higgs smiled and showed all of his teeth. "Just came to have a chat, Ju-Long me old chum. You looked lonely up here all by yourself."

"I do not require companionship," Ju-Long said, and turned away.

"Could have fooled me. You look nervous," Higgs said, as he lit a cigarette. He didn't offer one to Ju-Long. "Hearing things, are we? Scared of the dark, maybe?"

"I heard a gunshot," Ju-Long said, not looking at the sergeant. Higgs was an unpleasant man, distrusting of those who did not share his ethnicity or culture. It did not matter whether they were Chinese, Malay, or Lascar; he disdained them all. Or so it seemed, at least, to Ju-Long.

Higgs grunted. "Dayaks, probably. Maybe they've smartened up and done away with old Muda Saffir, eh?"

"I do not think we are so lucky as that."

Higgs chuckled, but there was no mirth in the sound. Ju-Long glanced at him. Higgs smiled around his cigarette and leaned against the guardrail of the tower. "I wouldn't call any of this lucky, me. Stuck out here in the middle of bloody nowhere, playing nursemaid to some old German Arkwright dug from God knows where, whilst said German does . . . what, exactly?" He blew a plume of smoke toward the forest.

"You do not need to know," Ju-Long said, with some satisfaction.

Higgs flicked ash from his cigarette. "But you do, innit?" He fixed Ju-Long with a calculating gaze. "Barely any daylight between you and the lieutenant, is it? His loyal Chinese killer."

"I am from Singapore."

"Semantics, innit?" Higgs blew smoke into Ju-Long's face. "You ain't a soldier, boy. At best, you're a mercenary; plenty of those in these waters. So why'd Arkwright hire you? Not just for your pretty face, I think."

"Perhaps he values loyalty, Englishman," Ju-Long said, softly. He met Higgs' gaze and held it. The other man was trying to provoke him—why?

Higgs chuckled and turned away. "Maybe. Fool not to, I suppose. Word is, he is not well liked, back in Blighty. Some scandal or other. Might be why he's out here, doing whatever it is he's doing."

"I do not know anything about that."

"No, you wouldn't, would you? You only joined us in Singapore—like that dotty old sausage-eater, Vogel." Higgs paused, as if a thought had occurred to him. "Odd coincidence, that. One day you show up, and the next, him. And then, all of a sudden, we're shipping out to this bloody nowhere island, scavenging equipment from some old compound on the other side of the island so Vogel can play mad scientist."

Ju-Long said nothing. Higgs smiled in a self-satisfied way and puffed on his cigarette. "I been watching you, Ju-Long. I think you're in this up to your pigtail, old boy."

"I do not wear a queue," Ju-Long said, absently.

"No, you don't do you? Proper barbarian like you, I can see why. But my point stands. Something is going on here, and I would like to know what. What exactly is it that Vogel is doing in that bloody lab of his? And what's being kept in those cells under our feet, eh? Tell me that, and I shall be content."

"Your contentment is not my concern, Sergeant," Ju-Long said. He paused. "But if you are bored, then I will alleviate your suffering. Take two men and go to the Maxon compound. I believe the shots I heard came from there."

"And so? That's on the other side of the island, practically. What does it matter?"

"It matters because I say it does." Ju-Long fixed the other man with a cold look. "The lieutenant might not be concerned but you do not allow a man to break into your home and then lock the door. If someone else is on this island, you will find them and stop them before they endanger this compound."

"You don't give the orders, you bloody—" Higgs began.

Ju-Long's hands snapped out and caught the other man by the front of his uniform jacket. Before Higgs could squirm free, Ju-Long swung him easily about and forced him back against the guardrail. One shove would be enough to send Higgs plummeting to the ground below. And from the look on his face, Higgs knew it.

"I answer to the lieutenant, Sergeant—and you answer to me. Is that understood?" He gave the other man a gentle shake. "Do you understand?"

"I—I do, yes, damn you! Now let me loose!"

Ju-Long pulled him back from the edge and released him. "If it is Dayaks, capture them. If it is Muda Saffir . . . kill him." He dismissed the man with a gesture. "Go."

Higgs hesitated, but only for a moment. Then he went, muttering imprecations the entire way. Ju-Long didn't mind, so long as he did as he was told. He looked up into the rain and felt a moment's satisfaction. It passed all too quickly.

He climbed down. It was almost feeding time. The thought brought with it a shudder of revulsion. The things imprisoned beneath the compound were becoming more restless by the day. Hungrier. Belligerent. He had counseled Arkwright to shoot them, before they became impossible to restrain. Thus far, Arkwright had ignored him.

As he reached the bottom, he spied a small hunched figure trotting through the rain toward him. "Is there trouble, Ju-Long?" Vogel called out. "After dark, with a storm bearing down on the island . . . it is an odd time for such activity, yes?"

Professor Vogel was an odd little man. He resembled a gnome from a German fairy tale, but there the resemblance ended. Like Arkwright, he was far too clever for Ju-Long's liking. Unlike Arkwright, Vogel had no master save his own curiosity. "I thought you were in the laboratory, Professor," Ju-Long said.

"I was. Now I am out here."

Ju-Long grunted. Vogel could be obstinate when he wished it. "You should go back inside, Professor. It is raining."

Vogel smiled politely. "I will not melt, my boy. What is happening out in the forest that requires soldiers?"

"Routine security," Ju-Long said. Sometimes he wondered whether Vogel were entirely sane. The old man seemed to drift in and out of reality. Then, maybe he was simply playing the part of mad scientist.

"Is that all?"

Ju-Long hesitated. "I heard a gun shot earlier."

Vogel's eyebrows went up in evident surprise. "Ah. When was that, please?"

"It was probably Dayak pirates having a dispute among themselves," Ju-Long said, swiftly. "If it is pirates, they will be dealt with. You have my assurance."

Vogel nodded. "You reassure me. Thank you, Ju-Long. Have you notified our host?"

Ju-Long frowned. Arkwright must not have thought it worth mentioning to the professor. "I have." He extended his arm. "Let us go inside, Professor. It is almost time for the evening feeding. You should stay indoors, just to be safe."

"Yes, yes," Vogel said, as he allowed Ju-Long to guide him back toward the buildings. "Just to be safe."

"From the pirates," Ju-Long said.

Vogel nodded. "Yes. From the pirates."

8

CONVERSATIONS

BULAN LAY ON HIS BEDROLL and stared up at the ceiling, listening to the rain. The main building of the compound was largely intact, despite orangutans having made it a nest. Open windows and a cleansing rain had dispersed much of the smell, but there was still a musky quality to the atmosphere that made it hard for him to relax. So instead, he lay and listened and pondered all that had happened since they'd left the island the first time.

At the time, he'd thought returning home to New York with Virginia would be the end of it. Happily ever after, the way the story books promised. But the scars of his time here ran deeper than he'd suspected. More than once he'd awoken, bathed in sweat, heart hammering—in fear of something he could not name.

Sometimes, in the dead of night, he became convinced that he wasn't Townsend Harper, Jr., at all. That it was just a dream, born of the fevered imaginings of a soulless thing. That none of this was real, that he was still here, still a monster among monsters. In those moments, he often found himself staring at his own reflection in a mirror, searching for the hidden horror beneath his skin.

He thought of Number Thirteen, with his jaundiced gaze and saw-blade teeth, and in his mind's eye the monster's countenance overlaid his own. Perhaps that was who he really was. Perhaps this was all simply a delusion. He took a deep breath and closed his eyes, forcing his mind away from the disturbing thought.

No one truly understood, save perhaps Virginia. Even Sing couldn't really comprehend what it had been like to live among Maxon's creations for all those months. To learn their personalities, their foibles. To see them as fellow intelligent beings . . . even if he had not always treated them as such.

That was the worst of it. The single black thought that gripped the underside of his mind however much he tried to shake it loose. He'd had a chance to make their lives better, and instead, had led Number Twelve and the others to their deaths. Their lives had been short and brutal, and he had contributed to that.

He had not simply lived among monsters, but had become one. He had been no better than Maxon or Von Horn. And here—now—his first instinct upon seeing Number Thirteen had been to attack. To lunge for the creature's throat. He could rationalize it; he'd believed Virginia had been in danger, after all.

But the deed was done, nonetheless. Even if they found Number Thirteen, would he ever trust them? And what if he did? What to do with him then? Where to take him? More importantly, where was Number Thirteen now? Was he close by, or did he have some lair elsewhere on the island? Perhaps he was drawn to the compound by instinct; Bulan couldn't imagine wanting to be near it otherwise. Then, how much did the creature know of his own origins?

Bulan had no answers. There could be no answers while Number Thirteen was loose. But how to capture the creature without harming him? Especially given Sing and Kazin's predilection for shooting first and asking questions later.

He thought of Sing. The old man was loyal, but he had his own ideas about how this matter should be settled. When it came down to it, would he allow Number Thirteen to live? Or would he seek to kill the creature, as he'd planned to do the first time? And who was to say that he wasn't right to do so?

The sad truth was, Number Twelve and the others, however pitiable they'd seemed, were dangerous. They were savage; predatory. Driven by unnatural urges and a fierce survival instinct. For a moment, he allowed himself to imagine what might have happened, had they escaped—had there been a female among them—had they reproduced and multiplied like natural creatures. What sort of society would they have made?

Somehow, he suspected it would not have been one kindly disposed to humanity. No . . . he'd seen enough of what they'd endured to know better. Monsters could only make more monsters. Sing was right about that, at least.

Maybe it would be kinder to put Number Thirteen out of his misery. But was he miserable? He thought again of that yellow gaze, and of the depths of intelligence he'd glimpsed there. There had been rage there, the fury of a thwarted animal . . . but also something that might have been curiosity.

Bulan recalled the missing picture of Virginia and could not help but wonder if it had not been a child's inquisitiveness that had driven Number Thirteen to take Virginia. Not out of any intent to harm, but simply to . . . know. To better understand this sudden intrusion into his isolation. Did he know who Virginia was, somehow? Or had he simply recognized her face and acted on impulse?

Too many questions. Bulan grunted and rubbed his face tiredly. He wanted to sleep, to rest, but his brain was determined to run in circles until it caught what it was chasing.

"You're not asleep, are you?" Virginia murmured. She lay beside him on her own bedroll, facing away from him. He'd thought she was fast asleep.

"No. You?"

"I was. But you kept sighing."

He smiled. "I'm sorry."

"You sigh very loudly, my love."

"Again, I'm sorry."

Virginia rolled over and looked down at him. "Apology

accepted. What's wrong?" She paused. "Besides the obvious, I mean."

Bulan let out a soft laugh. "Where to start?"

Virginia smiled and poked his arm. "I did say besides the obvious."

"I was just thinking."

"Were you thinking about having an ice cream soda at Benson's?" she asked, smiling gently. "Because I could go for one of those right about now."

"Well, I wasn't, but I am now," Bulan said, in mock annoyance. "Thanks for that."

Virginia chuckled throatily. "Happy to help, darling."

"I appreciate it. But no, I was thinking about why we came." Bulan looked at her. "And about how I needed to apologize to you."

Virginia frowned and sat up. "For what?"

"For putting you back into harm's way. You should be . . ." He trailed off. She leaned over him, her expression stern.

"Where? Home in Ithaca? Doing what, exactly? Worrying about you?"

"I just meant . . ." he began.

"I know what you meant, and I love you for it. But I will not be coddled. This is as much my home as it was yours. And both of us endured horrors here, and came out the stronger for it." She sighed and laid her head on his chest. "I understand that you're a ball of emotions right now. That this whole thing is not easy for you. But please—*please*—don't go down the road of doubt. Not now."

"I'm not. I just—are we doing the right thing?"

"We are. And we have to be strong, not just for ourselves, but also for him. For Number Thirteen. He deserves a second chance."

"Does he? Sing hates them—the monsters, I mean. Von Horn hated them too." Bulan stared at the ceiling as he spoke, and he knew that she felt the tension radiating from him. It had always been with him, that fear of what others might think of him. Even as a boy. And as a monster.

"But you don't hate them," she said. "Nor do I."

"No. I don't hate them. I don't hate him." Bulan interlaced his fingers behind his head. "I'm scared of him, though. And for him, but mostly of him. Of what he represents."

"What do you mean?"

"Number Twelve and the others were strong, but . . . fragile. They were out of sync with the world in a way I cannot quite explain." He glanced at her, wondering how to clarify. "The orangutans hated them. They wanted to stay with them, to live among them and—and breed with them. It sounds laughable and horrible but, I—I understood. They just wanted somewhere to exist without pain, without fear and . . ." He fell silent.

"And what?" she asked.

"And it was as if the world itself denied it to them. As if it knew they didn't belong here. Von Horn tortured them, the apes hated them, and the Dayaks killed them. Hate and pain and death were all they knew." He paused. "But Number Thirteen is different, somehow. The way he moved, the way he fought . . . the way he vanished."

"I understand," she said. "It's as if the world has accepted him, somehow. As if he belongs here."

"And that's what frightens me. He's not just a brute. Earlier, you asked me to define a soul. Well, I can't. But I know one when I see it, and looking into his eyes I saw . . . something. A spark of something. I've been turning it over and over in my mind. He is not like the others, at all." He looked at her. "I think your father succeeded. I think Number Thirteen, for all the hideousness of his appearance, is a—a man."

"The question, then, is . . . how did he wind up that way?" Virginia paused. "Uh-oh. I know that look."

Bulan closed his eyes. "What look?"

"That look, there." She poked his chin. "On your handsome mug. What are you thinking, Bulan?"

"I want to talk to him," he said. "But after that, I don't know what to do. Can he be, well, socialized? And who taught him German?" He hesitated, and then let the questions flow. "Was it Von Horn? Or is there someone else here?"

"I doubt it," Virginia said. She reclined with her fingers interlaced over her stomach. "There's nothing on this island of any real value."

"But it is possible," Bulan said, as he sat up. He ran his hand through his hair and stared at the far wall as he spoke. "Let's say it was Von Horn. He assisted your father, and knew everything about his process of creation."

"Not everything," Virginia interjected. "My father kept some secrets."

Bulan nodded, unsurprised. Though he couldn't help but wonder just what those secrets might be. But that was a question for another time. "Fine. Sing switched me with the body of Number Thirteen and no one suspected. Not your father and certainly not Von Horn."

"And then Doctor von Horn decided he wanted to marry me, to get his hands on my father's fortune," Virginia said. "Not that there was much of a fortune to be had, given how much of it my father had sunk into his research over the years. Besides which, I had my heart set on another." She looked at him, and he felt his own heart beat a little faster. "But no, you're right. Von Horn had no idea that you weren't Number Thirteen, until moments before the Dayaks took his head."

"And good riddance," Bulan said.

Virginia nodded in agreement. "Either way, we can be fairly certain that he didn't know another Number Thirteen even existed. As to the German, well, who knows? Maybe he encountered a shipwrecked sailor."

Bulan raised an eyebrow. "A bit far-fetched, don't you think?"

"What, you mean like monsters created in a lab?"

He grunted. "Fair point. I'd still like an explanation, though."

"So would I. But only one person can solve your mystery."

"Number Thirteen," Bulan said, with a sigh.

"There you go, sighing again." She smiled up at him. "Tell you what, we'll go look for him in the morning and ask him ourselves. What do you say?"

"And until then?"

"If we put our heads together, I'm sure we can think of something," she said, and reached up to wrap her arms around his neck.

9
FEEDING TIME

JU-LONG ENTERED THE OUTBUILDING that served as Arkwright's office and went immediately to the steel door set in the far wall. As ever, he hesitated before opening it. Not out of fear, but simple practicality. If there was something waiting on the other side, he gave it the opportunity to reveal itself. More than once, the things caged below had managed to escape. They only remained contained through his diligence.

He suspected that were it left up to Professor Vogel, the horrid things would have been allowed to roam free and feast upon whatever they wished. The old man seemed to see them as little more than precocious children, rather than as the savage brutes they truly were. Even Arkwright regarded them with a sort of benign paternalism. To view the captives as anything other than witless, destructive monsters was a mistake, in Ju-Long's opinion.

He placed a heavy hand against the door and counted silently to five, listening for any hint of an escapee. The scratch of claws on steel, the rasp of unnatural breath. They could not help but give themselves away. Even for mindless beasts, they were impatient.

When nothing revealed itself, Ju-Long retrieved the keys from the desk, unlocked the door and hauled it open. A familiar mephitic stink issued forth, causing the bile to rise in his throat. He choked it back and started down. His steps echoed eerily as he descended. The subterranean chamber had been built according to Arkwright's instructions and was, out of necessity, the most secure part of the compound. Higgs and the other enlisted men knew it existed, but not many more than that. Only three people had access to the chamber, and one of those was Ju-Long himself.

As he reached the bottom of the steps, he could hear the eager panting of the things below, echoing softly from behind a second steel door, as thick as the first. They were impatient. Starving. Arkwright liked to keep them hungry. Ju-Long thought it foolish; better a sated tiger than an eager one.

The cart containing the day's offal was waiting for him on the other side of the door. He'd filled it himself earlier in the day, from meat scraps collected from the camp kitchen. He'd made sure they were the worst leavings he could find. The beasts deserved no better.

The only light downstairs was provided by a single lantern, mounted atop the cart. As he pushed it down the passage, the light cast strange, unsettling shadows on the walls. The panting increased in fervor as he drew close to the cells. The sound of their eagerness never failed to send a chill through him. He was glad for the presence of the knife on his belt.

Ju-Long brought the cart to a halt in front of the cells. He paused for a moment, studying the shadows beyond the bars. There were eight of the beasts currently, though Arkwright intended to make more. For his part, Ju-Long thought eight was more than enough. He could just make them out, sitting hunched beyond the reach of the light. He could hear them breathing and the creak of their unnatural limbs. They stank of blood and excrement. The cells had not been cleaned in days. It was too dangerous.

He carefully filled a tray with meat and approached the cells. He hesitated at the last instant and that hesitation saved his life. Clawed hands erupted through the bars of the closest cell, slashing wildly at him. He roared out a curse and kicked the bars in frustration. "You will never know patience, will you?" he snarled.

The thing in the cell gave a guttural chuckle. Creation Eight. The youngest and most belligerent of the creatures. "I know patience," it grunted. Ju-Long hated this one the most. It had more cunning and it was better at aping a man than the others. That made it the most dangerous of them all. "Yes, I know patience," it repeated, moving slowly into the light.

It clutched at the bars with three clawed hands, and glared at him with a tiger's eyes, albeit set in the face of a rotting corpse. Stringy, fibrous strands of hair hung from its narrow head and its jagged teeth snapped in brief frustration. "I know that if I wait long enough, you will be careless," it gurgled, as it stepped back. "And then we will feast on your flesh."

As it spoke, more hands emerged from between the bars of the other cells, all clawing at the air. The beasts moaned like starving dogs and Ju-Long could not help but pause at the sight of their gleaming eyes staring at him.

No two of them were alike, save in the most general of proportions. All but the earliest pair might pass for men, though deformed ones, at a distance. Creations One and Two were hunched, insect-like things, with too many limbs and excretions of bone and keratin covering their twisted bodies. They were the dullest of the batch, with no ability to either mimic speech or comprehend it. Unfortunately, the others were cleverer.

Creation Three resembled a bat, though a wingless one. Creation Four looked as if it were slathered in barnacles, and Creation Five was the only female, with a vertical rupture for a mouth and eyes that glittered like the embers of Hell. Creation Six bore a resemblance to an overheated waxwork, and Creation Seven reminded him of an upright salamander. All of them were reaching for him, grunting, and hissing and moaning.

Angry at them and himself, Ju-Long flung the remainder of the offal onto the ground just shy of the bars. "You dare to make threats against me? I am a man—while you are not!" He watched as the other beasts scrabbled at the spilled meat, snatching up what they could and squabbling over the rest. He knew that if there weren't internal bars separating them, they might well have already killed one another. "You are nothing more than animals," he spat.

"Are they causing trouble again, Ju-Long?"

Ju-Long turned to see Lieutenant Arkwright standing at the entrance to the cell block. He had removed his uniform jacket and rolled up his sleeves, but was otherwise every inch the officer, as ever. Ju-Long sniffed dismissively.

"Nothing out of the ordinary. Just pretending to have an ounce of wit between them."

Arkwright chuckled and stepped fully into the cell block. The creatures whimpered softly as they caught sight of the coiled bullwhip that hung from Arkwright's belt. More than once, they had felt the touch of that lash, though not as often as Ju-Long might have wished. "I see you're still of the opinion that they are merely mimicking human speech, rather than having learned it." He peered into the first cell, at Creation One. It cowered away from him, grumbling piteously to itself. "That they lack all self-awareness. You believe them to be nothing more than beasts."

"That is what they are," Ju-Long said. It wasn't the first time they'd had this discussion. Arkwright, like Vogel, humanized the creatures in a way that seemed nonsensical to Ju-Long. They were not men, for men were not born in vats of simmering chemicals. Neither were animals, come to that. No, these things were less even than the beasts of the forest. They were abominations and did not deserve to breathe the same air as men. "There is no hope for them. They know nothing but hunger, and hate. You should destroy them all."

Arkwright prowled slowly down the line of cells, pausing for a moment before each one. "Tell me, Ju-Long . . . if these poor, misshapen creatures can only mimic what they see, how is it that they know hate?" He paused and glanced at Ju-Long. "If they do, is that not the fault of those of us around them?"

Before Ju-Long could stop him, he reached through the

bars of Creation Eight's cell and laid his hand on the creature's head, the way one might comfort a child. "How are you today, my lovely?" Arkwright murmured. "The blood on your lips tells me that you've eaten. Good. You must grow strong."

Ju-Long watched this display of misplaced paternalism with some apprehension. All it would take was one wrong moment and Arkwright would lose his hand—or worse. His own hand fell to his knife, and Creation Eight's gaze flicked toward him. Arkwright noticed the creature's sudden tension. "Do you hate him, my sweet?"

"Yes," Creation Eight growled. It stared at Ju-Long, eyes bright with malice. Arkwright smiled, as if pleased by this display.

"Why do you hate him?"

"He hurts us."

"Ah." Arkwright looked at Ju-Long. "You see?"

"Are you implying something, Lieutenant?" Ju-Long asked.

Arkwright shook his head. "No. I am merely providing the necessary punctuation to your amateur hypothesis. You say that they hate. But is that not an indication of intelligence?" He did not smile, but his eyes glittered with bleak amusement. "Does the lion hate the gazelle? No. It stalks and kills, yes—but out of hunger, not animosity."

"They hunger," Ju-Long said.

"I expect they do, given how little we feed them."

"On your orders," Ju-Long began. Arkwright cut him off with a gesture.

"Yes. But even so, if you believe that they hate us—hate you—you must concede that they are intelligent. And thus it follows that we must therefore be judicious in both words and actions around them. We must act and speak with purpose and without haste." He touched the bullwhip at his side. "We cannot afford to act out of anger, Ju-Long. What has been accomplished here must not be compromised. We must follow the letter of the law—my law." He paused and looked hard at Ju-Long. "Do you understand?"

Ju-Long gritted his teeth. "Yes, Lieutenant."

"Splendid. Make sure the doors are locked behind you when you have finished feeding them. I want no incidents, this close to the arrival of the next supply ship." With that, Arkwright turned and departed, leaving Ju-Long alone with the beasts.

Creation Eight chuckled wetly.

Ju-Long turned to face its cell. "You dare?" he hissed. Creation Eight stood. It was taller than a man; lanky and oddly proportioned. Its ugly gaze fixed on Ju-Long.

"I dare, yes. Because you are no more a man than we, Ju-Long. You are just another creature who belongs to Arkwright. You fear him, as we do."

"I fear no man—or beast, come to that." Ju-Long drew his knife and for a moment, considered where best to thrust it. Creation Eight chortled, as if it could read his thoughts. "Silence," he snapped. *"Silence!"*

Creation Eight snapped its teeth together, and the other creatures followed suit. They laughed and clawed at the bars, and shrieked with demonic joy. Creation Eight slid an arm through the bars and made a fist.

The others fell silent.

"We do not obey you, Ju-Long," Creation Eight said. "We hate you. And one day, we will devour you." It stepped back, out of the light. "I swear it."

Ju-Long stared into the darkness for long moments. Then he sheathed his knife and pushed the cart back out of the cell block. And then, as Arkwright had reminded him, he locked the two doors behind him.

And double-checked them both.

10
NUMBER THIRTEEN

NUMBER THIRTEEN—OR OTTO, as he thought of himself—carried the dead Lascar through the forest, back to the tunnels he called home. He had spent long months tunneling through the earth, digging until his claws were splintered and his fingers bloody. Despite this, it had taken less time than he'd expected. The Kind One had been very impressed, and had complimented him on his efforts, though Otto had shown him only the barest stretch of the extensive burrow he'd made for himself.

The truth was, Otto spent most of his days digging. His tunnels stretched across much of the island, a network of cramped passages that allowed him to move about undetected by those with whom he shared his world. The Kind One had warned him that the others would not be pleased to find him. That they would try to kill him, unless he stayed out of sight.

Or he killed them first.

It was the Kind One who had given him the name "Otto," as well as taught him German and English, and how to read. Otto was clever and his mind, the Kind One said, was like a sponge. He absorbed information quickly, though comprehension of what he had learned often came later, when he had the time to properly mull it over.

There was a small collection of books, down below. He had scavenged them from the compound, and taken great pains to preserve them from the dirt and the damp, even before he could read them. Since the Kind One had begun teaching him, he had come to appreciate them even more. From them, he had learned about the world beyond the island.

The world of men. Men like the Kind One, or the one named Maxon. Maxon who was his creator, though Otto still did not understand what that truly meant. The Kind One had tried to explain, but in a halting way—as if uncertain how much to share.

When he reached the pit, he flung the corpse down and followed it a moment later, dropping the considerable distance with an ease born of experience. For a moment, he paused, listening. Sometimes animals became lost in the tunnels. Hearing nothing, he turned his attention to the corpse. He probed the wound in the dead man's throat with a claw, and then brought the glistening talon-tip to his mouth.

It was sweet—so sweet.

Hungry now, he slit the dead man's belly open and began to drag out fistfuls of intestine. As he ate, he knew that the Kind One would not approve. Understand, yes. Approve, never. The old man did not consume flesh, indeed he apparently subsisted entirely on grains and vegetables, or so he claimed. Otto, however, could not deny his body's needs in such a way. The furnace in his belly demanded meat and to deny it for too long was to risk losing control.

As he gnawed on the slippery organs, he thought of the newcomers at the old compound—the Woman, in particular. He had never seen a woman before, save in the crumpled photo that even now rested in a secret place in his tunnels. That it was clearly the same woman seemed to him to be fate. He had dreamed of her since his first awakening in the forest, and now here she was.

She had almost killed him.

The thought stung Otto, painful as a hornet. He paused in his chewing. She had threatened him—why? Because of the Other. His chewing became more savage, blood cascading down his neck and chest as he feasted. The Other had attacked him, the way the Dayak had. The way men always did, save for the Kind One. But the Other was different. Stronger. Faster. Almost as strong as Otto himself.

That had disturbed him. He was not used to facing someone who was a match for him. Part of him longed to return to the old compound and renew the struggle, to prove that he was the Other's superior. But some instinct for self-preservation held him back. Perhaps later he would return and see. But for now he would eat his fill.

So Otto ate and ate, peeling the meat from the bone. He gave no thought to who his victim had been, save a flicker of hesitation as he recalled the man's frightened face as he had dropped down on him from above. He had been drawn to the compound by the sound of voices and new scents on the wind. Curiosity had given way to impulse. Both to feed his belly and to see who had invaded his territory.

Hunger sated, Otto sat back on his heels and studied his bloody hands. The sight did not revolt him, though he thought it should. Indeed, the blood seemed almost beautiful in the rain and the moonlight. His own fluids were black and sluggish. They did not flow or spurt like a man's. The Kind One said that his insides were not as those of a man; that they were . . . simpler, but more efficient, whatever that meant.

Otto absently wiped his hands on the ragged trousers he wore. He'd rescued them from the compound not long after his awakening. He paused, remembering that time of confusion and pain. His first memories were of the rain, and the dark. Of an all-consuming hunger lancing through him, driving him to hunt and kill everything that crossed his path.

He wondered if the others like him felt that way. Pity stirred in him as his thoughts turned to them, caged beneath the earth. The Kind One had assured him that they would soon be free, but that day never seemed to arrive. Perhaps he was simply impatient.

Otto was filled with a sudden desire to see the others. To speak with them. The Kind One had told him that it was not allowed; too dangerous, he'd said. But Otto was strong and something about his encounter with the woman had filled him with a strange sense of urgency. It was time that he met them. Past time, perhaps.

He carefully flensed more meat from the dead man, and bound it up in a large strip torn from the corpse's clothes. Then, parcel clenched in his teeth, he made his way for the tunnels he'd dug beneath the other compound. These were among those he had not revealed to the Kind One, knowing that the old man would be upset.

Otto understood. The old man feared that the men there would kill him. Otto was not a stranger to the idea of violence. He had waged a silent war on the Dayaks in his first year of life, hunting them and, yes, eating them, when the opportunity arose.

But these newcomers, these British, were different. More organized. More dangerous. He recalled when they had first arrived and the way they had plundered the old compound, stealing books and equipment. He had considered revealing himself to them, but thankfully he had thought better of it at the time.

The tunnels beneath the compound were more cramped than those of the forest, barely large enough for him to squirm through. He knew that those like him were kept underground, which made reaching them easier. He had probed the edges of the underground chamber several times, searching for weak points, which he had then marked for future use.

He used one of these now, tearing easily through the foundation wall and creating an aperture large enough to squeeze through and drop to the floor below. He crouched there, listening for any sign of a human presence. Satisfied that there was none, he at last turned his attention to his kin. They watched him from their cages, silent and guarded. It was clear that they did not know what to make of him.

Carefully, he began to feed them. They were greedy; hungry. They growled and snarled as they snatched the bloody meat from his hands. He watched them in wonder. They were like him, and yet not. Had they been created in the same way, if not by the same hands? He made to speak, but was interrupted before he could get the words out.

"Who are you?" the one in the last cell growled. Otto glanced at Creation Eight and hesitated. The newest of them was the most dangerous, according to the Kind One; the most clever, the most like his creators. Otto wanted to be friends, to talk to Creation Eight as he talked to the Kind One. But something in the other monster's gaze made him wary.

"Eat," he said, simply, as he offered a chunk of meat.

"No. I have already eaten."

"You . . . hunger still," Otto said. He could read it Creation Eight's body language, in his eyes. The same fire that filled his gut was in these others. They too burned with the same insatiable need that filled him, at times. The difference was, he rarely denied himself the pleasure of feeding his hunger. He hunted the forest the same as any predator, and as a consequence had grown strong.

But his wretched kin were not so lucky. They were kept prisoner, and starved, for reasons he could not comprehend. He knew that the Kind One wanted to help them, but could not. So he had decided to act on the Kind One's behalf.

"The law of Arkwright says hunger is necessary," Creation Eight said. He fixed Otto with a baleful gaze. "You break the law. Why?"

Otto leaned close. "Ich bin so wie du bist," he said, as the Kind One had taught him. "I . . . am one of you. I wish to help you."

"One of us?" Creation Eight's gaze flashed with anger. "You do not live in the dark. You lie!" A long arm shot from between the bars and grabbed a handful of Otto's scalp. He was yanked viciously against the bars, hard enough to rattle his brains against his skull and the world spun about him. The others were howling and gibbering now, excited perhaps by the sudden show of violence.

"Let . . . me . . . *go*," Otto roared, tearing free of Creation

Eight's grip. He rolled away from the cell and rose into a crouch, teeth bared. "Why do you attack me?"

"Where are your scars?" Creation Eight hissed. He thrust his arms out through the bars, showing off faded weals and newer, livid marks. "This makes you one of us! This makes you his creation!"

"I am not his," Otto said, fighting against the kill-urge as it rose in him. He wanted to tear apart the cell, and Creation Eight both. "I belong to no one."

"You feed us. Like Arkwright. Like Ju-Long. Soon, like them, you will make us feel pain. That is the way of things. That is the law."

"No," Otto said. "I will not hurt you."

Creation Eight leered at him. "Arkwright is the creator. Arkwright is the law. I will tell him of you, and we will see which end of the whip you receive."

"You will do no such thing, child," the Kind One barked, startling them both. He stood in the doorway, a ring of keys dangling from one hand. Creation Eight and the others fell silent, their eyes on the Kind One. "You would condemn your brother—why?" he continued. "Because he is free and you are not?"

"Yesss," Creation Eight said. The Kind One clucked his tongue.

"And that is why I call you child. Because you give a child's answer. You are hurt, and so you seek to hurt. How disappointing."

"Arkwright—" the monster began.

"Arkwright is not your creator," the old man said, firmly. "I am. That he has caused you pain, causes me pain."

"Then why do you not stop him?" Creation Five asked. Her voice was like glass scraping against bone. "Why do we hurt?"

"Quiet," Creation Eight snarled, silencing her. "Do not speak to him. He is not Arkwright. Arkwright is master."

"Do you need one so badly as all that?" the Kind One asked.

He looked at Otto. "This is why I warned you to leave them be, Otto. At least for now."

"I will tell Arkwright," Creation Eight repeated. The Kind One approached his cell and looked up at him. He said nothing, simply studied the looming monster.

"I am sorry, child. Sorry that I could not prevent all that has happened to you. You are so beautiful, all of you, and I could not stop him from hurting you. Forgive me."

Creation Eight grunted. "Forgive . . . ?"

The Kind One reached up and through the bars, as if to stroke Creation Eight's cheek. The monster jerked back out of reach with a shrill cry, and retreated to the far side of his cell. "No, no. Do not—I will not listen!" Like a recalcitrant child, he covered his ears and refused to look at the old man. Otto stared at the other monster in bewilderment, before turning his attention to the old man.

"I—" he began.

"Hush, boy. You must leave. Quickly. Before someone realizes you were here." He gestured to the hole in the wall. "Go. Back the way you came. I will cover the hole, though it will be discovered soon enough." He looked at Otto. "Oh, my kind boy. You are too gentle for this world, Otto."

Otto wanted to speak, to protest. Instead, he did as the Kind One asked him. The old man was right. If he was discovered, the men would kill him. And he did not want to die. He turned and leaped up to the hole, pausing only to glance back at the Kind One. "I am sorry," he said. "I did not mean to upset them."

The Kind One smiled. "All will be well, Otto. I will see to it. Now go."

Otto climbed back into the dark, and began to make his way home.

11
PATROL

SERGEANT HENRY R. HIGGS, in the service of His Majesty, King George the Fifth of the British Empire, cursed loudly as he navigated the tangled trails of the forest. Despite the obscenities that tumbled freely from his lips and the scowl on his face, Higgs was pleased. Ju-Long was clever—and dangerous—but he'd done exactly as Higgs had hoped.

When he'd overheard Ju-Long's request to Arkwright, he'd spied a chance to finally take a poke about the Maxon compound without either Arkwright or the ever-watchful Ju-Long breathing down his neck. While there likely wasn't anything to find, he needed to make sure. His father had been a stonemason and had instilled in him an aversion to slipshod work. So, he'd provoked the normally taciturn Ju-Long into giving him exactly what he wanted.

Higgs had no qualms about what he'd done. Ju-Long had no loyalty save to Arkwright, and Arkwright—well. Determining Arkwright's loyalties was one of the reasons that Higgs had been assigned to this expedition. Arkwright was ambitious and influential and too clever by half. Someone, somewhere, in the rarified atmosphere of Whitehall was worried that such a combination might lead to something unfortunate.

Perhaps it already had.

There were stories about this island. About what had gone on here a year ago. They had percolated through the ports and back to England, where certain men took notice.

Arkwright had been one of them, was working with others. All suddenly interested in the theories of a disgraced American academic. It was all fairy dust and nonsense as far as Higgs was concerned, but someone thought it was worth a punt. Strings had been pulled by shadowy benefactors and men seconded, and soon Lieutenant Arkwright was sailing to Singapore with his own small army.

"What difference does it make what we do, is what I'm asking," Baskin said, suddenly and loudly. Too loudly for the forest. Higgs turned his attention to the conversation taking place behind him. He stopped, fixing the two men with a stern look.

"Because we are being paid, Baskin. Now shut your gob."

"Half the time, I'm boiling bloody cabbages for tea is all I'm saying," Baskin countered. "Ain't you tired of playing dogsbody, Sergeant?"

Higgs sniffed. "Since you're asking, I am tired of hearing you two complain. So do me a favor and sew your lips shut, Baskin. Before I do it for you, eh?" Baskin and Fraser were both professional shirkers. Like most of the men seconded to Arkwright's little expedition, they were troublemakers—the sort of men that their former commanding officers would be only too happy to get shed of. The only one of them worth a damn was Arkwright second-in-command, Welles. God alone knew what he'd done to get seconded to this circus. Probably second-guessed some privileged blowhard or accidentally insulted someone. But he, like the rest of them, was expendable.

Fraser spoke up, scratching his neck. "Here Sergeant, what do you think about all of it? Think old Ju-Long is losing his wits in this heat?"

"I'd be surprised if he had any to begin with," Baskin muttered, warily scanning the sides of the trail. "Why the lieutenant keeps that Chinese around I don't know."

"Because lads, he knows better than to ask stupid questions

of his superior officer," Higgs said, pointedly. "Still, I don't trust him either. Far as we know, he could be working with old Muda Saffir."

Baskin and Fraser exchanged looks. "You think he could be, Sergeant?" Baskin asked.

Higgs turned away. "Probably not. But then, I don't know much about him. Do you?" It was a leading question; he didn't know much about Ju-Long, and wanted to learn more. Like Vogel, Arkwright seemed to consider him valuable but Higgs couldn't see why.

Fraser spat. "He let slip some things . . . I think he might have been a pirate before he signed on with us. He's a dodgy sort."

Baskin nodded. "He claimed to know these islands, that's why the lieutenant hired him. Only he hasn't done much guiding, has he?"

"He led us to this place, didn't he?" Higgs said, as he stopped again. The Maxon compound loomed out of the jungle like some forgotten temple out of Kipling. He felt a shudder of disquiet run through him as he considered the place. Something about it didn't sit right with him—hadn't the first time, either. It wasn't just the rumors. There was an atmosphere to the place; some of the old churches his father had worked on felt the same. As if the very ground had gone sour somehow.

Baskin felt the same way, clearly. He hawked and spat, and gave Higgs a pleading look. "We don't have to go in there again, do we?"

"Scared of monsters, are you?" Fraser asked, innocently. Baskin rounded on him.

"I'm just saying that there might be Dayaks in there. I don't like the thought of walking into a bloody headhunter ambush, do you?"

Fraser paled slightly and looked at Higgs. "It's not Muda Saffir then, is it?"

Higgs started toward the compound. "We don't know that it's anything. Come on." He led them to the foot of the palisade, scanning it for any openings or signs of habitation. Someone had trimmed the underbrush and overhanging branches, and recently.

Fraser noticed it as well. "Dayaks wouldn't have bothered to clear the brush," he said, quietly. He lifted his rifle. "Malays, maybe?"

"Maybe," Higgs said, alert now. In the first weeks of their arrival, while Arkwright oversaw the construction of the British compound, Ju-Long and the German, Vogel, had spent their days here, collecting machinery and books for reasons that still escaped Higgs. He'd accompanied them once or twice on these foraging expeditions, but could make neither heads nor tails of the strange equipment they'd collected.

Vogel seemed to know what it was and that was enough for Arkwright. But Vogel was another question mark for Higgs. The elderly German had joined them in Singapore, after a private conversation with Arkwright and Ju-Long. The three of them knew something about all of this, about what the American, Maxon, had been up to, and maybe they weren't the only ones. Perhaps someone else had come looking for that mysterious equipment and those odd books. Higgs wondered what Arkwright might say about that.

"Right, Fraser go around and check the gate and make sure it hasn't been tampered with. Baskin, you and me will go around this way." Higgs pointed at Fraser. "You see anything, you shoot first and ask questions later, yeah?" Thankfully, Fraser didn't argue. Higgs turned to Baskin. "That goes for you as well." He hefted his rifle. "Now come on. Let's get this done."

Higgs led Baskin around the far edge of the palisade, keeping one eye on the forest and the other on the compound. A preliminary search might yield some excuse to go inside, Baskin's hesitation not withstanding. If someone had been poking around, he needed to know about it, though he doubted they were still here, whoever they were.

"I don't like the idea of splitting up," Baskin murmured. "God knows who's watching us. There's probably sixty Dayaks hidden up in this place."

"And why would they be doing that, then?" Higgs said.

"Catch us. Kill us. Why do Dayaks do anything?"

Higgs grunted but didn't reply. Baskin made a good point, though he wasn't planning to admit it. The Dayaks were a constant danger. He and the others had seen them off twice now, but Higgs knew a probing attack when he saw one. Arkwright probably did as well, but he didn't seem inclined to worry. Maybe he wanted the Dayaks to attack. Or maybe he didn't think they'd be here long enough for it to matter.

That was the other thing that was beginning to worry him. He had the sense that whatever had brought Arkwright here, it was fast coming to an end. And so far, Higgs still wasn't sure why they'd come. He needed answers, and right now that meant he needed to get into this compound and see what he could find.

Around him, the forest suddenly went silent. No birds, no rustlings. A dead silence, such as he had never heard before. It sent a chill through him and he found that his palms were suddenly clammy on the stock of his rifle. The forest around him seemed more threatening somehow. As if it were waiting for—what? "Baskin, you see anything?" he asked, as he turned to the other man.

Baskin had stopped. He was looking back the way they'd come, a peculiar expression on his face. Higgs looked at him. "What is it?"

"I heard something."

"Heard what?"

"Something, I said. I don't know. *Something.* Like—like something following me. Like it was creeping up on me, ready to tap me on the bleeding shoulder." Baskin swallowed and stared into the forest.

"Dayaks?" Higgs asked. But the look on Baskin's face said it wasn't.

"Maybe the stories we heard in Singapore were true," Baskin said, softly. "Maybe there are monsters here."

Higgs stared at him. He'd heard the stories. They all had. The rumors about Maxon had made for fertile soil for new tales of superstitious dread to take root. Every sailor in these waters now knew the stories about buried treasure and guardian demons. At first, Higgs had even thought that might be why Arkwright had come. But it had been months and no treasure-hunting expeditions appeared to be taking place. Unless one counted the way they'd stripped the old Maxon compound. He looked up at the palisade—and froze.

He'd seen someone up there, just for an instant. Had they seen him? He waved Baskin to silence and waited. No outcry came. "Right. Let's go find Fraser. There's something going on here, and I want to know what."

"Right behind you, Sergeant," Baskin said, nervously. They moved quickly back the way they'd come, and the silence around them grew ever more oppressive with every step. Every fiber of Higgs' being screamed for him to flee. Instead, he pressed on until the gates were in sight—closed, as they should have been.

"Where's Fraser?" Baskin asked.

Higgs shook his head. There was no sign of the other man. He considered calling out, but common sense warned against it. If there was someone here, no sense alerting them too soon. Baskin made a sound, deep in his throat. Higgs turned to chastise him, but stopped as he saw the look on the other man's face. He thought Baskin had been frightened before.

Baskin pointed. A bloody handprint marked the wood, but not a man's hand. It was too large for that, and the fingers were not all in the right places.

Higgs bit back an oath. He had the sense that something, somewhere, had gone horribly wrong and all he could was play witness to it. He crouched and touched the mark. It was still fresh and the blood was warm.

Voices rose from behind the palisade. Someone was

heading for the gate. He rose quickly and waved Baskin back. Whoever it was, they'd find a pair of rifles waiting on them. And for their sake, Higgs hoped they had the answers he was looking for.

12

SING

SING LEE SAT ATOP THE ROOF of the old laboratory, his rifle across his knees and his eyes on the forest. The threat would come from there, whatever form it took. There were more than monsters here—men as well, dangerous ones. These islands were the hunting ground of pirates, including the despicable creature known as Muda Saffir.

He regretted not killing Saffir when he'd had the opportunity years ago, fleeting as it had been. He'd been a younger man then, aboard a supply ship bound for Borneo, and a pair of war-canoes had intercepted them in the Strait of Malacca. He'd had Saffir in his crosshairs before a cannonade from the ship had sent the Dayaks rowing for safety.

Sing was not against piracy, in general. A man had to make a living with the tools he was provided. He himself had engaged in a spate of privateering in his youth, along with Kazin. But there were pirates, and then there were *pirates*. Saffir was one of the latter sort; brutal and spiteful, with no concept of mercy.

He'd listened for news of the Malay when they'd returned to Singapore. He'd hoped the British or the Dutch might have finally put an end to him—or even the Dayaks, who were notoriously fickle when it came to their allies. But no such luck. Saffir was tenacious; a survivor, much like Sing himself.

The thought annoyed him and he turned his attention to the sky and the stars peeking out through the clouds. A part of him regretted agreeing to accompany his employers back to this awful place. Nothing good would come of awakening the ghosts that slumbered here. Indeed, they had already disturbed one, and paid a bloody price for it.

Sing had not known the dead men well, or at all, really. Kazin had been in charge of picking out likely men for the small crew necessary to sail the yacht. Nonetheless, it galled him. He had warned both Mr. Harper and Miss Ginny that what they were searching for did not exist; that Maxon had made only monsters. But they had not listened, and now all of them might have to pay for that hubris.

He glanced down into the courtyard and saw two of the Lascars on patrol. "Clear?" he called down. One, Esmail, looked up.

"Clear, Mr. Sing."

"Good. Stay alert." Satisfied, Sing settled himself back. But a moment later he sat forward again, and raised his rifle. Branches rustled out beyond the palisade. Kazin and the others had cut back what they could but the forest still pressed too close for Sing's comfort. He scanned the trees through the iron sight of the rifle, and fought down the sudden spike of nerves that had accompanied the sound.

Sing was no stranger to combat. He had fought pirates in his youth—and been one—and had killed his share of men, though he was careful never to mention this to his employers. He preferred that Mr. Harper and Miss Ginny think of him as kindly old Sing, rather than as Sing Lee, who had once killed men in alleys for money.

A flash of motion in the trees silenced these ruminations and he focused his attention on the canopy. Something heavy was moving through it, causing a commotion. Another flash— of orange, this time—and he sighed in relief as the intruder was revealed to be an orangutan. He wondered if it were the same brute from earlier. It vanished even as the thought occurred to him, disappearing back into the depths of the canopy.

"I am told it is considered bad luck to shoot one of those," someone said, from behind him. Sing stiffened and turned, to see Kazin making his way slowly up the other side of the roof. "If it is the same one that I saw earlier, it has been circling the palisade for the last hour or so. Probably wondering whether it is safe to return."

"What are you doing up here?" Sing asked. "You will slip and break your scrawny neck if you are not careful."

"The same could be said of you, old man." Kazin climbed onto the peak of the roof and paused to stretch. "Why are you perched up here like an ugly bird?"

Sing turned away. "The better to sight worms. Did you come up here just to insult me, old friend?" Kazin chuckled and clambered over to sit beside him.

"Not just that, no. I came to relieve you. You should get some sleep."

"I will sleep when we are off this island."

"Might be a while. Your employers are stubborn." Kazin sighed and held out a hand. "Ah well. At least the rain has passed."

"It will be back."

"And your monster?"

Sing sucked on his teeth and looked at the Lascar. "He will be back too, I expect. Why else would I be up here?"

"I did wonder." Kazin set his rifle aside. "Big thing, wasn't he?"

"Bigger than I remember," Sing allowed. He sighed. "I am sorry about Hamad and Comjee. I did not know them well, but they seemed like good men."

Kazin smiled thinly. "Comjee was a self-righteous prig and Hamad was a rapscallion of the worst sort. But thank you." He exhaled noisily. "Why did it kill them?"

Sing shook his head. "They are murderous brutes, these things. They have only anger where other men have souls."

"Why did this Maxon person make them? Was he a madman?"

Sing paused before answering. "Yes, for a time. Perhaps he is still mad. He wished to wed Miss Ginny to one of those things—the one stalking us now, in fact."

Kazin stared at him. "Is that why you . . . ?" He gestured airily. Sing nodded.

"I thought it best if she was to be married, better it be to a man with a soul."

Kazin snorted. "Oh we both know a soul is no guarantee of kindness. Remember Hoon Lo? He had a soul, of sorts. Or so the Christians maintain."

Sing grimaced. "I remember."

Kazin laughed. "I bet you do. It was because of him you had to sign on with Maxon in the first place. You needed to get out of Singapore quick after that, as I recall."

"The world is better without Hoon Lo," Sing said, loftily. "And I signed on with Maxon to support my wife and children. And grandchildren."

Kazin frowned. "I was sorry to hear about Aihan. She was a good woman."

Sing said nothing. His wife had died while he'd fought monsters. His children were long since married and with children of their own, and no interest in reconnecting with an old man they'd barely known. He'd imagined seeing them again, upon his return to Singapore but—no. Better to leave it. Better for everyone.

Kazin hesitated and then clapped Sing on the back. "My Leena passed on some fifteen years ago. The pain dulls but it never really fades."

Sing grunted. "Pain I can live with."

Kazin sniffed. "You are a stubborn old fool, you know."

Sing glanced at him. "As are you."

Kazin leaned back. "Agreed. And we are both of us too old to be hunting monsters." He patted the roof. "So this is where he did it, eh?"

Sing nodded. "It is. Though it looks as if someone has looted the place."

"Pirates," Kazin said.

"Why would pirates steal useless equipment?"

"It was metal, yes? Metal scrap can be sold." Kazin rubbed

his chin thoughtfully. "Though, now that I say it out loud it does seem to be a bit much like hard work for the average pirate."

Sing looked at him. "Did you hear any rumors about this place before we hired you? Anyone looking for Maxon, or the island?"

Kazin looked away. "The usual stories. Every sailor in Singapore has heard about the lost treasure of Pamarungs. They say the American, Maxon, buried a fortune in the forest, to hide it from pirates." He glanced slyly at Sing. "I do not suppose you know where it is, eh?"

Sing laughed. "Maxon spent all his money on books and chemicals. If there is treasure here, it was buried after we left."

Kazin sighed. "That is what I thought. Shame. I would like to be wealthy."

"In my experience, money does not bring happiness. Miss Ginny is wealthy, but no happier now than she was when she was living here." He knocked on the roof with a knuckle. "She is too worried about the sins of the past, that girl."

Kazin gestured dismissively. "I know you, Sing. You think of that woman as a child, the same way you thought of your daughters until they were married and gone. But she is not. Your Miss Ginny is more cunning than any pirate."

Sing made to protest but was interrupted by a shout from below. He saw Esmail running across the courtyard, carrying something. Quickly he and Kazin made their descent and intercepted the young Lascar. "Someone is out there," Esmail said, out of breath.

"Pirates?" Kazin asked.

"No. I found this." Esmail handed Sing a battered brown cap.

"British cap," Sing said. Kazin nodded.

"What is it doing here?" he murmured.

Sing grunted. There was blood on the cap, and fresh blood at that. Sing touched it and grimaced. He looked at Kazin.

"Still warm."

"We heard nothing," Kazin said, uneasily.

"That does not mean that there was nothing to hear." Sing looked at Esmail. "Tell us where you found this—*now*."

Esmail pointed to the gates. "There, just outside. I heard a noise, but I saw no one." He swallowed. "Do you think that—that thing has come back?"

"We will find out. Go tell Mr. Harper, quickly!" With that, Sing and Kazin hurried toward the front gate. "If you wish to hang back . . ." Sing began.

Kazin made a noise of disgust. "Now you are just being insulting," he said. Sing smiled but didn't reply. They reached the gates a moment later, and Sing stepped out into the forest as Kazin pushed them open.

Both of them froze as they saw the rifles leveled in their direction. Rifles held by British soldiers—two of them. "You there," one barked. "Don't move!"

"Be calm," Sing said. "We are no danger to you. Everything is hunky-dory."

"'Hunky-dory'?" Kazin muttered. Sing silenced him with a glance. He wondered where the soldiers had come from. Moreover, he wondered why they were here. The island was of no military importance, and held no resources.

"You pirates?" the soldier who'd spoken before demanded.

"I am a cook," Sing said.

"And I am a sailor," Kazin added.

"For who?" the soldier asked. "What are you two doing here?" The rifles did not waiver and Sing suspected that the soldiers wouldn't hesitate to kill them both, if provoked. Still, it was best to be careful with how much he told them.

"Doing nothing. I lived here once. Just visiting."

"Is that so? Just the pair of you?" The soldier peered suspiciously at them.

Sing glanced at Kazin. "Just us and some Lascars. For protection."

"Protection, eh? Baskin—get their rifles, if you please." The second soldier stepped forward and took Sing and Kazin's rifles. In the process, he dislodged the bloody cap from Sing's grasp. All eyes followed it as it fell to the grass.

The first soldier's eyes widened. "Bloody hell." He aimed his rifle at a point between Sing's eyes. "What have you done?" he growled. "Answer me!"

13

INTERRUPTION

IN HIS DREAMS, Bulan was back in the court of mystery, suffering the kiss of Von Horn's bullwhip. The world was red and black, as if there were no sun, only fire. The building heaved and creaked like a ship at sea, and the pain of the whip was almost a caress as he stalked its wielder. Around him, the other monsters capered, clad in crimson. Beneath his feet, the dead lay still and silent. He saw Sing there, and Maxon—and one other, whose face he could not bring himself to look at.

Von Horn screamed something, but the words made no sense as he—Number Thirteen—lunged with hands wide, all the better to throttle the last of his hated enemies. The whip was lost and Von Horn fell, and Number Thirteen crouched—squeezing, *squeezing*—until the man's struggles ceased. Around him the others sent up a wailing howl of triumph. He saw Number Twelve and Number Three crouch atop Maxon's body and begin to feast.

Without thinking, he too began to tear at Von Horn's flesh for a great hunger roiled within him. He moaned as skin parted beneath his scrabbling fingers and he began to pry loose fat coils of intestine. He could not stop himself; did not want to stop. He was a monster, after all, and this was what monsters did. They killed and they ate and nothing more.

He wanted to scream as he tore loose a section of intestine and raised it to his lips.

Instead he began to eat.

Bulan awoke with a start, and sat up so quickly that the world around him spun for a moment. He sat up, careful not to disturb Virginia, and cradled his head. The ache of sudden waking faded slowly and the world returned to its proper proportions. Yet he could still taste the blood on his lips.

Someone called out, from outside. Virginia stirred. "Is that—?" she murmured, disentangling herself from him.

"Esmail," Bulan said. He recognized the young Lascar's voice. He rose to his feet and padded to the doors, clad only in his trousers. "What is it, Esmail? Is something the matter?"

Esmail was waiting at the bottom of the steps, fidgeting nervously. He looked at once frightened and excited. "Someone is here, Mr. Harper," he said, loudly. "Soldiers!"

Bulan rubbed the sleep from his eyes, alert now. "Soldiers? What kind of soldiers?"

"British," Esmail said.

"There's a stroke of luck," Bulan said, relaxing slightly. "Where's Sing?"

"He went out of the gate with Kazin. But, sir . . . there's trouble." Esmail hesitated.

Bulan hurried down the steps. "What kind of trouble? Is anyone hurt?" He wondered if the soldiers were here looking for pirates. The British had a standing warrant for the capture of pirates in the strait, including Muda Saffir. It was possible they'd caught wind of him prowling about and come to check it out for themselves.

"Yes, but we do not know who," Esmail said.

Bulan paused and glanced back at the building. Virginia was inside, getting dressed. He looked at Esmail. "Stay here and guard Mrs. Harper, please. I'll see what's going on." The young Lascar set his jaw and nodded. Bulan hurried toward the gate, calling out for Habiboola and Amer as he did so. The other two Lascars raced to join him, hurrying from opposite sides of the compound as fast as their legs could carry them.

Bulan reached the gates before them, but paused before charging through. He could hear voices on the other side—Sing and someone else. English. Angry. He waved for the Lascars to wait where they were. No sense making things worse, if there was a chance to make them better first. He leaned close, listening.

"Where is he? What did you do to him?" the Englishman snarled.

"Who?" Sing asked, calmly.

"Don't play silly buggers with me, mate. The other soldier. Where is he?"

"I see no soldier," Sing replied. "Just a hat." He was silent for a moment. "I am Sing Lee. A year ago, I lived here, in this compound. Now I have come back, to pay my respect to old ghosts."

The Englishman laughed sourly. "I don't think so. I think you're one of Muda Saffir's curs. Come looking for plunder, have you?"

Bulan pressed his eye to a crack in the palisade wall beside the gates. His view was cramped, but he could just make out Sing and Kazin, held at gunpoint by two men in British uniforms. There didn't seem to be any more of them, thankfully.

"I know Muda Saffir," Sing said. "A kidnapper of young ladies. He and his pirates made trouble for us last year. If he were here now, I would kill him with my bare hands." A pause. "We are on the same side, you and I."

The Englishman laughed again. "I doubt that. But if we are, tell me where my man is. We'll call it a show of good faith, innit?"

Sing grunted. "I told you I know of no soldier. All I see is a hat."

"What's your business in this compound then? Not just laying old ghosts to rest, I'd wager. What did you come looking for?"

Bulan tensed. He glanced at the Lascars and gestured for

them to ease through the gates while Sing had the newcomers distracted. If they could get the drop on the British, they might be able to bring this matter to a peaceful resolution.

Sing cleared his throat. "A year ago I worked for a man named Maxon. A scientist. Wealthy. I help in his laboratory."

Something odd passed across the Englishman's expression. As if he were simultaneously startled—and pleased. "What do you know about this laboratory then, eh?" he asked, in a low tone. "Who sent you? Answer me!"

At that moment, the two Lascars stepped through the gates, their rifles aimed at the newcomers. "Drop your weapons," Amer called out. Several things happened very swiftly. First, the second soldier spun about to face the two Lascars, his rifle raised, even as his companion fired at Sing. But Sing jerked aside at the last moment, slapping the barrel of the rifle up so that the shot buried itself in the palisade. Then he leaped upon the Englishman, knocking him sprawling.

As shots sounded, Bulan took a few steps back and launched himself at the palisade. The impact shuddered through him, but the wood gave way and he launched himself through at the second soldier who was even then drawing a bead on Sing. He caught the startled soldier up with a roar and sent him flying into the palisade.

He spun to see Sing flung backward by the other soldier. The latter clawed for his sidearm as Kazin and the Lascars closed in. He managed to get off a shot, winging Amer. "Keep off me," the Englishman shouted. "Keep away!" He swung the weapon toward Sing, but before he could fire again, Bulan drove a fist into his jaw, flattening him. The soldier slumped limply to the grass.

Kazin helped Sing to his feet. Habiboola crouched beside Amer. "Clean wound," he said, as he bandaged the injured man's arm. Bulan nodded.

"Good. When you've seen to him, tie these two . . ." He turned—and cursed. The second soldier was gone; run off during the fracas. Or . . . his eyes lit on the fallen cap, with its telltale red stains. He retrieved it and looked at Sing, a sinking sensation in the pit of his stomach. "I don't think they were our only visitors."

Sing nodded gravely. "My thoughts exactly." He retrieved his rifle from where he'd dropped it. "This is not good, Mr. Harper."

"Any idea how many more of them there are?" Bulan peered at the hat and then at the palisade. Was Number Thirteen still here? Or had he fled with the arrival of the other soldiers? He turned, surveying the nearby trees and undergrowth for any sign of the creature, but saw nothing— no scratches, no broken limbs . . . just a bloody handprint on the palisade. Why? Almost as if he had been trying to—

Realization hit like a thunderbolt.

"Virginia," Bulan whispered. He turned and sprinted through the gates, the others shouting after him. He ignored them and pelted back into the compound, heading for where he'd left Virginia. The creature was wilier than any of them had suspected. He had drawn the attention of the British, caused a confrontation, and used the distraction to slip into the compound—but why? The answer was horribly obvious; the creature wanted Virginia and had seized the opportunity Bulan had so foolishly provided him.

"Virginia," he called out, desperately hoping to hear her reply. As he raced for the main building, he saw Esmail stretched out on the ground. He slid to a stop beside the young man and crouched to check his pulse. The Lascar was alive—only stunned, thankfully. Bulan left him and bounded up the steps, calling out for Virginia, his heart thudding painfully in his chest. He hit the doors at a run and stopped.

Virginia was gone.

He staggered against the doorframe, momentarily overcome. When he turned back to the steps, he saw that Sing, Kazin, and the others had arrived. "Miss Ginny," Sing began, before he saw the look on Bulan's face.

"She's gone," Bulan said.

"Number Thirteen?" Sing asked.

"Without a doubt," Bulan replied, his hands curling into fists. A shout from Kazin brought him and Sing around the side of the building, where it nearly abutted the palisade. The old Lascar was crouched beside a hole torn in the soft earth.

"This was not here before," Kazin said, as they arrived.

Sing and Bulan crouched beside the hole. Bulan touched the edges, and saw where a covering of grasses and sticks had been tossed aside. "He camouflaged it—ingenious." He felt something like pride as he considered the forethought required for such an act. None of the other creatures had ever displayed anything close to that level of wit. He banished the thought with an irritated flick of his head. "He must have waited until he was certain we were outside, come up through this hole, clocked poor Esmail, and taken Virginia."

"Or she went with him," Sing said. "She had a pistol, re-member? And we heard no shots." He looked worried as he said it, and Bulan couldn't help but wonder if he was right. "Maybe she is not a captive," Sing went on.

"It doesn't matter," Bulan said, firmly. "I have to go after her."

"Are you insane?" Kazin asked. "For all we know, that beast is waiting for you down there." He stood. "We should all go. I will send Amer and Esmail back to the ship and the rest of us will—"

"No," Bulan said, firmly. He looked at Esmail. The young Lascar was on his feet, but still looked dazed. "Get my sidearm and a lantern, please. I have a feeling I'll need both."

"I will go with you," Sing insisted, as Esmail stumbled off to retrieve the items. Again, Bulan shook his head.

"No, I need you to stay here and keep an eye on our guest."

Sing blinked. "The soldier? Why?"

"We were wondering who took the missing equipment. Perhaps we should ask him." Bulan turned to Kazin. "Keep watch. We'll head back to the ship when I have returned with Virginia, is that understood?"

Kazin looked as if he wanted to argue, but settled for a nod. Esmail returned with Bulan's pistol and a lit lantern. Bulan took both with a nod of thanks and handed the lantern to Sing. Then, with barely a grunt of effort, he dropped into the hole. As he'd suspected, it wasn't deep—barely seven feet. He landed in a crouch, pistol in hand, and surveyed the cramped tunnel leading away in the direction of the forest. When nothing attacked him, he reached up for the lantern. Sing handed it down. "Are you certain you do not wish me to come?" he asked, again.

Bulan shook his head. "They can't have gone too far." He smiled, trying to show a confidence he didn't quite feel. "But if I don't return after thirty minutes, feel free to come to my rescue, okay?"

Sing didn't return his smile. "Thirty minutes."

Bulan nodded, raised his lantern, and strode into the dark.

14
PLANS

PROFESSOR EGON VOGEL removed his spectacles and rubbed ineffectually at tired eyes. They were always tired these days. So were his legs and arms, his back—his mind. Like a machine pushed too hard for too long. Maybe it was simply age catching up with him at last. He considered himself a vigorous man, despite his advanced years. But then, didn't all old men think of themselves as young, until something disabused them of that fanciful notion?

He pushed himself back from his desk and stood, joints popping in protest. He went to the gramophone in the corner, selected a record from the small stash Arkwright had allowed him to bring, and set it to turning. The room was soon filled with the hearty voice of Ada Jones, belting out her rendition of "By the Light of the Silvery Moon." A favorite of his.

He moved to the center of the room and began his usual nighttime regimen of stretches, bends and twists. The routine was designed to keep him flexible in his dotage, to prevent him from ending up like so many men of his generation, confined to bath chairs. As he worked his joints, he thought of Otto.

Otto was becoming difficult. That was to be expected, of course. The boy was clever, and growing more so by the day. He devoured every book he was given, and had a facility for languages that bordered on the preternatural. He had his share of flaws—he was impulsive and his curiosity was all but ungovernable. Worse, his hunger was, to be blunt, bestial.

88

Vogel suspected that more than one Dayak had fallen prey to Otto's rending teeth before Arkwright's expedition had arrived on the island.

But that could be forgiven. The boy had been doing his best to survive alone in a hostile wilderness, with no one to show him right from wrong. Vogel was certain there was a gentle soul in that monstrous frame—the soul of a poet or a painter—but it would take time to nurture it to full bloom. Otto was an orchid; he needed tending, else he might wither on the vine. Vogel didn't like to think of what might happen then.

There were enough monsters in the world as it was. It did not require another.

But that was exactly what Arkwright wanted. Monsters. Fiends. Clawing, tearing, howling cannibal ogres, to be unleashed upon—who? Empires did not lack for enemies. It did not matter. Vogel had no intention of helping him.

He suspected Arkwright knew that, however. Had probably planned for it. Like Otto, Arkwright was too clever by half. Unlike the boy, however, there could be no forgiving his monstrousness. And if Arkwright even suspected that Otto existed—no, such a thing did not bear thinking about.

Someone knocked at the door, startling him. Then, "Professor? It's Lieutenant Arkwright. May I speak with you?"

Vogel checked his pocket watch and allowed himself a thin smile. "Speak of the devil and he shall appear," he murmured. He wondered if Arkwright's consistency in visiting at this time every night was intentional, or simply habit. Perhaps his patron was simply checking on him, the way he checked the compound's defenses, ensuring that a vital tool in his arsenal was still functioning as expected.

He gave his quarters a quick once-over before he answered. They consisted of little enough; a cot, a chair in the corner, next to a small bookcase loaded down with volumes pertinent to his work, and a small writing desk. Electric lights burned in the corners of the small room, casting a dull orange glow over everything. Nothing incriminating was visible. All was as Arkwright would expect it to be.

Vogel cleared his throat. "Naturally. Please come in."

The door opened and Arkwright entered, looking as inhumanly composed as ever. Even in shirt sleeves, he looked every inch an officer and a gentleman. He closed the door behind him and peered at the gramophone. "Have I interrupted you?"

"No. Is my gramophone bothering you?" Vogel moved to turn off the music.

"No, no. It's . . . an interesting choice, is all."

Vogel chuckled. "Despite what you English may believe we do not all listen to Wagner in our free time. Though, perhaps Mozart might be a better choice for a man of my age, eh?" He looked at his guest. "I am an old dog, but I can learn new tricks."

"An admirable quality." Arkwright looked around the room, as if scanning for enemies. Vogel waited for him to speak for several moments. But when nothing appeared forthcoming, he said, "Why are you here, Lieutenant? Is there something I can do for you?"

"Tell me about him. Maxon, I mean. What sort of man was he?"

Vogel shrugged. "A genius. But a flawed one." It wasn't the first time Arkwright had asked about Maxon. Vogel suspected that Arkwright had people in the United States searching for the professor even now, if only to ensure that their efforts here remained absolutely secret.

Arkwright smiled. "All geniuses are, I am told."

Vogel grunted. "Then I am glad to be a simple scientist."

"Is that what you are, Professor?" Arkwright asked. "A simple scientist? Is that why our successes of late have been so . . . limited?" He picked up one of Vogel's notebooks and flipped through it. Vogel wondered if Arkwright understood what he was looking at. It was possible. There was much he didn't know about his mysterious benefactor.

They had met in Singapore. Arkwright claimed to be a

military attaché to some governmental factotum in the rubber industry and Vogel had been doing his best to be invisible. His political leanings had earned him no friends in Germany and cost him his position at the University of Vienna. At loose ends, he had come to Singapore hoping to meet with Professor Maxon, whose theories he'd found intriguing and with whom he'd maintained a lively, if somewhat irregular, correspondence.

Instead, he'd met Arkwright.

Arkwright made a show of studying Vogel's small library, his expression conveying disdain. But Vogel could see the interest simmering in the Englishman's keen gaze. If Arkwright were truly as unimaginative as he wished to appear, he would have ignored the books entirely. Instead, every time he visited, he gave them an increasingly covetous examination. And why not, after all? What true man of learning could ignore the potential of the Jabirian corpus or the writings of Paracelsus?

Arkwright selected one of the texts—a French translation of *Concordance of the Sanguine Serpent*—and carefully thumbed through it. After a moment, he snorted and returned the book. "Alchemy and superstition," he said, in an almost accusatory tone.

"And yet you see the results for yourself," Vogel replied. Maxon's notes had been a hodgepodge of scientific theory and mysticism, all encrypted in a lunatic's cipher. It had taken him long months to translate the madman's scrawling into something useful. Maxon was undeniably a genius, but a thoroughly unstable one.

"Monsters," Arkwright said, flatly.

"Intelligent beings," Vogel corrected.

Arkwright sniffed and selected another book. "On that note, how are we progressing with the next batch?"

Vogel sat. "I am not sure I understand your question." In truth, he understood all too well. Arkwright wanted things done yesterday, as if time were just another soldier to be ordered about. "The womb-vats have all been sanitized and the necessary apparatus have been cleaned and inspected. But until the supply ship arrives, there can be no progress."

He leaned back in his chair, trying to get comfortable—a vain effort. Age had its claws firmly in him, despite all his exercises. Sometimes he fancied brewing himself a new body, but it was only a fancy. Once a man's soul had taken root, no amount of scraping could dislodge it from its chosen soil. He gave Arkwright a thin smile. "It seems we must wait until fresh chemicals and tissue samples arrive to continue the experiment."

Arkwright was silent for a moment, and Vogel idly wondered whether he'd gone too far. Arkwright's favor was a tenuous thing, hard to earn and easy to lose. He had a suspicion that if he sufficiently angered the Englishman, Arkwright would not hesitate to kill him and feed his body to the creatures in the cells. Arkwright sighed. "I am aware of all of this. What I meant was have you had any progress in regard to our desired results?"

"Your desired results," Vogel said, more sharply than he intended. "Not mine."

Arkwright dismissed this assertion with an absent gesture. "As you say. But the question stands." He fixed Vogel with his too-steady gaze, and the latter could not help but shift uneasily in his chair. Arkwright's composure was just short of inhuman. Even his rare instances of anger seemed calculated. "Can they be made more . . . pliable?"

"Docile, you mean."

"I am precise in my word choice, Doctor. Docile monsters are no good to anyone. Pliable ones, however, have a variety of potential uses. Not just militarily, whatever you might be thinking." Arkwright gave a tiger's grin and Vogel shivered.

"They can think and reason," he began, softly. "And while some are more enlightened than others, they all show a great capacity for learning. For independent thought. For all their grotesque appearance, we have created men." He swallowed and pressed ahead. "Why then do you wish me to investigate the retardation of their mental capacity?"

Arkwright gave a small laugh. "Isn't it obvious? I wish them to be stupid for the same reason I wish them to be sterile—so that what we create here does not eventually replace us in the grand scheme of things." He shook his head and turned back to the books. "We both strive for perfection in our own ways. It is the core of who we are, and why I entrusted you with this endeavor."

"For which I am grateful," Vogel began.

"Are you? I have my doubts." Arkwright glanced at him. "That search is what defines humanity. It is what separates us from the animals. It is what keeps us at the pinnacle of creation. But what if something else came along to knock us from our perch? They are stronger and more durable than we are . . . why risk them being more intelligent as well? No, what we have created is more than sufficient to our—to my—needs."

"Then why continue?" Vogel asked.

Arkwright turned. "Because sufficiency is all well and good, but there are improvements to be made. We are close, though. I want brutes, professor. Pliable and fierce. Remember that, for the next time."

Vogel cleared his throat. "And what of our current crop of subjects? Some of them . . . exceed your maximum threshold for intelligence. Creation Eight in particular."

Arkwright strode to the door. "We'll continue to observe them, and see what we can learn. Knowledge is always a useful thing." He paused in the doorway. "But if the next batch meets my expectations . . . well. The current crop will be quite redundant, won't they?"

A moment later, he was gone. Vogel sat in silence for long moments, considering the dilemma before him. Arkwright was pragmatic to a fault. There was no poetry in him to be exploited. To him, the beings they had created were nothing more than raw materials to be exploited and discarded, as necessary.

A shortsighted view, in Vogel's opinion. And an evil one. He had met only a few truly evil men in his long life. Some were deranged; others twisted by greed or lust. But Arkwright was worse, for he was driven by his ideals. He was the sort of man who would happily build his chosen future on a foundation of bones, if that was what he deemed necessary.

Vogel sighed and pinched the bridge of his nose. When he had first begun his correspondence with Maxon, he had never imagined it would come to this. But there was no turning back now.

One way or another, matters would be settled tonight.

15
FRIENDS

IRGINIA HAULED HERSELF UP out of the hole and paused to dust the dirt from her hands. The forest was dark and the grass was wet from the rain. It had been dark down in the tunnels, almost too dark to see, but her guide apparently had no difficulty navigating such oppressive gloom. Her father would have been pleased.

"Well, that was an interesting journey." She looked at her guide. Number Thirteen crouched nearby, watching her with what she hoped was curiosity, rather than hunger. "Care to explain why we had to make it, and so quickly?"

He grunted something in German and she had to ponder a moment what it might mean. She was forced to acknowledge that his mouth was not designed for human speech. That he could talk at all was a miracle. "It wasn't safe, is that what you're trying to say?"

He tilted his head, watching her. She settled back on her heels and studied him. There was blood on his hands and she felt a flutter of concern. He'd harmed someone; she could only pray it wasn't Bulan or Sing.

He'd surprised her, appearing so suddenly. She'd heard the gunshots outside and for a moment had been convinced that he'd had something to do with it. But as the sounds of struggle continued, she'd realized that he'd come to take her away. She'd considered shooting him—not fatally, just in the leg—but had decided to save that option for when it was absolutely necessary. Instead, she'd followed him, pausing only to check

Esmail's pulse. He'd only knocked the young Lascar unconscious, thankfully.

The tunnel had been a surprise; moreover, she saw convolu-
tions and split passages that implied it wasn't just one, but
many. It seemed that Number Thirteen was an industrious
sort. Her father, she thought, would have been pleased. The
tunnels, the speech, all of it showed the creature to be highly
intelligent—calculating—human in thought, if not appearance. She found the thought both heartening and disturbing
in equal measure.

Though Virginia didn't consider herself a scientist, she had
been raised by one. Looking at the monster more closely she
could see the similarities between him and his predecessors.
The bony growths that sprouted on his skin, his teeth and
claws, even the strange bluish tinge to his coarse flesh reminded
her of the others. Yet he moved without their pained awkward-
ness; and his strength was far in excess of theirs. Perhaps he'd
simply built up his muscles with all the digging.

As she'd followed him, she'd left discreet signs for Bulan—
hearts traced in the dirt. Her fiancé was almost certainly in
pursuit, or would be soon enough. He was as determined to
see this through as she was, if for different reasons. Bulan's
encounter with her father's work had changed him in some
fundamental way.

She knew in her heart that the man who had fallen in love
with her at the train station two years ago was not the same
man she now slept beside. Sometimes she wondered what
that Townsend Harper, Jr., had been like. Would she have
been attracted to him, or would she have dismissed him the
way she'd dismissed Von Horn? Was it Townsend she loved,
or Bulan? Was there any difference, or was it simply a matter
of semantics at this point?

Bulan had thought he was a monster; perhaps, in some
way, he still did. That was why he'd come. Because he felt
guilty about what he'd done as a monster. Whereas she felt
guilty for—what? What her father had done? Or maybe not.

Maybe it wasn't guilt driving her at all. But something else.

She cleared her throat. "Thank you for protecting me," she said, choosing her words with care. "I would rather be with my friends, but I appreciate your concern. I know only a few words in German, so I hope you can somehow understand me."

"I . . . understand," Number Thirteen croaked. She blinked, startled. So he could speak English! That made things easier. But before she could reply, he continued. "Many enemies here. Soldiers. Arkwright. You do not need friends. You will be with me now."

Virginia took a deep breath, fighting down the sudden surge of panic. She vividly recalled the horror of the moment she'd understood the fate her father had intended for her. How he'd believed his only option was to wed her to the so-called "perfect man"—this thing before her. Was he a man? Up close, he looked anything but. Maybe his appearance was due to Sing's interference. Or maybe her father was not the genius she'd always thought him to be. The thought nagged at her even as she tried to think of how to respond.

She licked her lips. "I want you to understand that I mean you no harm. I am a friend. My name is Virginia." She filed the name Arkwright away; something about it was familiar, but she couldn't say why just now.

"Virginia," he repeated, slowly, as if tasting the syllables. His eyes gleamed with—what? Not hunger, she thought. Not the physical sort, at least. She forced the thought aside and met his gaze.

"Yes. Do you have a name?"

"The kind one, he calls me . . . Otto."

"Otto. Okay then, Otto—"

He interrupted her. "Why are you here?"

She paused. That was a good question. "Why am I here?" she murmured. "Well, my friends and I—"

"Your friend—the *man*—he hurt me! Soldier of Arkwright!"

"No," she said, quickly. Arkwright again. Was he in

command of the soldiers? She was still drawing a blank on the name, though she was certain she'd heard it somewhere before. "He wants to help you. We want to help you!" She reached for him without thinking, and he flinched back out of reach. She paused, wondering if he had ever been touched in any way that wasn't violent.

"Soldier," he growled, flexing his oddly jointed fingers.

"No," she said firmly. "No, he's not. He wants to be your friend."

"Not a friend—*enemy!*" Otto's snarl echoed through the forest. She forced herself not to draw back, not to show fear. She didn't think he would hurt her, not intentionally. But he was still a monster, a predator. Her father might not have intended to make such creatures, but he'd done his work well. Otto, she fancied, would be a match for any leopard or orang-utan who thought to attack him.

"Who is this Arkwright?" she asked. "Is he on the island?"

"Arkwright leads the soldiers," Otto said.

She nodded slowly, digesting this. "When did he come here? Do you know?"

Otto looked down at the ground and scratched at it with a claw. "I have your picture." He glanced almost shyly at her. "I dream of you, sometimes. My pretty girl."

Virginia felt a chill that had nothing to do with the damp. "These soldiers, Otto . . . are they the ones who took the equipment from the lab?"

"The soldiers are dangerous. I will protect you from them." He moved closer to her and reached out to touch her hair. He stank of wet earth and blood, but she was careful to keep her expression even. "We will hide and they will leave and you will be safe."

"And then what?" she asked, gently. Otto looked at her in apparent befuddlement. She almost laughed. He reminded her of Bulan in that moment. Had Townsend Harper, Jr., thought of anything beyond meeting her when he'd set off in pursuit of her and her father? Otto shared that utter lack of forethought. He had seen her—wanted her—and acted, without considering anything else.

"You will be safe," he repeated. He drew his hand back.

"I have never been one to yearn for safety."

Otto paused, head cocked like that of a confused dog. "I . . ." he began, clearly bewildered. "I must protect you."

"Why?"

Otto stared at her. It was hard to read his expression, especially through the mass of long, matted hair that fell about his face. What features she could make out were not those of a man, and did not show the same play of emotions that a man's might. But when he snapped his teeth together, she took it to be a sign of irritation. "You ask too many questions," he grunted.

"I have been accused of that." Virginia sat back. "This is not going the way I wanted," she admitted, with a sigh. He had drawn away from her, and crouched as if on the verge of bolting. Was he frightened of her? It seemed inconceivable, given his raw strength. Then, what was he but an abandoned child? Feral, yes; fierce, but not fearless. Skittish, like an animal. But he wasn't an animal.

She decided to change the subject. "Let's not talk about soldiers or Arkwright, whoever that is—let's talk about the Kind One. The one who named you. What is his name?"

A twig snapped. Otto spun with a guttural snarl. Past his shoulder, Virginia saw a British soldier running down the jungle path, his expression one of panic. He stumbled to a halt as he spotted them and his eyes widened. He raised his rifle and Virginia lifted her hands to show she meant no harm.

"Don't—don't move you," the newcomer shouted. "Miss, you get up and get behind me, quick." His eyes flickered around nervously. She wondered if he was one of the ones who'd been at the compound. Was he running from Sing and the Lascars?

Her hand fell to her sidearm. "No," she said, as calmly as she could manage. "Don't hurt him. We mean you no harm."

"Do as I say," the soldier barked. "My god, what the hell is that thing? Get over here quick, before it attacks!"

Virginia frowned. That answered that. The soldiers clearly didn't know about her father's work. At least this one didn't. She snapped off a quick shot, splitting a low-hanging branch near the soldier's head and causing him to yelp. "Drop your rifle or the next one won't miss," she said, harshly. "I'm not kidding."

As the soldier hesitated, Otto leaped. Virginia cried out in instinctive warning but too late. The soldier pivoted and caught Otto a solid clout on the side of the head with the stock of his rifle. Otto stumbled back and toppled into the hole without making a sound.

So concerned was she with his fate that she momentarily forgot about the soldier until he was darting toward her to snatch the pistol from her grip. He elbowed her to the ground in the process and swung the rifle down to aim at her. "Don't move," he snarled.

"I'm not moving," she said, quickly. "I just want to check on my friend." She glanced down into the hole but it was too dark to see anything. It seemed impossible that even a lucky blow would have permanently injured Otto. But if he'd fallen wrong—broken his neck—even his durability must have its limits.

"Friend, is it?" the soldier grunted. He stepped back and gestured for her to stand. "On your feet, miss. We're going for a little walk, you and I. I have a feeling Lieutenant Arkwright will want to talk with you."

16

PURSUIT

THE SOUND OF THE GUNSHOT echoed through the cramped confines of the tunnel.

Bulan stiffened, ears straining to capture the direction the sound had come from. He'd already become lost and forced to double back a few times. The tunnels were a tangled molehill. They went in all directions, with no rhyme or reason. The thought of Number Thirteen scrabbling around down here in the dark sent a chill through him. How long had the creature been digging these tunnels, and what else might be down here with him?

Bulan hurried in the direction he hoped the sound had come from, casting the lantern's glow ahead of him. His heart was pounding in his chest as he clambered through the dark, subterranean corridors. Every so often, in the gleam of the lantern light, he spotted a heart drawn in the loose soil and knew that he was going in the right direction.

The hearts were a sign from Virginia. During the previous winter in Ithaca, when he would depart Virginia's home after his daily visit, he would blow her a kiss from the sidewalk. In return, she would draw a heart in the condensation on the glass of her front storm door. The hearts told him two things: first, that she was alive, and second, that she was allowed to move at her own pace.

He was beginning to wonder if Sing were right. Perhaps Virginia had gone with Number Thirteen of her own free will.

If so, what did it mean? He couldn't imagine her doing something so seemingly foolhardy without good reason.

Something appeared at the outer edge of the light, and Bulan slowed. Cautiously he approached the dark mass and swung the lantern up so that it was fully illuminated, revealing it to be Number Thirteen himself, sprawled on the ground. Bulan crouched beside the monster and checked for a pulse. It took him several attempts but he eventually found it; strong and steady. "Good job, Virginia," he murmured. "Not dead, but definitely out of our hair for the moment." Had Virginia somehow gotten the drop on the creature, and knocked him unconscious? If so, where was she?

Bulan stood. "Right then. You stay here and have yourself a nap, my friend." He raised the lantern and saw that they were at the bottom of a pit, much like the one he'd used to enter these tunnels in the first place. "Only one way out, I suppose."

He set the lantern down, tucked his pistol into the waistband of his trousers and began to climb. It was difficult, but not impossible. He dug his fingers and toes into the soft earth, heaving himself up before the soil could collapse under his weight. Was this how Number Thirteen did it? Or did he simply leap upward, like a wild animal?

Bulan pushed these thoughts aside as he reached the lip of the pit and hauled himself out. His muscles ached as he paused to catch his breath. There was a path ahead, cutting through the forest. Had Virginia gone that way? She must have. But why not wait for him? He scanned the ground, squinting against the weak light of the moon dripping down through the trees. There were footprints in the soil; he identified some as Number Thirteen's, and others as Virginia's . . . but there was a third set. Deep, which implied they belonged to a man. Not a Dayak, for no Dayak he'd ever met wore military issue footwear. A soldier then?

He rose and looked back in what he judged to be the

direction of the old compound. One of the soldiers had escaped—had he somehow run across Virginia and Number Thirteen? "Hell of a coincidence," he murmured as he retrieved his pistol. He glanced back down into the hole to check that Number Thirteen was still lying where he'd left him. "Wait right here, big fellow. We'll be back shortly."

Then he started down the path. The temptation to run was strong, but something told him to take it slow and hang back. Soon his caution was rewarded; he could hear voices ahead. One of them was Virginia's. She was talking to someone—her captor, he realized. "Impressive palisade," she said, loudly. "For protection from the local pirates? We had some trouble from them ourselves."

"Quiet," the soldier replied, gruffly.

"Does that mean the island is now a British protectorate?" Virginia asked, ignoring him. Bulan smiled. Virginia had no give in her; it was one of the reasons he loved her. "You're not answering many of my questions," she went on.

"Just keep moving," her captor said, sounding aggravated. Bulan fell into step behind them, adjusting the rhythm of his footsteps to theirs. It was a trick Sing had taught him, a way of following close without being detected. He paused as they reached the base of the palisade. The soldier called up to one of his fellows on the wall, and the gates began to open. If Virginia went inside, he'd lose her.

Bulan decided the time for subtlety had passed. He thrust his pistol into his waistband and stepped out into the open, hands raised. "Hey, hold on there a minute," he called out. Virginia's captor whirled, rifle at the ready. Bulan recognized him as the soldier who'd escaped them at the compound. The man's eyes widened in recognition.

"Stay right where you are," he barked.

Bulan paused. "It's okay," he said. "Please stay calm. I'm an American, okay?"

The soldier glanced at Virginia. "Friend of yours?"

"You could say that," she said.

"Fine, then. Step over here, Mr. American. And keep those bloody hands of yours up."

Bulan did as instructed, moving slowly. He could see men atop the wall, and more at the gate—but not too many. How many men were stationed here? Not more than a detachment, he guessed. Twenty or thirty men, at most—not counting the prisoner he'd taken and the unfortunate that had possibly run afoul of Number Thirteen. The soldier glanced at the man at the gate.

"Oi, Chapman—go get the lieutenant."

Chapman hesitated, looking at Virginia and then at Bulan. "Where's the Sergeant? And Fraser? Why ain't they with you?"

"Never mind that," Virginia's captor snarled. "Just go get the lieutenant!" He squinted at Bulan. "You tossed me around pretty good back there, mate."

"Sorry about that," Bulan said. "It was all confusion in the moment, you know? A misunderstanding." He looked at Virginia. "Are you okay?"

"So far," she said.

"Quiet, the pair of you," the soldier interjected, sharply.

"I don't think so," Virginia said. "I want to talk to Arkwright."

The way the soldier hesitated made Bulan wonder what Virginia had learned. Who was Arkwright? Was he somehow involved with Number Thirteen? "Virginia," he began. "Why don't we . . ."

"Hush, Bulan," Virginia said. She looked at the soldier. "Well? Are we going to stand here all night, or are you going to take us to Arkwright?"

"That can be arranged," the soldier said, with a smirk. He gestured to the gate. "Get inside, both of you. And no funny business!" As Bulan stepped past him, the soldier snatched his pistol from his waistband. "Oh, and I'll hold onto this for you, shall I?"

"Be my guest," Bulan murmured. He looked at Virginia. "Number Thirteen didn't hurt you, did he?"

She shook her head. "No. Everything was just peachy until—well."

The soldier shoved Bulan forward. "Shut up!" He turned to close the gate, and Bulan considered taking the man's rifle from him while he was distracted. Instead, he kept walking.

"Who's this Arkwright you asked about?"

"I don't know exactly, but I think he's in charge here," Virginia said, in a low voice. "I also think Number Thirteen is in danger. He thinks of these men as enemies."

"Can't imagine why," Bulan said, taking in the British compound. It was laid out in similar fashion to Maxon's compound, but it was substantially larger—the better to accommodate a large number of soldiers. "I didn't know you were fluent in German."

"I'm not. He can speak English."

"This just gets more and more confusing," Bulan said, with a sigh. "My time on this island was spent in total confusion, and that wasn't pleasant at all. So it's like Coach Weber at Cornell always says: when the going gets tough—"

"No," Virginia said, in warning.

Bulan smiled. "Show them who's tougher."

"Please don't," Virginia said.

"Too late," Bulan said, even as he spun on his heel and struck their captor across the jaw. The man fell back with a strangled yelp and Bulan retrieved both his pistol and the soldier's rifle. He tossed the latter to Virginia.

"I really wish you hadn't done that," she said.

"Something's not right here, we both know that," Bulan said. He could hear shouts, and the sound of men running across the palisade. They needed to get back out through the gate and into the forest as quickly as possible. "We need to—"

"Surrender immediately?" an unfamiliar voice interjected. "Yes, that would be rather advisable, given the circumstances."

Bulan and Virginia turned to see several soldiers trotting toward them, accompanied by a man who could only be their commanding officer. He smiled as he spread his hands as if in welcome. "Good evening. I am Lieutenant Arkwright. This is my compound, and these are my men currently aiming their rifles at you. Now, I suggest you let cooler heads prevail and hand over your weapons before things take an ugly turn, what?"

"I don't think so," Bulan said. "In fact, I think we'll be leaving." He reached down and grabbed the collar of the soldier he'd coldcocked. "And your man here is coming with us, at least as far as the gate."

Arkwright shrugged. "Baskin? Take him. He's no loss. Nor are the others, whom I presume you dealt with in some fashion." His cool gaze flicked to Virginia. "I hear you wished to speak with me, young lady. Might I ask why?"

Virginia hesitated, but before she could speak, Bulan jumped in. If Virginia had one flaw it was her curiosity. It had gotten her into trouble more than once, and now had again. "Listen, Lieutenant, your men attacked me and my companions and I want to know why. You want pirates, go look for Muda Saffir."

"Bulan," Virginia began, but he ignored her.

"We're scientists, damn it! From Cornell University in America and we've done nothing wrong!" Bulan dragged the soldier to his feet, but kept his eyes on Arkwright and the others. The gate was directly behind them, maybe ten feet away—if he could distract them, Virginia might be able to make it.

Arkwright paused. "Scientists, you say? I was thinking of releasing you, but now I've changed my mind. Baskin, be a sport and relieve him of his firearm, there's a good fellow."

Baskin twisted in Bulan's grip and rammed an elbow into the American's midsection. Bulan stumbled back, off balance. The soldier had only been playing possum, and as he turned, he drew a knife from his belt. He leaped on Bulan, and they fell back in a tangle. "I owe you for earlier, mate," Baskin growled. "And for Higgs and Fraser!"

"Bulan," Virginia cried.

"I'm fine," Bulan said, as he caught Baskin's knife hand by the wrist and elbow and gave it a vicious twist. The bone snapped with an ugly sound, and the soldier fell away from him, howling in pain. Bulan rose to his feet. "Now then, who's next?"

"Give the word, Lieutenant," one of the other soldiers said as he sighted down the length of his rifle. The rest of them followed suit, taking aim at Bulan. Virginia raised her own weapon. Arkwright looked at her, and then at Bulan.

"No need," Arkwright said. "We'll let Ju-Long handle this, I think."

Bulan hesitated. Ju-Long? He heard someone drop down from the palisade and saw a muscular figure—not in uniform—stride toward him. The newcomer removed his straw hat as he came, revealing a shaggy mane of black hair and a square, unsmiling face. Something about it struck Bulan as familiar, even as the man stopped in front of him.

"You like to fight," Ju-Long said.

"Pal, I've been fighting my whole life," Bulan said. Ju-Long smiled.

"This should be interesting," he said, as he tossed his hat aside. "Because so have I."

17

FISTICUFFS

U-LONG FELL SMOOTHLY into a martial stance, and was pleased to see the American do the same. They were of a similar size, both heavily muscled but in the way of men used to constant exertion rather than sculpted by exercise. That was good. He had not had a physical challenge in months; not since the last time one of Arkwright's creatures had escaped.

He decided to seize the initiative and leaped on the American, tackling him to the ground. The American flung Ju-Long off, rolled to his feet, and kicked Ju-Long square in the jaw as the latter tried to rise. Ju-Long lurched up and stumbled back, fists raised. The kick had been a good one; his opponent had some training. He rubbed his jaw. "You are not altogether unskilled," he allowed.

"You're pretty quick on your feet yourself," the American— Bulan—said. They circled one another, each waiting for the other to leave an opening.

"In Singapore, I heard stories about a man named Bulan. The Dayaks said he was a giant. A monster." Bulan flinched, ever so slightly. Ju-Long smiled. "Ah. Was that you, then? Are you the wild bogeyman the Dayaks fear?"

"Last I heard, Dayaks weren't afraid of bupkis," Bulan growled. His fist shot out like a steam-driven piston, and Ju-Long grunted as he blocked the blow with his forearm. He returned Bulan's punch in kind, aiming for the other man's kidneys. Bulan bent forward, like a boxer, and absorbed the punches higher up on his torso.

For a time, there was nothing save the sound of fists dancing across flesh, and grunts of pain and effort. Ju-Long found a certain serenity in moments such as this. All the complexities of the world were banished, leaving only the simplicity of kill or be killed. He could not help but smile as he caught a glancing blow on the head, and gave Bulan one of his own in reply. It seemed the American felt the same way, for he was smiling as well—a fierce grin, stained as red as Ju-Long's own.

The world turned on its axis as they hammered at one another, ignoring all save the opponent before them. They came together and broke apart like conflicting tides, with every crash sufficient to reorient their surroundings. Rarely had Ju-Long ever experience a fight of such pristine brutality. Here was a man who truly understood the beauty of violence. Who gloried in it, even as he strained to pummel his opponent into the dirt.

Alas, all good things come to an end, and this brawl was no different. Ju-Long saw his opening and took it, driving a palm-strike across Bulan's jaw. Bulan caught at him as he fell back, and they tumbled to the ground together. There, their struggles continued for a few frantic moments. The ballet had devolved into a brutal wrestling match. Ju-Long found himself on the ground, and Bulan atop him, raining down blow after blow.

Ju-Long's legs snapped up to encircle his opponent's waist, and he managed to roll Bulan onto the ground. He hooked his elbow around Bulan's thick neck and put him into a hold designed to squeeze the air from his lungs. Bulan flailed, trying vainly to hurl him off. Even now, his strength was impressive. But his discipline was lacking. The longer they fought, the wilder he became. In contrast, Ju-Long only became more controlled.

As Bulan's struggles began to weaken, Ju-Long allowed his attention to wander. Arkwright was still watching, but his men had taken the woman into custody and were escorting her away. "Finish him, Ju-Long," Arkwright called out.

"You've had your fun, but I would like to question him at some point."

Ju-Long was about to reply when he felt a tremor, not from his opponent, but from the ground below them. His eyes widened as two blue-gray fists erupted from the earth nearby. Startled, he released Bulan and made to rise—but too slowly. Something heaved itself up from the disturbed soil, and fixed yellow eyes upon him.

Time slowed to a crawl as he met that yellow gaze. At first he thought it was one of Arkwright's creations, somehow free of its cage. But it was different; more powerful. And its eyes too were different—there was no malice there, only anger. It sprang for him, lithe and swift as a jungle cat. He could not stop it as it caught him up and lifted him over its head, as if he weighed no more than a sack of potatoes.

As it held him, Ju-Long saw Arkwright staring at the creature in what might have been awe. Baskin and the other soldiers watched in frozen horror as it hurled him to the ground—hard. Ju-Long hit the ground and only just managed to roll with the impact. Even so, he found he could not force his body to move for several moments.

The world sped back up. Soldiers lifted their rifles, fear subsumed by instinct and training. But before they could fire, gunshots came from above and beyond the palisade. A sniper? Perhaps Bulan and the woman had not come alone. Or perhaps the monster had allies of its own. Ju-Long forced himself to his feet as Arkwright and the others scattered, seeking cover. The sniper continued to fire, covering Bulan and the woman as they ran for the gates. But two could play that game.

Ju-Long sprinted for the watchtower and the Maxim gun positioned there. As he climbed toward the observation platform, he saw the monster fling an unlucky soldier across the courtyard. Impossible as it seemed, the creature appeared to be participating in the rescue attempt—was it allied with Bulan?

He'd heard the stories, of course. The Dayaks had had plenty of them. Bulan the Monster-Tamer. Bulan the King of Beasts. Perhaps they hadn't been exaggerating. Given what he and Vogel had found in the old compound, it was possible that one of Maxon's creations had somehow survived and been found by Bulan. He pushed these thoughts aside as he reached the top of the tower. None of it mattered, in the moment.

The Maxim was waiting for him like an old friend. He spun it around on its pivot and took aim at the monster. It seemed the more immediate threat. Let the soldiers handle the others. He fired, chopping up the turf in the creature's wake as it raced across the courtyard, but didn't manage to hit it.

The creature leaped over a fallen soldier and turned, charging back toward Ju-Long and the watchtower. He depressed the Maxim, firing at it as the thing raced toward him. But it was fast—too fast. It leaped and struck the base of the tower, clinging to the wooden posts like some great ape. Feverishly, Ju-Long worked to free the Maxim from its mount, but to no avail. The creature began to kick and smash the support struts and soon the whole tower was swaying wildly. Ju-Long lost his grip on the Maxim as the tower pitched and yawed.

Somewhere below him, wood splintered and hemp split. The tower groaned like a wounded animal—and toppled into the courtyard, ripping loose from the palisade as it went. Ju-Long held on for as long as possible, but soon had no choice but to jump.

He hit the ground a half second after the tower, and tucked himself into a tight ball as heavy shards of wood thudded to the ground around him. Thunder echoed in his head for long moments after the dust had settled. He became aware of voices. Arkwright and—Welles? Or one of the others.

"They're gone, sir," a soldier said. "And no sign of . . . whatever that thing was." They moved through the rubble of the fallen tower, checking the damage. No one offered to help him up. Nor did he expect it.

"Should we go after them?" That was Welles. Second Lieutenant Welles, Arkwright's second-in-command. "I can form up a party."

"No," Arkwright said. "We'll assess the damage and then formulate an appropriate response." He nudged Ju-Long with his boot. "Are you injured, Ju-Long?"

Ju-Long groaned and rose to his knees. Arkwright snorted. "Glad to hear it." He looked down at Ju-Long, his expression one of disappointment. "I thought you were made of sterner stuff than that. How annoying."

Ju-Long bit back a retort. Arkwright was in no mood for it. He looked out over the damage and sighed. "Make sure the gates are secured and report to me when you're cleaned up, there's a good man." With that, he turned on his heel and strode away, not even waiting for a reply. Ju-Long might as well have been a servant.

Ju-Long pushed himself to his feet. He felt as if every bone in his body had been twisted out of joint. He could taste blood, and bruises were already forming on his arms and legs. He rubbed at his shoulder. It was a miracle that it hadn't been dislocated.

"Are you all right, Ju-Long?"

Ju-Long turned. Welles stood behind him, a look of concern on his face. "I am fine," Ju-Long said. Welles was a decent man; a rare thing, in Ju-Long's experience. He seemed to care about the men under his command in a way that Arkwright assuredly did not.

Welles nodded. "Good. I've set Chapman and a few of the others to seeing to repairs." He removed his cap and ran his hand through his hair. "Quite the eventful evening, eh?"

"Yes."

"I don't think they were pirates," Welles went on. Ju-Long didn't reply. Welles looked at him. "Scientists, they said. Think they have something to do with that equipment we hauled out of that old compound on the other side of the island?"

Ju-Long paused. Welles was intelligent; ambitious. But

Arkwright had chosen to leave him in the dark when it came to their true purpose on the island. Perhaps he didn't trust Welles. Perhaps he simply hadn't thought it necessary.

When he didn't reply, Welles said, "I heard you had a set-to with Higgs earlier. He hasn't come back, has he?"

"No," Ju-Long said, carefully. He flexed his hand.

"You sent him to the old compound. Him and Fraser and Baskin. Baskin says they were attacked. That Fraser is missing. And Higgs . . ." Welles lit a cigarette and offered the crumpled pack to Ju-Long. Ju-Long waved it aside. "Baskin claims that Bulan chap took Higgs prisoner."

"Is that what he says?" Ju-Long stared out through the gap in the palisade, at the dark forest. Something nagged at him, something Bulan had said. A name. Sing. Could it be—? No. But it seemed too much of a coincidence.

"Ju-Long?"

He blinked and looked at Welles. "What?"

Welles studied him for a moment and then said, "Tell Arkwright I'm taking a few men out to the old compound. See if we can find Fraser and Higgs."

"He already told you no," Ju-Long said.

"He didn't say no. He said after we'd cleaned up. Clean up is in progress. They have a head start on us, and I don't intend to lose any of our men." Welles paused. "You can come, if you like. We might well need the manpower."

Ju-Long hesitated, but only for a moment. "No. But I wish you luck." As Welles walked away, Ju-Long added, under his breath, "I think you will need it."

18

MERCY

PROFESSOR VOGEL DESCENDED into the darkness with only a small lantern to see by. There was some disturbance outside, and it had given him the perfect opportunity to do what needed doing. What he intended was foolish, perhaps, but necessary, he felt. In any event, his conscience would not allow him to do otherwise.

The creatures did not deserve the sad fate Arkwright intended for them. Moreover, neither Arkwright nor Ju-Long had visited them since their last feeding. That meant that the hole Otto had clawed through the wall had yet to be discovered. But as soon as they knew of it, the hunt would be on. The boy would be in great danger . . . unless Vogel obfuscated his trail. There was only one way to save all of them—only one path to salvation.

If they were willing to follow it. If they did not tear him to pieces first.

He closed the steel door behind him and set the lantern down on the table. In its watery light, the eyes of the prisoners gleamed like those of wild animals. But they were not animals, whatever Arkwright, and Ju-Long, thought. Animals could not articulate their pain with speech; animals could not beg for mercy, or swear vengeance. No, these were men and he intended to treat them as such.

Vogel stood in silence for a moment, his hands clasped behind his back, the keys dangling from his finger. Every so often, he gave them a jingle. The things in the cells watched him warily. Finally, one of them spoke. "What do you want?"

It was Creation Eight, of course. He had assumed the position of spokesperson almost instinctively. Fitting, as he was the most intelligent of them. And the most dangerous. Vogel decided to be truthful. "I have not yet decided," he said. "What do you want?"

Creation Eight clasped the bars of his cell and peered out at Vogel. "You stopped us from killing the Other. Why?"

"Why did you wish to kill him?"

Eight blinked. "He is not one of us."

"He is—and he is not," Vogel said. "He was created, as you were. But he matured alone, without benefit of friends or the guidance of his creators." Vogel paused. "Not that you have received much in the way of the latter, I admit."

"I will tell Arkwright about him. Arkwright will punish him."

"Will he? I do not think so. I think he is exactly what Arkwright is searching for, though he does not realize it. You, on the other hand—well. Arkwright is not pleased by you at all. In fact, he wishes to destroy you."

A murmur ran through them until Eight silenced it with a growl. "You lie."

"Have I ever lied to you?" Vogel asked, gently. He took a step toward Eight's cell, putting himself within reach of those deadly hands. "Have I ever deceived you, or harmed you in any way? No. For you are as my children."

"We are Arkwright's children," Eight insisted.

Vogel smiled. "Are you? It was not Arkwright who grew you from a tiny knot of proteins. It was not Arkwright who pulled you from your steel wombs and helped you take your first breaths."

"Arkwright taught us; Arkwright feeds us," Eight countered. He was growing agitated, and so too were the others. They growled and hissed, sensing something was in the air. Vogel wondered whether all of them felt as Eight did, or if it was only Eight's almost religious adoration of Arkwright that kept the others in line.

"And now Arkwright will kill you. Or, rather, he will send Ju-Long to do it." As he'd expected, mention of the latter's name caused Eight to snarl in rage. If Arkwright was God in their cosmology, then Ju-Long was the Devil. "He will send him tonight or tomorrow; maybe the day after that. But he will come. Perhaps he will poison your food, or shoot you through the bars of your cells. Maybe he will kill you one at a time, so as to prolong the pleasure he will no doubt feel at your destruction." At his words, Creation Eight shrieked—and the others followed suit. They clawed at the bars and slashed at one another in their frenzy.

Vogel continued. "He will kill you, but I do not wish you to die. I would see you safe—and free. Do you wish to be free?"

Eight grunted. "What is free?" He waved a hand, as if to encompass the space beyond his cell. "To be out there, you mean? Arkwright says we are not ready."

"How do you know, unless you have tried?" Vogel asked.

Eight studied him. Vogel could feel the weight of the creature's gaze; he knew that there were calculations of a sort going on in that corpse-like skull. Eight wasn't simply clever; Eight was cunning. More so, perhaps, than Otto. Otto, at heart, was a simple soul. He wanted, as a child wants. His calculations were those of a child, with little thought as to consequences. Wisdom would come to him in time, but at the moment he was largely ruled by instinct and impulse.

Eight, on the other hand, had learned every brutal lesson that Arkwright and Ju-Long had taught him. He knew what it was to be punished, and knew how to conceal things from those who might do the punishing. Unlike the others, Creation Eight was smart enough to lie—even to himself. And while he might not believe that Arkwright would kill them, he certainly believed it of Ju-Long.

"You will free us?" Eight asked.

Vogel held up the keys. "I will free you."

"Why?"

"As I said, I do not wish you to be hurt."

Eight grunted softly. Vogel felt a pulse of unease. Something told him that the creature didn't quite believe him. "You do not wish the Other to be hurt either," Eight said. Then, slyly, "You do not wish me to tell Arkwright about him."

"Once you are free, you may do as you wish," Vogel said, after a moment's hesitation. Even as he said it, he wished that he had phrased it differently. Eight might very well take it into his head to pay Arkwright a visit. Or Ju-Long. That would be unfortunate. But he could not take it back now.

"Maybe I will find the Other and kill him," Eight said, almost gleefully. He pressed his grotesque countenance against the bars. "Maybe I will tear him apart, and bring his head to Arkwright, as a show of my love."

Vogel took a deep breath. "Maybe you will. But that is a choice you must make on your own. I trust that you will see that he is not your enemy. He is your friend, or wishes to be at least." He looked at the others. "Otto is like you; and like you, he does not know where he belongs. Perhaps together, you all might find some measure of peace."

He turned to Eight's cell and opened it. Now was the moment of truth. He did not think Eight would harm him, but there was no way to be sure. He stepped back as the creature stepped out. Eight was taller than Vogel, and possibly taller than Otto as well. He was somewhat over seven feet in height, but gangly like a victim of malnutrition. His limbs twitched oddly as he stretched—then, in a flash, he lunged for Vogel.

Vogel held himself still as Eight's hand clamped down on the back of his neck. The creature leaned down, and his sour breath fogged up the lenses of Vogel's spectacles. "I could kill you now," Eight murmured. "I could twist your head off and drink your blood. I could smash your skull and eat my fill of what spilled out."

Vogel forced himself to meet the creature's yellow gaze.

"You speak as a child might. Perhaps Arkwright was correct. You are not ready."

Eight clicked his teeth. "I am. We are. You will free the others and let us out through the door." He tightened his grip on Vogel's neck. "You will let us walk among the men we hear above and Arkwright will know we are loyal."

"No, for they would kill you—whatever Arkwright might have to say about it." Vogel pointed to the hole Otto had made in the wall. "There is your way out."

Eight looked down at him, and then at the hole. "Where does it lead?"

"The forest. Freedom."

"Will the Other be waiting for us?"

"I hope so," Vogel said, and meant it. "I hope he will help you to survive, as he has survived." He hesitated, then touched Eight's chest. "I want only for you to survive, my child. That is all I have ever wanted."

Eight flinched away from his touch. "You are not Arkwright. You have no say over what we do, or do not do." The creature released him and gestured to the other cells. "Free the others, and we will go."

Vogel did. Soon, all eight of them were free of their cells. They milled about for several moments, sniffing, and stretching. He realized that they had never been so close to one another without bars between them. He wondered if it might lead to violence; but Creation Eight held the reins still. He gestured to the hole, and the others went, squirming into the darkened aperture like great worms.

Eight was the last to go. He paused to look back at Vogel. Then, he was gone. Vogel shuddered as he considered what he had seen in the creature's eyes—savagery, yes, but also an inquisitiveness. What might Eight learn, out there in the forest? He was still pondering the matter when he heard the steel door creak open. "Vogel?" the newcomer called out.

Vogel turned to see Arkwright stepping through the steel door, a look of concern on his face. "Ah, there you are Professor.

We've had a spot of trouble, I'm afraid . . ." His words trailed off as he took in the empty cells.

"Yes," Vogel said, "I heard the gunfire. It seems we have had some trouble down here as well, Lieutenant."

Arkwright lifted the lantern from the table and swept its light out to illuminate each of the cells in turn. "Where are they?" he asked. Vogel answered, though he did not think the question was meant for anyone in particular.

"Gone. Escaped."

"How?" Arkwright demanded, turning to him.

Vogel shrugged. "I do not know. It is . . . baffling." He had to be careful here, to say no more than was absolutely necessary. He had to give Arkwright no reason to suspect him, not just yet. He still had to collect his notes and make his way into the forest. He had to find Otto and get to the Maxon compound. Whoever these newcomers were, they might well be able to help him. And if not, well, there was always Muda Saffir.

"They picked the locks somehow?" Arkwright asked.

Vogel paused. "It appears that way, yes. I did warn you. They are quite clever."

Arkwright frowned. "They didn't go out through the court-yard. We'd have noticed them, even with all the confusion."

"No. Look here." Vogel directed Arkwright's attention to the hole in the wall. Arkwright stared at it in shock. Vogel hid a flash of satisfaction at seeing the other man so clearly surprised. It was rare that anything disturbed Arkwright's equanimity.

"Bloody hell," Arkwright muttered, as he shone the light into the tunnel. "An underground tunnel. Clever beasts. How far does it go, do you think?"

"I cannot guess. Out of the compound, at least."

Arkwright was silent for several moments. "You stay here and watch that hole. And say nothing of this to anyone. I will send Ju-Long down as soon as he is able." He looked at Vogel. "There was another of them, you know. It was here, earlier. With the Americans."

"They were American, then?" Vogel asked.

"Yes, but they aren't important. Did you hear what I said? There is another of the monsters—one not created by us, unless you have been working on your own time." Arkwright paused. "It was different from the ones we created. Stronger, for one thing. It made a mess of the palisade."

Vogel felt his heart clench in worry. "Did you—was it . . . ?" he asked, fighting to keep his voice even. He had not considered that Otto might have been involved in what was going on? That fool boy was going to get himself killed.

"No. It got away, more is the pity." If Arkwright noticed Vogel's expression, he gave no sign. He set the lantern down. "Remember what I said, Professor—say nothing of this. We will speak more later, after Ju-Long has taken over."

"Will you send him after them?" Vogel asked. Arkwright paused at the door.

"I have no choice, do I? They cannot be allowed to wander free, Professor. They are too dangerous . . . and too valuable. At least until the supply ship arrives." With that, he was gone, leaving Vogel alone. The old man sighed shakily and looked at the hole.

"Godspeed, my children. Godspeed."

19
YACHT

NIGHT.

The moon hung full over the water, painting the shallows in hues of silver. The deck of the yacht was dark, save for the glow of a lantern hung from the mast. A single Lascar stood on the deck, a rifle cradled in the crook of his arm. His eyes swept the horizon, alert for any approaching vessel.

That was why the Dayaks had swum out, rather than using their prahu. Muda Saffir watched in pleasure from the deck of the war-canoe as his men swarmed onto the yacht and took the Lascar's head. Not a shot was fired. The Dayaks scattered, searching the vessel for any other guards. "Excellent," he said. At his elbow, Riwut nodded.

"What now?"

"Pull us closer. That vessel now belongs to me and I wish to search it myself."

"You do not trust the others?" Riwut asked, amused. Saffir snorted.

"I barely trust you, Riwut. Certainly not them. Besides, all it takes is one fool to set a fire and then the vessel and whatever plunder we might get from it will be lost." He turned and gave the order for the prahu to be pulled up alongside the yacht.

"Do you actually believe there to be anything of value aboard?" Riwut asked as the hull of the war-canoe thudded against that of the yacht. Saffir shrugged.

"The vessel itself is worth something. There are likely things aboard worth more. Perhaps guns, even." With that, he leaped easily across the gap between the two decks and landed in a catlike crouch. He would no doubt regret his dramatics in the morning; he was getting older and his body was no longer that of a young man. But it served to remind his subordinates who he was, and that was worth a few aches and pains.

Riwut followed him. "If the treasure you speak of exists, I doubt it is aboard this vessel," the Dayak said, in a low tone. And in English, as well, Saffir noted. Riwut had as much to lose as Saffir himself, if their crew decided to turn on them. "They will be unhappy."

Saffir did not have to ask who he meant. The Dayaks were impatient; the British supply ship was a few days out, and that meant sitting and waiting. Not something they enjoyed. And, of course, Tijilik had told everyone about his encounter with the old man and the monster, which only made things worse. Impatience and fear were a bad combination.

"Let them grumble. So long as that is all they do. Looting this craft will occupy them for some time, especially if there is anything of interest aboard."

"And after?"

Saffir laughed. "We will go inland and flush them out. They will flee here, and we will have them. Easy."

"And then we will find the treasure?"

Saffir turned away. "Yes, Riwut. We will find the treasure." He headed for the main cabin, eager to have a moment's peace from Riwut's badgering and the heavy glances of his Dayaks. He closed the door with a sigh of relief and looked around. It was not as well appointed as he might have imagined. Quite bare, in fact. A bed, some shelves and storage. He'd expected more of Americans.

Then, these Americans were odd, weren't they? Strange and full of secrets. Secrets that could be his, if he were cunning enough. His hands clenched suddenly, balling into fists.

He forced himself to relax. Anger had its place, and this was not it.

After his failure to acquire anything of value during his brief partnership with Von Horn, his reputation had been badly wounded. The invincible Muda Saffir was no longer so invincible. The Dayaks thought him weak and that had meant few wished to sail with him. It had taken him months of small raids and setting supply ships afire to restore his name to a modicum of its former glory. He would not recover from another disappointment.

Perhaps that was why he could not let go of the idea of Maxon's treasure. In his rare moments of peace, he often wondered whether it had ever existed at all. Or whether Von Horn had been just as taken in as he had. The American had certainly seemed surprised by the books that filled the heavy chest they'd shed so much blood to acquire.

The thought drew his eye to the low shelf near the bed. More books. He pulled a few from the shelf in order to search behind them for a hidden cache or safe. But there was nothing. Not that he had expected it. Virginia Maxon did not strike him as a woman who valued such things. And Bulan—well. Who knew what such a man cared for?

Saffir flipped through the books disinterestedly. Though literate, he had little love of the written word. His parents had intended for him to be a clerk for the British or the Dutch; a good servant to men not worthy to lick his boots. Saffir had quickly had his fill of being ordered about by foreigners. A life of piracy seemed infinitely preferable to the doldrums of civil service. Though he was beginning to wonder if he'd made the right choice.

He sighed and turned, scanning the remainder of the cabin. It was clear that two people were sharing it. Bulan and Virginia Maxon. The thought of the woman inflamed him and he tweaked his moustaches in frustration. Where was she? Somewhere on the island, obviously. Looking for her father's treasure, no doubt. The compound? Possibly. No—almost certainly.

He'd visited the old compound only once, since his encounter with Maxon and Bulan. He'd gone alone, just to see. The place had struck him as . . . evil. Ordinarily, he was not a superstitious man, but something about that place had set hooks of ice into his soul. If the treasure was there, he felt it better someone else acquire it for him.

Not the Dayaks, obviously; they feared the compound even more than he did. They thought it a haunt of ghosts and demons and refused to consider even approaching it. Else he would have led them to take Virginia Maxon and the others prisoner already.

But was the treasure still there? Or had the British taken it? That was a thought he tried not to dwell on. If the British had it, there would be no getting it back; not without some stroke of good fortune. And, of course, why else would they have come to this place, if not to acquire Maxon's treasure? The British were as rapacious as the Dutch.

"It must be here," he murmured. "It must."

"Rajah?"

Saffir looked up to see Riwut entering the cabin. He looked unhappy. "What is it?" Saffir asked. "Has something happened?"

"Tawi wishes to speak with you," Riwut said, in a tone of warning. Saffir sighed and pushed himself to his feet.

"Which one is he again?"

"One of old Baru's lieutenants," Riwut said. Saffir grunted and tugged on his beard. Baru was one of the most troublesome of the Dayak chieftains he dealt with. The old man was of the opinion that he deserved more of a share of Saffir's spoils than he was receiving. He had seconded Tawi and several others to Saffir as watchdogs, to keep an eye on Saffir in his dealings. It wasn't the first time it had occurred, nor would it be the last.

Occasionally, however, one of the watchdogs tried its teeth.

There was only one thing for it when that happened. Saffir loosened his niabor in its sheath. "Very well. Let us get this done. I have more important matters to see to."

Tawi was waiting on deck, the head of the Lascar dangling from his fist. He'd been the first aboard, and had killed the guard with a single sweep of his blade. He threw the head at Muda Saffir's feet. "Well, Malay? Where is the treasure you promised us?"

"Not here, obviously," Saffir said, bluntly. The other Dayaks were assembled on the deck, watching closely. Challenges among pirates were not unknown. Piracy was an uncertain profession, with none of the ingrained social conventions of a tribe. Hierarchy was, at best, a suggestion. In the past, Saffir had used that to his advantage. Apparently Tawi wished to do the same.

"Then why did we come here?" Tawi demanded. Blood dripped from his blade to pool on the deck. "To steal an empty vessel?"

Saffir glanced around, gauging the mood of his followers. "Hardly empty. There is much of value aboard. Why, the furnishings alone would fetch a good amount in Singapore."

"Hardly a treasure though, is it?" Tawi said, with a mirthless smile. "Maybe there is no treasure, eh? Maybe it is all a lie, and the great Muda Saffir was taken in by a foreigner. Maybe he thinks to fool us all, if only to save his pride, eh?"

Saffir scratched his chin, and studied the moon. "My pride is worth a good deal, I admit. But I have never lied to you, my friends. The treasure—Maxon's treasure—is real, and I will have it. You will see. But if you do not believe me . . . well. I shall not force you to stay where you do not wish to be." He gestured to the water. "Swim home, by all means. I will keep your share for myself."

An approving murmur ran through the Dayaks at this. They valued bravado in a captain, especially one who was not a Dayak himself. But they also wanted plunder—and skulls for their longhouses. Saffir had promised them both, but provided little in the way of either recently. They needed a show of good faith. He'd hoped taking the yacht would quell their murmurings, at least until he could capture Maxon and the others, and force them to reveal the location of the treasure.

Unfortunately, Tawi wasn't the sort to be bought off with promises. "You talk and talk but say nothing, Malay. We will sail home, and I will offer up your head as a token of apology to my people."

Saffir drew his blade. "Then come, boy. Come and sing me a song of steel."

Tawi needed no further invitation. He charged forward with a wild yell, and Saffir met him, blade to blade. Tawi was a skilled warrior, but Saffir had been killing men for longer than the younger man had been alive. That said, youth had its share of advantages. The longer the fight went on, the more his age crept up on him, gnawing at his strength.

Saffir fought like a miser, letting Tawi tire himself out. He watched the Dayak's feet, his eyes, everything but the blade. The blade was nothing. A sword was only as good as the man who wielded it. Tawi was all rage and fire, a true Dayak.

And like all true Dayaks, he fought like a hero, without hesitation or consideration. When the moment came, Saffir almost laughed. Tawi overextended himself: a wild sweep, meant to remove Saffir's head in a single blow. He twisted away and slammed his own blade into his opponent's midsection, chopping through meat and muscle—pausing only at the bone. Tawi stopped short, his eyes wide in disbelief. Saffir met his bewildered gaze and smiled. "A good song, Tawi . . . but I have heard it sung better."

Saffir ripped his sword free and Tawi fell to his knees. Saffir circled the dying man, looking at the others as he did so. "I am Muda Saffir. I am a rajah, and have in me the blood of rajahs. I am a king and I have promised you blood and treasure. I will provide both, but you must be patient, my friends. Without patience, we are nothing." He paused as he met

Riwut's disapproving gaze. The Dayak did not care for such theatrics, though he understood the need for them. Saffir spun about and severed Tawi's head from his neck.

The Dayaks fell silent as the head bounced once—twice. Saffir shook the blood from his blade and smiled. He had them tamed—at least for another few hours.

"Now," he said, "Who will volunteer to lead a search for the Americans?"

20

INTERROGATION

WELL," VIRGINIA SAID. "Now what?" She sat on the rail of the porch that encircled her father's old laboratory. Bulan, Sing, and Kazin stood nearby, discussing what to do with the prisoner in low voices, as if to keep from disturbing her. It would have been amusing, had it not been so irritating.

At her words, all three men turned to her. Bulan and Sing looked somewhat guilty. Kazin simply looked thoughtful. "We have him," she continued. "What are we going to do with him? Any ideas?"

"I thought we intended to question him," Bulan said. She met his dark gaze.

"If so, I suggest we do so now, before his compatriots come knocking."

Bulan glanced at Sing. Sing sighed. "We should leave him. Leave this place. Let the British have it. They will be here before the night is out."

"And what of Otto?" Virginia asked. After their narrow escape from the British, she and the others had made it back to the old compound without incident. Otto had vanished as soon as they'd cleared the palisade, disappearing into the forest as quickly as he'd appeared. Virginia had filled the others in on what she'd learned from the creature on the way back. Moreover, she'd had a think on it herself.

It was clear to her now that Otto was a victim—her father's last victim. But also, in a strange way, his ultimate triumph.

He was everything her father had imagined his creations could be, and perhaps more. She was still trying to reconcile that in her head.

"A question for later," Bulan said, as he entered the laboratory. Virginia and the others followed. The soldier was sitting in the center of the room, far from anything that might help him free himself. Virginia studied their prisoner. Sing and Kazin had tied him to a chair and left him under guard. The Lascars had ignored the man's demands by the simple expedient of pretending not to speak English.

He looked up as they entered. "Who are you people, and what are you doing here?" It was the same question he'd been asking since they'd taken him prisoner. He was nothing if not single-minded.

"You seem to be confused," Sing said, in an amiable tone. "You are the one tied up. Not us. That means we are the ones who will be asking the questions."

The soldier glared at him. "I'm not saying a bleeding thing and I damn well won't—"

"You will not speak that way in front of a lady," Sing barked.

The soldier hesitated. Finally, he said, "I am Sergeant Henry R. Higgs, in service to His Majesty King George the Fifth of the British Empire, and I'll speak however I want . . . especially to a bloody Chinese." Higgs smiled as he said the last bit. Virginia wondered if the invective was calculated. Was he trying to make Sing mad?

Sing smiled coldly. "I see. We chased out all the cobras when we came in here. They do not like the light. But maybe we will blow out the lantern and leave. See what happens to Sergeant Henry R. Higgs then, eh?"

Bulan interposed himself between them. "Listen, Sergeant, I know being tied up is uncomfortable, but we should be able to talk this out in a civilized manner." He sounded apologetic, but Virginia could read the anger in his eyes.

So could Higgs. "Civilized men know enough to show proper respect for British soldiers," he said, carefully. But not hesitantly. He wasn't afraid. Was it simply ego? Bravado—or something else?

"Right, but as I tried to tell your superior, Arkwright—"

Higgs' eyes narrowed. "You've met the lieutenant, then?"

Bulan glanced at Virginia. "Yeah. We had an . . . unproductive conversation." He paused and then crouched before the bound man. "Look, we're here by chance. We didn't mean to intrude on any official operation of the British Empire. But now that we've been attacked by you and your fellow soldiers, well—we're not going to take that lying down."

Higgs snorted. "Bit of a mistake, innit? If I were you, I'd cut me loose and apologize. The lieutenant might see his way clear to going easy on you."

"We'll see," Bulan said. "Your actions escalated this, so now curiosity is getting the best of me. What are you boys doing here? What's the big secret?"

Higgs chuckled. "Got me, mate. I'm just sergeant, aren't I? I don't need to know, and they don't tell me. We have orders to guard the place, so we do. And we don't ask questions."

Bulan pushed himself to his feet and went to the window. "That's about what I expected. It doesn't matter. We're planning to leave. Our ship is anchored just offshore. But I'm reluctant to go until I get some answers." He turned. "Have you ever seen anything . . . strange on this island?"

Higgs sat as far forward as his bonds would allow. "It's the tropics, mate. Strange goes with the territory." His gaze slid to Virginia and she saw the hint of a smile on his face. "Only I think you're talking about something in particular, innit?"

Bulan started to reply, but Virginia spoke up first. "I don't think you know anything, do you, Sergeant?" She looked down at the man. "Or maybe you just don't want to."

Higgs licked his lips. "Maybe you should enlighten me, then."

"Scientific experiments." Virginia gestured about them. "Conducted with equipment taken from this lab. My father's lab. Arthur Maxon. Does that name mean anything to you?"

Higg's eyes widened, but only for an instant. His expression became masklike. "What are you trying to say, miss?"

"Did they tell you what was born here, Sergeant? Did Arkwright tell you what my father birthed in those metal vats you plundered?" Virginia crouched before him. "Monsters, Sergeant. My father made monsters. Soulless things, brewed up from chemicals. One of them attacked your compound earlier tonight."

Higgs cursed under his breath. "What happened?" he demanded.

Virginia ignored him. "I think your Lieutenant Arkwright is attempting to recreate my father's experiments. I think that's why you came here. Not just because it's secluded but because you needed my father's equipment. Because Arkwright is looking to brew up his own batch of soulless horrors. And you're complicit."

Higgs was silent for a moment. Then, he laughed. "Rubbish," he said. "Absolute rubbish!" He shook his head. "You almost had me, love, I admit."

Virginia stood. She didn't know what she'd been expecting. Maybe nothing. "Fine. You don't believe me?" She looked at Bulan. "I say let him go. Let him make his way back—alone—in the dark. If he survives, maybe he'll see we were telling the truth."

Bulan hesitated, and then nodded. "You're right. This isn't getting us anywhere." He looked at Sing. "Escort Sergeant Higgs to the gate and see him off. My apologies, Sergeant. You'll never see us again."

Higgs said nothing. Virginia left the other to deal with it as she went back outside. A few minutes later, she watched as Higgs was escorted to the gates by Sing and Kazin. There was something about the way he moved that set her hackles to stiffening. Not quite like a soldier, and definitely not like a man afraid for his life. The way his gaze roamed about, taking in his surroundings as if memorizing them.

He reminded her, in a way, of the men who came to visit

her father at the institution. Men from the government all had the same body language. Alert, but casual. Observant, but trying to appear anything but. They couldn't help it. She wondered whether Higgs was just what he claimed to be, or whether there were layers to this situation that she and the others weren't privy to. Maybe it didn't matter.

Bulan joined her. "That's it, then. He's off and running. Are you all right?" he asked. "You look a million miles away."

Virginia nodded absently. "We're doing the right thing, aren't we?"

"Letting him go? I hope so."

"No, I mean leaving." She turned away from him, rubbing her arms. "Otto is out there somewhere. I called him a monster in order to scare Higgs. I feel so—so ashamed. I should never have said that."

"You were saying what we had to say," Bulan began.

She shook her head. "No. He's not a monster. He's not some soulless thing."

"I know," he said, pulling her close. He sighed. "I wish we had more time. After what happened, we need to get off this island as soon as possible. I have a feeling Arkwright isn't the sort to let bygones be bygones."

"And what about Otto?" she asked.

"I don't know. If we run into him on our way to the yacht, maybe we could persuade him to go with us. But somehow, I doubt it. Other than with you, he doesn't appear to be the trusting sort, and I don't blame him."

Virginia was about to reply when she noticed Kazin climbing the steps to join them. Bulan looked at the Lascar. "Well?"

Kazin nodded. "He is gone. I sent Esmail and Habiboola to see him off safely. Make sure no monsters ate him too close to the compound, eh?" He pulled a pack of cheroots from his tunic and selected one. "Amer is fit to travel. You should collect your things. If we are leaving, we need to do so now."

Bulan nodded. He gave Virginia one last squeeze. "I'll see to our gear. You take your time." He was gone a moment later.

Virginia leaned her elbows on the rail and turned her attention to the forest. After a moment, she realized that Kazin had joined her.

Kazin offered her a cheroot but she waved it aside. He grunted and went back to looking out at the forest. After a moment, he said, "You think too much about souls."

Virginia looked at him. "Oh?"

Kazin nodded. "Sing does as well. A philosopher, that one. Thinks only the soul, or its lack, matters in the end."

"And what do you think?" Virginia asked, curious.

Kazin shrugged. "I think it does no good to worry about such things. This monster—"

"Otto."

Another shrug. "This monster has killed two of my men. It killed a soldier, and has probably killed others. It is a tiger, with a taste for human meat. You do not ask why the tiger eats men, you simply kill it before it can eat more of them."

"Is it so simple for you, then? I expect you've killed your share of men." She didn't mean the words to come out as harshly as they did, but Kazin didn't seem to mind. He nodded and puffed on his cheroot.

"More than most, less than some."

"And do you regret it?"

"Not a one."

"That is a lie and you know it," Sing said, as he stepped onto the porch. Kazin snorted and made to throw his cheroot away. Sing snatched it from his hand and took a puff. "Do not be so wasteful. This may be your last." He looked at Virginia. "You should not ask his opinion, Miss Ginny. He is an old reprobate."

"I have a feeling it takes one to know one," Virginia said, smiling slightly. Kazin laughed and took his cheroot back from Sing.

"She knows who she is talking to, eh?" he said.

"I am just a cook," Sing protested.

Virginia laughed softly. Watching the two old friends bicker was never anything less than entertaining. She'd had some doubts about Kazin, at first. But they were gone now. His manner was almost as reassuring as Sing's, though in a more stolid sort of way. The Lascar left them to their thoughts, heading back down to rejoin his remaining men.

Sing was silent for a time. Then, "I heard what you said to Bulan. I was not eavesdropping, but . . ." He trailed off. Virginia put her hand over his.

"You were eavesdropping," she said.

Sing looked away. "Have you thought that maybe what is best for Number Thirteen—for Otto—is a merciful death?" he asked, softly. "You know that there is no place for him in this world, Miss Ginny . . . and it is cruel to expect him to be what he is not."

Virginia released his hand. "You think we mean to make a house cat of a tiger. Is that what you're saying?"

Sing sighed. "I think you mean to try. I think you will be disappointed and maybe even hurt. He is not a man, or a child, or even an animal. He is something that does not belong in this world, Miss Ginny." He started for the stairs.

"And the sooner you realize that, the better off we will all be."

21

CREATION EIGHT

REATION EIGHT CROUCHED amid the vibrant greenery of the forest and waited. He inhaled the strange damp odors and observed the vibrant colors. The world was so much larger than he had imagined in his confinement. The sheer immensity of it had almost caused him to collapse at first, overcome by all of the new sensations now available to him. The feel of rain on his sore flesh; the crunch of loose soil underfoot; and the taste of fresh meat.

He did not know the name of the animal that he and the others had caught and killed. It had squealed and fought and that had made its meat all the sweeter. The others were still eating; gnawing the bones and supping the marrow. But he knew better than to gorge in such a fashion. Arkwright had taught them better. The others might be eager to forget those lessons, but Creation Eight held fast to the words of their creator. Moreover, he took comfort in them. Especially as confused as he was now.

He still did not understand why they had been freed. He wondered if Arkwright was testing their faith in him. If so, Eight would not be found wanting. He could not say the same for the others. He turned slightly, rocking back on his haunches, and peered at them.

They crouched in a tight huddle about the body of their prey, tearing at the pitiful remnants as if determined to inhale it, bones and all. The sounds of cracking and slurping rose like music, and he was tempted to join them.

Instead, he turned back to the forest. It was full of noises, big and small. Scents as well. The rush of information was confusing, and he was still getting used to it. He closed his eyes, listening to the hum of insects and the patter of raindrops falling from the canopy above. Then—something new.

Voices.

Eight's eyes popped open and he whirled to face the others. "Quiet," he snarled. The others fell silent at once. Eight turned back, senses straining. Soon, the voices grew louder and more distinct. Someone was coming along the forest trail.

Soldiers appeared. First one, then two—three. Finally, a strung-out column of five, moving warily through the growth. Had Arkwright sent them after Eight and the others? "I haven't been to the old compound yet," one asked, looking back at his fellows. "How much farther?"

One of the others answered him. "Just under a mile, but as slow going as it is through this muck it feels like a long haul, sir."

"Longer, if we get lost," another chimed in. "Which is a distinct possibility."

A fourth laughed sourly. "What are you worried about, Rogers—the bogeyman?"

The third man spoke up. "You didn't see that thing, Benchley. It was big and fast and it threw old Ju-Long around like he didn't weigh nothing at all."

"Tore apart the bloody watchtower like it was kindling," the fifth man added.

Eight bit back a snarl. They were talking about the Other. The one that dared defy Arkwright's law. He had now apparently compounded his blasphemy by attacking Arkwright. Was there no end to his wickedness?

"Stow it," the first man barked. He was in charge, Eight thought. A servant of Arkwright? The soldier paused and turned to face the others. "We're not after that thing, whatever it was. We're after Higgs and Fraser. We find them, we get back to the compound as soon as possible, right?"

"And what about the Americans, then, sir?" the fourth—Benchley—asked. "Are we just going to say bygones and wave ta-ta?"

"Chances are, the Americans have already made their departure, Benchley. If I were them, I'd have already scarpered. If not, we'll do what needs doing . . . and no more than that, are we clear, lads?" His tone implied he would brook no disagreement.

The one called Jones spoke up, after a moment. "And what about the lieutenant, then, Second Lieutenant Welles, sir? Only he told us not to leave, didn't he? I can't imagine he's going to be happy about our little expedition."

Eight's eyes narrowed. They had defied Arkwright? Why would they do such a thing?

"Arkwright can go hang for all I care," Welles snapped. Then, as if realizing what he'd said, he added, "He might not care about Higgs or Fraser, but I do. If they're alive, they might need our help. And if not . . . we'll avenge them." He sighed. "If you want to go back, I won't stop you."

Benchley and the others looked at one another. Then Benchley said, "Forget I said anything, sir. Let's press on, shall we?" The soldiers started moving a moment later, continuing on. Eight watched them go, curious as to where they were going. It seemed there was another compound. Was that where the Other had come from?

Eight flicked the thought aside and turned back to the others. It was clear to him now that the soldiers were fair game, though they too served Arkwright. If they had defied him, they had forfeited his protection. That meant they could be slain—eaten—without risking Arkwright's wrath. "Soldiers," he said. "We will follow them."

"Why?" Creation Seven asked, in his dull, gulping voice. "They might hurt us."

"They will not." Eight made a fist. "We are stronger than they are. Faster."

"And why should we hurt them?" Seven pressed.

Eight paused. He had said nothing about harming the soldiers. Seven and the others were watching him carefully. He'd had to remind them of his authority as Arkwright's favorite several times since they'd emerged from the hole in the forest floor. They'd wanted to scatter, to experience the world for themselves. He'd had to force them to stay together, until he understood why they'd been freed.

But now, he was starting to see it. Now, he understood. This was indeed a test—of loyalty, and love. Of their faith in the law of Arkwright. Arkwright had foreseen Vogel's treachery; it was the only explanation that made sense. He had allowed the old man to free them, even as he had allowed Ju-Long to torment them. All to test them.

"They are . . . meat. A gift from Arkwright. They defy him and we will punish them . . . for him," Eight said, carefully. The thought turned in his brain, and he began to wonder how one could defy Arkwright? It did not seem possible. And yet, it had occurred. Was Arkwright then not all powerful?

No. It was a test. Just a test.

"We will punish them," he repeated. "Eat them. As Arkwright wishes." He looked at his hands—all three of them. Good hands. Strong hands, meant for tearing flesh and breaking bones. He imagined doing that to the ones called Welles, who had blasphemed.

The thought of digging his claws into the red meat of Welles' heart sent a shiver of pleasure through him. Maybe, if they pleased Arkwright enough, he would allow them to do the same to Ju-Long. Would he squeal and fight the way the animal had?

"What of the Other?" Three asked, in his strange, shrill voice, interrupting Eight's reverie. Eight hated Three; not just because of his voice, but that was a large part of it. "The one Vogel protected?"

"What of him?" Eight said, as he rose to his feet. He sniffed the air. The soldiers were moving away, but there were other scents abroad in the forest now, carried on the evening breeze.

Unfamiliar ones. And blood as well. A sweet scent, tantalizing and wonderful. He wished to follow it, almost as much as he wished to kill the soldiers.

"What if we should come across him?" Three plucked an insect from a nearby branch and swiftly devoured it. Then, almost as an afterthought, "He fed us."

Eight spun and drove his two right fists across Three's jaw, knocking the other creature flat. The rest of them drew back, startled by the sudden violence. "He is not one of us," he snarled. He turned his glare on the others. "He does not know the law of Arkwright. He cannot be trusted."

"He is like us," Three said, almost apologetically. He crawled backward, out of reach. "He was kind. Like Vogel."

Eight grunted. "Vogel is not kind. Vogel lies." He looked at the others. "Vogel lies," he said again. "He tells us that Arkwright does not love us, but Arkwright does. Why else would he send those ones into the forest for us?" He gestured in the direction the soldiers had gone. "See? He gives us a gift of meat."

"No," Three said. Still arguing. Three liked to argue. Three thought that he should be in charge; a ridiculous notion that Eight had been unable to beat out of him, thus far. So did Seven, but he was quieter about it. "Arkwright feeds us. We do not take food ourselves."

The others nodded at this. Eight did not blame them. Three was correct, if in his own limited fashion. Arkwright was the provider—and the soldiers were what he had provided. It seemed obvious to Eight. He forced himself to remain calm. To tamp down the rage that filled him, to wrestle back the hunger that gripped him—to fight the urge to kill Three, and to eat of his flesh. If he gave in to it he would be no better than One or Two: a mindless eating machine with barely enough sense to follow its fellows.

"We will hunt them, as Arkwright wishes. We will kill and eat and show him what we have learned. When he sees what we have done, he will be pleased. He will show us love."

Eight looked at them, letting his gaze rest on each of his fellows in turn. One by one, they touched their scars and murmured Arkwright's name. Even Three, though he hesitated.

"There are others," Five murmured, in a hoarse voice. "I smell them. Not just soldiers. Can we eat them as well?"

"Yes," Four hissed. "We eat them too." She glanced at Eight for confirmation and he stroked her head. He nodded.

"Yes. We eat them too." He raised his hands. "Go. Scatter. Hunt. Kill all who cross your path, and feast well on their flesh. In eating his foes, we show our devotion. Only when all are dead will we return to him and accept his blessings."

They went. In ones and twos, until only Three and Six remained by his side. "We hunt with you," Six mumbled, through the shapeless hole he called a mouth. Three nodded, black eyes shining wetly in the gloom. His expression was unreadable.

"We hunt," he squealed.

Eight nodded, pleased. He clasped his hands before him and bowed his head. "In Arkwright's name, amen."

22

ARKWRIGHT

L IEUTENANT THOMAS ARKWRIGHT sat in his office and stared at the papers on his desk without really seeing them. Most of them were the daily reports by his subordinates, Welles, and Higgs. Others were letters from home—though not from family.

From a young age, Arkwright had been told he was meant for great things. He'd had the best education available to a young man of his social standing, and his advancement through the ranks had been nothing short of rapid. He'd been selected by men of influence to carry out their will in a variety of matters—including this one.

For a time, that had been enough. But as he'd come to learn more about his patrons and the world they inhabited, his ambitions had grown. It was as if there were another world, just out of the corner of his eye and just out of reach. Like Alexander, he yearned to conquer the unknown. To make his mark. This posting was to have been his first step on that path.

But now—well.

He rifled through the correspondence listlessly and looked at his guest. "You have been in these islands longer than I have, Ju-Long. I assume you know a bit about the local legends." He paused. "Tell me again of this . . . Bulan."

Ju-Long grunted. The big man looked the worse for wear, but looks could be deceiving. Arkwright knew that better than most. What was he, after all, but a mask? "Before your arrival, I heard stories of a white man the Dayaks called Bulan,"

141

Ju-Long said. "A huge, powerful warrior . . . a ferocious fighter." He flexed his fists as he spoke, and Arkwright knew he was replaying his brawl with the American in his mind.

"And what became of him?"

"I think we know," Ju-Long said, rubbing his knuckles. "He is not a legend. He is real and he is here. He is the one I fought."

"That woman called him Bulan, so I tend to agree. Why was he here, do you think?"

Ju-Long shrugged. "Who can say?"

Arkwright clucked his tongue chidingly. "Come now, you are smarter than that. You're no fool, Ju-Long. This Bulan was in Maxon's employ, wasn't he?"

Ju-Long frowned. "It is possible."

"I think it's more than that. I think it is damn likely. But why is he here? Maxon is confined to an institution in the States, last I checked." Arkwright sat back, turning the thought over in his mind. "Perhaps he has not completely abandoned his claim to this island—or its secrets." It was a disturbing idea. He'd been assured that Maxon was out of the game by his patrons. It just went to show that no plan survived contact with the enemy. "Perhaps his presence has something to do with our commandeering of Maxon's old equipment."

Ju-Long looked doubtful. "If so, why did he not try and stop us?"

Arkwright shrugged. "It could be he did not know until it was too late. However, he doesn't concern me as much as the other one . . . the blue-skinned monster . . ." He could not help but feel a faint whisper of anger as he considered the creature. "You told me that Maxon's creations were all dead."

"That is what I was told. I have heard nothing of the creature, save the usual Dayak nonsense about ghosts and devils. I put it all down to their encounters with Maxon's creations." Ju-Long hesitated. "I do know one thing—it is clearly allied with the Americans."

Arkwright was silent for a moment. He looked at the man

before him, weighing his words. Ju-Long was, in many ways, a gift. Mercenaries were untrustworthy, but only when money was an issue. When it was in ready supply, they were utterly loyal to the one holding the purse strings. Ju-Long could be counted on in ways that men like Welles couldn't. His subordinate was a patriot—a weakness, in Arkwright's way of thinking. Patriots were loyal to an ideal, rather than something tangible. It made them hard to control.

If there was one thing Arkwright believed in, it was control. But the current situation was becoming rapidly untenable. The monsters had escaped, the compound was damaged—and their presence had been revealed. Or would be, if the Americans made it back to Singapore. And what would happen then, eh? Nothing good. Once word reached his patrons, they would undoubtedly cut him off. He would be left to fend for himself, with neither the influence nor resources he needed.

"Indeed," he said. "It requires no great stretch of imagination to conclude that our blue-tinted friend is one of Maxon's creations. Left here as a watchdog, perhaps. Still, I have often wondered why Maxon left his equipment here. Did he intend to return?" The question bothered him, but it wasn't his main worry at the moment.

Ju-Long seemed to agree. "I do not know. I will ask this Bulan after I drag him back here." He thumped a fist into his palm. "If I don't kill him first. I will take some men and—"

Arkwright gestured sharply. "No. You'll be staying here with me. Your skills and knowledge are too valuable to be wasted hunting Americans—especially given the recent escape." He glanced at the steel door that marked the descent to the cells below. "I suspect that anyone out there now has a very slim chance of survival. That's why I ordered everyone to—what?" he demanded, as he saw the look on Ju-Long's face.

"Welles," Ju-Long said, simply.

Arkwright sat back. "Damn that fool. Let me guess, he went after Higgs."

Ju-Long nodded. "He took Jones and three others with him."

Arkwright closed his eyes and sighed. Welles was proving to be more of an annoyance than he'd anticipated. He'd wanted to give the creatures time to burn off any excess excitement before he made the attempt to liquidate them. Let them gorge on wild pigs and Dayaks, and then they would be easy prey. "Wonderful. I ask you, can this day get any better?" He leaned back and interlaced his fingers behind his head. "When did they leave?"

"Not long after the attack."

Arkwright grunted. "Fine. This might be a blessing in disguise. Welles was becoming troublesome. Frankly, I believe he was seconded to me to do just that."

"Sir?"

Arkwright cracked an eyelid. "Does it surprise you to learn that I have enemies, Ju-Long? I do. Both in the military and out. There are many who would like to see me fail. That is why they assigned me shirkers and malcontents—and Welles. Oh, and Higgs, of course."

"Higgs?" Ju-Long asked.

"He's a spy, you know," Arkwright said, absently.

"What?"

"He's not an enlisted man, though he does a very good impression. I sussed him out in Singapore. Military intelligence, I think. No doubt a watchdog assigned by Whitehall to keep an eye on me, even as Welles was, albeit on behalf of our superiors in the military. Posing as a sergeant was a masterstroke. High enough rank not to be out of the loop, low enough not to attract attention. My enemies are clever men, Ju-Long."

"But you are cleverer," Ju-Long said.

Arkwright gave him a thin smile. "I like to think so, yes. But I fear our time grows short nonetheless. That is why it is imperative that we successfully conclude operations here and erase any evidence of our presence."

"The monsters," Ju-Long said. Arkwright nodded.

"Yes, you get your wish after all, Ju-Long. They'll need to be destroyed. But first we must disassemble the equipment we took from the other compound and make ready to ship it to another location. This island is no longer suitable. We'll try elsewhere—perhaps in the Channel. Remote, but close enough that regular supplies aren't a problem." He looked at the bare walls of the office. "We must be ready when the supply ship arrives. If the Americans have already fled the island, as I suspect, then we don't have much time before someone starts asking questions we would rather not be answered."

Arkwright's patrons were secretive sorts; they might very well decide that the only way to maintain their privacy was not to cut him off, but to eliminate him entirely. They would kill Ju-Long as well, and Vogel. Anyone who might know anything about their reasons for being here would be a target.

But, if he could oversee the quick transportation of the necessary facilities to a safe location, and the disposal of the monsters—as well as problematic elements such as Higgs— then he might well stand a chance of emerging from this with his scalp intact.

He only needed a bit more time. He'd been observing Vogel long enough to have gotten a grasp on the fundamentals of Maxon's process. A few more months, another batch of creatures, and he might not need the old man at all. Then Vogel could join his precious monsters in oblivion.

"How did they escape?" Ju-Long asked.

"You saw the hole," Arkwright said. Ju-Long nodded.

"I did. It was dug from outside. Nor was there any damage to the locks or the cages. Someone opened them using the keys." He indicated the key-ring on the desk. "Though how he avoided being torn apart by the beasts, I cannot say."

Arkwright paused. He hadn't noticed anything untoward about the cages. Then, such things had never been his forte. But it did put rather a new and disturbing spin on things. "Vogel was lying," he said. Ju-Long nodded.

"He is too soft-hearted. He would rather see them loose than destroyed."

Arkwright sighed and pinched the bridge of his nose. Of course. He'd been so distracted by the appearance of the other monster he hadn't paid enough attention to what should have been obvious. Then, maybe he'd just assumed Vogel wouldn't have the courage to do something so rash. He shook his head. "What do you know about the man? You're the one who introduced us, after all."

Ju-Long frowned. "As I told you at the time, I know little. He claims to have been a correspondent of Maxon's, and he wished to buy Maxon's notes from Von Horn."

"A deal you brokered," Arkwright said, careful to keep any hint of accusation out of his voice. Ju-Long was an asset that needed to be managed carefully.

Ju-Long nodded. "But Von Horn betrayed me."

"And then you introduced him to me." Arkwright was silent for a moment, pondering the matter. It had all seemed like fate at the time. He'd been in need of someone with Vogel's background and the German had been more than willing to help. Perhaps he should have looked that particular gift horse in the mouth. But he'd let his ambitions blind him, certain that he could do away with the old man at his convenience. He tapped on his desk for a moment, considering his options.

If Vogel had released the monsters, he'd revealed himself as a definite liability. And this operation could afford no liabilities. And there was the matter of the other monster; could it have been the one to burrow into the cellblock? He could think of nothing else that might explain it. "I think perhaps I should have another talk with the professor, don't you?" He pushed himself to his feet. Vogel's quarters were just down the hall from his office. Ju-Long nodded and followed him out into the corridor.

Arkwright paused at Vogel's door. There was no music playing—an oddity. He waved Ju-Long back and knocked.

"It's Lieutenant Arkwright, Professor Vogel. I'd like to have a word with you, please."

No answer.

Arkwright tried the door. It was unlocked. "Vogel?" The door swung open. The room was empty. At this time of night, the man should have been there. There was nowhere else he was allowed to be. "Damn it all." He turned back to Ju-Long. "It seems your suspicions were correct." He strode toward the other man, fists clenched. Anger thrummed through him. How dare Vogel do this; did the fool not understand what was at stake?

Ju-Long grunted. "I think he plans to join the Americans. If they are involved with Maxon . . ." He trailed off, but he'd made his point. Arkwright paused.

"He freed the creatures to cause a distraction. Of course. Clever old man." He looked at Ju-Long. "Betrayals of this sort are usually motivated by one factor: profit. Find him, Ju-Long. If he is with the Americans . . . try and take them alive. I want answers, and I think they might be best placed to deliver them."

"And if I cannot?"

Arkwright retrieved his cigarettes from his pocket and lit one. "Then kill them all. Including Vogel. And burn the old compound to the ground while you're at it."

Ju-Long nodded and made to go, but paused. "What of the other monster? Should I attempt to capture it . . . for study?"

"No. Kill it as well." Arkwright turned away. "It can be examined well enough on a slab. Whatever secrets it holds, well . . . I'll tear them from its flesh myself."

23
MOONLIGHT

OTTO MOVED THROUGH THE FOREST like a ghost, slipping from shadow to shadow. After all these months, he knew every inch of the island by scent and feel. He could tell when something had changed. There was blood on the air—human. The Dayaks were on the move, prowling inland. And there were British patrols wandering the forest. It worried him. If any of them were to stumble over Virginia and the others, she might be hurt.

He did not wish that. That was why, when he had stirred himself from the soldier's blow, he had followed her scent to the British compound and rescued her from Arkwright. The Kind One would not be pleased that he had revealed himself to Arkwright. Now that the latter knew he existed, he would stop at nothing to capture Otto.

He leaped onto the trunk of a tree and scrambled up into the branches, his clawed fingers and toes digging into the bark like pitons. He paused there, and sniffed the air. The night gripped the island fully, and everything stank of rain. The tang of blood drifted from the direction of the sea. That was the direction the Dayaks had come from. He'd seen them earlier, passing beneath the branches as he leaped from tree to tree. They had not seen him; otherwise he would have killed them.

He still might, if only to keep Virginia safe. As his thoughts turned toward her, he retrieved the old photograph from the pocket of his tattered trousers. It was a picture of Virginia—

younger, happy. He traced her laughing features with the tip of a claw, wondering as always at the symmetry of that face. Not like his at all.

He had never really thought of himself in comparison to others. His face was simply . . . his face. His teeth were his teeth, his eyes were his eyes. That they did not resemble those of other people had not unduly concerned him. Until her.

Until the Other. Until the one called Bulan.

And now he knew. He hung his head and crumpled the photo in his fist. Then, realizing what he'd done, he carefully straightened it out against the bark of the tree before neatly folding it and sliding it back into his pocket. The photo was covered in a map of white bends and wrinkles. How many times had he crushed it or dropped it? Sometimes, he knew, he was careless with fragile things. His hands had not been fashioned for delicacy. No—they were the hands of a killer.

He studied them; the placement of the fingers, the talons, the odd network of fibrous veins that carried bile-black blood through his body. He could hear his own pulse, not rhythmic like that of Virginia or Bulan, but . . . arrhythmic and thunderous. Like a machine in the midst of malfunction. He had heard similar sounds while watching the Kind One—Vogel—create the others. The machines that had created him.

He remembered the machines—the humming and bubbling. The heat and the sudden chill as he was wrenched from his iron womb and cast into the forest. Awareness had come swiftly; too swiftly, he now thought. He had been left in the dirt, for the animals to eat. But he had quickly become the one to do the eating. That was the lesson the forest had taught him: Eat, or be eaten. Kill or be killed.

He had throttled his first Dayak a mere seven days after his awakening. He had killed a dozen others since then, and relished each. He had almost devoured the Kind One in the same way, the night he'd come to the compound. But something about the old man had made him pause. Perhaps it was the way Vogel had spoken to him. The Dayaks had never spoken to him. They had screamed and cursed, but never spoken.

Otto hunched forward on the branch, instinctively maintaining his balance even as he continued to study his hands. Why had Maxon made him this way? Why had the Kind One made Creation Eight and the others the way they were? Perhaps they lacked the ability to make men like themselves. Perhaps something had prevented them. A flaw in them, or in the machine. Otto banished such thoughts to the back of his mind.

None of it mattered. He was as he was, and there was no changing it.

Otto snapped his teeth together in sudden irritation. He was confused; angry. But he did not understand why. He wanted to see Virginia—to talk to her. She would understand, he was certain of it. Maybe she could explain why he was the way he was.

Maybe—

A snap of a branch pulled his attention below. Someone was coming from the direction of the Maxon compound. He crouched low on the branch so that he would not be easily visible if they passed directly beneath him.

It was a soldier. "Where's the bloody stream?" he panted. "I find the stream, I find the compound. Buggers could have at least given me my rifle back, but no." Suddenly, the man tripped, releasing a flurry of invective. Otto leaped noiselessly to another tree, closer to the soldier. The man was unarmed; tired.

Easy prey.

He was about to drop down onto the soldier when the wind shifted, and he caught a familiar scent. A chemical stink, mixed with old blood. He froze and watched as something pale and gray slid into the moonlight. The soldier saw it—saw *her*—as well. But it was clear that he did not understand what he was seeing.

"Hello," the soldier called out. He rose to his feet, brushing loose leaves from his uniform. "Do you speak English? I'm a bit lost, innit? Higgs is the name. I'm looking for the British compound—you know the one I mean?" He took a step toward her, and Otto could tell by his expression that he was trying to look harmless, though without much success. Something about the man put Otto on edge. Something about he way he smelled—Virginia! That was it. He'd been near Virginia!

Curious, he crept closer. Neither the soldier—Higgs—nor the other had noticed him. The latter would only remain oblivious to him until the wind shifted. Then she would be all too aware of his presence.

She took a step toward Higgs. And then another. Moving as lightly as Otto himself. "The place with the high wall," Higgs continued, oblivious to his danger. "Do you know which direction that is, love?"

And then Creation Five stepped fully into the light. She hissed softly, and the cleft in her skull flexed. Higgs froze, but only for an instant. "Stone the crows," he said. "She was telling the truth." Even as he spoke, Creation Four lunged out from the undergrowth and made to grab him. Otto was as startled as Higgs. He had not even noticed the other creature.

Higgs reacted with surprising speed. He booted Four back into the bushes the creature had sprung from, and snatched out a knife he'd apparently concealed in his boot. As Four went for him again, he slashed the creature with the knife, opening a wound in Four's arm. The creature wailed in surprise and stumbled back.

Higgs turned and fled. Otto followed, leaping from branch to branch. Below, Four and Five pursued their prey. How had they escaped? Were they the only ones, or had all of them managed to free themselves? He wanted—needed—to know. He easily kept pace with them as they closed the distance between themselves and Higgs.

He dropped from the trees just before they caught him. His sudden appearance startled all three and sent the two creatures stumbling back. Five was the first to recover. She studied him with unblinking eyes. "You," she said, in a hoarse rasp.

"Yes," Otto said. "You escaped."

"No," she said. "He opened the cages. Told us to leave."

"Who?"

"Vogel." Five clicked her teeth. "The one who helped you. He loves us."

"Yes," Otto said, momentarily at a loss. Why had Vogel done such a thing? Confusion warred with gratitude. If they were free, they might accept him as one of them.

"How do you know Vogel?" Higgs asked, from behind him. Otto turned slightly, so as not to lose sight of the others. Higgs stared at him. "What are you?"

Otto snorted. "You are a soldier of Arkwright. You know what they are. They were created by Arkwright, just as I was created by—"

"This can't be real," Higgs said. But something in his tone told Otto that despite his words, the soldier understood exactly what he was talking about.

Five hissed. "You talk to Creation Eight when you bring meat. You say we are the same, but we are not. Arkwright gives us food; Arkwright protects us; Arkwright loves us." She turned, showing off a road map of scars that marked the flesh from the nape of her neck to the backs of her legs. "He shows his love, by giving us these. They are the marks of his love. Do you have these?"

Otto paused. "No." He had scars aplenty, but none like those. Something about them set his stomach to roiling. Arkwright had done this. Arkwright was the enemy. There was no doubting it now. Was that why Vogel had freed them? To save them from Arkwright?

"Then you are not one of us," Five said, in an accusing tone. "And if you are not one of us, you must be our enemy." Four growled at this. Otto's hands tightened into fists. They wanted to fight—to kill. They reeked of incipient frenzy.

They had been caged too long; hurt and starved. Now they wished to hurt something in turn . . . the kill-urge, rising up like a snake out of the undergrowth.

"No," he said. "I am not the enemy." He gestured to Higgs. "They are the enemy. The soldiers of Arkwright are the enemy."

Higgs frowned. "Bugger." He turned and ran. Otto waited a few moments and then stepped aside so that Four and Five could lope past him. Five paused, to look into his eyes. Her gaze was odd; black and opaque. Not like his at all, he thought. The only one who had eyes like him was Creation Eight. The thought disturbed him for some reason.

"Enemy or not, we are hungry," she said. "We will eat him and ask forgiveness of Arkwright." She turned to go, and he caught her arm.

"Where are the others?" he asked, as his eyes traced her scars and then the red wetness that split her features. Something about it made him hungry. "Where is Eight?"

"Hunting, as we are," she said, pulling her arm free. "As you do. Maybe he will find you and teach you the lessons we have been taught." She backed away from him. "Maybe you will learn to love Arkwright as we do. And if not . . . we will eat you too."

She was gone a moment later, joining Four in pursuit of the soldier. Otto looked down at his hands. He had been clenching them so tightly that his claws had cut into his palms. Blood ran down his forearms. In the moonlight, it looked almost like the blood of a man—rather than that of a monster.

Why had Vogel freed them? Why had he not been told?

And why did they hate him so?

24
HUNTERS

I KEEP EXPECTING TO SEE HIM," Bulan said, scanning the trees that loomed to either side of the party. Sing led the way, and Bulan and Virginia followed close behind. Kazin and his Lascars hung back to ensure no one was following them. The forest was dark, but the moon was high and silver light painted the trail.

"I know," Virginia said. "But it may be that he wants nothing to do with us. We've done little save endanger him, after all." Bulan looked at her and then away. She was right. They hadn't meant to do any such thing, but nevertheless Otto was in danger, and it was all their fault. He sighed.

"I keep running the scenario through my head. He comes out of the forest and everything is friendly. He goes back with us to Ithaca . . ."

"And then what?" Virginia asked.

"Exactly," Bulan said, with a self-deprecating laugh. "We want to help him, don't we? But we don't really know how. We came out here without any real plan. We assumed we'd know what to do, and . . . we don't. I don't. I'm trying, but I don't. After seeing him . . . can you imagine him on a train? Or taking classes at Cornell? Because I can't. Maybe that's wrong of me, but I—I just can't. What do we do, Virginia?"

"I don't know." She took his hand. "But I do know that we'll figure it out together."

"We are almost to the beach," Sing called out from up ahead. "I recognize these trees. We should hurry. We will not

be safe until we are aboard the yacht. Perhaps not even then."
He paused, waiting for them to catch up. After a moment,
he said, "There is something neither of you have considered,
I fear."

Bulan looked at him. "Which is?"

"He may not wish your help." Sing looked at Virginia. "I
gave you my opinion earlier, Miss Ginny. But I will say it again
now. Number Thirteen is not a man—he is something else.
To try and pretend otherwise will only lead to great sadness
for all involved." Suddenly, he stiffened. "What was that?"

"What was what?" Virginia asked. Bulan gestured for her
to be silent. He'd heard it as well. Splashing—like someone
moving through water, and nearby. He raised his hand, signal-
ing Kazin and the Lascars to wait.

There was a stream nearby; it led all the way to the compound, and had been used as a supply of fresh water by those
in Maxon's compound. Someone was crossing it, coming from
the direction of the shore, and right toward him and the
others. "Soldiers?" Sing asked, softly.

Bulan shook his head. "Wrong direction," he murmured.
He had a sudden premonition and looked at Virginia. "Whatever happens, stay close."

The curve of the stream was just in sight, and the sounds
of splashing drew nearer. Then Bulan saw them. One at first,
then two—three. A half-dozen men in loincloths and robes
and headdresses, carrying spears and blades. "Dayaks," he
said, drawing his pistol. He heard Kazin curse, and the Lascars
raised their rifles, as did Sing.

The leader of the Dayaks, a burly man of middle age,
froze at the sight of them. For long moments, the two groups
stared at one another. Then, Habiboola fired. A Dayak
pitched backward with his head wreathed in a red mist. A
spear was launched from their ranks an instant later.
Habiboola stumbled back, clutching weakly at the spear
jutting from his chest. As he sank down, Kazin and the
others fired as the Dayaks charged to meet them. In moments,

the stream was red with blood and the forest was filled with the sounds of struggle.

Bulan found himself facing the Dayak leader. The man bared his teeth and came in low, sword looping out to carve open Bulan's stomach. Bulan twisted back, avoiding the blow, and responded with his fist. The Dayak stumbled and fell, senseless. A second leaped on him and Bulan stepped back, emptying his pistol into the Dayak. The man sank down, dragging bloodstained fingers across Bulan's chest and leg.

Out of the corner of his eye, Bulan saw a Dayak knock Sing sprawling. The old man managed to swing his rifle up at the last moment and fire, dropping his attacker. The Lascar, Amer, sank down, a Dayak blade in his neck. Esmail and Kazin fired as one, slaying Amer's killer. The last of the Dayaks went for Virginia, perhaps believing her to be easy prey. He was soon disabused of that notion. She fired once and the Dayak toppled, a neat hole drilled between his startled eyes.

Bulan stared about in shock. It had all happened so swiftly. He turned to help Sing to his feet, and checked on the others. Virginia was pale and shaking, but unharmed. Kazin was in one piece, but Esmail had sustained a deep cut on the arm. Bulan went to Virginia and took her in his arms. "Are you okay?"

She swallowed and nodded. "I—I never thought I'd have to use those lessons. More fool me, I suppose." Realizing that she was staring at the man she'd killed, he gently turned her away. Unfortunately, there were dead men everywhere.

"You're a better shot than I am," he said, showing her his empty weapon. Virginia laughed weakly and closed her eyes. Bulan held her tight. Her heart was beating so fast, and he felt angry at himself for bringing her, for putting her in such danger. She might have been hurt or killed; Sing too, for that matter. He was a fool—no, an idiot. Resolve hardened within him. Like it or not, it was time to leave.

"I know these Dayaks, or at least their tribe," Kazin said. He was kneeling beside one of the dead men. "They are allied to Muda Saffir. I think you have had dealings with him before."

He rose, his gaze falling on Habiboola's body and then away. "I heard tell he was prowling these waters, but I did not expect to see him here."

Bulan looked at the others. "We need to leave—now."

"No," a voice said. The sound was raw and unpleasant; like glass on bone. "No, you will go nowhere, meat."

Bulan felt Virginia stiffen in his grip. Sing cursed softly, under his breath as the speaker stepped into the moonlight. It—he—was not human. That much was immediately obvious. He resembled a corpse, one that had been stretched and broken on some medieval torture device. The limbs were too long, the torso too elongated. A face like a skull turned toward them, and awful, lamp-like eyes took in the dead with obvious greed. "Meat," the newcomer croaked. "So much meat, for us."

Virginia grabbed Bulan's arm. "Bulan—*they did it*. The British did it. Somehow, they made more of them."

Bulan nodded, but didn't dare take his eyes off the horror before him. Other shapes, indistinct in the shadows, moved behind the first. How many of them were there? Kazin lifted his rifle, but Bulan stopped him. "Wait. Give him the opportunity to express his intent."

Kazin stared at him. "Are you mad?"

"He is right," Sing said. "Not all monsters are monsters, eh Bulan?"

Bulan nodded. "Let's hope." He cleared his throat. "Who are you, friend?"

The creature studied him for several moments, as if puzzled by his words. He took the opportunity to study the newcomer in turn. The creature was starveling thin, his gray flesh pulled taut over muscle. Not as well-fed as Otto, though possibly just as strong. Deprivation hadn't made Maxon's creations weak; quite the contrary. Hunger and pain lent them strength. He wondered if the same was true of these.

"I . . . am the child of Arkwright," the monster replied, finally. He spread his arms—all three of them—and his hideous countenance twisted into something that might have been an expression of joy. "We are *all* the children of Arkwright." As he spoke, two more creatures moved into the moonlight. Each was as different from the first as they were from one another. Like Maxon's creations, their only commonality was in their utter distinctiveness. One resembled nothing so much as a wingless bat, while the other reminded him of a melted waxwork.

Virginia tightened her grip on his arm. "How many did they make?" she murmured. Bulan shook his head. They'd come here looking for just one monster. Now it seemed there were at least four loose on the island.

"I don't know," he said, "But if they're violent, they'll be all over us before we can fire or reload. Otto's a lot faster than me, and I'm for damn sure faster than most men."

"Suggestion?" Sing asked.

"Run for the ship, when I give the signal. Fast as we can. The beach should be just past the trees. Until then—keep your eyes on them." Bulan stepped forward, facing the trio of horrors. He felt his pulse quicken, but there was no fear. He had done this before. He had dwelled among monsters, and thought he knew them—even if he did not know these in particular.

There was a possibility, however remote, that they could be talked into leaving. A part of him wanted to try and save them, the way he wanted to save Otto. But Sing's words came back to him. What if they didn't want help? Still, he had to try. If he didn't, who would?

"What do you want?" Bulan asked, loudly.

"To eat," the waxwork gurgled. "Meat! *Meat!*" He took a step toward Bulan, mismatched fingers curling into cruel hooks. The three-armed one flung out a long limb, intercepting his companion.

"No. We eat the dead now—living, later." His ugly gaze fixed on Bulan and something that might have been a smile passed across his corpse-like countenance. Bulan swallowed, suddenly recalling his dreams. Maxon's creatures had been man-eaters as well. But not even Twelve had seemed this . . . gleeful about it.

The bat-thing grew agitated. "No! We hunt, but we do not eat—not unless Arkwright feeds us!" He turned on the three-armed creature and crouched. "You cannot eat. You break Arkwright's law!"

The three-armed creature wheeled about with disturbing grace. "Arkwright has given them to us. I have seen it. This is his law—and I am its voice."

"Your friend doesn't agree," Bulan said. It seemed these monsters were as aggressive as Maxon's creations, if not more so. And as prone to infighting. Perhaps he could use that to his advantage. "Maybe he thinks that he should be in charge. Maybe Arkwright would agree."

The three-armed creature glanced at him, eyes narrowed in what he took to be suspicion. This one was smarter than the others, he thought. The creature knew what he was doing, even if the other two didn't.

"Arkwright—Arkwright will punish us," the bat-thing chittered. He clawed at his wrinkled face, clearly unhappy at the prospect. "Arkwright will starve us! Because you have broken his law!" Then, with a shriek, he launched himself at the three-armed creature. Bulan stepped back, leaving the two monsters plenty of room for their tussle.

Their struggle carried them into the stream, and for a moment, Bulan had a hard time telling which of them might come out on top. Not that it mattered. He waved the others back, keeping one eye on the waxwork monster. Thankfully, it was utterly intent on the brawl. Bulan turned and gestured with both hands. "Go—*go!*"

Virginia and the others started running. Bulan followed, but paused only long enough to watch the end of the fight. The three-armed creature slammed his heavy fists down on his opponent's skull with a horrid, echoing crunch. The bat-thing twitched and fell still. The victor looked up at Bulan, and there was hate in his eyes and something else . . .

Joy.

A terrible, incandescent joy. One that Bulan knew well. The monster had learned to kill—and enjoyed it. But rather than pursuing him, the creature turned away.

Bulan fled.

25
OLD FOES

SING CURSED SOFTLY AND CONTINUOUSLY in Cantonese as he and Kazin led the way to the beach. The Lascar laughed sourly. "This is not turning out to be the ideal trip, eh?"

Sing glanced at him. "No. Not as such." He wondered if the monsters were following them. He hoped not. One encounter was enough, for his taste. He prayed that there were only two of the beasts.

"Could be worse," Esmail piped up, from behind them. Kazin turned and swatted the younger man on the back of the head.

"Idiot! Never invite trouble that way. You never know when the Jinn are listening." He turned back to Sing. "You were right. We should have left earlier, storm be damned. Now we have a whole pack of fiends to contend with—and Dayaks as well."

Sing grunted and glanced back at Virginia and Bulan. Their worries were evident; neither was especially good at hiding how they felt. Seeing the other monsters had shaken them to their core. In their heart of hearts, they had not expected anyone to recreate Maxon's experiments. Sing had known better. What man learned, others could put into use. It was one of the reasons he'd agreed to come: to ensure that Maxon's crimes were utterly forgotten. Virginia understood; she intended to do the same, he thought. To erase her father's sins, if only to give herself a fresh start.

161

But now, the secret was out. There was nothing more to be done, in Sing's opinion. Best to leave, and swiftly. If the British wished to unleash such horrors on themselves, they could suffer the ramifications. Of course, there was the question of how they'd come to learn Maxon's secrets. Sing had a suspicion that he knew the answer to that particular question—though he wished otherwise. But Bulan's description of his opponent at the British compound was unpleasantly familiar.

Ju-Long.

Sing frowned. *Oh grandson . . . what have you done now?*

Kazin gave a shout, and Sing banished his thoughts of family, and turned his attention back to the path. The trees were thinning, and the ocean was visible, stretching across the horizon dead ahead. The yacht was there, where they'd left it—but not alone. Sing skidded to a stop at the edge of the beach. Kazin and Esmail did as well.

A Dayak war-canoe was anchored beside the yacht, and there were lights dancing across the decks of both vessels. Kazin cursed virulently and glared at Esmail. "I told you. You see? The Jinn heard you."

Virginia and Bulan joined them a moment later. "What is it Sing? Why did you stop?" Virginia asked. Bulan pointed at the war-canoe.

"I'll tell you what it is: the absolute last thing we needed," he said, flatly. He looked at Kazin. "Any sign of . . . ?"

Kazin shook his head. "He is dead."

"Maybe not," Esmail began. "Maybe he escaped!" Sing recalled that the Lascar they'd left to keep watch on the yacht, Jabal, was one of Esmail's cousins. In reply, Kazin merely shook his head again. He looked at Sing, and his gaze spoke volumes. Jabal was almost certainly dead, or worse.

There was a shout, from farther down the beach. A band of Dayaks had come ashore and were approaching at a trot. At their head was an unpleasantly familiar figure—the self-proclaimed rajah, Muda Saffir. He looked older than when

Sing had seen him last, but no less self-important, in his silks and jewels. Sing had to admit, he cut a dashing figure.

The Malay spread his arms, as if greeting long-lost friends. "Ah, there she is—the woman stolen from me twice. But there will not be a third time, I think!" He stopped a safe distance away and crossed his arms. "Hello, sweet Virginia. You are as lovely as the day you so cruelly attempted to drown me."

Virginia laughed grimly. "You look older, Muda Saffir. Piracy not agreeing with you?"

Saffir laughed loudly. He was putting on a show for his followers, Sing knew. Pirates loved nothing more than a bit of drama. "I have been pining for you, my dear. And your father's treasure." He crossed his arms. "Fate smiles upon me this day, having delivered both of my desires into my waiting hands."

"You don't have me yet," Virginia called out. Her hand fell to her sidearm. Sing, Kazin, and Esmail raised their rifles. Bulan waited, still as a tiger. Saffir studied them, and Sing knew the pirate was weighing the odds. The Dayaks could overwhelm them, but at what cost? Saffir would not order an attack, unless he was certain he could win.

"What do you want?" Bulan growled, and his voice carried like thunder. Sing felt his neck prickle at the sound. Here was the voice of the man who'd thought he was Number Thirteen, not Townsend Harper, Jr. Here was the voice of Bulan. The Dayaks murmured among themselves. It was clear they had not forgotten the stories.

Saffir grimaced. "That should be obvious. I want her, and her father's treasure. Give them to me, and I will let you live."

"There is no treasure," Bulan said.

"Lies," Saffir shouted. "Why else would you come back to this cursed place, if not to retrieve something of great value?" He waggled a finger at them, as if chiding a child. "I am not a fool, American. Nor am I frightened of the stories. You are a big man, it is true . . . but just a man. And men can be killed. I should know, for I have done so many times."

"As have we," Sing called out. "You think you are the only man here to have shed blood, Muda Saffir?"

"Is that Sing Lee, eh? I remember you, cook. You tried to kill me as well." Saffir glowered at Sing. "I have heard that there is a price on your withered head, in Singapore. That the family of a certain Hoon Lo would like to have your queue for their wall. Perhaps I should take it, eh?"

"If you think you can," Sing replied. Despite his tone, he felt uneasy. Boastful as he was, Saffir was not usually the sort to talk freely. Why would he engage in banter, unless—ah. On a hunch, Sing glanced at the forest and saw a small group of Dayaks creeping swiftly and noiselessly toward them. He spun, and his rifle spoke. The Dayaks broke for cover, all save one who collapsed, screaming.

Saffir cursed and pointed at the group. "Capture the woman! Kill the men! Now!" His warriors raced toward Sing and the others. Kazin and Esmail fired as one, and Dayaks pitched into the sand. But the others did not slow. They were brave, if nothing else.

Virginia drew her own weapon and fired at Muda Saffir, but he was already scrambling for cover, calling down every manner of curse upon her head. Bulan caught her arm. "We need to go, now. Sing—Kazin—come on!"

Sing reloaded his rifle as he backed toward the trees. Bulan was right. The Dayaks outnumbered them ten to one, and would be upon them in moments. The only way they stood a chance was by retreating to a more defensible position. He glanced at Kazin. The Lascar nodded and gave him a sour smile. "You go. Take Esmail. I will cover the retreat."

"No," Virginia began. "You'll be killed!"

Kazin ignored her, and fired. Another Dayak fell, plucked from life. Sing hurried her back toward the trees, with Bulan's aid. "He is right, Miss Ginny. Someone must stay, to buy us time. Esmail, come!"

The young Lascar hesitated, staring at Kazin. Then, he turned and ran, quickly catching up with Sing and the others as they reached the tree line. Sing heard Kazin's rifle bark again and again, as quickly as the Lascar could fire and reload. He paused at the trees, and looked back. The Dayaks were almost upon Kazin, but the Lascar had not moved. Nor would he. Not one step back.

"We have to go back for him," Virginia said, fighting against Bulan's grip. From the look on his face, her fiancé agreed with her. "He can't stop them all!"

"No. But he will do as he must." Sing watched as the Dayaks closed in. Kazin shouted something and there was a sudden flurry of steel—an arc of red. A Dayak fell, clutching at his stomach. Kazin was good with a knife.

Not good enough, though. Not against ten men. When he fell, he did not get up again. And a moment later, a Dayak was hoisting his severed head like a trophy. Sing raised his rifle and fired, killing the Dayak. The others hesitated. Sing took the opportunity to rejoin the others. "Kazin?" Esmail asked, softly.

"He did as he was paid to do," Sing said, not looking at the young man. "Lascars are, above all, men of honor." He looked at Virginia and Bulan. "Kazin bought us a few minutes, but they will be regrouping even now. We must find shelter."

Bulan pointed. "I think—I think it's this way." But he sounded uncertain. Sing looked around. They had reentered the forest some distance from the trail. Nothing was familiar. From behind came the cries of the Dayaks, as they entered the forest in pursuit.

"We're all turned around," Virginia said. "It's hard to tell."

"We are lost," Esmail said, eyes wide. He clutched his rifle like a talisman, and rubbed at his injured arm. Sing glanced at him and felt a flash of pity. According to Kazin, this was the first time Esmail had shipped out.

"How can we lose a whole stream?" Bulan growled, his expression taut with frustration. In this moment, he reminded Sing of a wild beast, at bay. He reflected that the young man's time among the monsters had scarred him in ways more than the physical. "The compound. If we could just get to the compound . . ."

"Due east," Sing said. He squinted up at the cloudy darkness above. The moon shone through the clouds, but not so the stars. "But without seeing the stars, I cannot be sure of which way to go." Something crashed through the foliage nearby. He signaled Esmail, and raised his rifle. The young man swallowed, but followed suit. "If they come upon us, run—both of you. Esmail and I will hold them here."

"We will?" Esmail asked, glancing at him. Sing quieted him with a sharp look.

Virginia turned. "I hear something. Bulan . . . ?"

"Yes," Bulan said, crouching, ready to lunge. Sing frowned. The sound was coming from the wrong direction. Unless—had Muda Saffir sent more Dayaks inland than just that one party they'd encountered?

The undergrowth parted . . . and a group of British soldiers stepped into view. "All right then, you lot. Drop your weapons and raise your hands," one called out. Sing didn't. Neither did Esmail. The soldiers looked jumpy. Sing could only imagine what they made of the sound of gunfire. The one who'd spoken advanced another few paces. "I said drop your weapons, if you please. I'd hate to have to shoot you before I got to ask any questions."

"Look," Bulan began. "We haven't done anything wrong. Whatever is going on here, we don't care. We just want to leave." He paused, and Sing could tell he was fighting to keep his temper under control. "You people attacked us. Not the other way around."

"Doesn't matter," the soldier said. He stared at them down the barrel of an officer's revolver, his gaze cool and decisive. "Where's Higgs?"

Bulan and Virginia glanced at one another. Sing frowned. "We let him go," he said. "He ran. Into the forest. It does not matter. There are Dayaks on the beach."

"They can stay there, as far as I'm concerned," the soldier

said, without taking his eyes from Bulan, or lowering his weapon. "I'm only concerned about your lot. I ask again: where is Sergeant Higgs?"

"Second Lieutenant Welles, sir," one of his men began, eyes on the trees. Sing heard it as well; not the Dayaks, but something else. Something moving above them. He looked up—a flash of gray, in the branches. A smell, like sour blood and damp earth, and all too familiar.

"Bulan," he said, in warning. If Bulan heard him, he gave no sign.

"I will ask you on last time," Welles said, ignoring his subordinate. "Where is Higgs?"

"Sir!"

"What, Rogers?" Welles snapped, glancing at the other man.

Something crashed down out of the trees, falling upon an unlucky soldier like a meteorite. The unfortunate man screamed, briefly, just before his throat was torn open like wet paper by the clawed fingers of his attacker.

The monster rose from the body of its victim and bared jagged teeth in a pantomime smile. "We are still hungry," it said, its three hands flexing with what Sing knew to be eagerness.

"And now we will eat live meat."

26
MEETING

VOGEL CREPT THROUGH THE FOREST, moving with all the caution of an old man who could barely see in front of his face. He'd forgone a light, not wanting to risk being seen by one of the guards on the palisade. The moon worked well enough. So long as the clouds didn't interfere, he would make do. Otto would be waiting for him somewhere close by. He'd warned the boy not to go far. Hopefully, he'd listened.

He clutched his satchel to his chest as he went. Inside it were his notes on Maxon's process, as well as copies of Maxon's journals. Everything one needed to know to create life was in his hands. He was tempted to bury it deep in the forest, and let the island have it. But his conscience compelled him otherwise. These notes belonged with their creator.

Vogel had been planning his departure for weeks; almost from the first moment he'd come to the island. It had quickly become apparent to him that Arkwright wasn't to be trusted. That his patronage came with strings attached—the sort that could easily be used to throttle the unwary. Vogel had not survived the cutthroat world of Viennese academia for so long by being a fool.

Finding Otto had only crystallized this decision. Vogel knew what Arkwright would do, if he found Otto. The poor boy would be opened up on a slab like a Christmas goose. Vogel could not—would not—allow that to happen. Nor did he wish to participate in Arkwright's cold-blooded slaughter of the others.

But now, there was a new element to consider. Ju-Long had told him something about their visitors; enough to convince Vogel that they were who he believed them to be. It could hardly be a coincidence, after all.

Virginia Maxon had come back to the island. To claim her inheritance? Or maybe to destroy the remnants of her father's work. Either seemed possible. But Arkwright would not allow her to do either. He had plans, and no intention of letting anyone interfere with them. But Vogel had plans of his own.

Initially, he'd hoped to use the Dayaks to get him back to Singapore. They were pirates, and probably worse, but he thought the promise of money might buy him safe passage. It had seemed worth the risk, at the time. He'd begun to suspect that Arkwright was more observant than he let on. That he'd needed Vogel to teach him what he needed to know, but once the latter had done so, their partnership would come to an abrupt end.

A branch rustled overhead, causing him to pause. He looked up. "This is no time to play hide and seek with me, Otto," he murmured. A shadow passed between him and the moon. Something moving between the trees. "Otto . . . is that you? Ich bin hier, mein junge. We must speak." Another rustle of branches, but closer this time. As if whatever—whoever—it was, was quickly descending. He turned, following the sound. "Otto?"

A familiar, crooked form dropped into view. Creation One hissed and loped toward Vogel in ungainly fashion. One was the earliest of their attempts, and the most rudimentary. He lacked even the barest flicker of self-awareness; he was animalistic and unteachable. Vogel backed away as the monster closed in.

Then, from out of the dark, Otto lunged to his rescue. Otto collided with One, tackling the smaller monster to the ground. One squealed in surprise and anger, and attempted to hurl his attacker aside to no avail. The fight that followed was as brutal as it was brief. In moments, One was hurled into a tree hard enough to make Vogel's bones ache in sympathy. "Otto—enough," he cried out. For a moment, he did not know if Otto had heard him.

Otto stepped back. "We do not need to fight," he said. "We are the same, you and I. Do you understand?" He extended his hand, as if to help One up. Instead, the other monster leaped up with a scream and made to attack. Otto reacted so swiftly that Vogel could barely follow what came next. One moment, the monster was upright. The next there was a horrid cracking sound and One crumpled to the ground in a twitching heap. Otto stared down at the body, as if surprised by what he'd done.

"Why . . . ?" he murmured. "I did not want to do that."

Vogel reached up and placed a comforting hand on his shoulder. Or as close as he could manage. "This world can be very harsh at times. Sometimes we must do terrible things in order to prevent worse things from occurring. You saved my life, but at great expense. It could not have been avoided." Vogel took a deep breath. "Otto . . . I need your help. There are new people on the island . . ."

"I have met them," Otto said, turning to face him. His eyes glowed eerily, reflecting the moonlight. "The woman . . . the woman is the one in the photograph I found in the house of Maxon."

Vogel felt a moment's elation as his suspicions were proven correct. "Her name is Virginia Maxon. She is the daughter of the one who made you. I am confident that she and her friends are our friends. Listen to me closely: when you and I first met by accident out here, I warned you to stay away from Arkwright and the soldiers. That they were your enemies. Well, they are my enemies too, now. They are also the enemies of those I created—those like you." He looked down at One's body. "Like him. His name was Creation One."

He looked up at Otto, to see whether he understood. He thought so. He hoped so. "These beautiful beings, like you, were created by man. But some men are imperfect. Some men cannot help but corrupt everything they touch." He sighed softly and hugged the satchel more tightly to his chest. "Arkwright wishes to take a scientific miracle and twist it into something obscene."

Vogel crouched gingerly beside One's body, wincing as his knees and vertebrae popped. He stroked the dead creature's face. So unlike that of a man, but somehow all too human. "Given time, Creation One could have been as intelligent and as compassionate as you, Otto. But Arkwright will not allow us that time." He looked up at Otto.

"He wants to destroy them, Otto. All of them. Because they are more like you than we ever imagined that they could be. That is why I had to release them. So that they might at least stand a chance at survival, however slim it might be."

Vogel rose to his feet. Otto's gaze was opaque. It was difficult at the best of times to tell what the boy was thinking. "You and I must find Virginia Maxon and her friends and ask them to take us far from this island. They are our only hope. Arkwright will kill us both if he catches us. Do you understand?"

He waited, hoping that he'd made himself clear. Otto looked at him, and then at the body at their feet. His lips peeled back from his shark's grin. He gripped Vogel's shoulders gently, but firmly. "Yes, I understand."

"Good," Vogel said, with no small amount of relief. Otto released him.

"Do not worry," Otto said. "I will kill them before they kill us. We will all be safe." Then, he turned and was sprinting away, as fast as his legs could carry him. Vogel watched him go, his surprise turning to consternation.

"Children," he muttered, as he started in pursuit. "I really must sit him down and explain that there is more than one way to deal with an enemy." Otto wasn't thinking clearly.

He would attack the first group of uniforms he saw, and that would be that. Especially if Vogel's absence had been discovered. They would kill the boy, and Vogel too. Of that he was certain. They needed to get off this island—the sooner, the better.

His thoughts were interrupted by the sound of gunshots, coming from the general direction of the beach. He paused. That didn't bode well at all. Ahead of him, Otto paused, listening. "Virginia," he growled. Then he was off again, like a shot.

Vogel tried to follow, but stumbled over a root and fell to his hands and knees. When he managed to right himself, Otto was gone and he was alone. Vogel, not normally a man given to foul language, was nonetheless tempted to paint the air blue, as the Americans said. Otto was headstrong; foolish. He was only going to get himself hurt—or hurt someone else.

Vogel sighed and brushed dirt from his trousers. "Something is going on at the beach, so to the beach I will go," he murmured. As he straightened, he caught the glint of metal, reflecting the moonlight. He stiffened as several shapes materialized out of the gloom.

Dayaks.

Vogel adjusted his spectacles and did his best to hide his sudden fear. "Hello," he said, in English. "I do not suppose any of you speak German?"

"Not enough to matter," one of the Dayaks said, in English. He was bigger than the others, and older. A chieftain, perhaps. "You are the old man Tijilik met."

Vogel hesitated, but only for a moment. "I am."

"You wished to meet Muda Saffir. To tell him about his treasure."

"I did."

"Did?"

"Do," Vogel amended, quickly. The Dayak smiled.

"You will tell me."

Vogel stepped back. "You are not Muda Saffir."

"I am Riwut. I am Muda Saffir's loyal man. You will tell

me of the treasure, and then I will tell him." The Dayak's hand fell to the hilt of his blade. "Be quick, for I am impatient."

Vogel swallowed. "I will tell only Muda Saffir. Take me to him."

Riwut stared at him. Vogel met his gaze squarely, and held it. "I could take your head, old man. What then, eh?"

"Then you would have the head of an old man, but no treasure." Vogel forced a smile. "I do not think Muda Saffir would consider that an even trade, do you?"

Riwut was silent for a moment. Then, with a snort, he turned away. "Bring him. If he wishes to meet the rajah, then by all means, let him do so."

27

TURNED AROUND

BULAN RECOGNIZED THEIR ATTACKERS instantly as the same pair from the stream. The two monsters fell upon the soldiers with brutal abandon, and two of the men were down before the others registered what was happening. He heard Virginia cry out, but could not tear his eyes away from what was happening.

The waxwork monster clubbed an unfortunate soldier to the ground with one malformed fist, and then tore out his throat in a welter of crimson. The three-handed creature gutted another, opening the poor man up from throat to groin. One of the remaining soldiers rushed toward the creature, as if hoping to aid his fallen comrade. But the monster was too quick; he rose and whirled, smashing the soldier from his feet with bone-cracking force. The soldier flopped limply to the ground, and did not move.

Three men dead, in as many seconds. Not a single shot fired.

Bulan stared at the bodies, not quite able to believe it. He'd known how murderous the creatures could be; indeed, he'd used that savagery to his own benefit once upon a time. But time and his own mental scars had dulled the memory. Seeing it here, now, had brought it all back, all too vividly. The three-armed creature looked at him again. "Arkwright be praised," the monster said, yellow gaze fixed on him.

For a moment, there was only silence. Then, one of the surviving soldiers bolted. "Rogers," Welles bellowed. "Get back

174

here you coward!" He turned his revolver away from Bulan and onto the three-armed monster, and fired. The creature sprang away, swiftly clambering up into the trees. The other monster followed a moment later, before anyone could get a bead on it. Welles glanced at Bulan. "Where did they go? Do you see them?"

"Not far," Bulan said. He kept his eyes on the trees. They were up there somewhere, watching—waiting. "Sing?"

Sing shook his head. "No sign of them." He waved Esmail back. "Keep watch, boy. They will be back, and sooner than we expect."

"You sound like you know what these things are," Welles said, with obvious suspicion. Virginia laughed bleakly.

"You could say that. Though I expect your boss could tell you more. He's the one who made them. Or didn't you hear what that thing said?" She took a step toward Welles. Bulan reached for her, not quite sure what she was planning but all too aware of the revolver in Welles' hand.

"Virginia," he began.

"No, Bulan. Higgs might have laughed at the notion, but Welles here has damn well seen them with his own eyes." She took another step toward Welles, who gazed at her in consternation.

"Higgs . . . so you were telling the truth?" he asked, haltingly. "About letting him go?"

"Why would we lie?" Bulan asked, plainly. He shook his head. "All we wanted—it doesn't matter now. All we want now is to get off this damn island and go home."

Welles hesitated. His eyes widened and his revolver came up—too late. Bulan heard Virginia cry out and turned to see a Dayak holding a blade to her throat. More Dayaks, no doubt their pursuers from the beach, crept into view. "Let her go," Bulan said.

"Her life for the treasure," the Dayak barked, in Malay. Bulan understood, and replied in kind, even as he waved Sing and Esmail back.

"There is no treasure," he said. The Dayak was young; one of his arms was in a sling. His companions, unfortunately, didn't appear to be injured.

"Lies," the Dayak spat. "Muda Saffir says that this one's father hid it on this island. Says she knows where it is, and we are to bring her to him. I—Tijilik—will do so!" He hauled Virginia back, his good arm around her neck, the blade braced against her throat. "Surrender—or die!"

"That damn treasure again," Sing said, as he sighted down the barrel of his rifle. "Even a year on, they still seek it. Idiots."

Bulan motioned for him to be quiet, though he agreed with every word. Saffir had been obsessed with the treasure, as had Von Horn. Neither of them had realized it was nothing but a fabrication of their own greed.

Frustration boiled in him. Every moment they stayed here was a risk. Monsters in the trees and Dayaks on the beach. It was only a question of which got them first. He cleared his throat to speak, but Virginia beat him to it. She twisted in Tijilik's grip and said, "Listen to me: Muda Saffir is mistaken. There is no treasure! There is no gold, no diamonds . . . it was books in that chest. It was just books!"

Tijilik made to speak but was interrupted by a sudden crashing of branches from overhead. The Dayaks' attention was diverted, if only for a moment—but it was enough. Sing, Esmail, and Welles fired as one. Dayaks fell. Tijilik shouted a command and the two surviving warriors raced forward.

Bulan met them head-on. He crashed into the Dayaks as if they were opposing linemen, and sent them tumbling to the ground. Unfortunately, one shot back to his feet almost immediately, blade in hand, and nearly took Bulan's head. He heard Virginia cry his name, but had no time to answer. The blade looped out again, whistling as it cut the air. He twisted aside and slammed his fist into the side of the Dayak's head, knocking him to the ground. He wrenched the sword from the dazed man's grip and brought it down on the Dayak's head without thinking.

He turned to see the other rising, and slashed the sword out across his opponent's neck—again, on instinct. The Dayak slumped back, choking on his own blood. Panting, Bulan looked at the sword in his hand—at the blade, painted crimson—and flung it away from him. He could hear more crashing in the undergrowth. Dayaks, maybe. Or more soldiers. Absently, he reached for his handgun. In the heat of the moment, he'd forgotten it.

"Bulan—look out," Sing shouted.

Bulan looked up as a shadow fell across him. The waxwork monster pounced on him, knocking him to the ground. He flung the creature away, but realized that he'd lost his weapon in the process. The monster scrambled toward Sing, who was taking aim with his rifle. Nearby, the three-armed monster had managed to knock Welles to the ground and slap the pistol from his hand.

Bulan flung himself at the creature, and attempted to pin all three of his arms. The monster roared in fury and wriggled free before clubbing Bulan to his knees. The brute had a hell of a punch, just like Otto. Worse, he had three fists to use. Bulan rolled back as his opponent closed in. He rose, forearms in front of his head like a boxer, but took a few blows that made his thoughts rattle in his head. Luckily, the monster wasn't a practiced fighter—more like a wild animal.

Bulan backed away, leading his opponent away from Welles. Past the monster, he saw the soldier fumbling for his revolver. "Welles," he cried, as he avoided a punch that might well have torn his head off. "Shoot him!"

However, when the shot came, it did not come from Welles' direction. The monster howled as a bullet took him high in the uppermost shoulder, and he whipped around to face this new threat. Bulan peered past him and felt his heart sink. Ju-Long and a pair of soldiers stood at the far side of the clearing.

"Oh great," Bulan said, as Sing sidled toward him, attention split between the newcomers and the monsters. "Him again.

Just what we need. I've taken some hits on the football field, but none like that fellow can dish out."

Sing didn't reply, but something in his expression told Bulan that the old man recognized Ju-Long. Before he could ask, however, the three-armed monster spoke up. "At last," he growled, clutching his injured shoulder. "My patience is rewarded. Now we face one another without bars to protect you, Ju-Long. Arkwright has gifted you to me, so that I might show him all that I have learned."

Ju-Long gestured to one of the men with him. "Davies. Shoot that one."

But before Davies could do so, Sing fired. His shot, whether lucky or simply skillful, smacked the rifle out of the startled soldier's hands, causing him to yelp. The monsters took the opportunity to retreat once more, vanishing into the under-growth. Bulan seized the moment as well, springing on the second of the soldiers that had come with Ju-Long. He knocked the man to the ground and slugged him.

Bulan rose, soldier's rifle in hand, aimed at Ju-Long. A sound made him turn; clawed hands shot from the underbrush and caught the dazed soldier by the head. He was dragged into the shadows before he could make a sound. Bulan backed away, feeling sick. He heard a scream and spun, to see the other soldier yanked upward into the trees before Ju-Long or the others could act. There was an ugly series of sounds, and then the body tumbled to the earth to lay like a broken doll.

Up in the trees, the monster laughed. "We will have our accounting later, Ju-Long."

Branches rustled. Then . . . silence.

"Drop the rifle," Ju-Long said, aiming his own at Bulan. To his credit, the big man did not seem in the least perturbed by what had just happened. Then, perhaps he had been ex-pecting it. Bulan hesitated. The other man had him dead to rights, but maybe . . .

"Ju-Long, this is mad," Welles said. He was pale and wide-eyed. "Whatever is going on, on this damn island, I don't think these men are our enemies. Let's put the rifle down and have a chat, eh?"

Ju-Long didn't so much as look at him. "I am not one of your soldiers, Welles. I do as I please." He sighted down the barrel, taking aim at Bulan.

Sing appeared behind him, the muzzle of his rifle resting against the side of Ju-Long's head. "Do you? Drop the rifle, boy. *Now.*"

Ju-Long hesitated, but only for a moment. His rifle clattered to the ground. "Arkwright will not be pleased, Welles. These men cannot be trusted."

"Neither can Arkwright, it seems," Welles said, as he checked the cylinder of his service revolver. "But that's a conversation for later." He snapped the weapon shut. "For now, we've got a lady to rescue, which, in my book, takes priority."

It took Bulan a moment to register what Welles had said. He felt talons of ice clutch at his heart as he turned to where he'd last seen Virginia. She was gone, as was her captor. "Virginia? *Virginia!*"

"The Dayak must have stolen her away," Sing said. "Go, find her. Esmail, go with him. I will stay here and watch our friends." Seeing Bulan's hesitation, he added, "Go!"

"I'll get her, Sing. Be careful!" Bulan darted into the forest, in the direction the Dayak would have taken. He heard someone pursuing, and glanced back to see Welles and Esmail following him.

"I don't understand what any of this is about, but I know my duty when someone is in trouble," Welles said, as he caught up with Bulan. "If you're willing, I mean . . ."

Bulan nodded. "Thank you—Welles, was it?"

Welles grinned. "Second Lieutenant Welles, to be exact. But I don't expect that matters much at the moment, eh?" He paused. "Now why don't you tell me what's really going on here, while we look for the lady . . ."

28

REUNION

ING WATCHED AS BULAN AND WELLES vanished into the gloom of the forest. Then, he sighed and lowered his rifle. "Now, grandson, perhaps you had better tell me everything you know about all of this." He'd wanted a private word with his grandson before he revealed the truth of their relationship to Bulan and the others. He had a sneaking suspicion that he knew why Ju-Long was here—but he wanted to hear it from the boy himself.

Ju-Long turned. "You should not have come back here, grandfather."

"Oh? How is it that you are aware I was ever here in the first place, boy?" Sing looked his grandson up and down. Ju-Long was bigger than he remembered. He looked like a pirate; a killer. Was that what he'd become, in Sing's absence? "What has your mother been feeding you?"

"Mother and I have not spoken in some time." Ju-Long spoke stiffly; his face was a mask. "Not since father died. And you left." Sing wondered what had happened between his oldest daughter and her son. Ju-Long's father had been a sailor; he'd perished in a pirate attack, somewhere in the Strait of Malacca. He felt a flicker of regret as he considered what might have been. Should he have stayed, rather than going with Maxon?

"I taught you better than that."

Ju-Long grimaced. "You taught me nothing."

Sing snorted. Ju-Long was as petulant as ever. He'd never

180

learned to respect his elders. "I certainly taught you better than to enlist in the British army."

Ju-Long sneered. "I am no soldier. After you left Singapore to cook and launder the clothes of that American scientist, I also left. I went out to seek my fortune, as you did at my age. Unlike you, however, I chose not to become a manservant for wealthy Westerners."

"Is that what your mother told you?" Sing murmured. It was probably for the best. His relationship with his children had been strained even before taking service with Maxon. They disapproved of his past indiscretions, though they had not complained about the full bellies and new shoes his illicit activities provided. He pushed the thought aside; it was not seemly to expect gratitude, even from one's children.

"Mother told me little. What I know is what I have seen." Ju-Long bent to retrieve his rifle. "Do not happily gaze only at your feet as you follow behind others, because they might lead you into chains," he recited. "Do you remember telling me that?" He gestured sharply. "Yet that is exactly what you did."

Sing sighed again. Ju-Long had been a bad-tempered little boy; impatient and unwilling to reconsider his assumptions. It seemed not much had changed since they'd last seen one another. "Hardly. What I did, I did with eyes wide open. What I did, I did for your grandmother and your mother and your sisters. Had you not left, you would have known that every penny I earned working for Maxon went directly to your grandmother."

Ju-Long blinked, and Sing wondered if the thought had ever even occurred to him. "You still left," he said, stubbornly. "What was I to think?"

"I would hope you did not think so poorly of me that you would think I would abandon my loved ones." Sing paused. "Can you say the same? Now, why are you here, Ju-Long? How did you come to serve this Arkwright?"

"I do not serve Arkwright," Ju-Long snapped.

"And yet you appear to be doing his bidding nonetheless," Sing said. Then, more firmly, "Answer my question, boy. How did you come to be here?"

Ju-Long hesitated, and Sing could tell he was weighing his options. The forest had grown still around them. There were Dayaks abroad, and monsters. They did not have time for recalcitrance. He was about to say as much, when Ju-Long spoke. "After I went out on my own, I worked odd jobs around Singapore and met a number of . . . interesting people. One was an American named Von Horn—"

Sing hissed in shock. "Von Horn!"

Ju-Long smiled bitterly. "Yes, I thought you might recognize that name. And not just him—a German as well, named Vogel. He was also a scientist, and one who'd come looking for Maxon . . . or so he claimed."

"You doubted this?"

"I am not you, grandfather. I do not trust Westerners at their word." The way he said it, however, made Sing suspicious. He smiled mirthlessly.

"Did you trust Von Horn?"

Ju-Long looked away. "He had just entered into a partnership with Professor Maxon, to assist him in his experiments. He said Maxon needed money, and entrusted Von Horn with locating a partner for their endeavour."

Sing raised an eyebrow. "And how did you come into it?"

"I knew Vogel was looking to meet Maxon, and so I introduced him to Von Horn. The idea was that Vogel would join them here later, once funding had been secured. Once the money was in hand, Von Horn was to send a signal, letting us know when the time was right to arrive. As a gesture of good faith, he provided Vogel some of Maxon's notes to look over."

"Did he now?" Sing muttered. Things were starting to make sense now. Somewhere close by, a branch cracked. He turned and peered into the dark. Had the monsters come back? But when no further sound came, he looked back at Ju-Long. "Let me guess: Von Horn never sent the signal."

"No," Ju-Long said, sourly.

Sing grunted. "Because Von Horn was not acting on Maxon's behalf. He was a scoundrel, Ju-Long. A swindler. Once he had the money, he had no more need of you or Vogel. I would guess that Maxon never even knew of your conversation." Seeing the look on his grandson's face, Sing chuckled. "Do not feel bad, Ju-Long. Von Horn tricked us all—even that scurvy Malay, Muda Saffir. But how did this Arkwright become involved?"

Ju-Long shook his head. "I do not know. But he knows all about Maxon's experiments, and has plans for them."

"Plans you are helping him with," Sing said, somewhat accusingly. "Why?"

Ju-Long frowned. "He is influential; wealthy."

"But I do not think he is a good man," Sing said.

"Was Maxon?" Ju-Long's hands tightened on his rifle. "Do you hear that?"

"I have been hearing it," Sing said. There was something prowling about them now, slinking through the undergrowth. Not Dayaks, for they would have already attacked. "Perhaps Arkwright sent more soldiers to look for you . . ."

"No," Ju-Long said, flatly. He turned, rifle at his shoulder. The sounds were coming from either direction now. "Arkwright has given orders to kill you and your masters, grandfather. If I were you, I would leave this place."

Sing sighted down the length of his rifle, trying to follow the noises emerging from the undergrowth. Whatever it was, it would be on them in moments. "Is that why you came into the forest, Ju-Long? To kill us?"

Ju-Long didn't answer. Sing shook his head. "Your grandmother would be disappointed." Ju-Long tensed, but before he could reply, two forms erupted from the greenery on either side of them. Monsters, though not the same pair as before.

"Do you know these two?" Sing asked, not taking his eyes off of the disturbingly feminine creature stalking toward him. In the dark, with her grotesque features hidden, she might have almost passed for human.

"The one that's covered in growths is Creation Four," Ju-Long said, as he took a step toward Sing, until they were standing back to back. "The other is Creation Five."

"Are they aggressive, like the others?"

"They are animals," Ju-Long said. "They cannot think. They can only kill."

"Do they know what rifles are?"

"No."

Sing frowned, watching the creatures pace about. Neither had attacked, but he could read their body language easily enough. "They are keeping their distance. They must understand the threat, at least." His finger tightened on the trigger— then, abruptly, relaxed. His first instinct was to shoot. But he owed it to Miss Ginny to at least try another way. He took a deep breath and lowered his weapon. Ju-Long gave him a startled look.

"What are you doing?"

"Something foolish, I expect," Sing said, as he set his rifle on the ground and raised his hands. "I will do you no harm if you do me no harm," he called out. "We are friends, do you understand?"

"Friends?" the woman-thing rasped. "You are friends with Ju-Long?"

Sing hesitated. "I am." Seeing the way her bifurcated face contorted, he glanced at his grandson. "Did I say something wrong?"

"Unfortunately," Ju-Long muttered.

"Friend of Ju-Long," Creation Five growled, "We eat you as well!" With that, she bounded toward Sing, clawed fingers outstretched. Her compatriot did the same, rushing toward Ju-Long with a bellicose wail.

Sing ducked below her lunge, letting her form pass over

him to crash into Ju-Long, who was struggling with his own opponent. All three of them fell in a tangle, until Ju-Long managed to kick his way free and roll aside. Creation Five was on her feet before her companion, and she flung herself at Ju-Long, screeching like a wounded cat.

Instinctively, Sing jumped onto her back and wrapped an arm about her throat. Jamming a knee into her back, he dragged her off of her feet and sent her tumbling to the ground. As Creation Five fell, Sing spun and leaped, catlike, to drive a kick across the misshapen skull of Creation Four, knocking the beast sprawling.

"I had him," Ju-Long protested. Sing ignored him. Ju-Long raised his rifle, as if to finish off the dazed creatures, but Sing stopped him.

"No. Their actions are either instinct, or are guided by what they have been taught. Either way, they will react to violence with violence." He looked at his grandson. "Hate with hate." Ju-Long turned away.

"I do not have time for this. I have a task to complete."

"Which is?"

"What does it matter? It does not concern you."

Sing caught the younger man's arm and forced him around. "I say it does. What this man Arkwright has done here, it endangers us all. These creatures—"

"What creatures?" Ju-Long said, pointing.

Sing followed the gesture and saw that both monsters were gone; slithered away while their opponents were busy arguing. He grunted in frustration. "My point stands. These creatures should never have been created. But now that they exist, they must be dealt with."

"I was going to. You stopped me."

"Not that way," Sing said. "Kill them if they attack you, by all means. But they are no more to blame for this than Bulan or Miss Ginny . . ."

"Is this Bulan your new master, grandfather?" Ju-Long asked, with a sneer.

Sing turned, and something in his expression must have warned Ju-Long against further taunts, for the younger man took a step back. Sing took a deep breath and retrieved his rifle. At the very least, he could tell Miss Ginny that he tried. "The way you talk, it's as if you want me to be a servant or a slave. I am sorry to disappoint you, grandson, but I am neither. I live with Bulan and his father in a place called Ithaca, New York. But I do so as their guest. I am their friend, you see. And that is why I am here. Because they needed help, and so I came to help. Why are you here, Ju-Long?"

Ju-Long stared at him but did not reply. Perhaps he was wondering that himself. Sing shook his head and turned away. "It saddens me that you seem to hate these creatures so much, and yet you are so much like them. Miss Ginny believes that if they can be taught better, they might become something more than what they are. I do not know whether I believe her, but . . . I am willing to try." He started away, in the direction Bulan and the others had gone, but stopped and looked back at his grandson.

"And if they can change, perhaps you can as well. Remember that, Ju-Long."

29
HIGGS

HIGGS RAN LIKE ALL THE DEVILS OF HELL were on his heels. Maybe they were. What else to call such creatures, but devils? Only they hadn't come from Hell, had they? No, they'd come from Arkwright. Bloody Arkwright.

He panted and stumbled against a tree. He paused, listening for his pursuers as he caught his breath. He'd heard gunshots a few moments before, and wondered if Welles or Ju-Long had been dispatched to find him and the others. Maybe Baskin had made it back to the compound and told them what had happened. Maybe the creatures were already dead. Somehow, he doubted it.

"I wanted to know, I suppose," he muttered. Now he did. In a way, getting captured had been the best thing he could have hoped for. The Americans had spilled everything, probably hoping that he'd go back and cause trouble for Arkwright—which was his intention, more or less. Whatever Arkwright was up to, it wasn't cricket. Then, he'd already known that, hadn't he? Else he wouldn't have been assigned to keep an eye on the man. Someone, somewhere, knew that Arkwright was up to something. The question was, did they want to put a stop to it . . . or take advantage of it?

Higgs pushed the thought aside. His was not to reason why, to quote Tennyson. He stepped away from the tree, still listening for any sign of pursuit. Nothing from behind him. But something was up ahead, and coming closer. He drew his knife and took a tight grip on it. The blade had served him well enough last time. Whatever those things were, they could bleed, at least.

Thankfully, the knife proved to be unnecessary. A familiar face burst into view, panting and panicked. "Rogers," Higgs said, stepping forward. Rogers slid to a halt, and for a moment, Higgs thought the other man might shoot him.

"H—Higgs?" Rogers gasped. "You're not dead?"

Higgs sheathed his knife and tried for a grin. "Not for lack of trying. I'm all turned around, mate. Which way to home?"

Rogers shook his head. "We can't stop here. They'll get us!"

"Who, the Americans? They let me go." But even as he said the words, Higgs knew that Rogers wasn't talking about them. Not with the fear he saw on the other man's face. "You're not talking about them, though, are you?"

Rogers gave a high, stuttery laugh. "There's monsters out here, Higgs! Real ones! The stories we heard in Singapore were true!"

Higgs nodded. "I know, lad. Had a run with them myself, innit? Three, in fact. Showed them some good Sheffield steel and they buggered off right quick." He patted his knife, and hoped his bravado would serve to calm Rogers some. The other man was no use to him in this state.

Rogers shook his head, not really listening. "They're not human, Sergeant. They—they killed Benchley and the others!" He looked around wildly. "The forest is—is full of them. They're all around us!"

"Which is why we need to get back to the compound, right?" Higgs grabbed Rogers by the front of his uniform. "You and me, we need to talk to the lieutenant, don't we? Because I think he knows more than he's telling about all of this."

"He—the lieutenant—he told Welles not to come looking for you," Rogers said, hesitantly. "Do you—do you think he knew about those things?"

Higgs grinned mirthlessly. "Lad, if half of what that Virginia lass told me is true, he knows. Moreover, he might have made

the things—him and that withered old prune, Vogel." He had
no idea what he was going to do when he got back to the
compound. Mutiny was always an option, but for that, he'd
need to make sure Rogers and the others were on his side.

"Virginia," a deep, unpleasant voice growled, startling both
he and Rogers. Higgs turned to see the blue-skinned creature
he'd faced earlier standing entirely too close for his liking. The
damn thing was as quiet as a cat. "Where is she?"

Rogers made a high-pitched yelping sound and swung his
rifle up, but Higgs shoved the barrel aside before he could
fire. "Save the shot, lad. This one's a talker." Higgs stepped
past the soldier, to face the creature. It was one of the most
nerve-racking things he'd ever done, and every instinct he
possessed was screaming at him to run—to get away from the
thing glowering at him. Instead, he cleared his throat and
said, "Last I saw, she was in the old compound. The one I was
leaving when you tried to feed me to your chums."

The monster grunted, and Higgs suddenly wondered
whether the creature could tell them apart. Maybe they all
looked alike in their uniforms. Rogers spoke up, almost absently, "No, no, the Americans left the compound. They were
heading for the beach—they were attacked by—by monsters,
like you. They—they attacked us too." Higgs glanced at the
soldier. Rogers' voice was strained; he was on the edge of
breaking. "I—I ran."

"But she is alive," the monster growled, as he took a step
toward them. Higgs tensed. They'd only get one shot, if the
creature decided to charge.

"Sounds like it to me," he said, not taking his eyes off of
the creature. "Where'd you last see them, Rogers?"

Rogers hesitated, and then gestured back the way he'd
come. An instant later, the creature was gone. Higgs looked
at Rogers. "We need to get back to the compound. *Now*.
There's things the lieutenant needs to know." And, Higgs
thought, to see how much Arkwright already knew.

They moved as quickly as they could in the dark.

Higgs could hear intermittent gunfire from the direction of the shore. Someone was still alive out there. Maybe the Americans, maybe Welles. Were they fighting monsters, or someone else? Maybe the Dayaks had finally decided to have another go at the compound.

Higgs wasn't especially worried about any of that. He was more concerned about Arkwright. As far as he could tell, something had gone very wrong. Arkwright and his pet German had unleashed something hellish, and now they were all going to pay—unless Higgs could think of a plan.

The supply ship wasn't due for a few days. That meant no way off the island, unless they could commandeer the Americans' boat. But from the sound of it, the Americans might already be gone. In their shoes, Higgs certainly would be. So that left the compound, where Arkwright was bound to want to debrief him. There were two ways that could go. No way to tell which it would be, not until it was too late.

Higgs glanced at Rogers. The soldier was terrified half out of his wits. Most men would be, he figured. What would the others think, once Rogers got finished blathering about it? Arkwright would be lucky if he was still in charge by morning. Higgs thought he could use that for leverage, to keep his skin intact if nothing else.

But that meant making sure nobody caused a panic. He stopped and caught hold of Rogers. "Hold up. We need to have a chat."

Rogers looked at him wild-eyed. "We have to hurry—we can't—"

Higgs dragged him close. It would be safer to kill the other man, and it wouldn't have been the first time. But once that particular bell was rung, you couldn't take it back. And he might well have need of all the soldiers he could lay hands on before the night was out. "You say nothing about this when we get back, right? Mum's the word, innit? No screaming about monsters. Not until I say."

Rogers hesitated. "What—why?"

Higgs smiled. "Because I say so, there's a good lad." He patted Rogers' cheek. "Glad you understand. Now, off we go."

Another ten minutes stumbling along a moonlit path brought them back to the familiar clearing. There were men on the walls, watching the forest. Shouts greeted Higgs and Rogers as they stepped out into the open, and the gates began to open immediately. Worried faces surrounded them, and questions peppered the air—only to be silenced by the appearance of Lieutenant Arkwright.

Arkwright looked them up and down. He didn't look worried or even concerned. He looked as if he were contemplating the weather. "Rogers, you went with Welles. And Higgs . . . whom Welles went in search of. Where are the others?"

"The monsters," Rogers began, but Higgs silenced him with a look. Arkwright caught the gesture and frowned.

"What is it?"

"Perhaps we had best discuss it in private, sir," Higgs said, smoothly. "No need to get the lads all excited. Rogers, why don't you go have a sit and a ciggie, eh? Steady the nerves, innit? And keep your yap shut until I tell you different." He patted Rogers firmly on the arm and sent him on his way, before turning back to Arkwright. The lieutenant had a bemused expression on his face. He gestured to his offices.

"After you, Sergeant."

"Obliged, sir," Higgs said. The spot between his shoulder blades itched, and he wondered whether Arkwright was the sort to shoot him out of hand. He didn't think so, but he'd been wrong before.

When they were safely inside and away from any eavesdroppers, Arkwright said, "You'll pardon my rudeness, but I had hoped you were dead."

Higgs laughed. "And why might that be, sir? Surely I have not caused any offense."

Arkwright perched on the edge of his desk, and then drew his sidearm and set it down beside him. Higgs gave it barely a glance. "It is not so much what you have done, as what you are. Who do you work for, Higgs?"

Higgs considered bluffing, but it had always only been a matter of time until Arkwright sussed him out. Still, there was opportunity here. He reached into his jacket pocket and got out his cigarettes. "Same people you do, sir."

"I do not think so," Arkwright said.

Higgs selected a cigarette and tapped it on the crumpled pack. "Oh, I beg to differ sir—respectfully so, of course. I expect some of the same people paying for this expedition are the very ones who sent me to keep an eye on things."

"So you are a spy," Arkwright said. He set his revolver on his lap, the barrel pointed vaguely toward Higgs. But not aimed at him, not quite yet.

Higgs struck a match and lit his cigarette. "And you are a bloody alchemist."

Arkwright gave a bark of laughter. "That would be Professor Vogel, actually. I am more in the way of a gifted amateur, if we're being honest." He seemed tired to Higgs. Exhausted. Stress had a way of aging a man.

Higgs nodded, his eyes on the steel door set into the far wall. He'd always been curious about that door. "Was that where they were, then?" he asked, indicating it with his cigarette. "Is that why you had the foundations dug so deep?"

Arkwright was silent for a moment. "How much do you know?"

Higgs took in a lungful of smoke and released it into the air over his head. He was confident now that Arkwright wasn't planning to shoot him. At least not immediately. "Depends on how much you want to tell me," he said.

Arkwright smiled. "So, nothing, then. I thought as much."

Higgs grinned. "I know that nearly a year ago you paid a visit to a man named Maxon, currently in an American institution. I know that this same Maxon used to own that compound on the other side of the island. And I know that he got up to something nasty while he was here—and that you're doing the same. The question is, where you successful, or not?"

Arkwright was no longer smiling. He lit a cigarette of his own. "In a sense." As he spoke, he made a curious gesture. It was too intentional to be offhand, but when Higgs didn't respond, he relaxed somewhat.

Higgs frowned. A hand signal of some sort? He knew certain groups who used such things. Just who was Arkwright working for? He pushed the thought aside to concentrate on the matter at hand. "I'll take that as a yes. They're out there. I seen them. Nearly got eaten."

"A pity you didn't."

Higgs chuckled. "You would say that, I suppose. Still, I did not and thus we have a problem, do we not?"

Arkwright raised his pistol. "Not that I can see."

Higgs didn't flinch. This was a test, and one he'd passed before. He blew a plume of smoke into the air. "Now, is that any way to treat the only man who can get you out of this, body and soul intact?"

Arkwright hesitated; he lowered the pistol. Higgs smiled. "Now then, sir, you and I have much to discuss, I think."

30
PRISONERS

THE YOUNG DAYAK MARCHED VIRGINIA through the forest at sword-point. Despite his injury, he moved quickly and she had no opportunity to break away from him. She tried to talk to him, to make him see sense. When that failed, she decided to ask questions. "What do you plan to do with me?" she asked.

"Muda Saffir will decide," Tijilik said, in his broken English. "Keep moving." He gestured with his niabor for emphasis. Virginia shook her head, but kept walking. It wasn't the first time she'd been captured by Dayaks. They weren't the most considerate of hosts. Saffir probably wanted to question her about her father's supposed treasure. That it didn't exist was no impediment. The more she denied it, the more he believed she was hiding something. Saffir was as obsessed in his own way as her father had been.

"I was telling the truth back there," she said. "There is no treasure."

"There had best be, for your sake," Tijilik retorted. "Now be quiet."

"Or what?" She stopped and turned. "You can't kill me. And you can't drag me, not with that busted up arm. How did that happen, by the way?" She only needed a moment; an instant's inattention to break away and put some distance between them. Bulan was sure to be on their trail. She wouldn't allow herself to consider otherwise.

"Quiet," Tijilik snapped, bringing the tip of his blade up

194

to a point just below her nose. "Or I will take your head, and suffer the consequences."

"You will not, Tijilik," a new voice called out, startling them both. Tijilik lowered his sword as more Dayaks stepped out into the open. They'd appeared so noiselessly they might as well have been ghosts. Virginia spied an old man huddled among them; a white man. The speaker stepped into the open. He was older than the warriors around him, and heavily scarred. A chieftain, perhaps, but the one in charge, whatever his title. "She can join this one," he continued, indicating the old man. "I will take them both to Saffir."

"No," Tijilik said, firmly. "She is my captive, Riwut."

Riwut smiled. "So you go with us, then. Where are the others?"

Tijilik grimaced. "Dead."

Riwut's smile faded. "The British?"

"Yes—but not them alone." Tijilik shook his head. "I warned you. There are monsters in the forest. And they are hungry."

Riwut glanced at the old man. Virginia did so as well, wondering who he was. The old man met her gaze and adjusted his spectacles. Riwut grunted. "Monsters. Fine. We take these two back to Saffir and then we will hunt the monsters."

The old man cleared his throat. "If you harm them, I will not tell you where the treasure is," he said. His English was good, but his accent was strong. German. Virginia frowned. Was this the man who'd taught Otto to speak? What had Higgs called him—Vogel?

Riwut sucked his teeth like a man on the verge of fury. "You do not make demands, old man. I cannot take your head, but I can certainly take your legs."

"The monsters are not your enemy," Vogel continued, still looking at Virginia. "The British—they are the danger. Muda Saffir will agree."

"Muda Saffir is not here," Riwut snarled. A ripple went through the other Dayaks. Virginia knew from experience that Saffir's hold on them was likely tenuous. What was the old man playing at?

"No, but he would agree even so." Vogel patted the satchel he held, his gaze fixed on Virginia. "With what is in this satchel, I can make Muda Saffir the most powerful man in these waters. But if you harm me, or them—or Miss Maxon—he will get nothing. Is that a risk you are willing to take?"

Virginia blinked. The old man knew her name, knew who she was. He was trying to tell her something—but what? Then, all at once, she knew what he must have in the satchel. Vogel nodded surreptitiously as he caught her look of realization. "You will take me to Muda Saffir, and I will tell him what I want, in return for my knowledge," he continued, loudly. Every Dayak was looking at him now, even Tijilik.

"What about the treasure?" Tijilik demanded.

"That too," Vogel said, smoothly. This set the Dayaks into an uproar, and Virginia seized her moment. With them distracted, she took off running into the forest. Shouts erupted behind her, but she neither stopped nor slowed. They wouldn't kill her, she thought. Muda Saffir wanted that pleasure for himself. But she needed to put some distance between herself and them; Bulan and the others needed to know what she'd learned.

She wove between the trees, trying to retrace the route Tijilik had brought them. But in the dark, it was almost impossible. She had some moonlight to see by, but not much. Not enough. She could hear someone in pursuit behind her. Tijilik, maybe. Or one of the others. She slowed and hid herself behind a tree, shaggy with growth. Panting, she waited and listened. Her pursuers closed in—ran past. The forest fell silent.

Virginia waited.

Then, the soft crunch of a footstep. They hadn't run past after all. They were waiting for her to show herself. They knew she was close. She wondered if she could outlast them.

She never got the chance. Something large and brown,

with entirely too many legs, dropped onto her shoulder and began to crawl down on her chest. She forced herself to remain silent and calm, though it took every iota of self-control to do so. The arachnid paused, as if considering its options.

A long shape shot down and caught it. An arm—a hand—closed about the spider and crushed it. Then it rose, and her gaze rose with it. Something vaguely human-shaped crouched in the branches above. It gulped down the mangled remnants of the spider with every sign of enjoyment. Instinct took over then. She shoved herself away from the tree and leaped out of reach of the monster.

In doing so, however, she put herself into full view of her pursuer. Only one, thankfully. Tijilik. He grinned at her. "I knew you were here," he said. "I told the others to go ahead, just in case. But I knew you were here. I will drag you back—by your hair, if I must."

Keeping one eye on the branches where she'd seen the monster, Virginia rose slowly to her feet, grabbing a handful of mud from the ground as she did so. Tijilik had his niabor in his good hand, and he was matching her movements, obviously ready to intercept her if she tried to dart past. He crept closer, clearly under the assumption that he had her.

"You'll have to catch me first," she said. With that, she flung the mud full into Tijilik's face, blinding him. Tijilik cried out and swung his niabor, but Virginia ducked and the blade sank into the wet bark of the tree. Virginia lunged and shoved Tijilik over, knocking him off of his feet. As he scrambled up, clawing at his eyes, she wrenched his sword from the tree and extended it. "Go," she said. Tijilik froze. "Go," she repeated.

Tijilik reached slowly for the knife at his hip. "Riwut is a fool. And Saffir too. I will take your head, woman, and be well pleased." He bared his teeth at her, and she knew he was going to make the attempt. Her old fencing lessons came back and she stamped forward, the niabor lashing out. Startled, Tijilik leaped back. Virginia pressed her advantage. It wouldn't last long. When the other two returned, she would be out-numbered and overcome.

She steeled herself and concentrated on Tijilik. He was retreating now, his expression wary. Overhead, something heavy scuttled along the branches. Tijilik's attention was drawn upward, just for a moment. It was enough. Virginia swung the niabor out in a sharp arc. The impact of the blow nearly shook the blade from her hand. Tijilik stared at her, incredulous. Then his eyes rolled up in his head and he collapsed like a puppet with his strings cut.

Virginia stepped back, leaving the sword where it jutted from his neck. Her stomach churned and she turned away, fighting the urge to vomit. She looked up. The monster stared down at her, beady eyes glittering with what she took to be curiosity—or hunger. It began to creep down, its eyes never leaving her as it descended. It—he?—was only vaguely human-shaped; he reminded her more of some great insect, or even a reptile.

"Easy," she said, softly. "Easy, fellow. I mean you no harm." She spread her hands and tried to sidle away. The monster watched her, but every few moments, he cut his gaze toward the dead Dayak. He *was* hungry. The thought made her stomach squirm, but she stepped back, hands out. "Eat up, if you like. You'll get no argument from me."

The creature crept toward the body on all fours, keeping a wary eye on her as he did so. She wondered if he could walk upright. "What's your name then?" she asked, doing her best to keep her voice level and soothing. "Do you have one? A name, I mean."

The monster made a curious clicking sound, like some sort of giant cockroach. He caught hold of Tijilik's body and dragged it close, sniffing at it. Suddenly, the creature stiffened. He gave a bestial squawk and vanished into the undergrowth, leaving Virginia alone. She heard the sound of running foot-steps and turned to see Bulan burst into the open, followed by the soldier, Welles, and Esmail.

"Virginia!" Bulan cried, as she threw herself into his arms. "Are you okay?"

"Better now that you're here," Virginia said, with relief. She pointed to the undergrowth where the monster had vanished. "One of Arkwright's monsters is here as well. He went that way."

"I'll get him, miss," Welles began. Bulan caught his arm.

"No, Welles," he said, firmly. "Leave it. Those poor creatures are as much victims of circumstance as we are. As such, I don't intend to see them hurt, not unless we have no other options." Virginia could see that Welles wanted to argue, but remarkably, the soldier held his tongue. Bulan looked at him for a moment longer, then turned back to Virginia. "What happened, Virginia?"

"The Dayaks," Virginia said. "I saw more of them, heading toward the beach. They had a prisoner with them." She looked at Welles. "An old man. German."

"Vogel," Welles said, startled. "What's he doing out here?"

Bulan looked down at Virginia. She could read the worry on his face. "I don't know," he said. "But something tells me we need to find out, and quick."

"I might be able to help with that," Virginia said. "I don't know whether he was a prisoner, but he was definitely carrying something. A satchel. I think—I know—that it contained my father's notes on the creation of life." She bent down and retrieved the niabor from Tijilik's body, wincing a little as she pulled the weapon free of his neck. She watched the blood roll down the blade, and looked at Bulan.

"Muda Saffir doesn't know it, but I fear he now possesses a treasure far beyond anything he could ever imagine. And unless we act quickly, we're all in trouble."

31
ALLIANCES

T HE BEACH WAS QUIET, save for the crackling of the flames that steadily consumed the American's yacht. Muda Saffir watched the vessel burn with mild satisfaction. They'd stripped everything of value from it; burning it was, admittedly, an act of spite. But what was life without the small pleasures?

He'd sent several groups of Dayaks into the forest to hunt for Virginia Maxon and her friends, but so far none had returned. She was a wily one, that woman. Clever and dangerous. Under other circumstances, he might well have made a wife of her—but no doubt she would have made him regret such soft-headedness. Some women were wives; some were courtesans . . . and some were too dangerous to be let loose in the bedchamber. Virginia Maxon was of the latter group. No. Better that she died, but he would do her the honor of killing her himself. If that did not show his respect, he did not know what would.

A cry of warning rose up from the men he'd posted near the forest's edge. Riwut had returned. Saffir's second-in-command trotted across the beach to meet him. "We have a prisoner," he said.

"The woman?" Saffir asked, eagerly.

Riwut hesitated. "No. She . . . escaped."

Saffir growled wordlessly. He was annoyed, but not surprised. Maxon was clever. But she could not run forever.

And with her vessel currently burning to the waterline, there was nowhere for her to go. "Then who?"

"An old man."

"An old . . ." Saffir paused. "The German Tijilik spoke of?"

Riwut nodded. "The very same. He practically wandered into our hands."

Saffir laughed. "Well, by all means, show him to me. I find myself in need of some entertainment this evening!" Riwut hurried off to have their captive brought before him. Saffir waited impatiently, his gaze on the burning yacht. When he heard Riwut behind him, he turned back with a theatrical flourish.

The old man was pinned between two of the larger Dayaks. He looked small and frail next to his captors, but there was something iron in his expression. Old he might be, but he was no doddering ancient, to be intimidated by strength and aggression.

"You wished to meet me, then? Well, here I am." Muda Saffir stepped forward, arms wide in greeting. "Am I all that you hoped, old man?"

The old man frowned at him, and Saffir felt a sudden thrill of uncertainty. His guest did not seem impressed at all, or even the least bit worried. To cover his sudden hesitation, he gestured for his men to release their captive. "Let him go. What threat is he, eh? One withered ancient against men such as ourselves—ha!"

Saffir circled his captive. "What is your name, then? What should I call you?"

"My name is Vogel," the old man said.

"German," Saffir said.

"Yes."

"A spy?"

Vogel frowned. "I am a scientist."

Saffir grunted. "Like Maxon," he said. Vogel's eyes widened slightly.

"You know Professor Maxon?"

"Not well," Saffir said, carelessly. He glanced at the satchel in the other man's hand and snatched it away before Vogel could react. "What is this, then? Not the treasure you promised me, I think. Maybe it is a map, eh?" He turned away from Vogel, and peered at the papers within the satchel. "No, not a map." He tossed the bag to Riwut and turned back to Vogel. "Perhaps I should let my Dayaks take your head."

"Perhaps you should stop blustering and listen to me," Vogel said, unperturbed. Saffir almost gave the order to kill the old man then and there, but something in Vogel's tone gave him pause. He made a curt gesture.

"By all means, speak your piece."

"You seek treasure, yes? Gold, jewels—a king's ransom, yes?"

"Yes."

Vogel smiled. "Then you will be disappointed, I think. No such treasure exists."

Suddenly all too aware of the weight of his men's attention, Saffir laughed forcefully. "You lie. Why else would the British come, if there were not something valuable to be had?" He turned, looking at Riwut and the others. "Tell me that, eh?"

Vogel's smile didn't waver. "I did not say that there was nothing of value. Merely that it was not what you imagined. You say you knew Maxon. Do you know what he did?"

Saffir paused. "He made monsters. You have made them as well, I think."

"Yes. And I could make more with the notes in that bag your man holds." Vogel gestured to Riwut. "With those notes and the tools in the compound, I could make many monsters. For you."

Saffir snorted. He'd had similar ideas himself, earlier. But it was no longer as tempting as it had been. While an army of monsters might seem to be a good idea on the face of it, the truth was it would attract too much attention—and the wrong sort, at that. "A tempting thought, but I have enough trouble with my Dayaks."

Vogel shrugged. "Then you could sell those notes. You could name your price, to the right buyer. I would be happy to broker such a deal, if you like."

"You cannot trust him, Rajah," Riwut said, in a low voice. "At best, he is a madman. At worst—a sorcerer." Vogel stiffened at the accusation, but said nothing.

"A scientist," Saffir corrected, absently, as he studied Vogel. Saffir considered himself a good judge of character, and the old man struck him as being honest, if not entirely open. He was concealing something—but what? Riwut gestured dismissively.

"Whatever the word, he is dangerous. Let us kill him and leave this island. Let the British and the monsters kill one another."

"And what of what he promises, eh? Imagine how much certain parties might pay for the knowledge in his bald head." Saffir tapped the side of his skull for emphasis. "We could be rich men, Riwut."

"And what might it cost us?" Riwut shot Vogel a suspicious look. "What does he want in return for this valuable knowledge?"

"Let us ask him," Saffir said, with a clap of his hands. "Well? What is it you want, old man? I will spare you, if you like. A cut of the profits, perhaps?"

"I want to go to Singapore. With . . . my son."

Saffir heard the hesitation in his voice, and wondered what it meant. "Safe passage, eh? Fine." A thought occurred to him: if they intended to sell Maxon's work, they would need proof of its viability. A monster of their own. Just one. He looked at Vogel. "How many of them did you create, old man?"

"Eight," Vogel said.

"And how many survive?"

Vogel shook his head. "I do not know."

"We will need one of them. As proof that these notes are worth anything."

"It would be simpler to create a new one," Vogel said, after a moment. "The others will not return willingly to captivity."

"The big one seemed quite placid," Saffir said and smiled as Vogel flinched. *Ah,* he thought. *That's what you were hiding, eh?* "Why didn't you bring him with you? It would have simplified matters."

"I did not create him," Vogel said, flatly.

Saffir paused. "Maxon," he said. Vogel nodded.

"Yes. He is the last of Maxon's creations." Then, quickly, he added, "I can create more. As many as you like. But he is not part of this. Do you understand?"

"I do, but do you understand—where you are, and into whose power you have put yourself? I am Rajah Muda Saffir, old man. These waters are mine and all within them, my property, to do with as I see fit." Saffir smiled at Vogel and waved his own words aside. "But never mind. You tell me it is easier to make more—fine. Let us go. You will make more."

"I require certain equipment," Vogel said. "It is in the British compound."

"Can you not use other equipment?" Saffir inquired, in a level tone. He was beginning to see it now. Vogel wanted him to attack the British for some reason.

Vogel shook his head. "No, sadly. To even attempt to recreate it would require a fortune—which I do not possess. I do not suppose you do either."

Saffir laughed. "I have possessed many fortunes in my time."

"But at the moment . . . ?"

Saffir tugged on his beard and leaned forward. He was beginning to like the old man, despite himself. He didn't trust him, however. Like himself, the old man was an opportunist. Saffir respected that, but knew it only led to trouble, as it had with Von Horn. "I see no way of acquiring this equipment, short of the British handing it over. Which I do not see them doing. So we are back to you being of no use to me at all."

Riwut scratched his cheek. "We should kill him. We can find a buyer for these . . . scribblings without him." He shook the satchel for emphasis. Saffir considered it, but only for a moment.

"How many men do the British have?"

Vogel hesitated. Then, "Thirty."

Saffir looked at Riwut. "Half our number."

"They have guns and walls," Riwut said.

Vogel cleared his throat. "Arkwright has dispatched patrols across the island, to kill the monsters. The compound is lightly defended at the moment."

Saffir grinned and thumped his fist into his palm. "Ha! You see, Riwut. Fate has once again bent to my will. Truly, I am fortune's favored son. Very well. We will take the compound and slay everyone we find." He paused. "Except for Virginia Maxon. I want her alive." He smiled.

"There is an old matter to be settled between us."

32
MONSTERS

BULAN AND THE OTHERS carefully made their way back toward the coast. Welles took the lead. "Straight this way is direct north," he said, glancing back at Bulan. "If we miss the compound, we'll still find the beach. And from there I know my way back inland."

"Given what happened last time, I don't expect we'll receive much in the way of a warm welcome," Virginia said doubtfully. Bulan rubbed the back of his neck.

"Maybe. But we don't have much choice. We can't go back to the old compound—there's no way to secure it. Not against Dayaks."

"Perhaps we should try for the yacht," Esmail said, hesitantly. The young Lascar had spoken little since Kazin's death. Bulan suspected he was in shock. "Maybe we could sneak aboard . . ."

"There's no way," Bulan said. "I'd be surprised if Muda Saffir hasn't burned it to the waterline by now, as bad as he hates us." He felt a wave of guilt as he watched the Lascar deflate. Esmail hadn't signed on for any of this. Nor had Kazin and the others. Now they were dead. Just like Von Horn and Number Twelve and all the rest.

Bulan turned away and tried to wrestle the guilt back into its cage, in the underside of his mind. He hadn't intended for any of this to happen, but it had regardless. There was nothing for it now but to duck their heads and keep moving forward. At some point, they'd reach the end zone and that'd be the game. Or so he told himself. He was coming to realize that football metaphors could only carry a guy so far.

Virginia touched his arm. "Are you all right?" she asked, softly. "You have that look on your face again."

"What look is that?"

"The look that says you're wondering what we're going to do now."

"I admit, it's been on my mind," Bulan said, forcing a smile. Virginia nodded

"Mine as well. How many of them do you think there are?"

"The Dayaks? Or . . . ?"

"You know who I mean."

Bulan swallowed. "I can't imagine there are many. A handful at best. Otherwise Welles and the other soldiers would know all about them." He paused, considering the idea. Then, "Welles . . . can you think of where Arkwright might have kept those creatures?"

Welles glanced back at them. "I've been thinking about that myself, if I'm being honest. The only place that comes to mind is the subcellar under the main building in the compound. Arkwright had it dug out and reinforced. He told us it was a secondary armory . . . but it could just as easily have been a prison for those monsters."

"What reason did he give for you being out here in the first place?" Bulan asked, wondering how Arkwright could have hidden what he was doing. Welles laughed.

"Never been in the army, have you? Not big on explanations, your average superior officer. Do as thou art told, and that shall be the whole of the law." Welles shook his head. "The truth is, I knew something was rotten from the moment we got to Singapore. I just didn't know what it was that I was smelling. If I had known . . ." He stopped abruptly, his rifle up and aimed at the trees that loomed before them. "Listen. Hear that?"

Bulan did. Someone was running toward them through the forest. He tensed, ready to meet whatever new threat revealed itself. Esmail knelt, his rifle to his shoulder; Virginia lifted the niabor she'd taken from her captor.

"Miss Ginny! Is that you?"

Bulan felt relief wash over him. Virginia stepped forward. "Sing! Over here."

Sing appeared a moment later, moving with sure-footed speed despite the darkness. "Miss Ginny! Thank heaven you have been found." The hulking form of Ju-Long followed the old man, moving more slowly but no less surely. Bulan met the latter's gaze and, after a moment's hesitation, nodded. Ju-Long responded in kind.

"Thanks to Bulan and the others," Virginia responded. "We were just discussing our next move. And how many of those creatures might be waiting on us out here."

"Eight," Ju-Long said. "There are eight of them. And one other."

"Otto," Bulan said.

Welles looked at him. "That's the big blue one that came to your rescue earlier this evening, I'm guessing." He frowned. "Eight of the damn things. And you knew all about this, didn't you, Ju-Long?"

Ju-Long looked away. "I knew." He didn't sound so much regretful as annoyed, in Bulan's opinion. He looked at Sing, but the old man's expression was unreadable.

Welles took a step toward the other man. "Why were you out here, anyway? Not to look for me and the others, I think."

"Arkwright sent me after Vogel," Ju-Long said. "But I have seen no sign of him."

"I think I can help you there," Virginia said. "The Dayaks have him. He was carrying a satchel." She paused. "He was carrying it as if whatever was in there was valuable."

"The research notes," Ju-Long said, after a moment. "Maxon's notes. He took them with him. Probably hoping to sell them."

"How did he get my father's notes in the first place?" Virginia asked.

"Von Horn," Sing interjected. "He sold copies to this German, who in turn used them to ingratiate himself with Arkwright."

Virginia turned to the old man. "How do you know that, Sing?"

"Ju-Long told me." Sing glanced at Bulan. "You fought him, Mr. Harper, but Ju-Long can be trusted." Sing turned his gaze on Ju-Long. "Is that not so, Ju-Long?"

Ju-Long made as if to reply, and then turned and walked a short distance away. Bulan watched him for several moments, wondering what was going on in the other man's head. Welles joined him and said, in a low voice, "I don't know whether you consider your man a good judge of character or not, but if it were up to me, we'd leave Ju-Long tied to a tree somewhere."

Bulan stifled a laugh. "No love lost between you two?"

Welles hesitated. "Ju-Long is a mercenary. Arkwright is the one paying him, and if what you've told me is true, Arkwright is the cause of all this. That means my duty is clear—I have to put a stop to this. All of it." From the look on his face, he meant every word. Bulan nodded in agreement.

"We'll help, of course. I—*hsst!*" Bulan turned, listening. Ju-Long had tensed as well, his gaze sweeping across the nearby undergrowth. Esmail cried out, and Bulan spun to see something bulky emerge from the trees at a run. "Everyone back," he bellowed, as he moved to intercept the monster. He recognized it from earlier; the creature was covered in barnacle-like growths and had a simian gait, running on all fours and then on three limbs as it—he—closed the distance between them. Esmail raised his rifle, as did Welles, but Bulan flung up a hand. "No shooting! Not unless we have to."

The monster sprang at the last moment, and Bulan braced himself to meet his opponent's charge. The creature collided with him and nearly threw him from his feet. As he grappled with his attacker, he saw two more of the creatures emerge from the darkness. One darted toward Welles, while the other prowled after Virginia.

"Virginia, look out," he roared as he struggled to free himself from his opponent. Ju-Long had tackled the monster going for Welles, but Virginia was still in danger, with neither Sing, nor Esmail able to get a clear shot. But then a familiar figure dropped down from the shadowed reaches of the canopy above and crashed down atop the contorted, insect-like monster threatening Virginia.

Otto roared wordlessly and dragged the struggling beast into the air, hefting the creature over his head and hurling it into the one fighting Bulan. The two monsters fell to the ground in a squalling tangle. The third swatted Ju-Long aside and charged toward Otto, howling wildly. Otto met him head-on and threw him to the ground. By then, however, the other two had regained their feet and were bounding toward him as well. Bulan rushed to help Otto without a moment's hesitation, and to his surprise, he saw Ju-Long doing so as well. Together, the two of them managed to drag one of Otto's opponents away and they sent the beast stumbling back into a tree. The monster shook its barnacle-encrusted head and gave a low snarl as it started forward again—right for Bulan.

A rifle barked. The monster collapsed to the ground without a sound, and his companions fled into the forest, screeching. Esmail lowered his smoking rifle, his eyes wide. "I—I didn't mean to kill him," he said. "You said not to shoot, but he was heading right for you . . ." Sing patted the Lascar on the shoulder sympathetically.

"The others ran," Bulan began. He wondered if they could catch up to them . . . talk to them . . . but even as the thought occurred to him, he knew it was futile. Especially now.

"Not this one," Welles replied, aiming his weapon at Otto.

"Welles, put the damn rifle down," Virginia said, sharply. She stepped between Otto and the soldier. "Otto is no monster. He is our friend." She looked at Otto. "At least, I hope so. Are you our friend, Otto?"

Otto was silent for a moment, his yellow gaze resting on

Virginia's face in a way that made Bulan uneasy. Then, "Friend. My friends." He looked down at the monster Esmail had killed. He sank to his haunches beside the limp carcass and studied it. "What was this one called?" he asked, in a soft rumble.

Ju-Long crouched beside the body. "Creation Six," he said. "That leaves eight of them, counting our friend here." He indicated Otto.

"Seven," Otto said, solemnly. "I killed Creation One." Bulan could hear regret in Otto's voice—and a profound sadness. He knew that sadness well, for he'd felt it himself.

"And one of them killed one of his pals," Bulan said. "One with three arms. He smashed one that looked like a bat. Hit the poor brute until his head cracked open."

"Creation Eight and Creation Three," Ju-Long said. "Creation Eight is the cleverest of them, and the most dangerous. Creation Three often challenged Eight. It is not surprising that it ended that way. If we spy Eight, we must not hesitate. The others might listen to reason, though I find it doubtful. But Eight will not." He looked at Otto, and then away. "I warned Arkwright about them. He didn't listen. He thought he could control them—control Vogel. He's a fool. I wish I had seen it earlier."

"Vogel . . . you mean to say this Vogel freed them?" Bulan said. "Why?"

Ju-Long rose slowly to his feet. "A distraction, possibly. But I suspect that it had more to do with the fact that Arkwright intended to kill them. Vogel is too soft on them. He views them as children. Thinks a stern look is enough to keep their jaws from his throat."

"Arkwright intended to—why?" Virginia asked, horrified.

Bulan stared down at the dead monster. "The same reason your father planned to do the same. They weren't controllable. Too wild, too fierce—too much like men, in other words." He ran a hand through his hair. He was tired. Every muscle ached. But there was no time to rest. No time for anything except finding shelter. "We have to go. We have to get to the compound and . . . I don't know. Fix things, somehow."

"Arkwright will kill you," Ju-Long said.

"So we make sure that doesn't happen," Welles said, firmly. "As of now, Arkwright is no longer in charge of this operation. I will be taking command as soon as we get to the compound." He looked at Ju-Long. "Anyone here have a problem with that?"

Ju-Long smiled. "None at all."

"Good." Welles looked at Bulan. "I hope I can count on your support. I have a feeling I might need it. And as for your friend Otto, I—hold on. Where is he?"

Bulan turned. Otto was gone, as swiftly as he'd appeared. He looked at Virginia. "I think Otto has his own plan in mind," she said.

"Maybe so," Bulan said. "But I don't think we should stick around to find out what it is. Let's go. Come on."

33

LEADERSHIP

CREATION EIGHT CROUCHED over the body of Creation Six, not quite able to process the sight before him. He had killed Three, so he knew that death could claim them as easily as anything else. Yet somehow, it did not seem real. Six was dead and One was dead. Three was dead. Only five of them left now.

Five, and the Other.

The Other disturbed his equilibrium. That he existed at all seemed so incongruous to Eight. If Arkwright had not created him, where had he come from? Why was he here? Why was he free, where they had been caged?

"A soldier killed him," Seven said, prodding Six's lumpy skull. "I saw it." He and Creation Two had been with Six when he died. They had fled, to find Eight and the others, and brought them back to where Six lay.

Eight nodded, but did not reply, still lost in thought. He rubbed absently at the injury in his shoulder. The bullet was still lodged somewhere within the meat of his tendons and he could feel it every time he moved. But the pain was good. Pain brought wisdom. Arkwright had taught them that. Pain was wisdom and love. Only through pain would they learn purpose. That was why they were here, why they were free.

"The Other killed One," Creation Two hissed softly. Then, as if trying to explain, "But only because One attacked the Kind One. One was stupid." They had found One's body in a clearing not far away; he had been hurled against a tree hard enough to snap his neck. Two claimed to have seen it, and privately Eight wondered if Two were pleased. One and Two did not like one another. Too close in temperament and behavior.

The others began to snap and snarl at one another over this. Two and Seven and Six had attacked the Other, only to be driven back. The Other was stronger than all of them, save Eight. Even together, they'd lacked the strength needed to bring him down. What if the Other was stronger than he himself? Moreover, what if the Other was also being tested?

The thought perturbed Eight. It had risen suddenly in him, and now he could not shake it loose. This, their freedom, was a test. A test of their faith, of their love. But what if it was also a test to see which of them was worthy of Arkwright's love? What if Vogel was right? What if Arkwright loved the Other more? Was that why he had no scars? Was that why he had not been in the cages? The Kind One had claimed otherwise, but the Kind One could not be trusted. Eight knew this in his gut. Only Arkwright could be trusted.

Except—where was Arkwright? If he had sent the soldiers to be eaten, why had one of them killed Six? Was that part of Arkwright's test, or simply an accident?

No. No, there were no accidents. Arkwright was God. God had decreed that they be free. That they eat—or be eaten. To eat and grow strong, and prove that strength to God. Eight clutched his head, trying to stem the growing ache. New thoughts wormed their way into his mind; it was as if a web were being woven within his consciousness, linking one occurrence to the next in a grand tapestry.

The more they ate, the stronger they would be. The more blood he gulped down, the more his thoughts seemed to burn and flicker, moving with a quickness that startled him. Did the others feel it as well?

He looked down at Six again, and felt a wash of sadness, edged in satisfaction. Six had failed the test. As had One—and Creation Three. All had failed, and in failing, been proven unworthy of life. To eat was to live and to live was to eat. To grow strong and wise on flesh and blood. That was Arkwright's law, served to them in a gospel of pain.

Arkwright wished them to be strong. So they must eat. They must prove that strength. They must, they must. Else they would be nothing more than meat.

Eight snarled and the other monsters fell silent. "What does it matter why the Other did it? That it has been done is enough. Three of us are dead; five are left." He looked at Four. "You say that the Other . . . helped the soldiers?" he growled.

Four nodded, somewhat reluctantly. "Yes. I do not know why."

"I do," Eight said, as he rose to his feet. "It is another test. We must kill the soldiers. Kill the Other. That is the way we prove ourselves to Arkwright." He took a deep breath, relishing the spike of pain that radiated from the bullet wound. "We must show that we are strong, so that Arkwright will love us. We must kill all of them. It is the only way." He paused. There had been a noise, deep out in the jungle. The sounds of stealthy movement. He gestured sharply, and the others quickly ascended into the trees, out of sight.

Eight waited until the last moment to join them. He did it to prove that he feared nothing, but also because he was curious. The sounds of those approaching were unlike any he'd heard before. They were not soldiers but something else.

They revealed themselves even as he concealed himself in the canopy above. They were men, but dressed in feathers and robes, rather than uniforms. They carried swords and shields and spears and moved with eerie silence through the gloom. There were so many of them that, at first, they seemed like nothing so much as a tide of flesh. He tried to count them, but soon ran out of fingers.

"Who are they?" Five trilled, as she stared down at the newcomers in wonder.

"Meat," Eight said. And they were. Men were meat, whatever their appearance. Even so, these were strange men.

They smelled of blood. He wondered where they were going. He crept a short way down the trunk of the tree he'd chosen to perch on, listening, trying to make sense of their language. Unfortunately, it made no sense to him—until he caught a snatch of a familiar voice and spied the small, shrunken form of Vogel hurrying along beneath the trees. Eight tensed, ears straining to catch whatever Vogel was saying.

Luckily, the newcomer's leader called a halt beneath the trees. He was a tall man, and clad in silks and gold. "Well, Professor," he began. As he spoke, he drummed his fingers against the pommel of the blade sheathed at his side. "We have seen neither hide nor hair of these monsters you say haunt the forest. I hope you are not a liar. I would hate to have to kill you." He smiled as he spoke, but Creation Eight thought he was not amused.

Vogel cleared his throat and adjusted his spectacles. "Would you come out of hiding at the sight of fifty armed Dayaks? No. They will come, but only after you take the compound. The smell of blood alone will be enough to draw them from hiding." He hesitated. "I expect that they will be hungry."

"And then we will take our pick of the litter."

Vogel nodded. "Yes, yes. But remember, Muda Saffir, Otto is not a part of this. I do not wish him harmed. Do with the others as you like, but Otto is mine, yes?"

Muda Saffir gestured dismissively. "Of course, of course. The blue one is yours. The rest are mine." He laughed sharply. "I hope they are smart enough at least to come quietly. I would hate to have to kill them."

"And Arkwright?" Vogel asked.

Saffir laughed again. "Him it will be a pleasure to kill."

Eight's claws dug into the bark of the tree. They intended to kill Arkwright—inconceivable. Impossible. And yet . . . intriguing. If Arkwright could die, was he a god? To Eight, the answer was obvious. Perhaps this was not simply their test, but Arkwright's as well. The group below began to move once more, and soon were lost to sight. Only a few stragglers remained behind. Three warriors, talking among themselves.

These, he thought, they would take. Eight dropped onto one, slamming the unfortunate Dayak to the ground with bone-breaking force. The man died without a sound, save that of his splintering bones. The remaining pair reacted swiftly, drawing weapons. But before they could attack, or cry out in alarm, Five, Seven, and the rest pounced on them. The Dayaks died swiftly, torn to pieces by the frenzied monsters.

Eight watched the slaughter in satisfaction. Arkwright would surely be pleased by their ferocity. They were worthy of his love. More worthy than the Other? For who had he killed? What flesh had he devoured? How had he proved his love?

The questions circled within Eight's mind, tormenting him. Why would Vogel love the Other, and not them? Why would Vogel kill Arkwright, to spare the Other? Would Arkwright kill to spare them? No. No, Eight did not think so. Arkwright's love took a different form.

"You make too much noise. They might have heard."

The words came from above. Eight stiffened and looked up. The Other crouched above them, perched on a thick branch. Seven and the others stopped savaging the dead and followed Eight's gaze. They growled and snarled at the sight of the intruder, especially those who had fought him. The Other did not appear perturbed by this show of aggression.

"You spy on us," Eight said.

"I was listening. Watching." The Other swung down out of the tree and landed in a graceful crouch, over the body of one of the dead men. "You were too loud. You did not wait long enough. The Dayaks would have lagged farther behind, had you waited. They are arrogant, and fearless, and that makes them easy prey."

"You have killed them before?" Eight asked.

The Other nodded. "I have eaten many of them." He paused. "I have been very hungry, in my time. You are hungry as well, and hunger makes you stupid." The Other—Otto—rose to his feet, dragging the dead Dayak with him. He examined the corpse for a moment, and then threw it at

Eight's feet. "There are our enemies," he said, slowly. "Soldiers and Dayaks both. If we work together, we might defeat them."

Eight bared his teeth. "I do not wish to defeat them. I wish to devour them."

"To do that, you will need help." Otto sank to his haunches. "My help. I will aid you in this, give you all the meat you would wish . . . in return, you will not harm the Kind One." He looked, not at Eight, but at the others. Eight hissed softly.

"We do not need you," he growled. He flexed his claws in warning. Otto, like Vogel, could not be trusted. "We should devour you. We will devour you."

Otto rose slowly to his feet. "You can try."

Eight hesitated. The others were watching him now, and he knew that they would follow his lead. Or perhaps not. Four and Two were both greedily eyeing the dead Dayaks. Five and Seven hesitated, as if uncertain. What would happen, in a fight? Would Otto flee, or prevail? And if the latter, what then?

Eight knew that his hold on the others was precarious. He was coming to realize that, outside of the cells, his authority shifted moment to moment, and largely depended on how full their bellies were. How soon before Seven or Five challenged him, as Three had? Would they be pleased to see him beaten and devoured by the Other? In their place, he might be.

He knew that he could beat the Other. Otto was weak; Vogel had made him weak. But what if he wasn't as weak as Eight thought? No. Best to leave it for now. There was always later. Decision made, Eight grunted. "How will you aid us?"

Otto relaxed slightly. "I know how to get into the compound without being seen."

"The hole?" Eight asked.

Otto shook his head. "There are other ways." He smiled. "Better ones."

34
SAFETY

WELLES LED BULAN AND THE OTHERS back through the forest to the British compound. They lost their way more than once, and Bulan expected the Dayaks to fall on them at any moment, but they made it without further incident. As the walls of the compound came into sight, Welles motioned for them to stop. Lights beamed down from the top of the palisade and swept across the tree line. In the reflected glare of the lights, Bulan glimpsed men moving back and forth along the top of the wall.

"Let me go first," Welles said. "I'd rather the lads not take a plink at you, if we can help it. They're bound to be jumpy—especially if Rogers made it back in one piece."

"You can hardly blame him," Bulan said, feeling some sympathy for the soldier. "It's no picnic for us, and we've seen them before. I can only imagine how he must have felt."

"He is a coward," Ju-Long said, flatly. He pushed past Welles and headed for the gate, despite the other man's protestations. Welles sighed and hurried after him. Bulan watched them for a moment and then motioned to get Sing's attention.

"You and Esmail keep an eye on them. Virginia and I will watch for Dayaks."

"You don't trust them?" Virginia asked.

"Welles is still a British soldier. He'll do what's in the interests of his men, if not his mission. I trust him to do what's right—but what's right for him, might not be for us." He pulled her close. "One way or another, I think this will

219

be over by sunrise," he continued, in a low voice. "What are you thinking?"

"In regard to Otto, you mean?"

He nodded. Virginia sighed and looked at the trees. "When you came here, you took control of my father's creations. You became their leader. Otto might be able to do the same."

"And what—lead them away?"

"Maybe. Maybe they'd be happier, in the forest. Away from us." Virginia leaned against him and he wrapped an arm around her. "But I think he's out there now, and so are they, and they're watching—and waiting."

"The blood will drive them into a frenzy," Bulan said, grimly. "I remember that all too well. They were always hungry, always on the verge of starvation."

"Their metabolic processes are enhanced," Virginia said, absently. "They need constant fuel, or they start to break down. Like a fire snuffing itself out once it's used up all the oxygen in a room. My father was frustrated by it; he was still trying to correct the flaw when everything happened. That's why he wasn't worried about them escaping. If misadventure didn't claim them, their own bodies would."

"Otto is still here," Bulan pointed out.

Virginia chuckled bitterly. "Otto isn't picky about what he eats."

Bulan caught her meaning and shuddered. After a moment, he said, "I dream about that sometimes, you know. About what I might have done, had you not—had I remained . . ." He trailed off. Virginia touched his chest.

"But you didn't, and you wouldn't have, even if you'd never remembered who you are. You're a good man. Some things amnesia can't blot away."

Sing whistled and Bulan turned. Ju-Long and Welles had reached the wall of the palisade. A rifle shot echoed through the clearing, but Ju-Long didn't flinch. "It is Ju-Long, open the gates," he bellowed. A light swept down, fixing on him. Ju-Long spread his arms and gestured impatiently.

Welles gestured for Bulan and the others to come forward as the gates were pushed open. Soldiers stepped out, both carrying rifles and lanterns. "S—Second Lieutenant Welles, sir . . . is—is that you?" one of them called out.

"Who else would it be, Rogers? Or did you think I was dead?" Welles advanced into the light and gave both soldiers a stern look. The one he'd addressed as Rogers visibly wilted.

"I—I didn't—sir, I—I . . ." He caught sight of Bulan. "It's them!" He made to raise his rifle, but Ju-Long snatched it from his hands and made a show of checking it over.

"They're with us, Rogers," Welles said. He looked at the other soldier, who was watching all of it wide-eyed. "You understand, Jones?"

Jones nodded. "As you say, sir. But—ah—Rogers said that you'd been eaten, like. By monsters. That's why we've got the lights, sir." He indicated the top of the palisade.

Rogers was pale. "The sergeant saw 'em, and—and I did too! Lieutenant Arkwright put us on alert, told us to keep watch for them." Bulan glanced at Virginia. It seemed Higgs had survived his trip through the forest as well. That could be very good for them, or very bad, depending on how Higgs felt.

"Is anyone else out there?" Welles asked.

"Lieutenant Arkwright sent out Poole and a few others to reconnoiter." Jones hesitated. "They haven't come back yet."

"Dayaks might have gotten them," Sing said, as they followed the soldiers inside. Bulan looked around. The damage from their previous visit had been largely cleared away, but it appeared as if only the most basic of repairs had been undertaken.

Jones frowned and looked at the old man. "Dayaks?"

Welles cursed softly. "Arkwright doesn't know about the Dayaks yet. He's never taken Muda Saffir seriously as a threat, and unless we're lucky, I have a feeling we're going to pay for it before morning."

"We need to find the lieutenant and warn him," Virginia said.

"Look no further," a voice called out, across the courtyard. Bulan turned and saw Arkwright striding unhurriedly toward them, Higgs at his side. The sergeant looked positively cheerful, and he smiled widely when he saw them. Bulan wondered whether he was hoping to get his own back. "I am here and most eager to hear your report, Welles. Are these your prisoners, then?" He looked Bulan and Virginia up and down, before turning his attention to Ju-Long, utterly ignoring Sing and Esmail. "And where have you been? I thought I sent you to look for Vogel."

"Muda Saffir has him," Ju-Long said.

Arkwright paused. "Ah. Well. How unfortunate. I expect his head is decorating the prow of a war-canoe by now." He seemed more annoyed than saddened, Bulan judged. As if Vogel's probable demise was a personal inconvenience rather than a tragedy.

"I assume you've sent out patrols. How many of them have reported back?" Welles asked, intently. For a moment, Bulan thought Arkwright might not answer.

"None," he said, after a moment.

"How many men are still here?"

"Enough to see off any threat," Arkwright said, blithely. Welles hesitated.

"Then we should see to the defenses, sir. I have no doubt the Dayaks are planning something—perhaps an assault."

"They've already tried that twice before," Arkwright said. "Why risk it again?"

"Because Muda Saffir is an opportunist," Virginia said. "If I were him, I would have been keeping an eye on your compound here, waiting for the right moment to launch an attack. While you're distracted with . . . other matters."

Arkwright looked at her sharply. "Hello again, Miss Maxon," he said. He lit a cigarette. "I should have realized that it was you before. Your father is a brilliant man."

Virginia lifted her chin. "My father is mad, Lieutenant. Whatever brilliance is in him, it is overshadowed by lunacy."

Arkwright tutted. "Harsh words. Then, given what little I know of what occurred on this island perhaps your feelings are justified." His cool gaze slid toward Bulan. "And that would make you Townsend Harper, Jr., . . . or do you prefer Bulan?"

Bulan crossed his arms. "Call me what you like, Lieutenant, so long as you explain why you're here—and what you have to do with those monsters running around out there."

Arkwright frowned slightly. "Forgive me, but I don't think you're in any position to demand answers, sir. I am the authority here."

Welles coughed delicately. "Strictly speaking, sir, I wouldn't mind knowing about that myself—especially given what I've seen tonight. Why did we come to this island? What did you do with that equipment we removed from the Maxon compound?"

"That is above your pay grade, Welles." Arkwright motioned to Ju-Long. "Take his sidearm, please. I fear it is time to relieve my subordinate of his duties, at least temporarily."

"No," Ju-Long said.

Arkwright frowned. "That was an order, Ju-Long."

Ju-Long crossed his arms. "I am tired of taking your orders, Lieutenant. You ignored me when I said the monsters should be killed, and now they are running mad across the island. Vogel is missing and Muda Saffir is on the hunt."

Arkwright nodded. "Fine. Rogers, Jones, take Ju-Long and Second Lieutenant Welles into custody please. And these others as well." Rogers and Jones looked at one another. Arkwright's frown deepened. "I do believe that I gave you gentlemen an order."

Bulan moved to the side, keeping one eye on the soldiers, and one on Arkwright. Their confrontation was drawing the attention of the men on the palisade. When neither Rogers nor Jones leaped to obey, Arkwright glanced at Higgs. "Sergeant?"

Higgs smiled and shook his head. "No, I don't think so, sir." Arkwright's expression tightened and his hand fell to his pistol, but before he could draw it, Higgs had snatched it from its holster and backed away to join Welles. "Now, now sir, no need for that. We're just having a bit of a palaver is all, innit?"

Arkwright stared at the sergeant for a moment, and then relaxed. "So, is that how it's to be, Sergeant?" he asked. "I thought better of you."

Higgs grinned. "Merely taking advantage of an opportunity when presented, sir." He glanced at Welles. "None of this is sanctioned, as far as I can tell. Our lieutenant is off the reservation, as the Yanks say. Well out of bounds, all this."

Bulan watched Arkwright's face as the spy spoke, trying to read it and failing. Arkwright was adept at concealing his feelings. He just looked bored.

Welles took a step forward. Bulan heard men approaching from all directions—soldiers alerted to their commander's predicament. If things weren't cooled off soon, there'd be bloodshed. He caught Virginia's eye and was glad to see she'd noticed the approaching soldiers as well.

"What have you been doing, Lieutenant?" Welles demanded. "I saw those creatures with my own eyes. Are you responsible for their creation?"

Arkwright blew a plume of smoke into the air. "In a literal sense, no. That would be Vogel. In a broader sense, yes, I suppose you could say that I am. All for the good of the nation, of course. I am sanctioned by conscience, if not duty."

"To create horrors," Welles said, in a tone of disgust.

"Weapons, old boy," Arkwright said, evenly. "Like the gas we used on Brother Boer—awful stuff, but damned effective." He looked at Virginia. "They're immune to it, you know. Gas, I mean. Most forms of poison as well, including arsenic and cyanide. Durable as all hell, your father's creations. Shame about their looks, but one can't have everything." He puffed on his cigarette and smiled. "War is coming. A big one, full of all the sound and fury that industrialized nations can manage. Even the most idiotic politician can see it. And we must be ready when it does come."

"They aren't weapons, they're people," Bulan said, in a low voice. Arkwright looked at him and his smile turned thin and sharp.

"I can see why you might think so. And I admit, they are intelligent—clever—but most assuredly dangerous. Too dangerous, at present. Hence my intention to hunt them down and put them out of their misery."

There were soldiers around them now, looking confused and worried. Bulan counted ten in all. Welles seemed to realize what was going on and turned his attention to the men, but before he could speak, Arkwright said, "Men, Second Lieutenant Welles and Sergeant Higgs have proven themselves to be disloyal to the Crown. Take their weapons from them and confine them to the stockade, please."

For a moment, all was still. Bulan could see the mental calculus running through the enlisted men's minds. From what Welles had let slip, Arkwright was not especially well liked. Would they yield to his command, or fall in line behind a more acceptable authority figure in the form of Welles? Bulan tensed, waiting to move.

Then, men began to sidle in behind Welles. Arkwright was perplexed at first. When he realized what was occurring, his face flushed and Bulan thought he might say something. Instead, he turned away. "I will be in my office. Welles, you're in charge."

Welles seemed startled, and looked at Bulan. Bulan gestured. "Well, you heard him. You're in charge. What's first?"

35

ATTACK

VOGEL HUNCHED UNHAPPILY in the damp. Rain dripped from the leaves overhead. Dayaks flitted through the trees around him, readying themselves for the battle to come. Nearby, Muda Saffir peered through a spyglass at the compound, muttering to Riwut. Vogel didn't bother to eavesdrop. He thought he could guess what they were saying. His gaze slid toward the bodies of the soldiers they'd caught nearby.

Arkwright had obviously sent out patrols to look for him. But the Dayaks had caught these men first, and slain them swiftly and silently. For all that he had been told that the headhunters were savages, he had not expected to ever see such a display of bloody efficiency. The Dayaks had fallen on the patrol like shadows, striking them down before they'd even realized they were under attack.

The unfortunate patrol had consisted of four men, all known to Vogel. All dead. Poole had been from Manchester, and had had an affinity for American dime novels. Hutton had been an inveterate gambler; Roud and Spence had been serial malingerers, always looking to do something other than their assigned duties. Now their heads dangled from a branch, and their bodies lay in a bloody heap. Their rifles had been claimed by a quartet of Dayaks, who even now were creeping closer to the compound, using the undergrowth as cover.

Saffir's plan was simple; the rifle-armed Dayaks would fire at the men on the walls in order to draw the soldiers out. When the gates opened, Saffir and his men would race forward

226

and enter the compound, while Riwut lead a sortie toward the gap in the palisade left by the fallen watchtower. Privately, Vogel doubted Arkwright would fall for it. The man was no fool. But Saffir had the devil's own luck.

Vogel swallowed and looked away from the dead. Condensation from the rain fogged his glasses and he removed them in a vain effort to wipe them clean. Saffir snapped his spyglass shut and crept back to join the old man. "It appears you were correct, my friend. There is a gap in the palisade. And there are not so many men on those walls as I feared. Something going on inside has them distracted."

"All to the good, then," Vogel said, examining his glasses. "The equipment is in the largest of the buildings. Arkwright will have the keys."

Saffir grinned. "Good. I look forward to killing him. His skull will make a fine decoration for my war-canoe." He paused. "You will remain here, until the deed is done."

"No." Vogel put his spectacles back on. "I will go with you. I cannot risk your men damaging the equipment amidst their plundering."

"Or maybe you wish to try and escape in the confusion, eh?" Saffir laughed and clapped a hand onto Vogel's narrow shoulder, nearly knocking him from his feet. "A man after my own heart. Have no fear. We will do great things together, you and I. We will both be rich men!" Though he sounded jolly, Vogel knew it was an act. Saffir intended to kill him as soon as he had what he wanted.

The Malay was not a man who looked farther than his next meal, and his schemes were fragile things, easily undone and forgotten. He intended to take what he could and vanish. Perhaps he would sell the monsters to some interested foreigner, or Malaysian noble. The equipment as well. There were always buyers for such things, especially in Singapore. And in Europe as well.

Maxon's theories had not been devised from the aether. They had been built on a solid foundation; there were others who had done the same. Maxon was simply farther along in putting his theories into practice, at least as far as Vogel knew. There were a number of men who might pay well for the secrets of Maxon's process, if only to refine their own.

He watched as Saffir and Riwut saw to the disposition of their subordinates. The Dayaks had made an art of attacking places like this. Then, they had plenty of practice. Many of the warriors had bows or javelins, in addition to spears and swords. The palisades would provide little protection from a mass assault.

From speaking with Arkwright, he knew that the soldiers would fall back to the buildings in the event that the palisade was breached. Each of the compound's buildings had been constructed with a siege in mind, or so Arkwright had insisted. From there, they could theoretically hold out indefinitely. Unless, of course, Saffir decided to burn them out.

"According to our spies, the supply ship will be here in a few days," Riwut said, startling Vogel from his thoughts. "Perhaps we should try and keep the compound intact, eh? Make it look presentable, and take two fish with a single thrust."

Saffir grunted. "And how many soldiers will that ship have on it? No. I think we will take the compound, strip it of all value, and leave. Let the forest reclaim it, and the bones of the British. Once we have the equipment, and a monster to show off, we have no more need of this place or any supply ship."

"Is he still certain that these beasts of his will come, then?" Riwut muttered. He studied Vogel dismissively. "Because all I see is a fortress full of British soldiers."

Saffir looked at Vogel. "Well? Are you certain?"

Vogel tightened his grip on his satchel. He took a deep breath. "Tell me, how many men did you come here with?"

Saffir frowned. "About fifty. Why?"

"And how many are here, now?"

Saffir's frown deepened. "What do you mean?"

Riwut understood, however. "They are following us. Some of the men—I have not seen them lately. I thought they had wandered off to relieve themselves, or because they had sighted another patrol, but we would have heard something if that were the case." He grimaced and glared back the way they'd come, his eyes flicking from tree to tree, as if searching for any sign of something amiss.

Saffir growled low in his throat. "Treachery." His hand fell to the hilt of his sword, but his eyes were wide and there was fear in them.

"No," Vogel said, firmly. "I told you—they are hungry. Your men dawdled and were taken. They are probably watching us even now. Waiting to see what happens next." He gestured to the branches above. "They are like children, you see. Naturally curious, but also impulsive and aggressive. If they see an opportunity to indulge themselves, they will take it. That is why you must attack soon, so as to distract them from your men, yes?"

"Yes," Saffir said. "Yes. Of course." Saffir whistled sharply. A moment later, the stolen rifles spoke. The Dayak gunmen were not marksmen; not with rifles, at any rate. But they clearly had some familiarity with the weapons. Enough to raise shouts of alarm from the men on the palisade.

Riwut saw the look on Vogel's face and smiled. "You think we are too stupid to learn how rifles work, old man?"

Vogel shrugged. "I was simply wondering why you did not have more of them."

Saffir chuckled. "My allies are . . . traditionalists. They don't like things that smack of foreign influence. Swords and spears never run out of ammunition. Arrows can be easily produced, and they kill a man just as dead. And, of course, neither the British nor the Dutch like when their weapons fall into the hands of those they regard as lessers." He glanced at Vogel. "You see my cunning, now? They cannot afford to let these rifles remain in our hands. Our riflemen will draw them out and then we will storm the compound."

"If they come out," Riwut grunted. Saffir glared at him.

"Of course they will come out. That is what they do.

They come out, they try to flush out the shooter in order to chase them away. They have no knowledge of our true strength. Why do otherwise?"

"And what if they do not come out?" Vogel asked. "What then?"

Saffir paused, a look of calculation on his face. "Then we will fall back on tried and true methods. Riwut, how many of these fools count themselves archers?"

"A dozen, maybe. Why?"

"Fire the compound. That way, we can be sure they will come out."

"It might be too wet," Riwut said, doubtfully.

"And it might not be," Saffir said. "We will not know until we try."

"No," Vogel said, sharply. "If you burn the compound, you risk damaging the equipment!" Saffir turned and casually knocked the old man to the ground.

"Let me remind you that I do not take well to being told no," Saffir said, in a mild tone. "And rest assured, your precious equipment will not be harmed. Riwut, fire the outbuildings and the palisade. Leave the rest."

Riwut nodded and slunk away to pass along his captain's orders. Saffir crouched before Vogel. "If we are going to be shipmates, you and I, there are things we must be clear about. I am in command. You are useful, but not indispensable. You do what I tell you, and if you do not, I will kill you. Is that clear?"

Vogel swallowed. "Very much so." He sat up, wincing as his old bones creaked. "But let me be clear as well. Without me, you have nothing save what you can scrape from a burned-out compound. If that satisfies your needs, then fine. But I do not think it does." He held Saffir's gaze and did not flinch away from the anger he saw there.

Men like Saffir fed on weakness. He had met many like them in Vienna. Show even a moment's hesitation, and they would devour you. But like all bullies, they respected strength. Saffir grinned.

"You have bellyful of iron, old man. I hope I do not have to kill you."

"That makes two of us," Vogel said. He paused as something caught his eye—a flash of movement from above, as of something gliding through the trees. He looked up, but whatever it was, was gone. Even so, he feared he knew what he'd seen.

Saffir followed his gaze. "What did you see?"

"Nothing," Vogel said. He'd hoped Otto would remain far away from the compound, but clearly it had been in vain. But had he come alone—or with help? "You should be overseeing your men."

Saffir sniffed. "Do not tell me what I should be doing, old man. Still, you are correct. They cannot hope to succeed without their rajah." He rose to his feet, drawing his niabor as he did so. "Get up, old man. Destiny calls, and Muda Saffir will meet it head on."

36
OVER THE TOP

THE FIRST SHOT CAME AS A SURPRISE to Bulan, and he instinctively ducked beneath the top of the palisade. "They've got rifles," he said to Welles. Counting him, there were only ten soldiers on the palisade, plus Bulan, Ju-Long, and Sing. Ten more were scattered throughout the compound on guard for any attempts by the Dayaks to sneak inside.

Virginia was safe in Arkwright's office. She and Higgs were keeping an eye on the man. Bulan was certain there were more answers to be had from the lieutenant, but getting them would have to wait until they'd seen to the Dayaks.

"They've got our rifles, is what they've got," Welles said, bluntly. "Arkwright sent men out into the dark and none of them have come back. We should have figured the Dayaks might have some among them familiar with rifles." He sighted down the length of a rifle, peering at the trees. "Probably trying to draw us out."

"And?" Bulan asked, checking over his own rifle. The Dayak attack had come so quickly they'd barely had time to make even the most minor repairs to the broken palisade. One moment he'd been hefting a timber into place and the next he'd been scrambling up onto the palisade, a borrowed rifle in his hand. The Dayaks hadn't shown themselves, but he knew it was them.

"I'm not in any hurry to go back out there, are you?" Welles turned as several of his men returned fire. "Cease fire," he roared. "Leave it until you get a clear look at them."

He glanced back at Bulan. "As soon as they realize we're not coming out, they'll try and come in. That's when things will get tricky. I'm going to check on the others, make sure no one is getting too jumpy."

"Good plan," Bulan said. He glanced at Esmail, crouched nearby. "Esmail, go with him." The young Lascar hesitated, but only for a moment. Soon, the pair were gone, duckwalking along the catwalk and doing their best to keep out of sight of any watching Dayaks. Bulan watched them for a moment and found himself praying that Esmail would avoid the fate of Kazin and the others.

Pushing that grim thought aside, he finished checking his rifle and sank down, sitting with his back against the palisade. Sing crept toward him. "The Dayaks, then," he said. Bulan nodded.

"I think I prefer the monsters," he said. The shots were haphazard. They came every few minutes and never from the same direction. Or so it felt to him.

Sing sat beside him. "I would prefer to not be here at all."

Bulan sighed. "I'm sorry, Sing. You were right. We should have listened to you. Then we wouldn't be here in this mess."

Sing chuckled. "Miss Ginny was determined. You could no more have talked her out of coming than I could have. Besides, we are here now and must deal with the world as we find it. Wishing otherwise is simply a waste of time." He peered over the palisade. "They'll attack soon. Dayaks aren't known for their patience, and neither is Muda Saffir."

"I wonder if the same goes for Otto and the other monsters," Bulan murmured. Where were they? Somewhere close by, he thought. Watching—waiting. Would they be drawn to the attack, or frightened away? He hoped it was the former. The Dayaks were bad enough. The monsters would only make things worse.

Another shot struck the palisade, and Bulan heard Ju-Long curse. He looked past Sing to where the big man crouched behind one of the five heavy spotlights the compound possessed. Ju-Long noticed his attention and said, "If you had not ruined my Maxim gun, we would be better able to repel the enemy."

"If you hadn't shot at us, Otto wouldn't have broken your toy," Bulan replied. Ju-Long laughed and turned away. Despite himself, Bulan smiled. He was starting to like the big man. He wondered if Ju-Long knew anything about football.

He turned back to Sing, and saw that the old man had been watching the back and forth with Ju-Long, and he was smiling. "What?"

"Nothing. After this, you might consider hiring him. I think he will need employment when all this is done. I—ah. Even as I said."

Bulan followed the old man's gaze and saw a dozen shapes slinking out of the trees toward the main gates. He called out to Ju-Long, and the other man swung his light around. The Dayaks froze as the beam struck them. Bulan and Sing rose from behind the palisade and fired as one. A Dayak spun and fell with a cry. Several others threw javelins, forcing Bulan and Sing to duck back. The soldiers on the wall were firing now as well, and the Dayaks soon broke and fled back into the trees.

Gunfire crackled from the other side of the compound, and Bulan heard Welles shouting something. But he had no time to listen as something bright and burning arced over the wall to land inside the palisade. "Fire arrows," he called out. One of the burning arrows chunked into the catwalk and a soldier rushed to stamp it out. As he did so, a second arrow caught him in the neck. Bulan leaped to help him, but too late. The injured man fell from the catwalk with a gurgling scream, leaving Bulan clutching at empty air.

More arrows fell across the compound, and rifles barked in response. A light burst with a screech of broken glass, scattering burning filament across its controller and the palisade both. Dayaks came out of the trees, racing for the gates and the gap in the wall where the watchtower had once stood.

An arrow sliced across Bulan's bicep and he clapped his hand to the wound with a hiss of pain. Sing ducked as another arrow plucked his hat from his head and looked at Bulan. "They are coming, Mr. Harper—they are coming!"

Flames whooshed up with a sudden roar. Something had caught, despite the rain, and the fire began to spread across the palisade. Thick clouds of black smoke rolled along the catwalk, obscuring everything. He couldn't see Sing or Ju-Long, or much past his own nose. But he could hear well enough. From the sound of it, the Dayaks had reached the gates and were attempting to force them open.

Bulan tore off his sleeve and tied it around his injured arm as a makeshift bandage. Arrows punched into the catwalk, forcing him to dance back. He heard a crash from somewhere below him, as of dislodged timbers smashing into the ground. Feet thudded against the wood and a lean shape raced out of the smoke, niabor raised.

Bulan swung his rifle like a club and the Dayak fell with a crushed skull. A second headhunter leaped over the body of the first and swung his blade down. Bulan caught it with his rifle, but his opponent's momentum drove him back against the palisade. The Dayak leaned all his weight against the sword, threatening to send Bulan plummeting over the edge.

Then—hands as blue as those of a corpse emerged from the smoke and caught hold of his opponent's head. The Dayak's eyes bulged as his skull crumpled and split like a rotten mushroom. Bulan shoved the body aside with a cry of disgust and sought out his rescuer. But he saw nothing save smoke and the vague hint of obscene shapes moving through it. Even so, he knew that the monsters had come. Things had just gone from bad to worse.

"Mr. Harper," Sing called out, and Bulan turned to see the old man flapping at the smoke with his ruined hat. Ju-Long was just behind him, his face and arms streaked with soot. "Are you okay?" Sing asked, as they joined Bulan.

"For now. You two?"

"The Dayaks are in the compound," Ju-Long said. "I warned Arkwright that this would happen." He grimaced and checked his rifle. "I warned him about all of this."

"Some men don't know good sense when they hear it," Bulan said. Ju-Long snorted.

"Speaking from experience?"

"I've never been accused of having good sense," Bulan said. He coughed. The smoke stung his eyes and coarsened his breath. They couldn't stay on the palisade much longer. "Sing, I think Otto and the other monsters are here. We need to fall back. Find Welles—get to safety. I'll get Virginia."

"I can go with you," Sing began, but his eyes widened and Bulan heard the shriek of steel parting the air somewhere behind him. He flung himself aside, and Sing lunged past him to meet the charging Dayak. The niabor glanced off of Sing's interposed rifle and skidded across the old man's arm, releasing a spray of red into the smoky air. Sing fell back with a cry as Bulan hammered a fist into the side of the Dayak's tattooed skull, sending the man plummeting from the palisade.

"Grandfather!" Ju-Long cried, as he crouched beside Sing. Bulan had no time to ponder that revelation, for more Dayaks were racing across the palisade toward them. He snatched up Sing's rifle and fired, forcing the Dayaks to slow.

"Get him to his feet and get to the fallback point," Bulan said, as he fired again. A Dayak staggered as a blossom of blood sprouted high on his chest. But even as he sank back, there were more to take his place. Too many to fight. Worse, dark shadows loped through the smoky courtyard below. Dayaks or monsters, there was no way to tell, but he could hear men screaming and dying and knew that the defenses they'd mustered were crumbling. "Find Welles if you can. If not, hole up and I'll find you as soon as I've gotten Virginia."

Ju-Long looked as if he wanted to argue, but Sing merely nodded and said, "Be careful, Bulan. These monsters are not like the ones Maxon made. I do not think we can reason with them. Do not let your hope blind you to the sharpness of their teeth."

"I won't. Now go—I'll keep the Dayaks busy!" Bulan fired once more as Ju-Long helped Sing to his feet and headed for the closest set of stairs. Fire rose up, momentarily separating him from the advancing Dayaks. He only had a few shots left, and between the smoke and the heat his aim wasn't what it should have been.

The palisade gave a groan and he felt the planks beneath his feet vibrate ominously. The British had built the wall well, but it was still only wood and rope. The fire was weakening the section he was on. It was only a matter of time until it collapsed. A spear cut through the flames and pierced the planks between his feet. He cursed and retreated, firing as he went. The Dayaks were in no hurry, for the flames had spread to the walkway behind him. He realized with a sinking sensation that he was trapped.

One of the Dayaks called out to him, and the others laughed. Not mockingly, so much as good-naturedly. They understood the ridiculousness of the situation as much as he did. Hunting a man across a burning palisade was a good way to take a head, and lose your own in the process. But they had no give in them, and he knew they wouldn't retreat.

The Dayaks crept closer, wary of both his rifle and the reaching flames. Bulan sighted down the length of the rifle and weighed his options. But fate made the decision for him. Even as he pulled the trigger, the section of palisade they were on gave a thunderous howl; wood split and ropes frayed as the fire surged up and the whole edifice gave way, pitching both Bulan and his opponents to the ground below!

37

ANSWERS

VIRGINIA SIGHED AS THE DOOR to Arkwright's office was shut, and turned. Arkwright was seated at his desk. Higgs stood nearby with his revolver trained on his former commander. Virginia had volunteered to guard Arkwright, wanting to talk with the man privately. Higgs had decided to join them, without invitation. Virginia had a feeling she wasn't the only one who had questions for Arkwright.

She leaned against the wall with her arms crossed. "They'll need you on the palisade," she said to Higgs. Outside, gunfire crackled. Virginia frowned. The Dayaks had arrived, and quicker than she'd expected. From what she'd overheard, they were circling the compound for the moment, keeping to the trees. But they'd rush the gates sooner or later.

"The lads will see them off, never fear," Higgs said, confidently. "Welles is a good man. Got a clear head on him. And Ju-Long is a mean bugger. Between them, those head-hunters don't stand much of a chance . . . isn't that right, sir?" He directed this last part at Arkwright, who stared at him balefully.

"You disappoint me, Sergeant," Arkwright replied. "I thought we had an understanding." Higgs smiled and flicked through the papers on the desk. If he heard what was going on outside, he gave no indication.

"Oh we do, sir. We do. But, as the instigator of our arrangement, I felt it necessary to alter the terms slightly. You understand, of course."

Arkwright lit a cigarette. "I understand that you have no idea of what is going on here—the import of our undertaking is beyond you." He glanced at Virginia. "Either of you."

Higgs looked at Virginia, and then said, "The war effort, wasn't it? Gas and such, as you said earlier." He paused, his eyes scanning the papers. Virginia wondered what he'd found. Instead of asking, she kept her eyes on Arkwright. She didn't trust that he wasn't planning something. He reminded her of Von Horn; a man who never ceased scheming. "Unkillable soldiers for the war to come."

"That's part of it, certainly." Arkwright leaned back, the very picture of ease. "But there is more to it." He cut his eyes to Virginia. "Do you truly believe your father's theories congealed in a vacuum? That his madness, as you call it, was his alone?"

Virginia leaned forward. "What do you mean?"

Arkwright smiled. "Maxon was a cog in a great machine; a machine that has been running for centuries." He expelled smoke from his lips, and it wreathed his face for a moment, clouding his features. "A machine that will continue to run, whatever happens here. Those things out there, those over-grown homunculi . . . they are the future. Not just of warfare, but of labor. Imagine factories full of tireless workers, inured to even the most grievous of hardships. The applications are multifarious."

Virginia flushed with anger. "Is that why you came here? To make slaves?"

Arkwright leaned his head back. "Why does anyone go anywhere, Miss Maxon? Because it profits them. I came here because I was told to come. Because my patrons are part of the great machine, just as your father was, just as I am. Just as you are."

"Are you talking about a—a conspiracy?" Virginia asked, softly.

Higgs snorted. "He's talking rubbish is what he is. He's working for a bunch of rich toffs who want cheap labor, that's all." He glanced at her. "Dressing it up fancy don't make it magic, love. Arkwright here is just giving himself airs."

"But it is magic, of a sort," Arkwright said. "The power to control life and death, to improve upon God's design. That's a quest worthy of any man. Your father knew that."

Virginia glared at him. "The only thing my father got from his quest was a stay in an institution. I suspect your superiors won't be so accommodating. Will they hang you, do you think? Or just have you shot?"

Arkwright leaned back in his chair, the very picture of ease. "I expect I will be promoted. Lauded, even. If any of us make it out of here, that is."

As if to punctuate this grim statement, there was suddenly a great crash from outside that shook the office to its foundations. Virginia whirled toward the window, her heart in her throat. Higgs did the same, a look of surprise on his face. "Bulan," Virginia cried out.

"I expect he's dead," Arkwright said. She turned back and saw that he'd drawn a revolver from somewhere inside his desk. He aimed it at her with a cold, hard smile, and she realized, belatedly, that they should have done a better job checking the desk. "But never fear, you'll join him soon enough."

He fired and she flinched back, but the shot wasn't meant for her. Higgs crumpled to the ground, firing his weapon even as he fell. Arkwright cursed and fled out the door as Higgs' shots pursued him. The sergeant fired until the revolver was empty, and then slumped back. Virginia was at his side a moment later. Higgs tried to speak, but nothing came out save a thin whistle. He smiled weakly at her, and then, he was gone.

Virginia raced outside to see flames spreading across the palisade, despite the rain. Greasy smoke rolled across the compound, choking the air, and she could see men locked in battle near where the watchtower had once been. The Dayaks were inside the compound. She looked around frantically, but Arkwright was nowhere to be seen.

She looked again toward the fallen section of palisade. That was where Bulan had been. She hurried toward it, silently praying that he'd managed to escape before it had collapsed. But as she drew closer, her hope dimmed. The section was a burning mass of wood and smoke painted the air black. "Bulan," she called out, coughing as she did so. *"Bulan!"*

A sound caught her attention. Was that a groan of pain—or someone calling her name? She got as close to the fire as she dared, trying to see past its glare and the stinging shroud of smoke. If he was alive, he might be trapped, pinned beneath a fallen beam or—

The Dayak erupted from the smoke, blade in hand and his flesh blistered and raw from the flames. Instinctively, Virginia dropped to one knee and shot him. Two more appeared, howling like wolves as they raced toward her. She shot one, and her revolver clicked dry as she swung it toward the other. She fell back as he closed in—but he never reached her.

Bulan appeared out of nowhere, falling upon the headhunter like a tiger. He carried his opponent to the ground and cracked the Dayak's head against the hard-packed earth. The Dayak went limp and Bulan rose. He was streaked with blood and soot, and there was a red-stained bandage wrapped around his arm. Burns stood out against his flesh beneath the tatters of his shirt, but he seemed otherwise in one piece. "Virginia, are you . . . ?"

"I'm fine," she said, tossing her empty pistol aside as she ran to him. They held each other tightly for a moment. "I thought you were dead."

"Takes more than that to kill me," he said, brusquely, as he released her from his grip. He sounded exhausted. She felt the same. But something told her there was no time to rest. Not now, and maybe not soon.

She stepped back and picked up the Dayak's blade. "What's happened? What do we do now? Where can we go?"

"Welles and the others are making a fighting withdrawal to the laboratory building. The Dayaks aren't trying to set fire to it, for some reason. I came to get you and Higgs and Arkwright. Where—?"

"Arkwright's gone. Higgs is—is dead."

Bulan shook his head, and seemed momentarily at a loss. But he recovered soon enough. "Damn. We'll worry about him later. We need to get to safety."

"No safety," a voice gurgled. Contorted, inhuman shapes prowled toward them through the smoke. Virginia recognized the creatures Ju-Long had called Creation Eight and Creation Four. Eight studied them with malign interest, one hand on the head of his fellow creature in an almost paternal gesture. "Not for you, or any flesh. Tonight, we prove ourselves worthy of the life bestowed upon us by our creator—we do as he made us to do, and in doing, we show our love for him."

"Arkwright," Virginia said, softly. "He's talking about Arkwright." She swallowed and said, "He is not your creator." Bulan tried to pull her back, but she ignored him. There had to be a way to get through to these creatures, to make them see that things did not have to be this way. If she could get through to Otto, she could get through to them. "Do you understand? My father is the one who devised the process by which you were created . . ."

Eight tilted his head, studying her. "Your . . . father?" He seemed amused. "Arkwright is our father. He made us. He taught us. He showed us love. See?" He lifted one of his arms and showed the scars there. Virginia flinched back, horrified by the sight of the old wounds. What sort of torture had Arkwright inflicted on these creatures?

"That's not love," she said. "If he loved you, he would be here and not scuttling off to hide while you and your kin die." The words came fast, and she saw that at least some of them penetrated, for Creation Eight's eyes narrowed slightly. Had he come here looking for Arkwright—and if so, why?

"He set us loose, so that we might prove ourselves," Eight said, but his tone was speculative rather than assertive. As if he were asking himself a question. "And so we shall." He lifted his hand from Creation Four's head. "Eat of their flesh, brother. Eat, and show your love. As I will show mine."

As he spoke, Creation Eight stepped back and vanished into the smoke. Now left to his own devices, the barnacle-covered monster eyed them greedily. "Eat you, prove my love," he grunted. A long tongue lashed across his blistered lips as he took a step toward them. The monsters flexed thick fingers in anticipation. Bulan pushed Virginia back.

"When I say go—go. Don't look back."

"Bulan," she began. Up close, she realized just how large the creature was. He was covered in ropey muscle beneath his bumpy hide, and his arms were longer than a man's—more like those of an ape. This creature, she knew, was stronger than Bulan. Hand-to-hand, he wouldn't stand much of a chance.

"Don't look back," he repeated, his eyes on Creation Four.

The monster scrambled toward them, alternating between four legs and two as it charged. Bulan moved to meet it, visibly bracing himself for the impact. Virginia took a step back, but hesitated, unwilling to leave him to his fate. She tightened her grip on the sword in her hand, and flinched away as her fiancé and the creature crashed together violently. Bulan was at an immediate disadvantage; Four's long arms shot out to grab him, and he was forced to avoid them, leaving himself open for what followed. Four struck Bulan on the head and chest, sending him to one knee with a series of swift, heavy blows.

Bulan shot to his feet and drove punches into his opponent's midsection. Four staggered, but closed the gap between them, clawing for Bulan's throat. They grappled for a moment, wrapped in a shroud of smoke. Virginia felt as if her heart were about to burst from her chest and her world narrowed to a single tunnel of focus. Time slowed to a crawl.

When the moment came, she reacted more quickly than she ever had before. Creation Four and Bulan spun in an awkward gavotte, hammering at one another with their fists— and for an instant, the creature's broad back was presented to her. She lunged with the grace of a trained fencer, and felt a shock run through her arm as the niabor bit into the mud-hued flesh of Creation Four. The creature stiffened and reeled, screeching like an injured animal. Virginia released the blade and scrambled back, out of reach of those too-long arms.

Creation Four spun toward her, his face contorted into a mask of perplexed fury. In that moment, his eyes were not those of a hungry monster, or even a wrathful man. Rather, it was the gaze of an aggrieved child; confused as to why such pain had been inflicted upon him and uncertain as to how to fix it. He took a step toward her, then another—then, toppled forward with a soft groan of resignation.

Virginia looked down at him, her mind crowded with pity and revulsion. She hadn't meant to kill him—had she? Panting, Bulan crouched beside the pitiful hulk and checked for a pulse. A moment later, he stood. "We should go. I don't believe those two came here alone. I'm fairly certain Otto led them here."

"Otto?" Virginia asked. Mention of him broke her from her pall of shock. "Why would he do that? He must know how dangerous it is."

Bulan frowned and tore the sword from Creation Four's back. He extended it to her, hilt-first. "Honey, I hate to say it, but I think he's counting on it."

38

DUEL

OTTO LEAPED THROUGH THE WAFTING SMOKE and landed heavily on the roof of one of the compound's outer buildings. Fire arrows smoldered nearby, unable to catch the roof alight. He scaled the incline of the roof and perched at its top, peering across the courtyard. It was hard to see anything, given the smoke, but he managed to spot a group of soldiers hurrying toward one of the central buildings. They were pursued by Dayaks. And the Dayaks were pursued by the monsters, though they did not yet realize it.

Creation Eight and the others had broken away from him the moment they'd entered the compound. He hadn't expected them to stay by his side, but it was still painful to see them go. To know that it was unlikely any of them would see the sunrise.

The Dayaks were everywhere throughout the compound. More of them than he'd ever seen in one place before. Creation Eight and the others would eat well, if their prey didn't kill them. He still wasn't sure which result he preferred. Eight and the rest of Arkwright's creations reeked of madness. They had endured so much pain that he wondered if there was anything else in them now.

He'd shown them how certain trees hung over the compound palisade, and how they could use them to get inside without being noticed. Then, given the confusion, that wasn't as much of an issue as he'd feared. No one had noticed them yet, though he knew several of the monsters had already claimed their first victims.

In any event, he wasn't interested in the Dayaks or the soldiers, or even in filling his belly. Instead, he was searching for Vogel. He'd spotted the old man as he led the other monsters into the compound. If Vogel was a prisoner, Otto intended to free him. And he would kill anyone who stood in his way.

He prowled across the rooftops of the compound, ignoring the scenes of violence that unfolded below. Arkwright's soldiers were outnumbered, and the Dayaks were eager. But the latter did not have it entirely their own way. More than once, he spied a small knot of soldiers hunkering down behind makeshift barricades and the bodies of many Dayaks scattered around them. Regardless, it was a foregone conclusion that the compound would fall. Either the Dayaks would take it, or the fire would.

He felt a flicker of anxiety as he realized that he'd seen no sign of Virginia or her friends. Were they dead too? Or had they managed to escape? He pushed the thoughts aside. Vogel was his priority. He would find Virginia afterward.

A wild burst of laughter caught his attention, and he crouched low on the edge of the roof. Down below, a large party of Dayaks moved across the courtyard. He recognized Muda Saffir immediately. And beside him, Vogel. "You see, old man?" Saffir crowed, a British rifle cradled in the crook of his arm. "I said it would be simple, and it was!"

"And how many of your men have you lost?" Vogel replied.

Saffir waved this aside as if it were of no importance. "Warriors can be replaced. When they hear of our victory here, the chieftains will be eager to replenish my numbers. Rajah Muda Saffir will once more be the most feared captain in these waters. And the richest, as well, if you are not lying." He looked down at Vogel and tapped the hilt of his sword. "If you are lying, well . . . my war-prahu shall have a new skull upon its bow. Now, which of these is your laboratory?"

Vogel gestured—then paused. The old man had seen something. Otto followed his gaze and saw two forms creeping
through the smoke toward the party of Dayaks. The wind
shifted and the smoke thinned, revealing Creations Five and
Seven. They'd clearly been stalking the group for some time.
Even as the Dayaks noticed them, Creation Five raced toward
the group, wailing hungrily. She bore one to the ground and
her mad rush scattered the rest. Muda Saffir fell back, cursing,
as Five tore his screaming warrior apart and began stuffing
steaming chunks of flesh into the vertical wound she called a
mouth. As Saffir and the others began to recover their wits,
Creation Seven sprang onto a Dayak as well, and tore him
limb from limb with a bellow of gusto.

Saffir shoved Vogel to the ground and snatched a spear
from one of his warriors. Without pause, he sent it hurtling
toward Seven. The monster, too preoccupied with the spasming
body in his grip, didn't notice the spear until it was too late.
The blade caught him high in the neck and he stumbled back,
clawing at the missile and howling in agony. At Saffir's
command, several Dayaks closed in on the wounded monster,
in order to finish him off. As they did so, Otto leaped down
among them, and with every blow of his fists, a Dayak fell
and did not rise.

It was too late for Seven, however. Otto turned his attention
to Saffir and Vogel. The Malay stared at him in wonderment,
even as he raised his rifle. "By the Prophet, he is a magnificent
beast is he not?"

Vogel stepped between Saffir and Otto. "No! Do not harm
him. You promised me!"

Saffir shoved Vogel aside. "So I did. But I said nothing
about this other one." He swung his rifle up and fired. Five
screamed piteously as Saffir shot her. She collapsed across the
body of her victim and clawed uselessly at the wound in her
belly. Saffir laughed at her writhings. "Not this one, either, I
think. Too fragile, eh?"

"Stop," Vogel shouted. "Leave her be!" In reply, Saffir fired again—this time putting his shot square between Creation Five's black eyes. Her head snapped back, and her screams were silenced in an instant. Otto roared and pounced on the Malay—but too slowly. Saffir whirled and fired for a third time. The bullet skidded across Otto's ribs, and knocked the wind from him. He fell in a heap before Saffir.

"Is this then the best of them?" Saffir chortled as he kicked Otto in the ribs. "A dog would have more sense than to charge a man with a rifle. When we make ours, I shall insist that they be bred with some cunning—if only to prevent such foolishness, eh?" He laughed, and the Dayaks joined him.

Otto rolled over and Saffir leaped back like a startled cat. He swung the rifle around to fire again, but Otto caught the barrel and tore the weapon from his grip. He slammed the weapon against the ground, shattering it, and flung the pieces away. Saffir retreated, a look of horror on his face. "Monster," he breathed.

"Yes," Otto said. "And a hungry one." He took a step toward Saffir and the Malay cried out to his Dayaks for help . . . but none of them moved. Otto paused, curious. The Dayaks retreated and one tossed a sword at Saffir's feet.

Saffir looked at the Dayak in shock. "Riwut—what is the meaning of this?"

Riwut crossed his arms. "You have led us far, Rajah. But if you wish to lead us farther, you will show us that you are worthy of it. Slay the beast, as you swore you would. Take its head . . . or we will take yours."

Saffir stared at his subordinates for a moment, and then snatched up the sword. "Very well. I will dispatch this fiend and then you, Riwut, you treacherous cur." He turned toward Otto, paused, and then lunged more swiftly than Otto had anticipated. The Malay was fast and Otto only narrowly avoided the blade as it whistled past.

They circled one another, and Saffir made several probing slashes with his sword. Otto easily avoided them and leaped for his opponent with a roar. Saffir ducked beneath his sweeping arms and carved a bloody stripe across his ribs. Otto staggered and swung a fist, nearly taking Saffir's head off. The Malay danced back, panting.

"You fight like an animal—a brute," he wheezed. "You are no match for a true warrior." Otto could hear the doubt beneath his bravado. He wondered how long it had been since Saffir had had to fight his own battles. He rushed the Malay, intending to snatch the sword from his grip, but Saffir surprised him again and Otto grunted as the Dayak blade chopped into his shoulder.

As Otto staggered back, pain shooting through his nerve endings, Saffir roared and tore the sword loose, readying it for another blow. Desperate now and driven into a frenzy by the pain, Otto lunged and caught the Malay by the skull. He glared down into Saffir's wide eyes—so full of fear and hate and greed, all mingled together. When he could bear to look at them no longer, he put them out. Saffir screamed and writhed in his grip like a snake caught by an eagle.

His screams became shrill as Otto's talons dug deeper, into the soft tissues behind the sockets—into the bone. When he had hooked it sufficiently, Otto *pulled* . . . and Muda Saffir's head came apart like a rotten gourd. He let the twitching body fall and looked at the frozen Dayaks. They stared at him in shock, but it quickly turned to anger.

"Shoot it," Riwut grunted, lifting his rifle.

The other two Dayaks tensed, ready to end Otto's life. Then, a pistol spoke—once, twice, three times. All three warriors fell dead.

A tall figure strode out of the roiling smoke. For a moment, Otto thought it was Bulan. Then the wind shifted and he saw that it was Arkwright. The Englishman smiled coolly as he emptied the spent shells from his revolver. He stepped over the dead Dayaks and advanced toward them, reloading briskly. "I suppose I should thank you, my ugly friend. Muda Saffir was quite the annoyance." He looked around at the burning compound, then at the bodies of Creation Five and Seven, and sighed. "A shame, really. Still, this compound will be easy enough to replace, as will they. So long as I have Professor Vogel here, and Maxon's notes, all the rest can be rebuilt." He snapped the pistol shut and aimed it at them. "On that note—come here, Vogel."

"No," Vogel said, clutching his satchel close. "No more monsters, Lieutenant. No more plans. Our time together has ended."

"Has it?" Arkwright's smile widened and he swung his revolver in Otto's direction. Injured as he was, Otto hauled himself to his feet, teeth bared. "I think not. In fact, I think it is just beginning." He studied Otto with interest. "Magnificent beast. Better than all the rest. When did you brew him up? And how did you manage to keep him secret, eh?"

"I did not make him," Vogel said.

"Ah, a mystery then. Pity we shall never have a solution." Arkwright cocked the revolver. "Magnificent or not, you are too dangerous to leave breathing."

"No," Vogel said, and stepped between them, though Otto tried to prevent him. "You will not harm him!"

"But I will, unless you agree to come quietly," Arkwright replied. Otto tensed. He was not sure he could reach the man before he fired, but he had no option save to try. Could a gun kill him? He suspected it would, if it hit something vital. "I do not need him, Vogel. He is a clearly a strong-willed sort and that does not fit my design in the least. But I will spare him and allow him to live out his days on this island, if you come with me now. And if not . . . " His finger tapped the trigger of his weapon and his smile was a slash across his face. "Decide quickly. There are still Dayaks about, after all."

"Do you fear them?" a voice growled, from somewhere beyond the smoke. Arkwright frowned and turned, searching for the speaker. Creation Eight stepped into view, his lamp-like gaze sliding across the bodies of his fellows before returning to Arkwright. "Do you fear these Dayaks? Is that why you allowed us to be freed?"

Arkwright smiled widely—falsely, Otto thought. It was the fear-grin of a terrified animal, not an expression of welcome. "There you are, my sweet one," Arkwright said, watching as Creation Eight prowled toward them, his three hands coated in blood—Dayak or British, it was impossible to say. "I am glad to see you. I thought you were lost forever."

"No. I waited. Watched." Eight tilted his head, studying his maker with a flat gaze. It was impossible to tell what he was thinking.

"You always were the clever one," Arkwright said. "And the others?"

Eight glanced at Otto. "All dead. I saw the Dayaks stab Creation Two with their spears, and the one you call Bulan slew poor Creation Four. Only he and I remain."

"Well. That is convenient." Arkwright made as if to turn, but instead fired his revolver into Eight's barrel chest. The monster fell back without a sound and lay still. Arkwright laughed as he turned the weapon back on Otto and Vogel. "There now. All done. And past time too, I should say." He raised the revolver.

"Now then . . . where were we?"

39

RESOLUTION

ARKWRIGHT SMIRKED AT THEM over the barrel of his service weapon. "I'm curious, Professor. How long have you known about our friend here?"

"Since we arrived," Vogel said, stiffly.

"And all that time, he's managed to hide himself from us? How clever of him. Did you teach him that, or did he already know?"

Vogel swallowed, his eyes on the pistol. Otto had eyes only for Eight's fallen form. There was something wrong—some tremor of motion in the limbs. It might have been a trick of the smoke or the shadows, but he thought Creation Eight was still moving.

"He knew," Vogel said. "Otto is clever."

"Is he cleverer than our batch?" Arkwright asked. He waved Vogel's reply aside. "Never mind. The answer to the question is before me. He's alive and they're dead. Clearly, he's smarter. Stronger, too." He paused for a moment, his expression considering. Then, "You know, Vogel, I've changed my mind. I think your friend there should come with us. The brute is clearly far in advance of these wretches we made. I have no doubt that with the secrets we wring from his flesh, we will succeed in our quest." Arkwright gestured with the smoking revolver. "And if not—well."

"It is true, then."

Creation Eight's voice was a ragged snarl. The monster sat up; he pressed one hand to the wound in his chest.

252

Arkwright stepped back, face pale with surprise as the creature clambered slowly to his feet.

"You are a liar," Creation Eight said. "A false god. False law." He advanced on his maker, a deadly gleam in his eye. Arkwright lifted his revolver, but before he could fire, Creation Eight caught his wrist in an unyielding, if almost gentle, grip. Arkwright's eyes widened in surprise.

"What are you doing? Release me at once!"

"Do you love us, Arkwright?" Eight asked. "Did you ever?"

Arkwright grimaced. "What are you talking about?"

"The old man claims that you would have killed us. That is why he released us. I thought you wished us to prove ourselves, to show you how much we loved you and how well we had learned what you tried to teach us. But I see now that what the old man said is true. We were nothing to you." Eight tightened his grip on Arkwright's wrist. "Nothing but *meat*."

Otto heard bones splinter and the revolver fell from Arkwright's twitching fingers. Arkwright's mouth moved, but no sound came out. It was as if he could not conceive of what was happening. "I thought you loved us, but now I think that you fear us. That is why you kept us in cages. The Other was not caged. Was it because he was loved? Answer me!"

Arkwright yowled in pain as Eight shook him. Then, through gritted teeth, he said, "What would something like you know of love? Ju-Long was right. I should have killed you all sooner and spared myself the trouble . . ."

With a growl, Creation Eight lifted the struggling Arkwright into the air and tore the man apart in a welter of red. Arkwright made no sound as he was rent in twain. What was left of him flopped wetly to the ground. The creature looked down at his hands, as if he could not quite believe what he had done. Then, he reached up to taste the blood. His expression became rapturous and awful. Something in it sent a chill through Otto. It was not the look of a blood mad beast, but something worse.

"Arkwright was the law . . . Arkwright was life," Creation

Eight grunted, turning his ugly gaze toward Vogel and Otto. "Now I am the law—I am life." He stretched out a glistening finger in Vogel's direction. "And I say you will make more of us, little man. Make more to replace the dead. And I will be their lawgiver and life-giver."

"I would not do it for him, and I certainly will not do it for you," Vogel said, white-faced. He stared at the monster in horror. Eight gave a guttural laugh.

"You will. It is your purpose. Arkwright said so. You will make more." Eight's gaze flicked to Otto. "And you will help us, brother." He held out a chunk of Arkwright to Otto. "Come. I will feed you, as he fed me. I will teach you, as he taught me. Together, we will hunt Dayaks and soldiers, until none remain to defy us."

Otto took a half step toward Eight. A part of him yearned to taste the red, to surrender to the kill-urge and join his kinsman in slaughter. But Vogel's voice stopped him. "Do not listen to him, Otto. He has learned Arkwright's lessons too well."

"Quiet, or I will make you meat as well," Eight said. He looked at Otto. "He is nothing. Do not listen to him. I know the truth. And you know it too. You knew that the others were weak. That is why you brought us here. So that they would die, and prove themselves unworthy. But I still live, as do you. And together, we shall make a new kingdom here, in this place."

"I did not—I only wished to help," Otto protested, but knew in his heart that Creation Eight was speaking the truth. He had brought Eight and the others here to die. To use them, as Vogel had said Arkwright intended to use them. And he felt sick at the realization. He faltered and clutched at his wounded shoulder. Was he any better than Arkwright, or Muda Saffir?

As if sensing weakness, Creation Eight took a step toward him. "Join me . . . join me, or I will tear you apart and eat your flesh." His bloody hands curled into fists. "I shall show you my worth, even if I must kill you to do it. Then I will eat the old man's legs, so that he cannot flee. I will devour him piece by piece, until he agrees to make more of us."

Otto heard the savage intent in those words and gently pushed Vogel back. Creation Eight was insane. The others had been mad, but this was something altogether more malignant. There was a sickness in him. Creation Eight would not stop until he had what he wanted. Vogel caught his wrist. "Otto—you are injured," he hissed. "We must flee."

"If we run, he will chase us," Otto said, not taking his eyes from Creation Eight. "And he is injured as well." The bullet wound in Eight's upper shoulder still leaked black blood, as did the more recent wound in his chest. But the other monster seemed unimpaired. Otto, unfortunately, couldn't say the same. The pain from his wound was beginning to fray the edges of his perceptions. It would heal in time, but the latter was something he was in short supply of at the moment.

"They hurt us, but we survive," Creation Eight said. "We are meant to survive. But if you cannot see the truth of it, then I will end you here." His eyes rolled in their deep sockets. "I will build a kingdom on these ashes, and feast on the flesh of those who would stop me."

Otto lunged and Creation Eight flew to meet him. They came together in a rending maelstrom of claws and teeth. Both of them were bleeding, which only added to the ferocity that drove them. The kill-urge rose up in Otto like a flood tide and the world narrowed to the face of his opponent. They hammered at one another, clawed and bit—broke apart and circled one another.

"Fool," Eight growled, gingerly touching a wound Otto had torn in his side. "I am life. I am law. You cannot deny me."

"Not my law," Otto snarled. "Not my life."

Eight gave a bleak laugh. "You are blind. We were made to kill. To eat. Deny that, and you deny your purpose." He pounced on Otto and they fell together in a tangle, punching and biting at each other. As they rose up, Creation Eight grabbed Otto's wrists and dug the talons of his free hand into the red meat of Otto's wounded shoulder. Pain exploded through him, and he howled his agony to the dark skies above. The strength went out of his legs and he slumped back. Creation Eight let him fall to the ground.

"You are weak. You are not fit to survive." Eight turned away, as if searching for something. He stooped and retrieved Muda Saffir's fallen sword. He peered at the blade for a moment, and then licked at the blood that stained the weapon. He grunted in satisfaction and turned back to Otto. "I knew you were weak. I knew it, though I hoped otherwise. But better that you die here, before you taint my new kingdom with your weakness." He raised the sword over his head. "Goodbye, my brother."

"Otto!"

Blearily, Otto saw Virginia hurrying toward him, accompanied by Bulan and a few soldiers. Creation Eight turned toward them with a low snarl and brandished the sword. "These—these are the ones who have made you weak. Arkwright made me strong, and I killed him." He looked back at Otto. "Will you become strong, when these are dead? Let us see, eh?"

With that Creation Eight spun and bounded toward Virginia, two long arms stretching out to her, the third holding the sword over his head. Otto scrambled to his feet and leaped onto his opponent's back. He hammered at Eight's head and shoulders with his fist, and the monster stumbled, taken off-balance by this frenzied assault. The sword fell from his grip.

The two of them whirled in a slow pirouette, and Eight's voice dissolved into shrill gibbering as Otto locked his hands about the other creature's throat. In that moment, he wanted nothing more than to silence Arkwright's creation. But Creation Eight fought back with the fury of a mad thing, driving blow after blow into Otto's midsection and sides. Otto felt some of his ribs give way as Eight hurled him to the ground.

Otto rose, and felt the heat of the fire at his back. Creation Eight charged him, roaring. Otto threw himself aside and Creation Eight hurtled past him and into the greedy inferno. The monster screamed in pain and thrashed at the flames that rose up to consume him. He fought the fire as if it were an enemy that could be defeated, and for a moment, he was lost to view. But his screams continued, growing in volume.

Otto went to the fallen sword and picked it up. It felt odd in his hands; unnatural. Creation Eight had staggered to the edge of the fire. He collapsed out of it, his flesh cruelly blistered and split by the immense heat, and his mane of wiry hair burned to a crisp. He stank of burning meat and as he raised his head, Otto could see that his eyes had boiled in their sockets. But he still lived, somehow. He crawled blindly away from the heat, muttering unintelligibly. There was a chance, however slight, that he could survive. That he might heal, as Otto had. And what then?

"Otto," Vogel began, reaching for him. But Virginia caught the old man's arm. She met Otto's gaze and nodded tersely. Behind them, Bulan held the soldiers back, and his face might as well have been carved from granite. Otto looked down at the sword in his hand, and then at the broken husk of Creation Eight.

Some things, he knew, could not be fixed.

Otto raised the sword and brought it down on Creation Eight's neck. The monster's head rolled free as his body collapsed. Otto tossed the sword down and turned to face the others. "It had to be done," he said. "They all had to die."

"And what about this one?" one of the soldiers called out. He and the others had their rifles leveled in Otto's direction.

"Put your weapons down," Virginia said. "Otto is our friend. Aren't you Otto?" She reached out her hand. Otto hesitated. He glanced at the burning palisade, and past it, to the dark forest that had been his home for so long. Then he placed his hand into Virginia's.

"I am your friend," he said.

40

CONCLUSION

BULAN SIGHED AND RUBBED his injured arm. Rain fell over the charred remnants of the compound. Only the innermost buildings had escaped the fire unscathed. The few soldiers who remained had set up a watch rotation, just in case the Dayaks returned. Though, given how many of the latter still lay scattered across the compound, Bulan didn't expect them to come back in a hurry.

With the death of Muda Saffir, and the fire, the Dayaks had broken off their attack and scattered into the forest. But the damage was done, and Bulan and the others had spent the morning accounting for it all. It wasn't quite a victory, but neither was it a defeat.

"Less than half the men who came to this island are still breathing," Welles was saying. His arm was in a sling, and his uniform was covered in soot. He, Bulan, and the others crowded Arkwright's office, out of the rain. Sing and Esmail had made coffee and sandwiches. Bulan had greedily devoured his sandwich, though he was trying to savor the coffee. "And of those, half are wounded. Three of them won't last the day."

"I'm sorry," Bulan said, unable to meet the other man's gaze. "I can't help but feel that this is partially our fault."

"It's not," Welles said, firmly. "Nor is it entirely yours, Professor." He gave Vogel a hard look. "The blame is Arkwright's and he's paid for it. That suits me. When the supply ship arrives, we'll get a ride back to Singapore. You all are welcome to come, especially given how Muda Saffir burned your yacht to the waterline."

"I think we shall take you up on that," Virginia said. "It's time we got back to Ithaca and left all this behind."

"If we can," Sing said.

Welles nodded. "In the meantime, what I'm worried about now are those damn monsters. How many of them are still out there, waiting for us to let down our guard?" He looked around warily as he spoke. Bulan understood his caution. Otto was nowhere in sight, but he was still in the compound as far as they knew.

Bulan had half expected the monster to vanish as he had all the other times, but instead Otto had perched himself atop the remnants of the palisade and kept watch. For what, none of them could say. Dayaks, maybe—or maybe he was thinking things through. In his place, Bulan knew he would be.

"I found Creation Two, over near the palisade," Ju-Long said. "The Dayaks had killed it. Though it cost them five of their number to do so, judging by the bodies."

"I killed Creation Four, I think," Virginia said. "I wish it hadn't come to that, but . . ."

"He gave us no choice," Bulan said. He wrapped his arm around her and squeezed. She patted his chest and gave him a sad smile.

"Otto killed Creation Eight," she said.

Vogel sighed, and Bulan could see that the knowledge weighed on him. "And the Dayaks killed Five and Seven. That is all of them, then. All save poor Otto." He looked toward the window. "He is alone again. I had hoped . . . but no. It was not meant to be."

"Maybe it was," Virginia said, softly.

Vogel turned. "Eh?"

"Have you considered that he might have done it knowingly?" Bulan asked. Vogel gave him a startled look. Bulan continued. "He might have brought them here knowing—hoping—that they would be killed. Given their behavior . . . ."

"They did not know any better," Vogel protested.

"They never would have," Ju-Long said, firmly. "Arkwright did not want men. He wanted expendable monsters and that is what he got. If this . . . Otto recognized that, it proves that he, at least, is no fool."

"Knowingly or not, it was a blessing in disguise, if you ask me," Welles said. "I can't imagine what Arkwright was thinking, helping to create things like that."

"Who was he working for?" Bulan asked. Vogel removed his glasses and pinched the bridge of his nose. Suddenly the gnomic little man seemed incredibly tired.

"I do not know. I assumed someone in the British government. Perhaps I was wrong."

Welles tossed the book he'd been flicking through on the desk. "Maybe. Maybe not. That might explain why poor Higgs was here. Sometimes the right hand does not inform the left as to what it is planning. It could be he was working to a secret brief."

"Or maybe his masters aren't affiliated with the government at all," Virginia said. She turned to Bulan and the others. "My father was—is—acquainted with some . . . unconventional individuals. Even as a girl I knew that some of his colleagues were not proper academics, but more akin to . . . esoteric theoreticians."

Vogel nodded. "Yes. While Maxon and I shared some peers, I had heard that he often dealt with dilettantes. Dabblers in fringe science." He looked at the collection of odd books and frowned. "Perhaps Arkwright was working for someone of that inclination, yes?"

"I'm guessing you're not talking about proper scientists, then," Welles said.

"No," Virginia said. "This stuff—all of it—needs to be destroyed. Every last bit of my father's work, and what Arkwright made of it, must be forgotten." She glanced at Vogel, who looked as if he wished to argue. "You understand, I hope, Professor. My father's dream must die here."

Vogel sighed. "And what of Otto, eh? He is not dead."

"That can be fixed," Ju-Long said, bluntly.

Bulan rounded on him. "For pity's sake, haven't we done enough to him?"

Ju-Long held up his hands in surrender, but his smile was hard and cold. "It might be for the best. Like Creation Eight, he is not a man, and he will not fit into a man's world."

"Ju-Long is right—rude, but right," Welles said, in a mild tone. "Otto, whatever his virtues, is still one of those things. He has claws and fangs. He's stronger than a bull and damn near as fast as a leopard. Hell, he's already healing from that sword wound he took. Even with the best of intentions, there is no way he will be accepted by any civilized society."

"And who says that I wish to be a part of your civilized society?" Otto growled, from the doorway. He loomed there, eyeing them through a curtain of stringy hair. Bulan felt a twinge of guilt. They had been discussing Otto's fate as if he had no say in it. Otto flexed his odd hands. "I have seen enough of what it entails to have no interest in it. I will stay here, on my island. Alone. I will live out my days in the forest and when I die, my bones will molder here, forgotten."

"You could come back to Ithaca with us," Bulan began. Otto gave a guttural laugh.

"Why? To meet my maker? No. I will stay."

"Except you can't," Welles said, softly. Otto looked at him, and the soldier blanched beneath that yellow gaze. "What I mean to say is, the stories about Maxon's monsters are in every port in these waters. And, well, someone sent Arkwright here. There's no telling if they might try it again. You might not have your privacy for very long."

"He is right, boy," Vogel said, sadly. "You are too valuable to be left alone. Soon enough, when word of what happened here spreads—as it must—they will come for you. Maybe they will be British, or German or even American . . . but they will come."

"Then I will fight them," Otto said, flatly. And, for a

moment, Bulan almost believed that his determination would be enough. Otto had lasted this long, after all. He was strong; savage. A monster's hide, and a tiger's heart.

Virginia touched Bulan's arm. "Bulan . . ." she said, gently. He looked at her, and then at Otto. The latter was staring at him in that peculiar way; half defiant, half pleading. Like a child who has been given a hard choice.

"What do you want to do, Otto?" Bulan asked, in a quiet voice. Otto blinked.

"I told you. I want to stay here."

"I don't think you do. Not really. So what do you want?"

Otto was silent for long moments. His yellow gaze slid first to Virginia, then Vogel and back again. With a grunt, he turned and made as if to go. Bulan hesitated, then followed.

"Hold on . . . let's talk about this."

"There is nothing to talk about," Otto growled, as he left the building and stepped outside. The rain was falling hard now, drumming along the rooftops and wiping away even the lingering odor of smoke. He looked up and then started toward the palisade. He moved at a trot at first, but soon picked up speed.

Bulan followed, not quite sure what he would do if he managed to catch Otto. How to talk to him—how to explain? He wondered how to make him see that they only wanted to help? Talking wasn't working.

"Leave me be," Otto snarled, as Bulan drew close.

"No. Not now. We came to this damn island to find you, and I'm not leaving you here alone—not again!" Bulan's hand snapped out and caught Otto's uninjured shoulder. He wrenched the monster around to face him, and Otto's hands snapped out to close around his throat, just as they had the first time that they'd met. But this time, there was no terrible pressure behind that grip. Bulan looked into Otto's eyes, searching for anger or hate, or even hunger. But all he saw was a deep well of sadness.

"I led them to death," Otto said, so softly that Bulan almost missed it.

"You did what you had to do," he said, as he reached up to remove Otto's fingers from his throat. "Even as I did, when I thought I was you."

"Except you are not me. I am me and they were like me." Otto hunched forward with his head bowed. "Vogel told me—he warned me—but I did not understand until now. I knew that they would die, and if they did not, that I would have to kill them." He stared at his hands and, after a moment's hesitation, Bulan caught the creature in an awkward embrace. Otto stiffened, and then relaxed. He slowly slumped against Bulan like a recalcitrant child, yielding to the affections of his parent.

"I did not want to kill them," Otto murmured.

"No," Bulan said.

"I do not know what I want." Otto extricated himself from Bulan's grip and stepped back. "For so long, I wanted to meet her—Virginia. And now I have, and . . ."

"And what?" Virginia asked, from behind them. Bulan turned to see Virginia and the others watching them with expressions ranging from sadness to confusion to unease. "Tell me, Otto, please . . . what do you want to do now?"

"I do not know," Otto insisted. He turned away, but did not move to leave. Instead, he simply stood in the rain, a grotesque statue, imposing and yet pitiable. At a loss, Bulan looked at the others. Vogel cleared his throat.

"I will stay with him. It is not right the boy should want for company, yes?"

"Neither of you can stay here," Virginia said. "You heard Welles . . . someone will come looking and I doubt they'll be friendly sorts." She looked at Bulan, silently urging him to do something, say something. But what?

Bulan took a deep breath. Then, "You say you don't know what you want. Fine. But what do you dream of, Otto?"

Otto glanced at him. "Dream?"

"Yes. When you sleep, what do you dream?" Bulan asked, hoping, wishing that the answer was not the one he feared. He prayed that Otto did not share his red dreams.

Otto was silent for a time. Then, finally, he said, "I think . . . I think I dream of a place. A place where I am welcome. Where I am not be hunted or attacked." He clenched his clawed hands and looked at them, and in his yellow eyes was a very human look of yearning. "Where I can find . . . peace. Can you help me find that place?"

Bulan hesitated. He looked at Virginia, and thought back to when they'd left Ithaca. She took his hand and nodded. "We will," she said. "Won't we, Bulan?"

Bulan looked at Otto. Was there truly a man there—or only a monster? Time would tell. Until then, could they do any less than their best for him? He extended his hand to Otto, and the monster took it, after a moment's hesitation.

"Yes, we'll help you, my friend. One way or another, we'll help you."

EDGAR RICE BURROUGHS UNIVERSE™

WEiRD WORLDS™

DEAD ON VENUS

TRANSCRIBED BY MIKE WOLFER

FROM CAPTAIN CONOVER'S REPORTS
ARCHIVED AT THE OFFICES OF
EDGAR RICE BURROUGHS, INC.,
TARZANA, CALIFORNIA

ERB
INC.

The FAVONIA

DESIGNERS: ERICH VON HARBEN & JASON GRIDLEY
VESSEL CONSTRUCTED AT TYLER SHIPYARDS AND AERONAUTICS,
SANTA MONICA, CALIFORNIA, U.S.A.

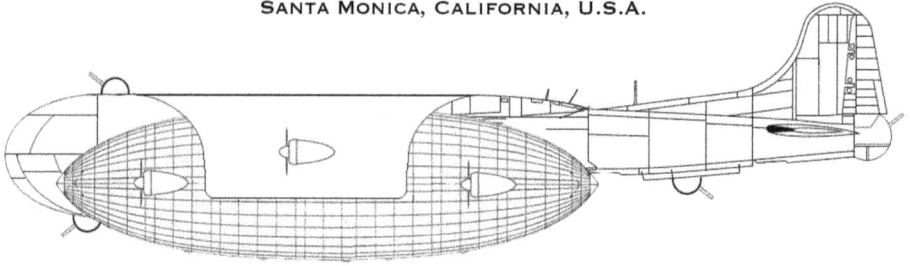

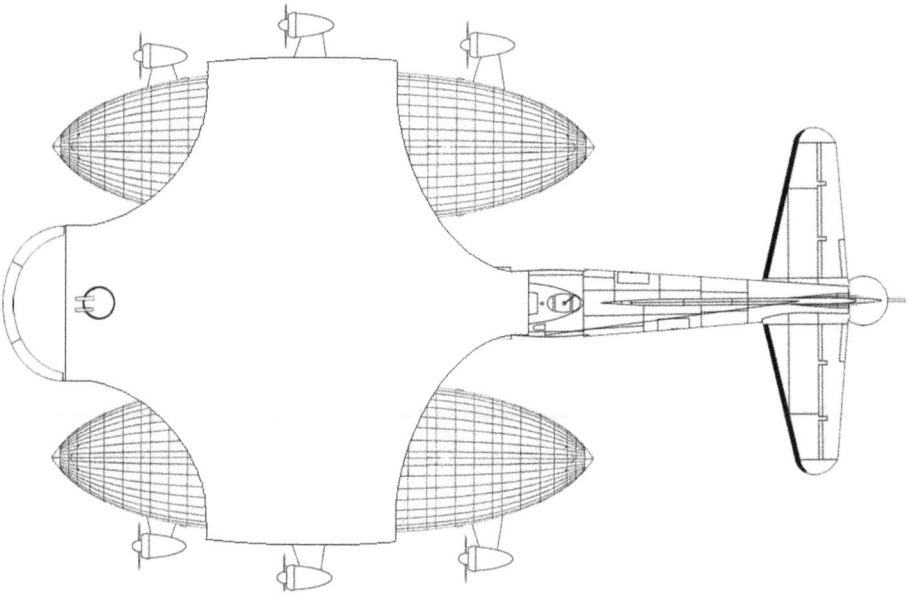

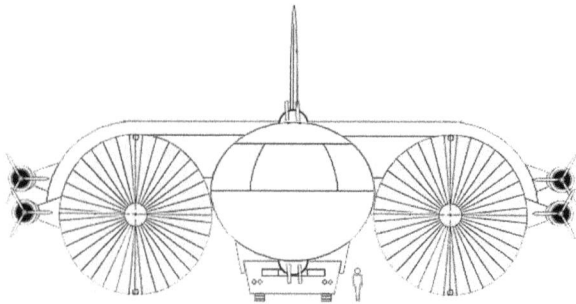

LENGTH: 158 FEET
WIDTH: 98 FEET
FUSELAGE HEIGHT: 38.5 FEET
HEIGHT OF TAIL: 47.5 FEET

The FAVONIA
CARGO CRAWLER
AUTONOMOUS ALL-TERRAIN EXPLORATORY VEHICLE

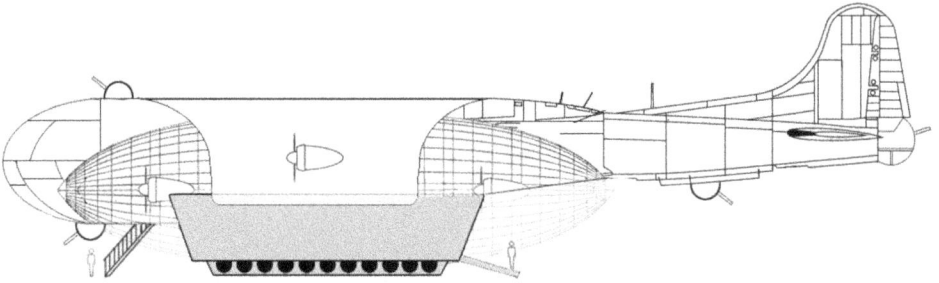

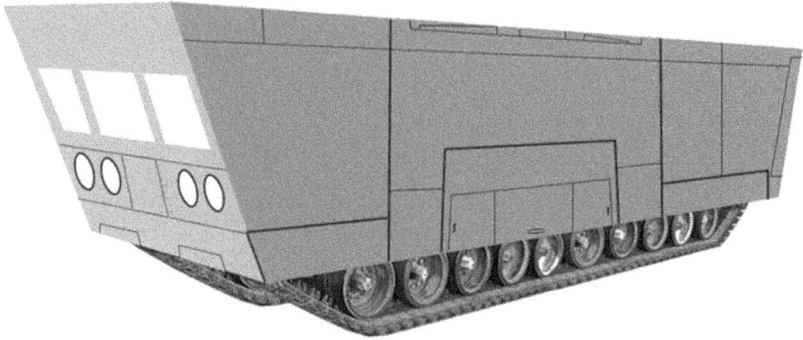

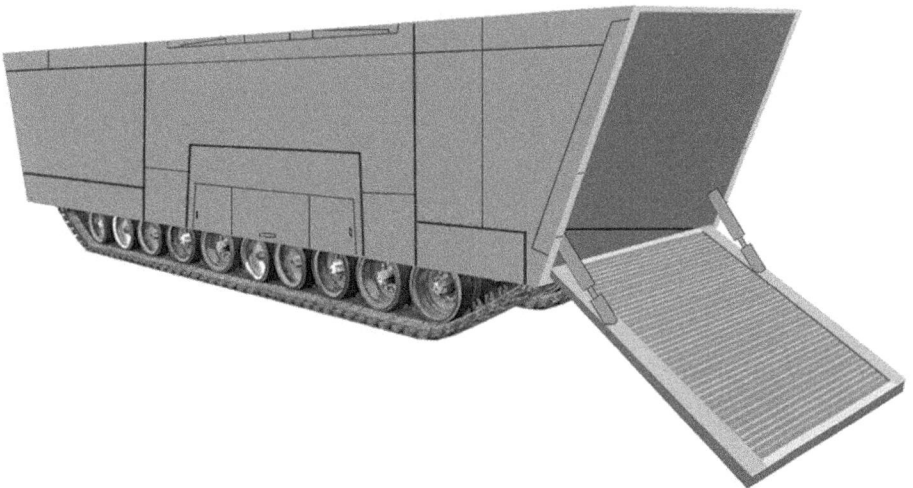

LENGTH: 52 FEET
WIDTH: 16 FEET
TOTAL HEIGHT: 15 FEET
CARGO HOLD HEIGHT: 12.5 FEET

PLANET OF MYSTERY

THE MAJESTIC VACUUM AIRSHIP *FAVONIA*, which I proudly captain, glided hundreds of feet above the treetops of the steaming Venusian jungle. At least, that's what the voice over the radio told us; we were traversing the stormy skies of the planet Venus, or as the voice called it, Amtor.

My name is Captain Douglas W. Conover. Earlier that week, my crew and I had departed Tyler Shipyards and Aeronautics in sunny Santa Monica, bound for the "polar opening," as it's been called, a dimensional anomaly near Earth's North Pole through which the select few who know of its existence may hopscotch into Pellucidar, the primeval world at the Earth's core . . . or to somewhere else. Our mission was to go somewhere else. With the proper electronic and Gridley Wave doohickeys, we intended to unlock a side passage and travel to a world unknown. There, we would gather readings, photos, and samples, and return to Earth. It was a purely scientific expedition, and I speak for every brave member of my crew when I say the thrill of adventure held its thumb firmly on the "what the heck" ends of our personal safety scales to tip them in favor of bounding into the uncharted void.

That's exactly what we did. The *Favonia*, designed by the aforementioned Jason Gridley and an archaeologist with deep pockets named Erich von Harben, passed through the polar opening and deposited us in the skies over a mysterious planetoid, its exact location in our universe undetermined at that time. What we hadn't counted on was that it wasn't a planetoid at all but some form of gigantic living creature whose intense brainwaves scrambled our "skeleton key" device, which should have allowed us to return to Earth.* That's what ship's mechanic Nathan Weinberg insists, at any rate.

Instead of beating a hasty retreat back home, we jumped from the frying pan into . . . what?

Static crackled over the P.A. system of the *Favonia*'s auditorium-like control room at the ship's fore, a chamber that houses the pilot and communications dais. Present were the entire crew, meager as they numbered, and their faces registered shock and dismay. They had thought we were going home. So had I.

"How did you get here? Over," the excited voice from the radio asked. He had introduced himself as Carson Napier of California, but how he ended up on Venus was a mystery. I knew I might only have seconds to process a load of information and arrive at the best possible decisions for my crew, whose lives were in my hands. Just because some radio jockey sounded sincere didn't mean we could trust him; for all we knew, he had an army somewhere in the jungle below with guns trained on our belly. With that in mind, I needed to proceed with extreme delicacy until we knew one way or the other if he was a friend or a crackpot.

Seated beside me at the piloting console, Aito Sato had read my unspoken caution and voiced it. "If they think we're enemies, the *Favonia* can't fly fast enough to evade whatever weapons they might have." I nodded in agreement and depressed the button on the radio transmitter.

"We're here quite by accident, Napier." I said. "Frankly, we're lost. If this is a restricted airspace, please advise on a course that will take us over neutral territory. Over." Before the

---

*See the bonus novelette "Weird Worlds: Voyage into Terror" in the back pages of *The Land That Time Forgot: Fortress Primeval* by Mike Wolfer (Edgar Rice Burroughs, Inc., 2025).

wide window that stretched across the width of the *Favonia's* nose, botanist Vivian Ouellet was joined by Waranji, our Chief of Security, and Tafari, the only other member of Waranji's team on our exploratory mission. Nathan Weinberg stood at the base of the control dais, and beside him was Brahk Zahla, the alien scientist who had joined our crew on one of our previous excursions. All had their eyes on the incredible vista before us.

The entire upper atmosphere of the planet was an unbroken sheet of murky clouds, through which not a single ray of sunlight passed, yet there was still dim illumination of the landscape, indicative of late afternoon or early evening. At a lower altitude that I estimated to be about a mile up floated a secondary layer of clouds, oddly underlit by an undefinable natural light source. To our port towered a forest of enormous trees that made the giant sequoias of Yosemite look like matchsticks, their crowns disappearing into the clouds. To starboard lay dark jungles, and beyond those, shadowed mountainous terrain. Several miles ahead of the *Favonia* lurked a still, dark mass, a black mirror that might have been of a body of water. Vivian and Waranji looked to be exchanging speculative words while Tafari was snapping away with his Brownie.

Napier's response shook me from the wonder of it all. "Restricted airspace?" he laughed. "No such thing here on Amtor, at least not yet. Until I got here," he said proudly, "air travel didn't even exist."

I had so many questions and didn't know which to ask first. Cruising aimlessly over a foreign world seemed less appealing than being wheels down and getting our bearings. Still, it was unknown if we could trust the voice claiming to hail from California.

"Actually," Napier continued, "when I saw you flying in from the horizon, I had to wonder if your craft was some crazy invention of a friend of mine. Over."

"Oh?" I responded. "Who would that be? Maybe I

know him. Over." I didn't really mean it, but I thought I'd humor the faceless voice.

Carson Napier earnestly replied. "You ever cross paths with a guy named Jason Gridley? Over."

Every last member of the crew spun to look at each other, then toward me and Aito on the control dais. It was like watching one of those time-lapse films of a flower blooming. That was what I saw spread across each of their faces after Napier's statement.

"Well, how do you like that?" I said, slapping my knees. I depressed the transmitter button. "Mr. Napier, you pinned the tail right smack on the donkey's . . . anyhow, Gridley did design this ship! If you'd be so kind, can you provide coordinates for a safe landing spot so we can speak face-to-face? Since our vessel has hovering capabilities, we won't need a landing strip, just something nice and level to set down on."

"You can hover?" Napier said more to himself than to me. "Leave it to Gridley."

Carson (as he asked me to call him) went on to explain that the inhabitants of Amtor have a highly erroneous understanding of their planet's geography. They subscribe to the theory that their world consists of a saucer-shaped disk floating upon a molten sea, mistakenly believing that what is in reality its south pole is located at the perimeter of the saucer, whereas its equator actually exists at the saucer's center. Additionally, the inability of those on the surface to view the stars due the two impenetrable cloud envelopes that surround the planet makes Amtorian cartography highly unreliable. He simply could not provide his precise coordinates, even as he wished as much. But Carson had a simple solution: He suggested we continue our current heading until we reached the sea, then decrease our altitude and skim the coast until we came upon his flying vessel, which he called an *anotar*. He told us we'd find the plane resting on pontoons in the water. He further explained that the shoreline was composed of a strip of sand and rocks that stretched for roughly two hundred yards before meeting the tree line, wide enough for the *Favonia* to set down, he figured. He and his three companions would meet us there.

"Let me confer with my crew, and I'll get back to you," I told him. I cut all six engines to bring the *Favonia* down to a sluggish glide, then called Waranji to the control platform.

"What do you think, Chief?" I asked my Waziri friend. Aside from the massiveness of Waranji's muscular bulk, his instincts were his greatest asset. He'd never steered me wrong yet, except that one time in Honolulu.

The security chief crossed his arms across his barrel chest and looked to the huge transparent Harbenite windscreen as he thought. "Aito indicated he needs to dismantle the 'skeleton key' device to hopefully correct the malfunction. Night is approaching, so it would be unwise to continue stumbling through the dark on a world unknown to us."

"Yeah. We might hit a tree," I interjected sarcastically, even though that eventuality was entirely possible. Perhaps even probable.

"This Carson Napier sounds sincere," Waranji mused. "With adequate regard for safety, landing would be acceptable."

"Agreed?" I asked Aito. He shook his head with confidence. "I'll fire up the props, find us a nice solid place to land, and we'll see what this Carson Napier is all about. Who knows," I added, "he might be able to help us find our way out of here."

I did just as Carson suggested and cruised the *Favonia* straight toward the vast, dark ocean, then looped back to fly parallel to the coast while keeping a close eye on the altimeter. While I maneuvered the ship into position, I continued my conversation with Carson, who gave me a brief overview of Amtor. At the recommendation of our faceless host, I maintained an altitude of three hundred feet, high enough to keep us out of reach of the "extremely nasty creatures" known to infest the waters of Amtor. As we followed the coastline, none of us saw any such beasts, but that wasn't from a lack of trying. After the things we've seen on our voyages, Carson's word was good enough for me. Within minutes, Tafari spotted the airplane tethered to a large boulder, but we saw no people below.

"How's it look, Weino?" I asked into the ship's intercom. Nathan had taken a position in the *Favonia*'s forward gun turret beneath the ship's nose, while Brahk kept watch from a similar turret on the underside of the fuselage. This gave us eyes on the ground. We couldn't be too careful.

"Looks clear, Captain," came Nathan's reply, thick with a Brooklyn accent. "But I'm not seeing any people below." Brahk made a similar report.

"If everyone will take a seat, I'm going to bring us down." I directed those on the command deck to buckle up in the jumpseats installed around the base of the command dais. "You boys downstairs," I said as casually as possible, "keep your fingers on the triggers of the fifties, just in case." The *Favonia* wasn't a warship by design, but knowing we have four gun turrets—each housing twin Browning .50 calibers—goes a long way toward calming cases of the jitters.

Gently as a feather, the *Favonia* landed on the clearest patch of sand near the airplane. Night was on its way, so I hit the floods to illuminate our surroundings, but anything could have been lurking beyond those dark jungle trees. Almost immediately upon touching down came the sound of seat belts unbuckling. I had to smile to myself; being lost on another world with no control over where we might end up sure didn't affect the crew's thirst for adventure. Vivian and Tafari rushed toward the front windscreen while I gathered Aito and Waranji to outline our plan of attack. Well, hopefully not "attack." With luck it would be a plan of diplomacy and nothing more.

I stood with my arms crossed, putting together all the pieces in my mind: mixing them, matching them, rearranging them. Everything kept coming together into the same picture. Waranji and Aito waited patiently, but they've been around me long enough to know that when I remove my captain's hat and smooth my hair, I'm ready to share my plan, or so I've been told.

Not one to disappoint my crew, I did just that—fit my cap back in place—and smiled. "Here's what we're gonna do. Waranji and I will go out and meet this Carson, while the rest of the crew stays put. Aito, that will give you time to see if you can figure out why the skeleton key is on the fritz."

Aito interjected. "This is interesting: I scanned the radio frequencies up and down the dial, and the only thing coming through was the communication from Carson. It's almost as if his transmitter is the only one on the planet."

"Well, maybe it is," I said, looking to Waranji. "I think we should leave Tafari on board to stand watch, would you agree?" Waranji nodded in the affirmative. "Now, I know Vivian's going to be chomping at the bit to get out there and retrieve some biological samples, but one thing at a time. We don't know anything about this guy. Heck, the whole thing is crazy. According to every egghead scientist on Earth, Venus doesn't have a breathable atmosphere. But Carson says it does. It doesn't make sense. Which leads me to the bumblebee suits." I referred to the formfitting black-and-yellow high-altitude flight suits we have on board, each fitted with a helmet and oxygen supply. "We'll need them if Carson's pulling our legs about the air being breathable, and the Harbenite plating will provide us protection against . . . whatever. I'm also thinking about the psychological advantage of the suits."

"How so, Captain?" Waranji asked.

"Think of it this way," I responded. "We can't be sure what we're walking into, despite how cordial this Carson is. We won't know who has the upper hand until we go out there. So I say we make a visual impression that we mean business by wearing the bumblebee suits. Of course," I considered, "if Carson and his friends are wearing something more outlandish than us, that blows my idea. But let's give it a shot."

Waranji looked at me warily. "We *will* carry weapons, correct?"

"Sidearms. Holstered. Unless you detect anything amiss," I said, patting his steely shoulder. Why a natural-born warrior like Waranji, who hails from the same neighborhood as Tarzan, would need a gun anyhow was beyond me, but as I said, I trust his judgment, Honolulu notwithstanding.

"And if all is deemed safe," Vivian interjected, "you'll run right back and get me, won't you, Captain?" Mrs. Ouellet had approached me from behind as quietly as a cat, but I pretended to know she was there all along.

I turned and smiled reassuringly. "Yes, ma'am," I said, giving her a wink. She pursed her lips, rolled her eyes in mock contempt, and uttered a clipped laugh.

"You can save that Conover charm for whoever that is out there in the jungle," she said. "Who knows? Maybe it will work on them." That Vivan is a firecracker, but for all of her bravado, I knew she was worried about her husband Jerry back in Santa Monica. I suspected that she wondered if she'd ever see him again. I shared a similar sentiment. Exploring the surface of Venus isn't an opportunity that pops up every day, but I'd sure have felt better knowing that when we were done, we'd be making a direct nonstop flight to Santa Monica, where we'd shortly thereafter sit around the barbecue grill sipping mai tais.

I wrapped up my briefing, and the crew got to work. While Brahk stayed below in the belly turret to keep an eye on the outside, Nathan ran out a "bug" (my nickname for our motorized atmospheric probes) to get readings. Nathan then took Brahk's position while the Rolodon Xinnar scientist analyzed the collected data. Carson was right. There *was* oxygen on Venus. How about that? While Waranji and I suited up in the *Favonia*'s science lab, Aito kept the conversation going with Carson, writing down every bit of what the man said. Except for Nathan and Brahk at their lookout posts in the underside turrets, we all reconvened on the command deck within minutes. Aito kept the intercom keyed open so Nathan and Brahk could hear what we discussed in the control room.

"So let me get this straight," I said, rubbing my hand over my face; I needed a shave. "Venus—more precisely Amtor—has dozens of nations."

"Some technologically advanced, some primitive," Aito replied. "Some, as he said, barely even human."

I scoffed at the suggestion. "Yeah, we'll see about that. And his radio set is one of a kind?"

"In a sense, yes," Aito explained. "Some nations have wireless communication technology, but nothing with the range of Carson's transmitter. One nation—Havatoo—isn't exactly on good terms with his adopted home of . . ." He checked his notes. "Korva, he called it. As a gesture of peace, Carson offered the Havatooans a radio transmitter-receiver of his creation, so the two nations' leaders can effectively communicate long-distance."

"To negotiate verbally before they resort to taking up arms," Waranji concluded.

"Exactly," Aito responded.

Vivian asked a vital question. "So where are we now? Korva?"

Aito explained. "No. Carson and three representatives of Korva flew in their plane to a neutral territory where they're awaiting the arrival of a Havatooan diplomatic party. Carson was warming up the transmitter for its presentation when he spotted the *Favonia* and radioed us. In the jungle"—Aito motioned to the darkness beyond the ship's windscreen—"there's an ancient fort, deserted for centuries. He set the meeting there because he didn't want to risk entering the city of Havatoo. Seems there's a standing order by Havatoo's ruling body that he should be executed."

"Well, doesn't that sound encouraging?" I said in frustration. I shook my head and glanced at Waranji, who gave it some thought.

"His crime?" Waranji asked.

Aito shrugged. "He didn't say, and I didn't ask."

I didn't like the sound of that at all. "Well, that's just swell.

We'll keep our holster flaps unsnapped, right?" I looked to Waranji, who nodded in agreement. "Let's get going. I don't want to raise suspicions by keeping our mystery host waiting."

"Be careful," Vivian implored.

"You can bet on it," I said.

Waranji and I now stood at the base of the metal ladder leading from the disembarkment chamber beneath the *Favonia's* nose. Above us, Nathan gave a thumbs-up through the clear Harbenite globe encasing the forward gun turret. Because they were unneeded, we left the bumblebee suits' bubble helmets and oxygen tanks on board, which offered us added flexibility. *Venus.* I was standing on a sandy beach on *Venus.*

The *Favonia's* floodlights reached just far enough to wrestle with the increasing darkness that seemed intent on devouring us. I raised my hand to block the strong peripheral light from the ship. As my eyes adjusted to the gloom, I detected a ghostly illumination similar to moonlight, even though the thick cloud layer above would have prevented that. Does Venus even have a moon? I couldn't remember. Anyhow, the underside of the lowest cloud formations dimly glowed by either natural phosphorescence or from reflected ground light radiating from some unknown source. Whatever the case, it felt as if the planet wanted us to see just enough to keep us terrified.

As always, Waranji was on high alert and scanned the dense jungle before us for any threats. Strange squawks and howls occasionally pierced the silence. Whatever was making the haunting noises, they didn't sound like any birds I'd ever heard. Maybe they were the "animal people" Carson had mentioned.

I depressed the radio communicator button on my bumblebee suit. "Aito, any news from Carson? Over."

"I've been watching the clock," Aito responded. "He said we're a half hour's walk from the fortress, so they should be here any minute now. Over."

"Keep me posted on your progress with the skeleton key, you hear? Over."

"Sure thing, Captain. Over and out."

I couldn't help but marvel at what I could see of the jungle at the edge of the floodlights. For a good old Earth boy who knows that grass is green, the purple-and-pink ground cover and foliage left me feeling off-kilter. I shared my amazement with Waranji.

"It's almost like being on another planet, isn't it?" I jested. Waranji didn't respond. "It's a joke," I said. Still silence. Then I turned to look at him. The two hundred and fifty pounds of muscle on his six-and-a-half-foot frame were tensed. He looked like a panther ready to pounce. His hand hovered over the holstered sidearm at his hip, and his eyes were narrowed in that way he has. I didn't need to ask. Waranji had heard something. My eyes grew wide, and I held up my hand to block the glare of the floodlights above us.

Carson had arrived. I'm not sure what I was expecting, but it wasn't what I saw anxiously stroll out of the blackness. If you picture a stereotypical Californian, that's Carson. Blond hair, blue eyes, barely any clothes, like a surfer up in Malibu. He was a muscular guy, around six feet tall, and looked to be around thirty years old, was my guess. He wore a loincloth woven of fine fabric and decorated with an intricate pattern. On his feet were sandals with straps that wrapped around his calves up to his knees, and a short cape lay over his back. I wondered if the cape might be a designation of his diplomat status, along with the clasp at his clavicle embedded with a large cerulean jewel. He excitedly greeted us with a wide smile of dazzling teeth. Waranji and I both had our eyes on the sleek, odd-looking pistol holstered at his hip and the sword hanging from his belt. That's right. A *sword*.

"Welcome to Amtor!" he exclaimed. "I'm Carson Napier!" We had figured that one out already.

Under Waranji's watchful eyes, I stepped forward to greet Carson, and we shook hands. "I'm Captain Douglas Conover of the airship *Favonia*, and this is Waranji, our chief of security."

Carson must have noticed Waranji's stern demeanor. Instead of leaning in to shake Waranji's hand, he chose to salute him with a smile. "Nice to meet you, Chief!" He craned his neck to look between us. "That is some ship you've got there. The *Favonia*. Just incredible. What's that underneath?"

Carson was referring to the huge Harbenite shoebox with tank treads clamped snugly to the underside of the fuselage and between the two vacuum tanks on each side of the ship that give us our lift. "We call that the Cargo Crawler. It's an autonomous land vehicle used for the storage and delivery of supplies. Not only can we drop off your groceries, but we can deliver them right to your door."

"That's genius," Carson whispered, duly impressed.

"That's Gridley for you," I said. "How is it that you two know each other?" Not that I would have been able to tell if he was lying, but I still thought I'd quiz him to see if his story sounded straight.

"After my stint as a stuntman," Carson explained, "I went into rocket development."

"Wait. A stuntman? As in . . ." I made motions like I was fighting the Invisible Man.

Carson laughed. "Exactly. Some years back, I met Jason at an exhibition of rocket cars in Hannover, Germany. He's one smart cookie, that guy."

I recalled Gridley mentioning his fascination with rocket cars, so I gave Waranji a wink to let him know I thought Carson was on the up-and-up. Waranji noticeably relaxed his posture but still kept his palm over his sidearm.

"Listen," Carson asked with conviction, "do you know if Jason eventually made it back to Earth?"

Carson's knowledge of Jason Gridley's unwilling barnstorming tour of the cosmos a couple of years back was all I needed to hear to seal the deal that this guy was sincere. "How did you hear about Gridley's predicament all the way out here on Venus?" I asked him.

"Because Jason Gridley paid me a visit during that

predicament," Carson explained with a deadpan delivery. "Did he make it back?"

I explained that Jason had indeed safely returned to Earth, to which Carson breathed a sigh of relief. Then he snapped his fingers as if he just remembered something, turned, and gave a whistle toward the blackness of the jungle. "I almost forgot about my companions. But don't let Duare know I said that, huh?" he whispered from the side of his mouth. I wasn't sure what that meant or what a "Duare" was, but he didn't sound fearful—more like a schoolkid uneasy about being in trouble with his girlfriend.

Then I saw her. Like Lana Turner descending the staircase in *Ziegfeld Girl*, she strode from the dark recesses of the jungle behind Carson, her head held high and her eyes cautiously on the two strangers to Amtor. Regal doesn't even begin to describe the young woman. Though she looked no older than twenty, she carried herself like the Queen of England. Carson had judiciously kept his sword sheathed when he met us, but this woman had no intention of concealing the ornate, jeweled dagger she conspicuously gripped in one hand. Her tanned body was wrapped in crimson silk, which was wound about her torso and chest like a boa constrictor. Encircling her neck was a loosely worn silken scarf of shimmering gold, its long ends draped over each of her shoulders to fall behind her. The woman's voluminous and wavy dark hair was worn in a style that would make any hairdresser jealous, and the golden tiara and many necklaces, rings, and pieces of arm jewelry that completed her ensemble had to put up a tough fight to compete with the beauty of the woman who wore them. In contrast to her regal attire, she wore a holstered pistol at her hip, similar to Carson's.

Two others approached from behind her, one male and the other female. Both were dressed similarly to their counterparts, each possessing the same dark eyes and hair as the woman who had come to stand beside Carson. As the others joined us, the old sky dog in me could immediately identify the woman in red as the "girlfriend" I had mused about earlier.

Carson introduced her as she warily eyed Waranji and me. "This is Duare, Janjong of Vepaja and Royal Emissary of Korva." The woman radiated sophistication. We couldn't help but bow rather than extending our hands to shake. "And this is Ero Shan and Nalte," he said, introducing the man and the woman behind Duare. Just as their companions carried those odd, sleek guns in holsters, so did Ero Shan and Nalte.

Nalte appeared to be the same age as Duare and exuded a less formal demeanor; her silk wrapping was a shade of aquamarine, and she wore far less jewelry. As for Ero Shan, he was easily a match for Waranji in terms of size, and the leather harness he wore around his chest that held a sheathed sword against his back screamed "warrior." If Carson was the stuntman, this guy could have been the leading man. All three Amtorians were physically striking with perfectly chiseled facial features. Any one of them would look right at home on the cover of a Hollywood movie magazine.

"I am Captain Douglas Conover," I said, but my introduction fell flat.

Carson explained. "They don't speak English."

Of course they didn't. I looked at Waranji. "The translators," I suggested. He and I carried small Xinnarian earpieces supplied to us by Brahk Zahla, devices that translate any language into the one spoken by the wearer. We slipped them into our ears as I explained their function to Carson. The Amtorians could not understand us, but at least we would be able to understand our hosts.

Carson introduced us to his friends, and then Duare spoke with the no-nonsense voice of a diplomat. "From what nation do you hail, and what brings you to this region?" I understood her words perfectly, but I would need Carson to translate my response. I looked to him for help, but his attention was on Duare.

In their tongue, Carson began to explain our translation

devices, but before he could complete his thought, she cut him off with the raise of an eyebrow.

"Good," she said. "Since they only speak your Earth language, I can speak freely to you, Carson." Before Napier could stop her, Duare launched into a stream of well-composed suppositions. "Who are they, and how do we know we can trust them? They could be spies of Havatoo, or worse, considering our proximity to Kormor. And look at that vehicle. I recognize a warship when I see one. Our diplomatic mission is already a risky endeavor for the four of us. Why would we entertain these travelers when they might fire upon us with the weapons at their hips, or have you not noticed those?"

Carson sheepishly raised his hands to stop Duare's little speech. He explained that while we did not speak Amtorian, we could understand her every word. Her face went ashen, but only for a moment. She recovered, lifted her chin, and spoke directly to Waranji and me.

"Perhaps the two of you would like to answer my questions?" she said without flinching.

I looked at Waranji and smiled. "I like her," I admitted, and the big Waziri smirked back at me.

Carson made an impassioned peace pitch, and the janjong—which means "princess"—visibly relaxed her pose and her features softened, as did those of Nalte and her mate. The big guy placed a hand of friendship on Waranji's shoulder, who reciprocated the motion on the shoulder of Ero Shan. After the initial tension of the meeting had passed, it looked like we had made friends.

Over the next several minutes, Carson explained more about their presence at that location, and I gave him a brief overview of our predicament. After consulting with Waranji and getting his A-OK, I radioed the *Favonia* standing patiently behind us. Nathan answered my call from inside the nose turret. I turned and gave him a wave.

"What's goin' on out there, Cap?" the Brooklynite asked suspiciously.

"Everything's A-OK here, Nathan," I assured him. "What Mr. Napier told us over the radio checks out. While we're out here, we're going to take a walk and do some sightseeing."

Nathan was incredulous. "Are you sure that's a good idea, Captain? With all due respect, I mean. Over."

After getting a nod from Waranji, I assured Nathan the situation was well in hand. "There's an abandoned fortress in the jungle where Carson and his crew are meeting with some others who are due to arrive tomorrow morning. They're on some kind of peace mission. Since Aito needs time to sort out the skeleton key, we'd be crazy to pass on an opportunity to get a lay of the land. I also think it's safe enough for someone else from the ship to join us."

Within minutes, a bumblebee suit–clad Vivian had descended the ladder and stood with us. Introductions were made, and Duare and Nalte were quite cordial in their welcome to our ship's botanist. I don't know anything about Amtorian politics or social customs, but I figured letting them know one of our team was a woman might reassure them.

"Shall we?" Carson asked, gesturing toward the jungle.

Waranji and I exchanged a glance. Vivian was nothing but smiles. She tugged at the strap of the canvas sample bag over her shoulder. "I'm ready," she said enthusiastically, and with that, we turned and marched into the darkness, led by Ero Shan and Carson.

Conversation was light and casual as we trod through the jungle at a mild incline. We walked upon a wide path of interconnected and ancient stonework, thirty feet in width. The road must have once assisted the occupants of the fortress in moving supplies to and from the seacoast. Ero Shan took the lead with a small handheld lantern similar to a flashlight. Dozens of feet above us loomed a cathedral ceiling of creepers and hanging moss, and Vivian delighted in stopping briefly to collect leaf and bark samples from the foliage as we passed. She secured those in small glass vials and stored them in her sample bag. Nalte seemed intrigued by Vivian's actions, and the two appeared to hit it off. At one point, Mrs. Ouellet shared her translation earpiece with the young Amtorian woman, and Nalte was flabbergasted when the device translated Vivian's words to her. Nalte excitedly shared the device with Ero Shan, then Duare, and all three took turns being profoundly shocked by the capabilities of the little translator. Waranji being Waranji, his focus was unbreakable as he scanned every dark recess between the boles as we continued our jaunt to the fortress.

While Carson kept a watchful eye for some animals he called "zangans," he elaborated on his precarious stature among the Amtorians. In his adopted home nation of Korva, he was considered a hero; in fact, he had been bestowed the title of "tanjong," the equivalent of "prince." However, the nation of Havatoo, whose emissaries he and his friends awaited, had deemed Carson an enemy after he had engineered the escape of Duare, who had fallen into their hands. The ruling council of Havatoo had declared Duare genetically inferior and scheduled her for "humane" execution before she and Carson escaped from the city of self-appointed physical and intellectual elites. It was hard to imagine anyone considering Duare "genetically inferior." Not from my perspective, nor Carson's. Ero Shan had originally hailed from Havatoo before he defected, but he too had come to realize both the wickedness and the invalidity of his people's belief in eugenics. With Carson and Duare's past exploits in mind, it was indeed a precarious situation into which they had voluntarily placed themselves. Meeting with the enemy to extend a peace offering, way out there in the jungle, without a battalion of soldiers to back them up, seemed like an insane proposal to me. But that's exactly what Carson offered the nation of Havatoo, and I suppose it said a lot about the fearlessness—and maybe foolhardiness—of his character.

After hiking for one quarter of a "kob" (one kob being an Amtorian unit equating to two and a half miles), the trees and underbrush cleared considerably, and we left behind the dense growth for a fairly clear area of low tangled roots and ferns, roughly the size of a baseball field. At its center lay the crumbling gray ruins of the fortress, the rendezvous point where Carson and his companions had chosen to meet the Havatooans. The place fairly reeked of jungle rot and stale puddled water, but I've smelled worse; I've walked the battlefields of Europe during World War II, after all.

The place loomed over us like some dark specter, or even a hungry beast waiting for us to march into its mouth. The perimeter of the fortress was ringed by a twenty-foot-tall wall of huge stone blocks arranged in a patchwork formation. Plant life completely covered the top of the wall and was joined to the ground cover below by a thick network of ivy and vines. The jungle was doing its best to eradicate the abandoned structure and all vestiges of the humans who had constructed it. Two great metal doors, pitted and rusted, dominated the wall our group approached.

Carson noticed my perplexed look. "They won't open," he said in answer to my unspoken question. "Maybe with a few drums of lubricating oil and picks and chisels, but they might as well be welded shut. We can get in through here." He pushed open a small human-sized portal inset at one of the door's lowest edges. The hinges screeched in protest. One by one, we filed through the opening to the interior courtyard.

After securing the door's locking crossbar, Ero Shan suddenly spun. In a flash, he had drawn his pistol and thrust out an arm to one side to shield Vivian, Waranji, and me. Before us in the courtyard stood a dozen armed men wearing black-and-gold loincloths and harnesses. Based on the reactions of our Venusian friends, the presence of the newcomers was not anticipated.

2

A Creeping Terror

PRESUME ONE OF YOU IS TANJONG CARSON," a commanding voice rang out, and then one of the men stepped forward. "I am Korgan Sentar Lok Marr. Present yourself, Tanjong Carson." A pistol and sword hung from opposite sides of the speaker's waist, and twelve soldiers stood at attention behind him. With but a gesture from their leader, the men performed a choreographed drawing and brandishing of their swords, culminating in the weapons' tips being thrust into the ground and twelve sets of hands clasped over the butts of their hilts. It appeared to be an exaggerated display of both "armed and ready" and "we're willing to listen first."

His back straight and head held high, our Californian friend walked calmly forward and stood before Lok Marr. "I am Carson, Tanjong of Korva. I am honored to make your acquaintance, and I applaud the wisdom of the Sanjong in agreeing to the overture made by Taman, Jong of Korva."

While Carson conversed with the leader of the new arrivals, I looked to Duare for an explanation of the similar-sounding words. "'Jong?' 'Sanjong?'" I whispered. I didn't want to miss a bit of what was transpiring, understanding the politics taking place before me and my crew might prove vital, whichever way things went.

Duare whispered back to me while keeping an eye on Carson. "The ruler of our nation of Korva is Taman; his title is 'Jong.' Havatoo, however, is not ruled by a single jong.

Instead, the city is guided by the recommendations of a quintumvirate, called the Sanjong. The body of the Sanjong is composed of five individuals from five designations of Havatooans: *ambad* (psychologist), *kalto* (chemist), *kantum* (physicist), *sentar* (biologist), and *korgan* (soldier). This man, Lok Marr, has been tutored in two of those disciplines, as denoted by his title korgan sentar."

"A soldier biologist, huh?" I said to Waranji. "Pretty odd combination."

"Almost like something you would find on another planet," Waranji cajoled, getting back at me for my earlier jest.

Ero Shan could not understand our words, but he read my unease. "I was once a korgan sentar, Captain Conover," he said, "so be consoled that well do I know the stripes of this tharban." I had no idea what that meant, but I took it as a disparaging comment directed at the leader of the Havatooans.

Carson beckoned Duare to join him in speaking to the visiting dignitary and his security force, while Ero Shan and Nalte conversed with each other in hushed tones. As the diplomatic overture with Lok Marr continued, Waranji, Vivian, and I took stock of the fortress interior.

The courtyard was overgrown, but less so than outside the walls. I dug my heel into the vines and moss carpeting the ground and found not earth beneath but pitted stone slabs, similar to cement. My motion disturbed numerous insects that scurried for refuge, some of which resembled the bugs and burrowers of Earth . . . but only somewhat. Looming over us rose a castle-like dwelling of at least three stories with a peaked roof of ceramic shingles like that of a Japanese pagoda. At one time, a tower must have risen from the center of the roof, but all that was now visible was a truncated circular base at the pagoda's central peak. The stone and wood remnants of the tower lay about the yard, while most of the structure had found a final resting place within the castle, having smashed through the roof long ago. Dark rectangular windows fitted with corroded metal bars dotted every surface of the bleak walls. Had this been a fortress or a prison? I couldn't be sure. The stone staircases leading to the tops of the ramparts were carpeted by moss and vines, and I could only guess that the wide marble steps fronting the castle's main portico had once been opulent; I could see vestiges of several railings, and tall poles lined the steps. The poles might have once hosted flags, or they might have supported a weather-resistant covering. In the center of the courtyard stood a table, upon which sat the radio transmitter-receiver unit Carson had invented. It consisted of a rectangular bronze box, the face of which contained several gauges and dials, along with a microphone like those used by radio station announcers. On the ground beside the table sat a larger metal case with heavy electrical wires feeding up to the amplifier; evidently, this was a battery of some sort. Other wires snaked away from the table, up one of the stone staircases, and then to a dish atop a collapsible metal radio tower, twenty feet in height, erected at the top of the barricade wall. Waranji pointed out the dry-rotted crates and other wooden constructs that had been overtaken by the Amtorian flora that covered everything. These discarded relics of the former occupants were piled at the bases of the fortified walls. It looked to me like there had been one final, cataclysmic battle before the stronghold was abandoned.

I looked up at those monstrous, moss-encrusted walls, the castle windows peering down upon us like black eyes in the darkness. A chill ran up my spine. How many had died here? If there were such things as ghosts on Amtor, surely they lurked in the dark halls of the abandoned castle. Maybe they stood beside us in this very courtyard.

Nalte's voice pulled me from my internal deliberation about the existence of spooks. "I do not like it," she said adamantly. Without Carson present to translate, all we could do was listen.

"What do you think she means?" Vivian asked. "Waranji? What do you think?"

The big guy surveyed all around us but said nothing. Finally, his eyes landed on Ero Shan, who apparently had already read our minds.

"Nalte is uneasy about the arrival of the party from Havatoo," Ero Shan explained. "We did not expect them until tomorrow morning." He turned to Nalte to allay her misgivings. "You know these jungles better than anyone. There are incalculable dangers here, particularly this close to Kormor. Lok Marr likely allowed for additional travel time because of those dangers, but to his good fortune did not encounter any."

"Or," Nalte said with a stern look, "they intended to arrive early to set a hideous death trap for us. Have you not considered that, Ero Shan?"

Ero Shan shifted nervously and seemed to be carefully choosing his words. "I have not considered that and I shall not, for we are not dead, are we?"

I noticed then that Nalte's palm lay firmly upon the pistol at her hip. She meant business. "That the Havatooans have not slaughtered us does not negate the possibility of that being their intent. This could be the last adventure. This could be the last second for all of us, and here we stand like oblivious *mistals* sitting in a targo web." The young lady didn't exactly have the most rosy outlook on life, but then, I had no idea what she had lived through, or what unknown threats lurked within and without the walls of the fortress.

"What is Kormor? What . . . Kormor?" Vivian asked suddenly. I realize now that she was attempting to change the subject. Nonetheless, she made a good point. We had heard several references to Kormor, and my curiosity was also piqued: Why did everyone seem to fear Kormor, whatever it was?

Ero Shan and Nalte exchanged a silent look. She pursed her lips as if summoning the nerve to speak, but whatever she had to say would have to wait. Carson hailed us, and together we approached the newcomers and their commander.

The Havatooan guards—well, korgan? Korgans?—anyhow, none of the twelve moved a muscle as we approached, which was mighty cordial of them. Carson introduced us to Lok Marr, but in doing so, he failed to mention we were from Earth. There was no point in complicating matters by interjecting aliens from another world into their mission of diplomacy, after all. I had already gotten the drift that the whole premise was dicier than Carson wanted to admit.

Lok Marr eyed Vivian, Waranji, and me from head to toe, and then back again. Our bumblebee suits made us stick out like sore thumbs. My fingers were crossed that would be a good thing.

"From where do you hail, Captain?" Lok Marr asked inquisitively, a hint of suspicion in his voice.

Carson stepped in to speak for us. "I know it is a strange concept to fathom, as it is said that all upon Amtor speak but a single tongue, but these three royal envoys come from a land so very distant that they do not speak our language. However, I have learned to speak theirs. They are from the kingdom of . . . Santa Monica, in the land of California." Lok Marr looked puzzled. "Their home lies far across the Trabol Joram, beyond even Ganfal Island and Malpi. They have traveled far and attend this most auspicious occasion by happenstance, as they would join Korva and Havatoo in matters of international diplomacy." He sure laid it on thick. Now we were "royalty." Imagine that.

"I have never heard of this land, California," Lok Marr said skeptically.

Carson fabricated an immediate and plausible excuse. "The Californians are of such high intellectual and scientific advancement that before now they have not ventured beyond their borders, for fear of their technology being stolen and used by tyrannical nations against innocents."

Lok Marr mulled it over before his features finally softened. "Your people are indeed wise, Captain. Havatoo welcomes further strengthening of ties with other lands, as the Thorists frustratingly remain a consistent threat." He thought for a moment, then arched a brow. "But what brings you here, now? The arrangement my nation made with Korva for this meeting was highly secretive . . ."

I spoke up immediately with a fib of my own, even though only Carson would understand me. "Korgan Sentar Lok Marr, it was not our intent to intrude on this sensitive mission. Our vessel is on a simple exploratory voyage. When we saw Tanjong Carson's anotar on the beach, we stopped to ensure the vessel's crew had not suffered an accident. It was compassion that brought us here." Carson bobbed his head in agreement and translated my words for the Havatooan.

"Very well," Lok Marr replied, apparently satisfied with the explanation. "Our arrival was hastened by uneventful travel, but we would be fools to attempt a return to Havatoo before daybreak. My men and I shall remain here until morning."

At this point, Carson turned to me and my crew members, saying that he would have loved to catch up with the current events on Earth, but duty called, and he needed to attend to his fragile negotiations with the Havatooans. As the rest of us fell back out of earshot, he began a rudimentary explanation of the radio transmitter to Lok Marr, who did not seem overly impressed with the device. Short-range wireless communication technology did exist in Havatoo, in a form; however, no radio transmitter capable of spanning the width of the great sea separating Havatoo and Korva had yet been invented. My take was that Lok Marr wanted to maintain an air of indifference to prevent the power dynamic between their peoples from shifting too far in Korva's favor.

Lok Marr's attitude changed after Carson switched on the transmitter. The apparatus crackled and hummed, and after it warmed up, Carson radioed far-off Korva. Within seconds came a response, acknowledging his transmission. Though they maintained their stoic demeanors, the members of the Havatooan security force eyed one another in astonishment.

During the demonstration, Waranji, Vivian, and I occupied

our time silently observing and soaking in the fact that we were standing on another world.

Vivian ran her hand over the mossy stones of the barrier wall and looked up to its top. Overhead, the sky was now black, with an occasional shimmer of luminescence across the low-hanging cloud cover that looked to me like lightning. None of us could see a single star in the heavens, as if a stifling ebon blanket lay heavily upon the world, and as the minutes passed, a dense fog thick with moisture began to creep over the fortress yard.

"I think I'll check in with Aito," I said, and depressed the communicator button on the collar of my bumblebee suit. What I received was only static, but at last Aito's voice came through, though he spoke only a few words before the signal once again fuzzed out.

Assuming my communicator was on the fritz, Waranji called to the ship with his device, but obtained a similarly disappointing response.

"What do you think, Vivian?" I asked.

She gazed up at the descending fog upon the courtyard and the flashes of light overhead. "My guess is an atmospheric disturbance. Could you make out anything Aito said?"

I turned to Waranji. "Did it sound to you like he said 'hours'?" Waranji nodded. "Well, at least that's good," I concluded. "If I'd heard the word 'never,' I'd be worried." I watched Carson and his companions among the Havatooans. "You know . . ."

Waranji knew what I was about to suggest. "We could return to the ship," he said, finishing my sentence for me. "I have been watching our hosts. Everything seems quite cordial, but Carson and his team are greatly outnumbered should anything go awry."

I winked at my security chief. "Just what I was thinking. Are you okay hanging around here for a bit," I asked Vivian, "just to make sure things stay kosher?"

Vivian was squatting on the ground, watching an odd little

insect crawling among the roots, some kind of centipede with wings. She looked up at me and smiled. "You'd have to drag me away, Captain," she laughed. With that, I radioed the *Favonia*, and though I had no idea if Aito was receiving a clear signal, I spoke slowly and explained we would remain with Carson and his team a while longer. The response I received was spotty, but I did detect the words, "sounds good." And so, the three of us settled into our self-appointed roles as glorified playground monitors. If only we knew then what we know now.

Carson's presentation of the radio went over well enough and had wound down, the conversation among all the Amtorians assuming a more casual tone. Several of the korgans were tasked with building a fire in the center of the courtyard, but just about the time they had gathered enough scrap lumber from the overgrown edges of the compound, it started sprinkling. It was decided to move things indoors, out of the elements and into the gloom of the dilapidated castle.

"Will you and your friends join us, Captain?" Duare asked cordially. I called over to Carson to assist with translation for his beauteous companion. He excused himself from his conversation with Lok Marr and strode over to where my crew and I had gathered near the entryway of the exterior wall.

I addressed Janjong Duare, with Carson's help. "We are grateful that you have entertained our unexpected presence, and we have already learned much about your world that will be scientifically invaluable to us," I began. "We are only on Amtor temporarily, and I should return to our vessel to oversee our imminent departure. However, I am concerned for the safety of you and your friends, as the Havatooans outnumber you. Therefore, I will commit to remaining as long as necessary, Janjong." I turned to Carson. "What's your take on their attitude? Any warning bells?"

"Nothing out of the ordinary," Carson replied. "Korva and Havatoo are long-standing rivals, so we always keep up our guard when it comes to them." He looked to the sky and brushed a raindrop from his forehead. "I can't ask you to endanger you or your crew by staying. It's probably not necessary anyhow. Lok Marr seems like a generally level-headed guy. Our philosophies about genetics might not align, but man-to-man, I think we have nothing to fear from them. It's up to you whether or not you stay," he concluded.

Behind us, the korgans were making quite a racket, as they had begun pulling on the castle entrance's large double door, trying in vain to free the hinges of decades of rust. With a loud crack, they succeeded, but as one, the men fell back from the towering panels of the immense gate after pulling them outward several feet. Something was in the castle foyer, moving and bobbing within the pitch.

Let me tell you about the spiders on Amtor, or as they call them, "targos." They're nasty-looking creatures, with legs covered by black hair, and a yellow spot over each of their eight eyes. If that doesn't sound like such a big deal, consider their bodies are the size of a St. Bernard's, with each leg probably spanning fifteen feet. If that wasn't enough to curl your toes, their fangs inject a deadly venom that kills within seconds. The Amtorians wisely fear the arachnids, but they rely on the creatures to supply them with *tarel*, the monsters' web silk, which is used to make everything from ropes to cloth for apparel. Imagine wearing a pair of long johns woven from spider silk. No thanks, pal.

The korgans hurriedly retreated to the base of the worn marble steps, while others rushed toward their fellow soldiers with guns drawn. Within the black portal, the body of the targo lowered to the floor, before rising suddenly and letting out an ear-splitting shriek. Waranji, Vivian, and I all cringed involuntarily; none of us had any idea spiders had voices, but I suppose on Amtor, anything is possible. With its intentions announced, the beast struck outward with one incredibly long, pike-like leg, barely missing the nearest korgan, who had dived to avoid the thrust. Other attacks followed suit, but the men were all outside the reach of the hideous creature.

To my dismay, Carson and Lok Marr held a none-too-panicked battlefield conference, their voices measured and precise. What seemed like a nightmarish scenario to me and my crew members appeared to be a mild inconvenience to the Amtorians and nothing more.

Carson shouted over to Ero Shan and Waranji, and the two rushed to his side. After a brief consultation, the two warriors bolted toward the castle, each to one of the construction's two front corners.

Vivian gripped my arm. "What are they doing?"

I'll admit, I was unsure what they hoped to accomplish until I considered that Waranji and Ero Shan were the largest and most muscular of all of us. The fact that none of the Amtorians fired their weapons was the second clue as to their plan. "I think I know what they're up to," I told Vivian. "Watch."

From their respective positions, Ero Shan and Waranji inched toward the double door, their backs to the mossy stone wall. As they did, several of Lok Marr's men tossed burning pieces of wooden debris toward the open portal, ensuring the targo would remain within the web-shrouded chamber. Carson shouted. Simultaneously, Ero Shan and Waranji applied their muscular bulks to the mighty doors. The hinges wailed in protest as the warriors exerted their prodigious strength. The metal scraped against the stone entryway, and with a resounding hollow boom, the doors were successfully closed, sealing the targo within the castle.

Nalte explained the rationale of the maneuver to our trio of incredulous Earth people. "The targo is an extremely dangerous and deadly creature, but the tarel it produces is vital to us. The first instinct might be to kill the targo on sight because of its ugliness, but unless it is attacking, it is best to let the targo live because of the tarel it produces. The targo has claimed the castle as its lair. It is welcome to it. If we leave it alone, it will leave us alone."

I shot a glance at Vivian. "Let sleeping targos lie, she says, huh?"

"Why not?" she replied. "But if it gets a thorn in its paw, don't ask me to pull it out." Vivian laughed. "I don't need any new friends."

Our hearts leaped into our throats. There was a pounding on the iron door, just a few steps behind us. Three hits: *bang, bang, bang!* The sound echoed across the courtyard—then silence. I glanced around the enclosure. Waranji and Ero Shan were walking back toward us after sealing the castle doors, and Carson and Lok Marr were approaching as well. Duare and Nalte were cautiously backing away from the door, so I figured Vivian and I should do the same.

"Was that you who knocked?" Carson asked in mild concern.

"No, sir," I replied. "Do you or Lok Marr have any other men due to arrive?"

Lok Marr did not understand my words, but he asked a similar question of Carson, who assured the Havatooan that his group consisted only of him, Duare, Ero Shan, and Nalte. "What of these strangers from Santa Monica?" he asked suspiciously.

I held up a finger to halt the conjecture, but three more solid bangs on the door came before I could respond. We all took another step back. I radioed the *Favonia* to see if one of the crew had followed us out to the fortress but was met with only static. "I don't think it's one of my people," I said.

Carson approached the door and listened through the corroded metal. By then, raindrops were tapping consistently on the jungle foliage. "Who's out there?" Carson called into the air in both Amtorian and English. There was no response. "Identify yourself!" Nothing but silence and raindrops.

"Step back." Lok Marr snapped his fingers to summon one of his soldiers. The man approached the door with sword in hand, and following his commander's orders, he raised the locking bar and pulled open the door. The korgan was tensed and ready for anything. The hinges ceased their squealing, and through the portal in the wall we saw a man, or what looked like a man. It was difficult to tell in the darkness.

"Who are you?" the korgan demanded.

Silence.

"I said . . ."

The sentence died on the soldier's lips. From his back protruded the bloody tip of a long, steely sword. The korgan collapsed onto his back, his sightless eyes staring into the blackness of the weeping sky. All of us fell away from the open door as the attacker lunged toward us.

Perhaps "lunged" is too powerful a word. More like shambled, but that would conjure an image far less deadly than what faced us. The man—if that is what it was—stepped awkwardly through the doorframe. From head to foot, the thing's skin was being eaten away by fungus, its hair matted to what looked like a fleshless cranium, dripping with swamp ooze. The clothing was in tatters, and the thing wore no armor; the only indication that it was a warrior was the bloody sword it gripped in bone white hands. But its face . . . How can I describe the countenance of the thing that trod toward us with liquid sloshes? It was as if the air had been sucked out of the head with a vacuum pump, pulling the cracked skin taut against the skull. There were no lips around the mouth; the decayed, yellow teeth were in full view, jutting from the gums to affect a sardonic grin. The dead eyes were the most unnerving feature of the face. They were watery and a sickly pale yellow, the color of the irises bleached out long ago, with each orb sunken into a dark socket. The thing moved like a marionette on strings, with unnatural jerks and spasms, but somehow it maintained its footing as it made directly toward us.

"What in Sam Hill is that?" I yelled to Carson. I turned

to find the Earth castaway looking down the barrel of his raised pistol, aimed at the corpse-like thing. The look of regret upon Carson's face gave me pause. It was not just regret. It was pity.

"Stand back," Carson said calmly, and with that, the tip of the bronze gun flashed with a burst of light. Not a sound was uttered by the weapon, nor did a bullet fly to its mark; instead, the upper portion of the attacker simply melted into nothingness. Flesh, bone, and muscle were instantaneously erased, leaving only the spindly legs attached to the hips, which wobbled before falling to the ground. With suddenly no hand to hold it, the sword dropped as well.

"My God," Vivian whispered.

Waranji's eyes were wide. "And mine, as well," the Waziri said.

Lok Marr began issuing orders to his men as he jogged in their direction. The soldiers sprang into action, climbing the stone staircases to take lookout positions atop the wall. Ero Shan jumped to the open iron door inset in one of the two main gates, slammed it shut, and pounded the locking bar into place. Vivian couldn't tear her eyes from the remnants of the corpse and squatted before it, prodding the exposed skin with a twig.

"This wasn't alive," she said, flabbergasted. "It's in a state of advanced decomposition." She stood and brushed her hands together. "What are we looking at here, Mr. Napier?" I could tell the wheels of her scientific mind were spinning a mile a minute, trying to comprehend the putrid thing lying on the ground before us.

"And what is *that* thing?" I asked, pointing at the weapon Carson was returning to the holster at his hip.

"The Amtorians call it an r-ray pistol," he said. "Yeah. I couldn't believe it either, the first time I saw one fired. It destroys only living—or unliving—tissue, but against human attackers, that's all that's necessary, as you saw."

I wiped rain from my eyes and looked at the remains on the ground. "You're saying that thing was human?"

"Once upon a time, yes," he said, a note of sadness in his voice.

"That," Duare interjected, "is why we fear nearby Kormor, Captain Conover. You see, Kormor is the City of the Dead."

3
ASSAULT OF THE DEATH CORPS

WARANJI SHOT ME A WARY GLANCE. Not at all worried he would be stepping on the toes of his captain, he turned to Duare and posed the questions that were on all our minds. "Janjong, can you please explain what you mean? You say this . . . *man* was already dead?" he said, pointing toward what was left of the corpse at our feet. "How great is their number?"

Carson translated Waranji's queries, after which the unflustered princess explained the ghastly subject as if she were describing something as mundane as eating an ice cream cone during a Sunday afternoon walk on the Santa Monica pier.

"Near our present location is the city of Kormor," Duare explained. "It is a vile, sickly place, a true reflection of its monarch, Skor, the mad jong of Morov. There can be found a handful of living beings, as is Skor, but all others are dead men who have been brought back to life to serve the every whim of their master until their destruction."

I shook my head in disbelief. "Sounds like one of those hoodoo-voodoo movies your pals in Hollywood make," I remarked to Carson.

"Oh, it's real enough," the castaway Earthman said firmly. "I've been to Kormor. So has Duare. We were both prisoners of Skor, for a time. In fact, that's where I met Nalte, locked away in a tower, the subject of the Jong of Kormor's diabolical experiments. Had we not escaped together, her fate would have been eventual death and rebirth as a, shall we say, thrall of Skor."

I glanced at Nalte and assessed her physical beauty. "You're comin' in loud and clear," I responded with a sigh of disgust. The radio jargon in my turn of a phrase jogged my mind back to a pressing matter. "Are there a lot of these dead men in the jungles around here? I need to warn my crew aboard the *Favonia*."

"This one shouldn't even be here." Carson pointed to the thing lying on the ground before us. "Skor devised some kind of scientific process to bring life to dead men that's part chemical, part hypnosis, and quite possibly, part magic. But even though they walk and talk and think, his soldiers are dead and are dependent on Skor's power to keep them moving. I'm not exactly sure what range that encompasses, but I do know that if they stray too far from Skor's mental emanations, they're worthless."

"Mental emanations?" Vivian asked skeptically.

Carson smiled with assurance. "That's correct. I know that might be difficult for a true scientist like yourself to digest, but mental projection is a very real thing. I practice it myself. It was taught to me by a Hindu mystic named Chand Kabi." Carson shot me a smirk. "More hoodoo-voodoo, I know, but trust me, I'm on the level."

I nodded. "I'll take your word for it. Now. About their numbers."

Carson pointed off into the distance. "Kormor is about five miles from where we are now. From our prior adventures, we know Skor can control his soldiers at least up to a mile away from his present location. After our escape from Kormor, a couple of them attacked Nalte and me in Havatoo, roughly a mile from Kormor on the opposite bank of the Gerlat kum Rov."

"Gerlat . . . what?"

"The River of Death," Carson revealed.

"City of the Dead, River of Death. Walking dead men.

Cheery neighborhood you've got here, Carson." I was trying to lighten the mood, but I could tell from the faces of the others that it didn't work.

Carson looked at his friends proudly. "I made Skor look like a fool when we escaped from him, and apparently, there's nothing more important to him than his ego. Why else would anyone surround themselves with mindless servants and soldiers who unquestioningly obey his every command? I proved he is not the god he imagines himself to be. I'm sure Skor would like nothing more than to see me dead."

Waranji, Vivian, and I exchanged uncomfortable glances. This guy Carson seemed to have a penchant for collecting enemies. The more I heard, the more I realized wandering into a dark, unknown jungle on an alien world was a risk we should not have taken.

Carson continued. "It appeared to me that the complete mental command Skor has over his undead slaves starts to wane about one mile beyond wherever he is at the moment, so for this gentleman to attack us here . . ." He tapped the legs of the corpse with his sandal. "That means Skor isn't in Kormor. It means he's very near." Carson translated for his companions, who looked none too happy about the prospects of his theory.

Duare scowled. "The question is, 'Why is Skor nearby and not in Kormor?'" Her eyes latched onto Carson's, and then the two turned to Nalte and Ero Shan. The dark-haired warrior looked up at the rain falling from the blackened sky. He then scanned along the perimeter of the wall until his eyes fell upon the true objects of his search: Lok Marr and his men. The drizzle was becoming a full-on rain shower.

Without a word shared between them, Carson and his Amtorian friends slowly unholstered their r-ray pistols and held them inconspicuously at their sides.

"Lok Marr," I whispered. "He tipped off this Skor fellow that you'd be here. This was a set-up."

Carson nodded.

"Hang on," I said, and proceeded to activate the radio

transmitter-receiver button on the collar of my bumblebee suit. I was receiving nothing but static, but I crossed my fingers that the information I relayed was being picked up by Aito in the *Favonia*. I instructed him, Nathan, and Brahk to be on high alert for human attackers and to shoot to kill. I left out the part about those attackers being zombies; if I had, they would have thought their captain had lost his mind. I received no response in return.

After a hushed consultation with me, Carson gathered himself, took a deep breath, and began to stride toward the Havatooans at the center of the courtyard. "I'm going to have a little talk with the korgan sentar and let him know our plans," he said through clenched teeth.

In that instant, I saw Carson Napier in a whole different light. Up to that point, he had portrayed himself as a happy-go-lucky beach bum from California, but that's not who I saw stalking toward the opposing contingent. His step was now commanding like that of a true warrior. He didn't look back, but all of us—Waranji, Vivian, Duare, Ero Shan, Nalte, and I—showed our support and marched behind Carson through the muddy roots. Where it was all going was anyone's guess, but none of my crew was about to abandon a fellow Earthman on that dangerous world.

Lok Marr tipped his chin to acknowledge our party's advance toward him and seemed unaware of our suspicions. "Tanjong Carson, my korgans report no more of the Kormorian warriors in sight," he said with administrative pride. He sure was putting on a good act.

"That's good to know," Carson said, "since my friends and I will be leaving. Now. We have fulfilled our part of the peace overture and delivered the radio transmitter-receiver, and I trust it will strengthen the diplomatic relations between Korva and Havatoo."

Lok Marr seemed both surprised and nonplused by the announcement. "In the rain? There could be more of Skor's undead warriors lurking out there in the dark." His statement was delivered without a trace of warm concern, and I was sure it was a bluff meant to hide his ulterior motive. He continued. "It would be far safer for you and your friends to remain here within the fortress, under the protection of my korgans." Yep. I knew it. It was a trap.

Ero Shan scoffed at the suggestion. "We can take care of ourselves without you or your men."

Duare bowed at the waist. "Korgan Sentar Lok Marr, please deliver our warmest regards to the Sanjong. Upon our return to Korva, Jong Taman will contact your superiors via the radio to ensure its functionality. With that, we take our leave." No two ways about it. We were ready to hightail it out of there.

Lok Marr made one last attempt to delay our departure. "Janjong," he said, addressing Duare, "surely you recognize the dangers of venturing outside the walls of this fortress . . ."

"And what of the dangers inside its walls?" Ero Shan could not hold his tongue. I gulped hard, but was reassured knowing that Waranji stood directly behind me.

The implication inherent in Ero Shan's words would not go unchallenged, and the korgan sentar stepped forward to stand just inches from the larger warrior's face, his tone seething. "An accusation, is it? Speak plainly, Ero Shan. What foul deed do you attribute to a royal envoy of the Sanjong of Havatoo?"

Nalte pushed forward to wedge herself between her mate and the angry leader. "The same foul deed that I now accuse you of!" she exclaimed, her eyes flashing.

Overhearing the commotion, three of Lok Marr's men moved closer, weapons drawn. Out of the corner of my eye, I saw Carson take Duare's hand.

"You and Skor have orchestrated a trap for Tanjong Carson, is that not true?" Nalte looked dead into the eyes of the Havatooan commander.

Lok Marr's face twisted in anger. "You accuse us of treason? You accuse Havatooans of conspiring with our most sworn enemy, the most hated scourge of Morov? There!" Lok Marr pointed toward the doors of the perimeter wall. "Do you not see the body of a brave Havatooan korgan, slain by an agent of Skor?"

Duare spoke up, her voice dripping with the confidence of a seasoned diplomat. "Indeed, we do, Lok Marr. But how else can you explain the appearance of one of Skor's soldiers so far from Kormor? How can you explain the coincidental presence of a deadly enemy of Tanjong Carson at a secret meeting location known only to the four of us and your diplomatic party?"

Lok Marr turned to me, a smirk upon his lips. "Perhaps you should ask that question of these three oddly attired strangers, of whose homeland I have never heard." Bluffing or not, he had a good point. We were strangers. Why should they trust us? Carson and Duare remained stoic, but Ero Shan and Nalte turned suspicious eyes on me and my crew. Somewhere in the distance, thunder rolled. The rain began to fall even harder.

That's when we heard it. It was a low rumble and a cracking of sorts, like a great timber being split, followed almost immediately by a heavy thump that seemed to reverberate off the stone walls protecting the fortress. Almost simultaneously came a sudden crashing through the high tree limbs and wet leaves above us as a dark shape sailed over the outer wall. The object thudded dully upon the roots and mud of the courtyard, not thirty feet from us, and lay still. To both my dismay and relief, the projectile did not explode as I had expected.

Two of Lok Marr's men approached the thing with swords drawn and began to prod at the object, which appeared to be nothing more than a large burlap sack tied with a length of cord. I heard one of the soldiers ask, "What is that horrible smell?" and then it happened. The bag moved! The soldiers took a step backward and raised their weapons, and we all held our breaths.

With surprising speed, a sword blade thrust through the rain-soaked material and sliced across its length, and from within the sack rose another dead man, this one clad in crude rusty armor. The hideous walking corpse had suffered broken bones upon its unceremonious landing; one of its shoulders and part of the rib cage were crushed inward, shards of its shattered skeleton jutting from wounds that oozed a sickly black substance. I could not believe what I was seeing. Skor's assassin appeared immune to pain as it grinned and hissed, blade in hand. The sound we had heard seconds before must have been a catapult that vaulted the horrid thing among us.

Before we could digest the ramifications of what was transpiring, a sustained volley of odd sounds filled the air. All around us, sacks began thudding into the courtyard from all sides of the fortress. One after another, the putrid missiles thudded sickly against the unyielding ground like sacks of meat . . . because that is exactly what they were. As the projectiles plunged through the fog and rain, I could hear the faint sounds of bones cracking upon impact, but grave bodily injury did not stop the phantoms from ripping free of the burlap in a furious display of savagery, their dull yellow eyes trained on the targets of their assault: the living—*us*.

As the enemies revealed themselves, I noted that not all appeared to be dead men; some were emaciated like unwrapped mummies, while others looked nearly living. The glazed stare of their yellowed eyes was all we needed to see in order to know from which side of the cemetery gates they had crawled. In contrast to the polished armor of Lok Marr's korgans, the protective coverings of Skor's troops looked like they were requisitioned from an Amtorian museum, their surfaces marred and dulled by rust and patina.

Lok Marr immediately rallied his troops, at least the ones not on lookout atop the walls; those four korgans were unfortunately cut off from the rest of us on the ground. Dozens of undead warriors now stood in the swirling fog. We were surrounded and appeared to be outnumbered three to one, but the hideous things just stood there. Waiting. All of the checkers were being put into position on the board, but no one was making the first move. Waranji and I had drawn our Colts, even though there was probably very little a .45 slug could do against an attacker who was already dead. Still, we'd give it our best shot.

"Why didn't I bring a gun?" Vivian tugged in frustration at the strap of the sample bag on her shoulder. Duare must have read Vivian's body language. She handed the botanist the ornate dagger she had brandished when we had first met her.

"Can you fight?" Duare asked. It was more of a command than an inquiry.

Vivian directed her response to Waranji and me, knowing only we would understand her words. "I can fight like a wolverine, if necessary," she said to quell any concerns we might have for her.

More bags continued to be lobbed over the walls, several falling behind us and effectively cutting us off from the only identified egress from the fortress. Between the darkness, the swirling fog, and the drenching rain, it was difficult to determine just who were enemies and who were korgans. Not wanting to risk hitting one of their own with stray r-ray fire, our friends and their Havatooan counterparts stowed their pistols in favor of swords.

"We're going to do this the old-fashioned way," Carson explained. He made several slashes in the air like a pitcher warming up on a baseball diamond, and then he and Ero Shan joined Lok Marr, who had gathered six of his korgans to our group. In the center of the courtyard sat Carson's vaunted invention. That bronze box, now sitting forgotten in the rain, was the reason they were there in the first place.

"What are they waiting for?" Waranji whispered. It was odd that the attackers weren't doing what they were obviously made for. But as we watched, the entire contingent, to a man, stiffened as if a soundless call had reached their ears. Suddenly, all turned their heads in our direction and they began their lurching march toward us. A soundless call was exactly what they had heard.

"Skor has reached out with his mind and given the command!" Carson shouted. "Get ready, my friends!"

The nightmare legion shuffled forward, their dead stares locked on the living intruders to their realm.

"They're mindless," I observed. "Like a bunch of African army ants."

"Not so, Captain," Carson replied. "Don't underestimate them. They can think, and they can reason. They're unable to resist Skor's orders, but dead or not, they're still men. Treat them as such and we might live to tell about it."

The clank of metal upon metal rang out like a starting gun, and the battle was joined. The korgan farthest from us had deflected a blow by a zombie and was now engaging it, but before the unfortunate warrior could react, two more of the fiends diverted their march to join their undead compatriot. Together, the three quickly overwhelmed the korgan, who fell to their slashing blades. In seconds, the defender collapsed to the ground. The trio of assassins grinned as they trod upon the fallen soldier in their march toward us.

I nearly jumped out of my skin when Waranji's Colt erupted to my right. As I spun, I saw the result of his shot; a dead man, not twenty feet from us, had been hit, an upper quadrant of his head missing from the eyebrow up. The thing wiped the palm of one hand across its face to clear its eyes of the black ooze that dripped from the grievous wound, slung the fluid to the ground, and laughed. It was the most hideous sound I had ever heard.

Carson shouted out. "Save your ammo! The only way to stop them is complete dismemberment!" That bit of sage advice had me wishing I had even a pocket knife on me.

Mayhem erupted on all fronts as Lok Marr and his korgans engaged the reanimated corpses. Several of the fiends were felled in the first wave of attack, but the overwhelming number of them kept the korgans on offense, despite their kills.

Waranji and I kept Vivian safely behind us as the creatures advanced through the rain. Gnarled fingers reached out, swords were raised. Without bladed weapons, we knew it was going to come down to speed and fists. Ignoring the sword tips now only inches from us, Waranji and I did what the corpses least expected: we rushed the bums. Together, we pushed into them and began serving up knuckle sandwiches, pounding into the closest four attackers. With each punch I delivered, I could feel brittle bone give way beneath my blows and putrid flesh puddle and recoil from my strikes.

One of the dead men was taken aback by my attack on him, or perhaps it was because of the rain, but in any event, he dropped his sword. I immediately threw myself upon the weapon, rolled, and jumped to my feet behind him. With a thrust, I skewered the creature's midsection. The thing only spun in place, dropped open its lower jaw, and erupted with a laugh straight from Hell.

It was only then that I truly understood. As reprehensible as his earlier recommendation sounded, Carson was right.

I kicked my attacker in the stomach and knocked it into one of its allies. Both fell to the ground. Everything was a blur, and I gave not a single thought as to what I was doing. I threw myself upon the two, snatched the sword from the second man's hand, and—God help me—began hacking at them like a madman.

Never in my life had I experienced a sensation quite like that, and I hope I never do again.

Within seconds, the red haze of berserker rage cleared, and I stood over the scattered remains of what had once been two warriors. I had no time to be revolted by what I had done, as I was suddenly struck from behind in my midsection. I spun in place to find several of the dead warriors advancing on me, one of them gripping his sword with a look of confusion. In a flash, I realized I had been stabbed, but thanks to the Harbenite plating woven into my bumblebee suit, the deadly blow was halted. It was just me against three. Even with a sword in my hand, the odds did not look good.

Waranji launched himself at the trio of attackers, his massive bulk scattering them like duckpins. With both fists covered in the black gore of battle, the mighty Waziri grabbed two of the invaders by the heads and smashed their faces together. A shower of fetid fluid erupted into the air. Without a whiff of concern, Waranji discarded both bodies he still held, then crouched to prepare for the onrush of three more of the creatures. I quickly looked behind me. Nalte and Duare were each flanking Vivian. Good. I ripped free the sword I had thrust through the zombie warrior I had destroyed.

"Waranji!" I yelled. He caught the sword I had thrown to him, and with one fluid motion, he brought it into a full arc to sever the head of the closest enemy. But that did not slow his momentum. To his left, a living corpse lost a sword arm; to his right, another was bisected diagonally across the chest; and beneath his heavy boots, the head of another who had fallen to the muddy ground erupted under Waranji's stomp. Despite our defensive maneuvers, we were powerless to prevent the attackers from slowly backing us away from the walls and toward the remnants of the stone outpost at the courtyard's center. The vaulting of troops over the walls had ceased, but enough of them were already within the compound to overtake us.

I paused a moment to take quick stock of the battlefield. Through the swirling fog and downpour of rain, I could see that at least two of the korgans from atop the walls had descended to join the fray, but so furious was the swinging of swords and falling of bodies that I quickly lost sight of our dubious allies among the dead men. The suggestion to refrain from using the r-ray pistols was wise; if I had one in my hands, I wouldn't have clear enough vision to make an accurate shot, nor would any of us.

Duare, Vivian, and Nalte stuck closely together, but it was no fearful huddle. All three women were working in tandem to protect one another while also preventing stray corpse warriors from drawing too near our retreating group. Each of them had by then secured swords taken from fallen attackers and brandished the weapons like pros. Jerry Ouellet would have been duly impressed if he could have seen his botanist wife swinging a sword; heck, I was about ready to ask her for pointers myself.

The voice of Carson cut through the din of battle. "Everyone to the castle!" he ordered.

"What?" Vivian shouted in response. "But that huge spider!"

"No choice," Carson called out as he slashed an attacking dead man, then kicked it away from him. "We'll have to kill it when we get in there. If we get in there," he growled solemnly.

Waranji and Ero Shan were covering our flank as we inched toward the castle, still a good fifty yards away. Despite our current precarious situation within the fortress, my mind was also with the rest of the crew aboard the ship. While my right sword hand deflected attackers' blows, I reached into my helmet ring with my left and hit my suit's communications switch. "Conover to *Favonia*! Come in, *Favonia*! Do you read me? Over!"

Static. I blocked a downward slash and skewered a walking corpse through the chest.

"Conover to *Favonia*, come in! We're under attack here! Over!" I shouted. Nothing but interference.

And then it hit me: Carson's radio transmitter. That came in loud and clear on the *Favonia* even when we were still airborne and miles out from the fortress. My eyes shot to the bronze transmission station sitting in the rain atop the table thirty feet away from me. It was only thirty feet, but it was a long thirty feet. I had to chance it.

My thought of reaching the transmitter would have to wait. I was grabbed from behind by a pair of strong hands and pulled backward. I could not see my assailants, but I could tell there was more than one. I tried to maintain my footing while I was swung in a circle. I felt sharp and repeated impacts against my back and could only conclude they were knife thrusts, dulled by the impenetrable Harbenite plates in my suit. The toe of my boot caught under one of the more prodigious aboveground roots. Down into the mud and roots I went, my attackers piling onto me. I began throwing wild punches with my free hand, hoping to connect with something, but again and again my fist slipped off slimy, rain-coated faces. I had only a matter of seconds before one of them went for my unprotected head, and then it would be lights out for good.

A face rushed into my field of vision, mouth agape to expose what few rotting and chipped teeth it had managed to retain. My attacker must have figured that if its dagger couldn't stop me, it would just bite my face off. The stench of rotting flesh overwhelmed me as the teeth pressed closer, only held at bay by my forearm across the thing's neck. The weight of the others atop my intended murderer pressed the horrid mouth closer and closer. The air was being squeezed out of me. I couldn't breathe and started to see stars.

One of Ero Shan's mighty hands came down upon the head of my attacker, and he dug his fingers into the sickly yellow orbs, bursting them both. He ripped upward, pulling the howling corpse from me like you'd hold a bowling ball. With his other hand, he slid his sword edge across its throat. Ero Shan flung the severed head across the courtyard and dropped his sword to continue his attack, pulling the other two dead men from me.

"I need to radio my ship!" I shouted, pointing to the bronze transmitter. "Cover me while I run to Carson's radio!" Ero Shan got the gist of what I was saying and nodded in acknowledgment, then ripped an arm from one of the undead soldiers and used it as a club to beat the other. I scrambled to my feet and bolted through the pouring rain toward the wooden table ten yards away. From behind me, Vivian called out my name in concern, but I couldn't stop. I had to warn Aito, Tafari, Nathan, and Brahk on the ship. It might just save their lives.

My previous battlefield experience had been in the Army Air Force, going head-to-head against the Luftwaffe over

Europe during World War II. As I mentioned earlier, I had seen the carnage in the fields and trenches up close on several occasions. All of those terrible memories I had hoped to erase came flooding back to me as I crossed the rainy courtyard; over the bodies of both foes and allies; through the mud and the muck, and the blood. As I neared the transmitter, I hoped that Carson had incorporated his earthly sensibilities into the design of his radio, because I ran the risk that I would reach the contraption and have no idea how to operate it. I drew closer, finally placing my hands on the wet table. I cleared the raindrops from the gauges on the face of the unit and was pleasantly surprised to find it looked very much like a good old RCA back on Earth.

Relieved to have reached my destination unscathed, I turned to look back at the battle. Pulling myself from the middle of the fracas allowed me to see just how outnumbered our forces were. At least half of Lok Marr's men lay dead on the ground. The fact that dozens of Skor's warriors were lying among them did not make our odds look any better. Just as many of the undead creatures were still on their feet. I needed to make it snappy and call the *Favonia* to warn them what was happening out there in the darkness.

I turned my attention back to the transmitter-receiver just as a shadowed figure reached out of the fog, lifted the radio, and smashed it to the ground. A heavily armored boot came down on the copper-colored box, shattering the dials and sending sparks flying. It was one of Lok Marr's korgans!

"What the hell is wrong with you?" I screamed, just as a bolt of lightning illuminated the courtyard. In the dark, we couldn't see much of the korgans' faces, but in that flash of light, I got a good look at this man's face . . . and his hideously yellowed eyes. Here was the traitor among us; here was the man who had fed Skor the information about Carson's presence at the fortress! Lok Marr's ranks had been infiltrated by a dead man, one who could still pass for living.

He began to draw his sword, but I beat him to the punch

and flipped the wooden table at him. I couldn't give the guy a chance. I knew what I had to do. In a flash, I tackled him, knocking him backward off his feet. We splashed into the mire, and I brought my sword to bear against the dead man's throat. I tried to tamp down the revulsion of what I was about to do, and it all got worse when the thing began to laugh.

He looked at me with those dead yellow eyes, and a smile spread across his bluish lips. He then spoke one curious word. "Freedom." I don't have to tell you what I did next.

I wiped the thing's black blood from my suit and rose from the muck to gather an assessment of my friends' well-being. They were massed together, moving backward up the castle's rain-slicked marble steps, and were surrounded by two score of the undead warriors. At least Waranji, Vivian, Carson, Duare, Nalte, and Ero Shan were all accounted for, along with Lok Marr and three surviving members of his brave squad.

And then it happened. In unison, three ghoulish warriors charged up the steps, swinging their swords wildly. Lok Marr and Carson rushed to the fore, swords flashing, but the maneuver of the dead men was a distraction; six of them made a second rush, met by Waranji and Ero Shan. As I said, the pouring rain had made the marble steps slippery, and I watched as one of Ero Shan's feet got out from under him, sending him to his back. The attackers were merciless, and even though I was rushing headlong toward the confrontation, there was nothing I could do but watch as one of the dead men brought his sword hilt down on the head of Ero Shan, while another thrust his blade into the abdomen of the dark-haired warrior. Ero Shan's scream of pain was matched by Nalte's horrified shriek. She threw herself upon the dead men hovering over her fallen mate. I ran as I had never run before, but I was so far away. So far. Vivian and Duare joined Nalte, hacking into the attackers, while others pushed up the stairs to replace those who fell. I heard Waranji's voice, booming a defiant war cry, only to be drowned out by a crack of thunder from the heavens.

I was front row center at the last stand of my dearest friends.

My heartbeat was pounding in my ears, but even so, I still heard the crashing from above as at least two dozen more projectiles were catapulted into the compound. Skor really wanted Carson dead. He wanted all of us dead. There would be no escape for us now.

The gathering of undead warriors upon the steps made it impossible for me to reach the others who were making a valiant effort to defend themselves and the fallen Ero Shan. I had to do something. Anything.

"Over here, you bunch of mindless geeks!" I shouted, waving my arms over my head. My outburst had the desired effect. The warriors ceased their attack and turned in my direction. Inside the bumblebee suit, I could feel the sweat trickle down my sides as, all around me, I heard the sounds of ripping burlap. I had to look. Rising from the ground into the pouring rain were fresh troops of the zombie corps, swords at the ready. Yellow eyes and exposed toothy grins were on all sides. I was surrounded.

The sound reverberated across the courtyard and seemed to shake the entire stone wall fortifying the outpost. What new weapon of Skor's created the din I could not guess, but it came from the direction of the huge metal doors barring entrance to the fortress. Again it sounded, again the wall shook. Even the undead seemed taken aback by this development. The sound was repeated, a thunderous boom. Something was hitting the fortified metal doors. Whatever it was struck again, and between the newly made cracks around the doorframes, beams of light cut through the gloom of the courtyard.

"What is that?" Carson yelled over to me.

"I was about to ask you the same thing!" I responded.

The answer to our question revealed itself within seconds. One thunderous crash later, both fortress doors burst inward from their ancient frames, and a flood of light blinded us all. I wiped the rain from my face and held up a hand to shield my eyes. There, through the frame of the fortress wall and over the fallen metal doors, plowed the *Favonia*'s Cargo Crawler!

The intent behind the Crawler's construction was quite simple: It was a pack mule. Since cargo space was limited within the fuselage of the *Favonia*, we could fill the Crawler with supplies to be delivered to Pellucidar, for example. Once the ship landed, the Crawler could detach from the main vessel and transport the cargo across whatever terrain we encountered. But seeing it now, tearing over the downed metal doors and across the muddy, vine-covered courtyard, it looked a whole heck of a lot like a battlefield vehicle. Friends and foes alike froze in their tracks, and after the Crawler came to an abrupt, skidding halt, the top access hatch was flung open, and a figure emerged.

It was Tafari, staring down the barrel of an M-1. "Give the word, Captain!" he shouted.

"None of them backed against the castle or the guys in black and gold; they're all friends!" I yelled. "Everyone else . . . enemies!"

One of the corpse warriors on the marble steps snapped out of his amazement and swung back to his human targets. Closest to him was Vivian, protectively covering Nalte, who wept over the prone form of Ero Shan. The warrior raised his sword, but before he could strike, a report rang out. From fifty feet away, Tafari hit the thing dead-on in the back of its neck. Black gore sprayed out at Vivian and Nalte, and the thing shuddered, but did not fall. Even at that distance, I could see the puzzled look on Tafari's face. The dead man swung his arm over his chest, preparing to slash both Vivian and Nalte, until the fist met the side of his face.

With part of the undead fiend's neck already torn away, Waranji's punch easily ripped the warrior's head from his shoulders and sent it tumbling through the fog.

Skor's fresh recruits were now only twenty feet from me.

I shouted again to Tafari. "Bullets won't stop them! You bring a shock gun with you?"

"Yes, sir!"

"Give that a try," I yelled. "Who's driving?"

"Nathan, sir!"

"Tell him to circle the courtyard while you take out as many of these zombies as you can!" Tafari's face went blank. "And if anything gets in Nathan's way," I added, "tell him to mow 'em down!"

Tafari dropped through the hatch as a warrior came within striking range of me. I parried his blow, and another, and then kicked my attacker backward as I heard the engine of the Crawler rev. The zombie stumbled but regained his footing, his rotting brow curled in murderous contemplation. Two others moved in from the fog to flank him, and the mouths of the three dropped open in terrifying laughter. They didn't laugh for long. I leaped clear as the Harbenite treads of the Cargo Crawler ground the trio of undead attackers into hamburger as it plowed over them at top speed. Nathan spun the vehicle sharply to bring it back around, plunging me into the spotlight of the headlamps. Though I couldn't see Nathan, I shot a thumbs-up at the Crawler's windshield and charged back toward the allies.

As I ran, I slashed my way past attacker after attacker until I reached the marble steps, and bolting between the enemies, I reached the two great doors of the castle where the others had gathered. Waranji had managed to carry the body of Ero Shan over his shoulder and was placing him down against the wall with the help of Nalte, tears streaming down her face.

"Any suggestions, Captain?" Waranji asked, his bumblebee suit stained with Ero Shan's blood.

"Let's see what your man Tafari can do," I replied, "and cross your fingers."

As if on cue, the Crawler ground to a stop perpendicular to the bottom of the marble steps. There must have been a dozen dead men surrounding us, with another two dozen still milling about in the courtyard and shambling in our direction. Tafari scrambled from the top hatch and stood atop the Crawler. In his hands, he held a shock gun, one of Brahk Zahla's alien inventions that had already come in handy once on our voyage. Tafari aimed for the enemy nearest the top of the stairs and fired a dart into its back. The light on the rifle's ovoid generator unit flashed from yellow to blue, and he pulled the secondary trigger. A bolt of blue-white electricity arced from the gun to the dart. As the electric charge surged through its frame, the corpse-like warrior stiffened, dropped its weapon, and stood shuddering. The shock gun had worked!

Lok Marr slashed down the stunned warrior. "Perhaps we will not die today," he shot to Carson. The Californian only smirked and decapitated a second warrior, standing stock-still after being jolted by Tafari's next shot.

Carson's suggestion that we treat the enemies as living men was not without merit. For the first time since the battle had begun, the tide began to turn, and now in the dead eyes of the warriors could be seen a glimmer of fear. We had backed the attackers down from the stairs and onto the root-covered courtyard, where they continued to fall to Tafari's shock gun and our flashing blades. But as high as my spirits were, it all came crashing down when I saw the legion of Skor's soldiers approaching us. Every last dead man not yet engaged in battle had amassed together in a wide phalanx, marching toward the Cargo Crawler like a wave.

"We need to get inside the castle!" Carson commanded.

I snapped my fingers. "Yeah. Let's do that. Right after we evict the current tenant." I winked at Carson, and he caught my drift. "Tafari!" I shouted. "Get inside and stay inside, got it?"

"Yes, sir," the Waziri soldier shouted. He descended into the Crawler and locked the hatch.

With Waranji at one of the castle doors and Carson and me at the other, we pulled with all our might until the hinges began to squeal in protest.

"Hurry!" Vivian shouted, pointing toward the marble stairs. There, Skor's men were ascending, slashing at the air with their swords only twenty feet from us.

"Keep pulling!" I shouted at no one in particular as I strained against the resistance of the enormous double door. Lok Marr and the last three korgans rushed to our aid, and together, we successfully heaved open the towering gate. "Take cover!" I shouted to Duare and Vivian, but rather than run, they stayed at the side of Nalte, who cradled Ero Shan's body.

The bloodthirsty warriors crested the stairway just as the ear-splitting shriek rang out. We dove away from the open doors as the hideous targo rushed forth from the blackness, its body held aloft by its thrashing legs. The nightmare creature barreled toward the amassed attackers, tearing into them with inhuman rage. Bodies were skewered by pike-like legs; others were ripped apart by the fangs of the beast. The thing was unstoppable, skittering down the steps while sending torn bodies flying. It reached the Cargo Crawler, easily surmounted its twenty-foot height, and scrambled across the courtyard, decimating Skor's ghastly troops as it passed. Judging from the destruction it left behind, I imagine the targo had suffered enough annoyance from us humans and wanted nothing but out. In a flash, the gigantic spider scaled the far wall of the compound and disappeared into the rain-drenched blackness of the jungle, leaving trampled and savaged corpses in its wake.

It was over. We had won. Across the vine creepers and mud of the courtyard were strewn the bodies of dozens upon dozens of warriors; some had bled red, others black. The rainfall had ceased, and a deathly stillness enveloped the fog-shrouded fortress. Lok Marr's remaining korgans marched forth on the grim task of assessing the fallen attackers, to either ensure their demise or quicken the final departure of the wounded. Tafari again popped up from the Cargo Crawler's top access hatch, and I gave him the "all clear." Then a jolt of sorrow surged through me as I heard Nalte's voice behind me. Ero Shan! Brave, stalwart Ero Shan was now . . .

"Alive! You're alive!" came Nalte's euphoric scream.

I rushed across the slick marble to the castle facade where Waranji had laid Ero Shan. The dark-haired warrior now sat upright, but he was buckled forward in intense pain. He gripped his side with both hands to prevent further blood loss, and Nalte wiped the blood from his face, which trickled from the gash on the top of his head. He was now being inspected by Vivian.

"This needs to be stitched up," she said to Nalte, as Lok Marr approached with concern.

The Havatooan korgan sentar kneeled at Ero Shan's side and inspected his abdominal wound. "Yes. You are in luck, my friend," Lok Marr said. "The sword passed through your flank without hitting any vital organs.

"How can you tell?" Nalte asked with frantic sarcasm, almost as if she wanted to hear the worst possible outcome. But by then, I had learned that was just how she was, always looking on the gloomy side of things.

Lok Marr smiled as he put a comforting hand on Ero Shan's shoulder. "The subdiscipline of my sentar class ranking is the medical arts," he explained. He looked to the castle's open doors. "There should be enough tarel in there for me to sew you back together."

"Lok Marr," I interjected, "during the battle, I was attacked by one of your men. He was a traitor, a dead man, masquerading as living. *He* was the one who told Skor of Carson's presence." Carson's eyes grew wide, and he translated my words to Lok Marr.

"Which man is it?" the Havatooan demanded.

"He's dead," I admitted. "It was the soldier who smashed the radio set."

Upon hearing my words, Carson cursed under his breath and pounded a fist against the lichen-covered wall behind us.

He hadn't known about the destruction of the transmitter. For a few moments, he sat there fuming. Then he sighed and rose, a lopsided grin on his face. "Well, it's back to the drawing board, I suppose."

Waranji, Vivian, and I convened with Tafari and Nathan on the open rear door ramp of the Cargo Crawler. They explained how the messages from my bumblebee suit had been coming through: garbled, but still decipherable, which is why they had decided to charge to the rescue. But even better news followed: Aito was certain he had gotten the *Favonia*'s skeleton key into reasonable enough working order for us to attempt a return to our home planet.

With that information in hand and exhaustion weighing heavily upon us, we bid farewell to Carson and his friends. We also thanked Lok Marr and his men for their courage and assistance, which they graciously accepted. I still didn't like them, but I had to admit they had spunk. Meanwhile, Carson assured us that he and his companions would be fine, so my crew and I boarded the Cargo Crawler for the return jaunt to the *Favonia* . . . and hopefully an eventless trip back to good ol' Mother Earth. I'll tell you about how that all panned out some other time, if you haven't written off all of this as just a bunch of hogwash.

POSTSCRIPT

IDO HAVE AN ADDENDUM to make regarding Carson Napier. When we left the fortress, we had hoped for the best for Carson and his friends, but it wouldn't be until months later that I would hear about what had occurred after the Cargo Crawler rumbled away into the jungle.

While Lok Marr attended to Ero Shan, Carson continued his conversation with the Havatooan, and their previous suspicions about one another were laid to rest. All were relieved that Ero Shan would live, though he would need immediate medical attention. To achieve this, Duare entered the castle to gather tarel, which Lok Marr would use as surgical sutures. But curiously, she did not return, raising suspicions. Carson made an immediate search of the castle. Luckily, Duare's path through the web-coated interior was easily followed, leading Carson to an open door at the castle's rear. Beyond the door was the back courtyard, beyond which he spied a crude ladder propped against the fortress' protective outer wall. At the ladder's base lay a length of shimmering gold silk on the ground. It was Duare's scarf!

It all struck him like a bolt of lightning: Skor's target was never Carson, it was Duare, and now she had been kidnapped by the fiend!

Back with the others, a frantic Carson relayed the news, donned a couple of pieces of armor and leather boots from one of Skor's destroyed warriors, and headed for the gates.

Nalte urged Carson to allow her to go with him, but he assured her that Ero Shan needed her by his side. Likewise, Lok Marr needed to perform surgery on Ero Shan, but offered his men to accompany Carson. Napier was thankful, but refused. Foolhardy or not, it was a battle he must fight alone, and he fearlessly plunged into the darkened jungle of Amtor.

I know how it all ended, but that's Carson's story to tell.

ABOUT THE AUTHORS

RETURN OF THE MONSTER MEN ™

A professional author since 2007, JOSH REYNOLDS has more than thirty novels to his name, three of which won the Scribe Award, in addition to have written numerous short stories, novellas, and audio scripts. Born and raised in South Carolina, he now resides in Sheffield in the United Kingdom with his wife and daughter, as well as a highly excitable dog and something he hopes is a cat. A complete list of his work can be found at joshuamreynolds.co.uk.

WEIRD WORLDS ™
DEAD ON VENUS

A professional writer and illustrator for more than thirty years, MIKE WOLFER is the author of the Edgar Rice Burroughs Universe novel *The Land That Time Forgot: Fortress Primeval* as well as three prior ERB Universe prose novelettes. Additionally, he has been a key talent working on the canonical ERB Universe comic books, including Jane Porter, Victory Harben, Pellucidar, The Land That Time Forgot, The Monster Men, and The Moon Maid. Best known for his Widow series, Wolfer is also the creator of the Daughters of the Dark Oracle franchise, and has worked on numerous licensed properties.

EDGAR RICE BURROUGHS: MASTER OF ADVENTURE

The creator of the immortal characters Tarzan of the Apes and John Carter of Mars, EDGAR RICE BURROUGHS is one of the world's most popular authors. Mr. Burroughs' timeless tales of heroes and heroines transport readers from the jungles of Africa and the dead sea bottoms of Barsoom to the miles-high forests of Amtor and the savage inner world of Pellucidar, and even to alien civilizations beyond the farthest star. Mr. Burroughs' books are estimated to have sold hundreds of millions of copies, and they have spawned 60 films and 250 television episodes.

About Edgar Rice Burroughs, Inc.

Founded in 1923 by Edgar Rice Burroughs, one of the first authors to incorporate himself, EDGAR RICE BURROUGHS, INC., holds numerous trademarks and the rights to all literary works of the author still protected by copyright, including stories of Tarzan of the Apes and John Carter of Mars. The company oversees authorized adaptations of his literary works in film, television, radio, publishing, theatrical stage productions, licensing, and merchandising. Edgar Rice Burroughs, Inc., continues to manage and license the vast archive of Mr. Burroughs' literary works, fictional characters, and corresponding artworks that has grown for over a century. The company is still owned by the Burroughs family and remains headquartered in Tarzana, California, the town named after the Tarzana Ranch Mr. Burroughs purchased there in 1919 that led to the town's future development.

In 2015, under the leadership of President James Sullos, the company relaunched its publishing division, which was founded by Mr. Burroughs in 1931. With the publication of new authorized editions of Mr. Burroughs' works and brand-new novels and stories by today's talented authors, the company continues its long tradition of bringing tales of wonder and imagination featuring the Master of Adventure's many iconic characters and exotic worlds to an eager reading public.

Visit **EdgarRiceBurroughs.com** for more information.

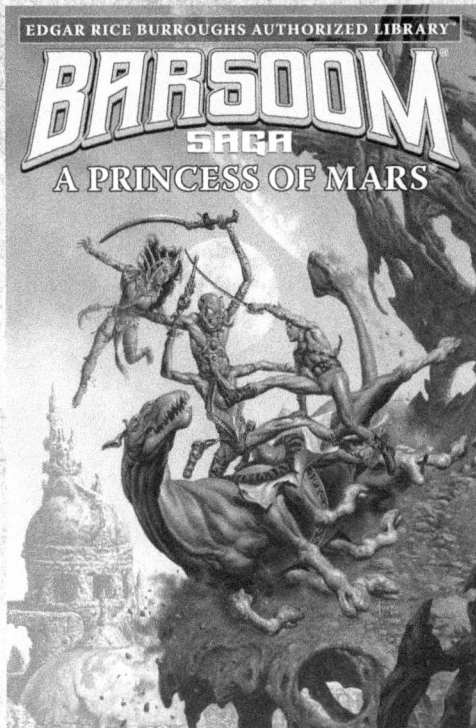

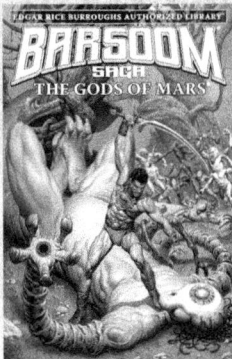

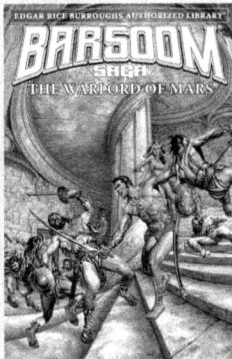

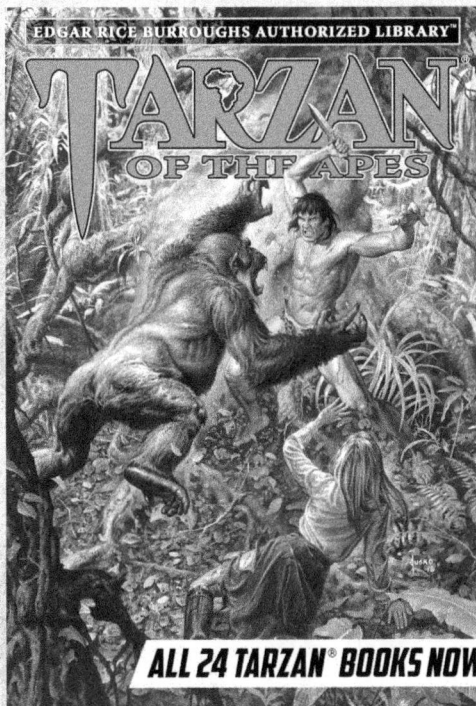

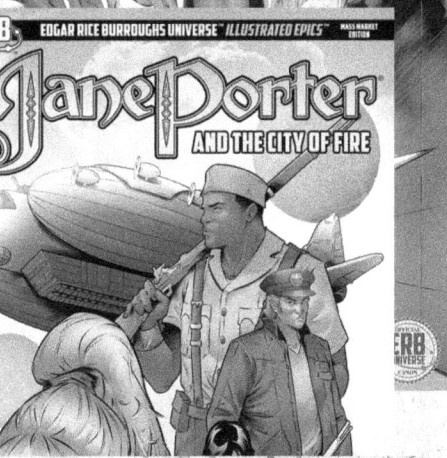

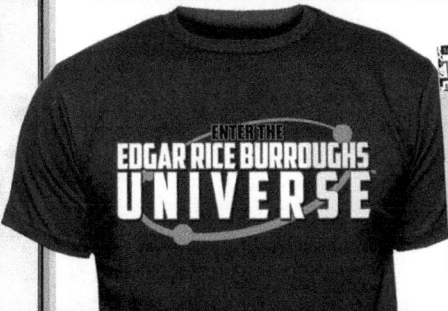

www.ingramcontent.com/pod-product-compliance
Ingram Content Group UK Ltd.
Pitfield, Milton Keynes, MK11 3LW, UK
UKHW040635031125
8725UKWH00044B/617

9 781945 462917